A Count of Courage

Book 2 in the Last Call Series

**

Nancy Moser

Mustard Seed Press

Overland Park, KS

THE BOOKS OF NANCY MOSER

www.nancymoser.com

Fantasy Books

A Slice of Sky (Book 1 Last Call)
A Count of Courage (Book 2 Last Call)

Contemporary Books

If Not for This
An Undiscovered Life
Eyes of Our Heart
The Invitation (Book 1 Mustard Seed)
The Quest (Book 2 Mustard Seed)
The Temptation (Book 3 Mustard Seed)
Crossroads
The Seat Beside Me (Book 1 Steadfast)
A Steadfast Surrender (Book 2 Steadfast)
The Ultimatum (Book 3 Steadfast)
The Sister Circle (Book 1 Sister Circle)
Round the Corner (Book 2 Sister Circle)
An Undivided Heart (Book 3 Sister Circle)
A Place to Belong (Book 4 Sister Circle)
Senior Sisters (Book 5 Sister Circle)
The Sister Circle Handbook (Book 6 Sister Circle)
Time Lottery (Book 1 Time Lottery)
Second Time Around (Book 2 Time Lottery)
John 3:16
The Good Nearby
Solemnly Swear
Save Me, God! I Fell in the Carpool (Inspirational humor)
100 Verses of Encouragement — Books 1&2 (illustrated gift books)
Maybe Later (picture book)
I Feel Amazing: the ABCs of Emotion (picture book)

Historical Books

Where Time Will Take Me (Book 1 Past Times)
Where Life Will Lead Me (Book 2 Past Times)
Pin's Promise (novella prequel to Pattern Artist)
The Pattern Artist (Book 1 Pattern Artist)
The Fashion Designer (Book 2 Pattern Artist)
The Shop Keepers (Book 3 Pattern Artist)
Love of the Summerfields (Book 1 Manor House)
Bride of the Summerfields (Book 2 Manor House)
Rise of the Summerfields (Book 3 Manor House)
Mozart's Sister (biographical novel of Nannerl Mozart)
Just Jane (biographical novel of Jane Austen)
Washington's Lady (bio-novel of Martha Washington)
How Do I Love Thee? (bio-novel of Elizabeth Barrett Browning)
Masquerade (Book 1 Gilded Age)
An Unlikely Suitor (Book 2 Gilded Age)
A Bridal Quilt (Gilded Age novella)
The Journey of Josephine Cain
A Basket Brigade Christmas (novella collection)
When I Saw His Face (Regency novella)

Dedication

To my dear husband Mark.
We've been married fifty years—
years filled with love
laughter
tears
resilience
patience
and many counts of courage.
I love you forever.

PROLOGUE

CASHLIN

We are quiet as we approach Legalis, each in our own thoughts. I'm thankful there *is* a city to go to, as there's no way we can ever return to Regalia—at least no way we know of. But I'm angry that we never knew Legalis existed. Never knew anyone existed beyond our walls.

Lieb faces Legalis, as if studying it. "It doesn't have a solid wall like Regalia, but the buildings are all connected."

They look just as impenetrable.

"They're pretty," Solana says. "All different heights."

"But oddly no windows," I add. "You would think they would like the view."

He shakes his head. "I don't see any doors either."

"You're right," Helsa says. "I don't see a way in."

"That man we met, Jass. He got out somehow," Solana says, looking left and right down the expanse of buildings in front of us. "But the city seems to go on forever, in a massive circle."

"Great," Helsa says. "More Rings."

They're being negative again, which makes *me* feel negative. And impatient. "We'll walk the perimeter until we find an entrance."

"That might be a long way," Lieb says. "I'm tired of walking."

So am I. I'd hate to lead them left when the entrance is to the right. I peer at the cloudy sky. "Keeper? You're our provider. Provide us with directions. Which way to the entrance of Legalis?"

"Are you expecting a map to fall from the sky?" Helsa asks.

Actually . . .

But then I see it. The clouds part. A slice of sky opens up. A beam of sunlight shines down on the right edge of the city. I laugh aloud and point. "There! There's his map for us. There, we'll find the entrance."

Lieb takes Helsa's hand. "Come on, Sa-Sa, let's go!"

She shakes his hand away and glares at me. "Prove to me that's a sign from the Keeper."

I feel sorry for her. Being pessimistic has got to be exhausting. Has she always been like this, or have I inadvertently done something to make her so skeptical?

I think of a good comeback. "Prove to me it isn't him, Helsa."

So there.

**

Up close, the stucco buildings are taller than I expected, at least four stories high. Sand is swept up against them, as if they've risen out of the earth from below.

There is no well-traveled path around the city, which implies two things: those who live there stay there, and Legalis doesn't have many visitors. It makes me wonder what business Jass was on to be leaving the city so casually.

He said Legalis has protocols regarding strangers. And rules. I've had enough rules. And councils. And Enforcers. And trials and exile. It would be nice to find a place where people could have friends from all walks of life, and use their gifts to live fulfilling lives of purpose, doing good for one another. Plus, a place where everyone could freely talk about the Keeper.

Is Legalis such a place?

I hope we find a way inside soon. Our food was long ago eaten, and I don't want to sleep outside when we're so close.

Finally, as we follow the curve of the buildings, I see a door. Lieb and Helsa see it too and run ahead.

"This is it," Solana says.

"Whatever *it* is."

"*It* is anything that gets us out of this desert," she says. "Hopefully, *it* is water, food, and a soft bed."

I agree on all counts.

As we get closer I see that Helsa and Lieb stand a good twenty feet back from the entrance. Something has made them stop short.

Solana and I catch up and see why they stopped. There's a large sign on the door that says: DO NOT OPEN. KNOCK.

"That's not very welcoming," Solana whispers.

Helsa looks at me. "You do it, Cashlin. Knock."

"Why me?"

"This is your exile. Get us inside."

Keeper, help us. I knock on the door and step back.

There's no answer, so I knock again. And step back again.

Finally, the door cracks open and a middle-aged woman squints at the sunlight.

I smile and greet her. "Hello, we're—"

"How many?" she asks gruffly.

"Four."

She opens the door wide and we walk into a small room that only has a single chair and a small table. A waterskin is hooked over the back of the chair, and a loaf of half-eaten bread is on the table. Crumbs are everywhere—including on the woman's chin. A book and a pencil share space with the crumbs.

"Close the door behind ya," she says.

Lieb closes it, and it takes our eyes a moment to adjust to the dim light of a single lamp hooked on a wall. The five of us are a tight fit in the small space.

The woman wears all white like the man in the desert, and has one black stud on her shoulder. I wonder about its significance. Is it a symbol of rank? "State yer business in Legalis."

"Sanctuary," I say.

"We've come a long way," Solana adds.

"We're hungry and thirsty," Lieb says.

For once, Helsa remains silent.

"We appreciate you allowing us into your fine city," I add.

She seems unmoved by my flattery and sits at the table with an *oomph*. She opens the ledger to the last page. "Names?"

"I'm Cashlin, and this—"

"Just name the names, I don't needs to know who's who."

How cold. "Cashlin, Solana, Helsa, and Lieb."

She writes them down with tedious care, as if she's not used to writing much.

"What's your name?" I ask.

She blinks as if no one's ever asked her that. "Durth."

What a horrible name. "Well, Durth, though we know nothing about Legalis we're eager to—"

Durth tosses the pencil aside and slaps the ledger closed. She shoves her chair back and goes to a door, opening a closet that has shelves inside. Then she pulls out four wads of white fabric and tosses them at us. "Put 'em on."

I hold one up and see it's a simple caftan. "Over our clothes?"

"Don't be ridiculous."

"We're just visiting," Helsa says. "I'm fine with the clothes I have on."

Durth shakes her head adamantly. "Everybody must wear the uniform of Legalis. Change."

"Here?" Solana asks.

"Here." She hands each of us a white tie belt.

We all turn away from each other and undress. The caftan has a slit at the neck and long sleeves. There is no shape whatsoever. I tie the belt around my waist, then fold my white dress from Regalia. Since it's white at least I'll have a change of clothes.

When I turn around I see that Lieb has put his many-colored vest under the robe. The robe covers it, but I see a smidge of it at the neckline. I point at my own neck and he pulls the robe up to cover it.

Solana's robe puddles on the floor around her. "Do you have one that's shorter?"

Durth retrieves a pair of scissors, kneels on the floor by Solana, and proceeds to cut eight inches off the bottom. The cut is not straight — which I suspect bothers a seamstress like Solana as much as it does me.

She gets up with a moan and points at the floor in a corner. "Toss yer old clothes and shoes there." Then she pulls out a basket of sandals, tied together in pairs. "Put some on."

We find sandals that fit and stand in a row, ready for whatever comes next. I feel very exposed. By giving up our old clothes it's like we're fully giving up our old life.

"Where you from?" she asks as she shoves the basket back in the closet with her foot.

"Regalia."

"Wrong answer."

I'm confused. "It's the only answer we have."

She shakes her head. "You are from the desert."

Solana takes a shot at it. "Yes, we came through the desert, but we're from Regalia."

"Not no more, you ain't. You are prohibited from saying the word 'Regalia' here."

"But you just said it," Helsa says.

The woman points a stubby finger at her. "Watch it, girl."

Solana and I both flash Helsa a look. Now is not the time to make waves.

The woman scratches the back of her neck, picks something off, looks at it, and flicks it to the floor. "Back to what I was sayin' . . . " She glares at Helsa. "If anybody asks where yer from, you say yer from the desert. Or say you were saved from the desert. Understand?"

"I suppose that's technically true. But why can't we say *Regalia?*" I ask.

"Do you understand?" she asks again, more forcefully.

We all say yes.

She returns to her chair, sighs deeply as if she's bored, and clasps her hands on the table. "Here's what you needs to know. First and foremost, you must blend in." She eyes me. "Though with that red hair of yours . . ." She takes a new breath. "Anyway, there will be no flaunting that yer outsiders."

"But won't people know we're not from here?"

She scowls at us. "They'd better not."

"What happens if they do?" Helsa asks.

Durth touches the stud on her shoulder. "Ya get one a these."

"What *are* those?" Lieb asks.

"They are called Faults. And you don't want to get many or you'll regret it."

"Who gives the Faults out?" I ask.

"Fault Finders. And they're everywhere." She leans forward and lowers her voice ominously. "They're always watchin'."

Sounds horrible.

"Finally, you must learn the motto of Legalis — and live it. Listen carefully: duty, deference, dedication, dependability." She glares at us. "Repeat 'em."

I look at Solana. "Duty . . ." she says.

I remember the next two. "Deference. Dedication."

"And?" Durth asks.

Lieb's face lights up. "Dependability!"

"There you go," Durth says. "Say 'em all now."

We repeat them together. "Duty, deference, dedication, dependability."

She slaps her hands on the table. "That's it. Yer done here." She points at another door. "Go outside and walk to the first door on yer right." She raises her arm in a salute. "All hail, Legalis!"

Her final words are unnerving.

"Where are we going?" Solana asks her.

"Your cells."

Cells? I've had enough of cells.

"Go on with ya," she says. "Or leave the way you came."

We do as we're told and enter a street teaming with people.

"Everyone wears the same thing," Solana says.

"We leave a land of fashion and come to a land of conformity," I say.

"It *will* make it easier to blend in," Solana says.

Though the buildings are of different heights, they are unadorned white boxes with windows poked in them. There is an occasional exterior stair leading to a higher level. The street is a mixture of sand and dirt.

What do they have against color?

We get a few curious looks, but far fewer than we would have gotten if we'd worn our own clothes.

But then . . .

"Helsa?"

Helsa turns toward a man's voice. She gasps, then runs to him. "Papa!"

Papa?

Solana and Lieb squeal and run to him too. There are hugs, kisses, and tears.

"Papa, I can't believe you're alive!"

Her exiled father lived through his exile as we lived? Thank you, dear Keeper!

Solana motions for me to join them. "Devin, I'd like you to meet a very special friend, Cashlin —"

Suddenly, I feel an inner nudge that propels me to say, "Oria."

My friends look at me, confused.

"Since when?" Helsa asks.

"Since now." We don't need to have this discussion at the moment.

I hold out my hand, but he shakes his head. "No handshakes allowed. But it's nice to meet you."

"And you."

Helsa puts her arm around his waist, but he suddenly looks nervous and removes it. "No touching."

No touching? But they hugged each other.

Devin looks upward at a huge clock. In fact, I see clocks on the face of every building.

Then he asks, "Where are you supposed to go?"

"The first door on the right," I say.

"To our cells," Helsa says.

"I know the place. Let's get off the street so we can talk. But quickly. It's nearly time for the hourly Count."

"Count of what?" Solana asks.

He urges us forward. "Hurry."

"Are we in trouble?" I ask.

"Not yet."

Have I traded one prison for another?

Chapter One

Oria

I'm in a cell. Again.

It's in a different land, but the cell is strikingly similar. Strikingly bleak.

There are only two narrow cots. No window. The biggest difference is the absence of bars. Actually, there's no door either. The cell Solana and I share is more of a stall than a room. Helsa and Lieb are in the one next to us. It's just us four. Obviously not that many visitors come to Legalis. A table with two benches sits in a shared space. An open privy is too close.

Lovely.

I sit on my cot listening to the joy playing out in the next stall. It's a miracle that Helsa found her father alive in Legalis. He was exiled months ago. The family reunion makes me think of my own mother and brother back in Regalia.

I will never see my family again. The lack of contact with anyone who shares my blood and history is sobering. Yet along with the lack comes a portion of relief because I will never again have to endure their disapproval. Unfortunately, the relief brings with it a wave of guilt. The conflicting feelings make my head spin, but my thoughts speak the truth. They loved me as long as I did what was expected of me, as long as I owned the elevated status of Premier Patron that brought them a higher standing and perks by association. I was a means to a better end.

They did *not* love me when I pushed the boundaries of Regalia by interacting with other Rings, working toward justice against an abuser, or bent the rules by wearing a plain white dress instead of the expected finery. And they did not understand me talking about the Keeper in private, much less in public. I disgraced them before I was exiled, while I was exiled, and I can only imagine the consequences they are enduring in my absence.

Regarding the Keeper, I pity their closed minds and hearts. What they don't know *will* hurt them as much as what I *do* know about the Keeper helps me.

I stop the thought. Helps me? I look around and wonder if help is the right word.

Talking about him has hurt me, for I was exiled into the Swirling Desert for my faith. That he parted the sand so I could safely walk *in* rather than being swept *away* is evidence of his mercy. The fact Solana, Helsa, and Lieb ran after me is a special blessing. How brave they were! Courage had nothing to do with me getting through the desert. I had no choice. But their choice — choices — came from a courageous trait I envy.

We could use some of that courage now. I don't like how they look to me for guidance as if I know what I'm doing. I'm as ignorant as they are. They've believed in the Keeper longer than I have. I'm a rookie at faith. I'm a rookie at making decisions. I'm a rookie at being a rebel.

What do I have to show for any of it? I'm a stranger in a very strange land. In Regalia I lived a privileged life with the best house and the best garden in the Patron Ring, with servants to answer every whim. Marli, Dom, and Irwin . . . what are they doing now? Did they get in trouble for their connection with me? With him? For their faith was stronger than mine.

I run my hand along the rough blanket on the cot. From lofty thoughts of courage and faith to me wondering if I'll ever sleep in a soft bed, enjoy a hot bath, or eat my favorite foods. How fickle and shallow I am.

Durth rushes into our building, and past me to the next cell. "Quiet! I could hear you on the street!"

I move to the edge of my cell to watch the exchange.

"We're just celebrating," Devin says. "This is my daughter, my mother, and Lieb is like a son —"

"I don't care. I just want *you* outta here. Quickly, before the hourly Count."

"Don't leave, Papa," Helsa pleads.

"Fine," he says. "If I can't stay then let's all go. Come with me. Quickly."

As they pass my cell, Solana invites me along. "Follow us."

I do as she says, choosing to follow someone in-the-know rather than sitting alone in my cell, chewing on a hundred questions.

There are far fewer people in the street now. Due to the mysterious Count?

"Hurry to my unit!" Devin says.

What will happen if we don't get where we're going before —?

I squeal as loud chimes peal. I look up and see two clocks nearby. Both are ringing. There's a cacophony of chimes from multiple clocks, all sounding at once. I want to stop and put my hands over my ears, but I don't dare. I feel the sounds reverberate in my chest.

"In here!" Devin opens a door and we rush inside. Oddly, he reaches into a bowl of pebbles, then sets two white pebbles and four black pebbles on a small exterior shelf built into the wall. He closes the door and only then takes a breath. "We made it."

When the chimes finish their awful noise, I point toward the door. "You put six pebbles on a ledge outside. Why?"

"It's for the hourly Count. Everyone needs to report how many people are in their unit: white pebbles for however many residents are inside, and black pebbles to represent the visitors who've run inside for cover."

"Cover? From what? Can anyone run into your home?"

He nods once. "As I can run into any building if I'm caught away from home. No one can refuse entry or be refused entry."

"Someone comes around and keeps track?" his mother asks.

"The Counters."

"But why pebbles?" I ask. "Why not just write it down somehow?"

He smiles a cynical smile. "Because writing is frowned upon."

"Frowned upon?" Solana asks.

He nods once. "It's not a law exactly —"

"I can't imagine why it would be," I say.

"But writing and reading are discouraged. I'm not sure you can get a Fault for it, but why risk it?"

I throw up my hands. "That's absurd."

He nods. "A lot about Legalis is absurd. You've heard it said that knowledge is power? Think about it: books provide knowledge, and writing can lead to an exchange of ideas, therefore . . ."

This is crazy. "They don't want people to learn?"

"They do not."

Helsa stares at the door. "Back to the counting . . . do they check every house to make sure the count is accurate?"

"Not every house every hour, but often enough that I'm not willing to test it."

I realize something. "You set out two pebbles for the residents? Who else lives here?"

He raises a finger, then calls out, "Elum?"

A tall man with a graying beard makes his presence known by stepping out of a room where I see two cots. He nods at us.

"This is Elum. Elum, this is my mother, Solana, my daughter, Helsa, family friend Lieb, and new friend, Oria. They've traveled here from..." He hesitates at the word, then whispers, "Regalia."

Elum's gray eyebrows rise slightly, the only indication that he is surprised.

"Nice to meet you," I say.

He nods as a greeting, making me wonder if he can speak.

"By the way," Devin says. "Although this is our unit we don't actually own it. No one owns anything in Legalis. I was assigned to stay here. Elum was here first." Devin motions us toward a table with two benches. "Please."

I sit on a bench with Devin and Elum. Nearby there's a small fireplace with a hanging pot, and a built-in counter with some cups, bowls, and a basket of bread on it. There is no adornment anywhere. No pictures on the walls. No pretties to brighten the room. No curtain at the one window.

Devin flattens his hands on the table. "I still can't believe you're here."

"It's a miracle," Solana says.

He looks at me. "Helsa said you were exiled and the others ran after you?"

"That's right. The sands parted. Did they part for you too?"

"They did. But no one came with me." He smiles at his daughter. "I'm so thankful the three of you came, but what about your mother?"

Solana and Helsa exchange a glance and I feel sorry for what they are about to say.

"She died, Devin," Solana says, reaching over to grab his hand. "She grieved to death. Over you."

He is clearly stunned and his expression collapses in on itself. He blinks over and over as if trying to blink the truth away. Then he says, "She was always delicate in mind and body, but I never imagined . . ."

Solana squeezes his hand. "She missed you desperately."

"I missed her too. All of you."

"But we're here now," Solana says. "We thank the Keeper for *that* miracle."

He nods, but his features are drawn with sadness. A happy reunion followed by the slap of grief.

Suddenly, the door is flung open and a man barges in. His eyes scan over us, then he leaves.

It's completely unnerving. "A Counter?" I ask.

"One of many."

"Why do they count?" Lieb asks.

Devin draws a deep breath. "The first thing you have to know about Legalis is that there are laws about everything, from what we eat, to what time we sleep, to how many may gather, and—"

"Why?" Lieb asks again.

"Because they want to control us completely."

"Why?"

Devin gives a sigh of resignation. "I wish I knew."

The notion of the Count bothers me. "They count every hour?"

"On the hour. Until ten. Then there's a curfew until it starts up again at seven in the morning."

"What happens during the curfew?"

"Nothing — or nothing we can see. No one is allowed outside. At all."

"It sounds ridiculous. "How long do we have to stay in here now?"

"Until we hear a single chime after fifteen minutes."

"All this counting doesn't allow people to relax for more than . . . forty-five minutes," Solana says.

"Which is the point."

I already feel the weight of the restrictions. "Who makes all these laws?"

"The Law Commission which is run by the Notables. The Notables are the elite here, the ruling class."

"Notables?" Helsa asks. "What an arrogant name."

"For arrogant people." He sighs. "I don't want to completely depress you about your new home but —"

"Home?" Helsa asks. "Are we stuck here?"

He seems surprised by the question. "You can't go back, daughter," he says. "The Swirling Desert is a mighty barrier in both directions."

Solana looks pensive. "Since the Keeper created a way for us to walk *into* the desert, couldn't he let us back in?"

"Do you want to go back?" Devin asks. "Your family is here now."

But *my* family is there. And my friends. And my status. Do I want to go back? Would I be allowed back if I somehow got there?

"Legalis is regimented but it's livable," Devin says.

"It doesn't sound livable to me, Papa," Helsa says.

I think of the restrictions in our past and present lives. "Both Regalia and Legalis are very set in their ways," I say.

He thinks about this a moment, then gives me a nod. "That's a good observation, Cashlin."

"Oria."

"Right." He makes a face. "Mother introduced you as Cashlin. I remember there being a Patron Cashlin."

"Which is me."

"Why the name change?"

I look down and hesitate. "My answer is going to sound presumptuous, but since your mother told me you are a man of faith I want to explain with full honesty. The Keeper gave it to me."

"The Keeper gave you a new name?"

I have to tell the whole story. "He appeared to me in my garden — twice. In person, as real as you are to me now."

"Hmm," Devin says. "That's quite . . . a story."

"It's not a story. It's the truth," I say.

Solana comes to my defense. "Oria doesn't lie, son."

He raises his hands in surrender. "Sorry. I didn't mean to doubt, but I've never heard of such a thing."

"I don't take the experience for granted." I don't need others to believe me for it to be true. But back to the name change . . . "The Keeper said the name Cashlin suited me for a long time, as it means vain. But he told me one day I would be called Oria — one who is humble in spirit and manner."

He looks doubtful again. My words *do* sound pompous. I set out to change his impression of me.

"In our second meeting the Keeper said I would know when it was time to make the name change, and even though I don't feel I've achieved those qualities yet, when I got here and met you . . . the time seemed right to officially make the change. Maybe the name will help me *be* humble in spirit and manner."

I'm relieved when he smiles. "It's a good goal for all of us. And the Keeper must think you're special to visit you like that."

"I don't know about that but—"

He points at me. "Look at you, being so humble about it."

Suddenly we hear a commotion outside and run to the window. We see two men wearing black robes and hoods that completely cover their heads except for their eyes. They have a man backed up against the wall across the street. A woman stands in the doorway, pleading with them.

"What's going on?" I ask.

Devin takes a look. "Our neighbor was probably late getting inside again." He sighs. "I feel for his wife. I've seen him test the law before. I guess his time is up — literally."

"Those men look so ominous, all dressed in black," Helsa says.

"They are the Fault Finders. And yes, they are to be feared."

"Durth, the woman at the entrance to Legalis, mentioned them," I say.

Lieb nods. "She says they're always watching."

"That, they are." He motions for us to return to our seats.

"What happens to your neighbor now?" Solana asks.

"He'll probably be put in jail."

"For how long?"

"It depends on how many Faults he's earned." He touches the black stud on his shoulder. "I think he had five or six."

"Durth mentioned Faults too."

He explains. "In Regalia we called them demerits." He touches the stud again. "But here we have to wear our Faults on our shoulder for everyone to see. It's demeaning."

"That's horrible," I say. Elum doesn't have any studs. I wonder how unusual that is.

"How did you get your Fault?" Solana asks.

"I broke a bowl in the street."

No one says anything for a beat.

"That's it?" Helsa asks.

"I'd taken a bowl to the food booth to make carrying our allotment easier, and I tripped and it broke. I cleaned it up right away, but someone must have turned me in."

"What law did you break?" Solana asks.

He recites it. "'Do not treat possessions recklessly.'"

"Wow," Lieb says. "I'll be extra extra careful."

"Someone turned you in, Papa?" Helsa asks.

"It happens. It's hard to trust people. There are a lot of tattletales in Legalis. Turning others in for breaking a law is a way to get some of your own Faults removed."

Lieb looks worried. "I would never turn any of you in."

"I know you wouldn't," Devin says. "But a lot of people get into it."

"Do the number of Faults represent how many you've gotten in a lifetime?" Solana asks.

He shakes his head. "Just in a year. There's a Zero Day where everyone can take off the studs and throw them in a huge barrel outside the Sanctuary. Then it all starts over."

"How long ago was Zero Day?" Lieb asks.

"A few months ago. Right before I got here."

"How many Faults until you get arrested like your neighbor?" Helsa asks.

Devin shrugs. "It depends. The system is unpredictable — which is something else Regalia and Legalis have in common."

His words hang in the air as the restrictions of our new home settle in. No touching, no reading or writing, no being outside when you shouldn't be, no breaking bowls . . .

Devin studies Lieb. "Are you wearing your memory vest under your robe, boy?"

Lieb pulls the neckline down proudly. "I am."

I remember Lieb telling me about the vest. "He told me it was his weave of the world."

"My world," Lieb says. But he frowns. "I don't know if there are any new scraps to add to it, to remember this place."

Maybe that's for the best.

Devin points to the neckline. "You need to cover it better or else you might get in trouble. It makes you stand out."

Solana examines it. "Do you have a needle and thread? I could stitch the shoulder seams so they'd pull the whole robe higher."

"We do," Devin says. "They give us some to repair tears."

While he gets the supplies, Leib starts to remove his robe, then realizes he's not wearing any pants. Devin brings him a blanket from the bedroom.

I wish he could wear the vest for everyone to see. In its own way, it's piece of art.

Solana gets to work on the robe and Lieb points at the bread in the basket, "I'm hungry. Is there a law against eating bread today?"

Devin chuckles. "There isn't. Elum, let's get some bread and cheese for our guests."

As Helsa and Lieb help the men, I have a moment alone with Solana. "What do you think?" I ask.

She's turned Lieb's robe inside out and swiftly sews a straight row of stitches. "I think it's going to be tough living here. Chances are we'll break laws without even knowing it."

"I really don't want to push boundaries again," I say. "I did that enough in Regalia."

She motions around the room. "And look what it got you. Us."

"I wish I knew the bigger picture; what we're supposed to do here."

"I didn't mean to eavesdrop," Devin says, "but I have an answer to that." He and Elum bring a bowl of cheese and a loaf of bread to the table and everyone sits. "Maybe you can help the Exiled."

"The Exiled?" I ask.

"They're similar to the people we called the Devoted back home. Actually they *are* the Devoted from back home. All of them were exiled from Regalia and ended up here. Many have been here for years."

"How many are there?" Solana asks.

"I'm not exactly sure. We only know a handful. Since we're supposed to blend in it takes time to get to know people enough to share." He hands his mother the bread. "Faith here is complicated. Unlike Regalia where faith is banned, everyone in Legalis *has* to believe."

"That sounds like a good thing," I say.

"It's not. They aren't being taught about the Keeper, but are forced to believe in the Judge."

It sounds ominous.

"We saw a Relic back home that implied the Keeper is a judge," Solana says.

Devin shakes his head. "This Judge is not the Keeper. This Judge is vindictive, controlling, and quite a bit scary. Bowing down to this Judge is required. Fear is a way of life here."

It sounds awful. "Unlike Regalia, it sounds like faith isn't outlawed it's out-lawed. Too many laws."

Lieb shakes his head. "Too many laws make me tired."

"I agree completely," Devin says. "It's taken me months to find a few of the Exiled. Knowing who's who and what people believe is hard. People don't sit around and chat about their beliefs because they're too busy surviving. And speaking against the Judge . . ." He glances over his shoulder at the window, then lowers his voice. "It's hard to know who to trust."

"How can we help, son?" Solana asks as she ties a knot in the end of the seam and bites the thread off with her teeth. She immediately rethreads the needle to sew the other shoulder seam.

"Tomorrow is Sanctuary Day. Everyone is required to go to the Sanctuary. You need to see firsthand what passes for faith in Legalis. You need to see the Judge in person."

Lieb shakes his head. "But you said it's scary."

"It is."

"How so?" his mother asks.

"You'll see."

I'm curious and very wary. What have we gotten ourselves into?

I jump when a single bell chimes.

"That marks the quarter hour, so it's safe to get you back to your cells—once we finish our meal, and Nana gets Lieb's robe fixed."

"Can't we sleep here?" Helsa asks. "I'd sleep on the floor."

"Sorry, my love, but you can't. New arrivals have to stay in the cells."

"How long?" Helsa asks.

He shrugs. "For me it was three days, but I've heard it's never the same. When they decide it's time, you'll be given work assignments. If you're not there when they want to tell you . . ." He reaches out and squeezes Helsa's hand. "I'm sure we'll have plenty of time together. I promise."

"What kind of work assignments?" I ask.

"Whatever they want you to do. Again, the goal is to blend in." He passes a plate of cheese. "You need to eat quickly, and then go."

I take note of his word choice: you *need* rather than you *should*. I already feel the restrictions of Legalis weighing me down.

Chapter Two

Solana

I ache all over.

No one is up yet, and I try not to moan when I turn over on my cot. Sleeping on the ground in the desert, and now on this hard cot . . . I'm too old for this. I get situated as quietly as possible. I don't want to wake Cashlin—Oria.

Oria. A special name, given to her by the Keeper. I didn't get a new name. Of course I also didn't see him. Or get to talk to him. At least in person anyway.

I shake my head against the cot. Jealousy is not constructive and won't serve any of us here in Legalis. Anywhere, period.

What a wretched place. Better than the desert, but worse than Regalia. I know that's not a fair thing to say as we've only been here a few hours but at least in Regalia we had a reason to get up every morning. Factory work wasn't fun, but it could be satisfying. We were creating something from nothing. Durth says our new jobs won't start until the day after Sanctuary Day. Tomorrow. For *this* is Sanctuary Day.

I should sleep. Who knows what the day might bring and what new laws will be thrown at us?

"Solana?" Oria whispers.

"I'm awake."

"Want to go outside and talk?"

"What about the curfew?" I ask.

"Just outside the door?"

We tiptoe out to the street. The white buildings reflect the dim light of the coming morn.

We stand in an alcove to stay out of sight. The night air smells used, as if the tedium of the day has not been completely shuffed off.

I whisper the first question. "What do you think about all the laws? I mean, Devin got a stud for breaking a bowl."

"They make no sense. No touching? I don't go around touching people in public, but to know it's against the law? What purpose does it serve? It's bizarre."

"It's good we're safe and fed, but I'm nervous. Devin is nervous, and he's been here for months. He's not one to talk about his worries, but I see it. So *his* anxiety is mine."

"Is there a list of the laws?" she asks. "Otherwise how can we *not* break them? I don't want my shoulders covered in Faults."

"Maybe they show mercy to newcomers."

Oria scoffs. "I doubt mercy is a Legalis trait."

"They do have Zero Day."

"Probably out of necessity or else people would run out of shoulder space."

I stretch and enjoy the pull of it. "These old muscles don't like mornings. Or cots."

Oria nods. She probably hurts too because she is used to sleeping in a soft bed.

"What do you think about Elum?" I ask. "He never said a word. Do you think he *can* talk?"

"I don't know. I wonder how he and your son met."

I feel bad for not knowing. "We should have asked. We should have talked to Elum. We ignored him."

Oria nods. "You're right. I felt overwhelmed with all there is to learn, but I should've been polite. We were in *his* unit."

"Agreed."

Oria leans against the wall and gazes at the cloudy sky. "The Keeper led us to Legalis but they don't seem open to him."

"The Judge . . . it sounds awful."

"Being afraid all the time sounds awful."

Suddenly a Fault Finder walks into view, stops, and points at us. We stiffen and gasp.

"Mind the curfew!" He doesn't yell, but his tone makes it clear we're in trouble.

"We're so sorry," Oria says.

"We just got here yesterday."

He hesitates, then shoos us inside.

I hate this place.

**

Devin stops by to lead us to the Sanctuary. The streets are full to overflowing with people headed in the same direction. A mass of humanity, sour-faced and plodding. There is no enthusiasm. They don't want to go, they have to go. I notice everyone has multiple black studs on their shoulders. It's only a matter of time until I earn my own.

"What happens during the hourly Count?" Helsa asks. "It must be a mob to get everyone inside at once."

"That'd be a lot of pebbles," Lieb says.

Devin smiles. "On Sanctuary Day there are no Counts."

Oria slaps her hand against her chest in mock horror. "How dare they do something so . . . so humane?"

Devin's shrug is disconcerting. He used to be a rebel, a man full to overflowing with faith. Of course, such passion did get him exiled, but seeing him here in Legalis . . . he seems too complacent. Where is my firebrand son?

We turn a corner and see our destination. The white buildings part for a public square that culminates in an enormous building that must be the Sanctuary. It's covered in white stucco like all the other buildings, but it's massive in breadth and height, over double the height of everything surrounding it. There's a balcony overlooking the square. I wonder what dignitaries show themselves there. The Law Commission or Notables? Or the Judge?

We follow the crowd inside, people without a choice.

I look upward and see a large opening in the roof. The sunlight shines at an angle toward a loft at the front. High on the wall above it is a four-pointed star lying on its side. There has to be symbolism in it and I'd like to ask Devin, but don't dare right now because no one is talking. The silence is deafening. Even the children are somber.

We stand shoulder to shoulder facing the front. Because I'm short, I can't see a thing. Devin looks down at me, realizes the problem, and says, "Let's move forward." He pushes through the crowd and the rest of us follow. We end up front and center. Other than a better view, I'm not sure it's a smart place to be.

Twenty-feet in front of us are two black-clad men sitting on a raised platform, facing us—one, whose face is covered in a black hood. More people in black sit on five rows of chairs on either side, facing the middle. The fact they are seated and we have to stand speaks volumes about our respective status.

The maskless man on the platform stands. Adorning his black robe is a gold medallion that matches the four-pointed star. He walks to the center and I feel a stir of anticipation around me. His face isn't covered like the Fault Finders we saw, but it's clear he has power; he's to be feared. "Who's that?" I whisper to Devin.

"Ivar, the acting Head Notable." He puts a finger to his lips to silence any more questions.

The man raises his hands. "Let us repeat the motto of Legalis." The crowd joins him: "Duty, Deference, Dedication, Dependability. All hail, Legalis!"

I glance at Oria. These are the words Durth taught us. The way the voices echo in the large room makes me shiver. It's like they're brainwashed. There's nothing inherently wrong with any of the words, yet when they are repeated as a chant, the words leave a chill in the air.

Duty. Deference. Dedication. Dependability. The motto is all about being beholden to someone more powerful.

When I look at the people standing to either side of us, many look straight ahead as if in rapt attention. But a few meet my gaze and look away. One woman holds my gaze and shocks me by rolling her eyes. Apparently, not everyone in Legalis embraces the slogan. Yet what choice do they have but to pretend to be loyal?

The woman's eyes move to Devin and there's a brief exchange between them. I wonder if she's one of the Exiled.

I turn my attention back to Ivar.

The Acting Head Notable — what an arrogant title — begins to list what he calls the "Directives of Legalis." Again, everyone recites in unison.

"Directive number One: Nothing is above the all-powerful Judge of Legalis."

I shudder and want to yell, *The Keeper is higher!*

"Directive number Two: Never question the Notables of Legalis."

How many are there? If the people in the seats are Notables, I'd guess there are about one hundred.

"Directive number Three: Never speak against Legalis or the Judge."

Are there any rebels here?

"Directive number Four: Never miss Sanctuary Day."

I'm not sure forced faith can ever be a good thing.

"Directive number Five: Never speak against those who have authority over you."

Back to forced loyalty.

"Directive number Six: All lives belong to Legalis. No violence."

I agree with no violence. But my life is my own, and is a gift from the Keeper.

"Directive number Seven: Never touch anyone in public."

I look at Devin as he recites the Directives, and he skims his hand along mine. I see no benefit in such a Directive. People need to touch people: shake hands, hug, touch a shoulder . . .

"Directive number Eight: Never take anything that has not been given to you by Legalis."

Even though Legalis doesn't seem very generous?

"Directive number Nine: Never lie or deceive."

I agree, and suddenly a truth comes to me: there's a difference between never lying and never telling the truth. I fear Legalis may be missing the truth part.

"Directive number Ten: Never desire anything beyond what you are given by Legalis."

They've successfully put themselves in total control of people's loyalty, love, lives, and longings. They should put *those* words on their four-pointed star.

The second man up front stands. He wears a masked hood with his black robe.

"A Fault Finder?" I whisper to Devin.

"The Head Fault Finder."

I fear him more than the Head Notable. The man scans his audience. "Last week there were fifty touching Faults, thirty-four Count Faults, twenty-one food Faults, eighteen insubordination Faults, and twelve adaptation of prescribed design Faults, for a total of one hundred and thirty-five Faults against the Notables and the Judge. This is an increase of thirteen from the previous week. If such blatant acts of disobedience are not curtailed there will be repercussions. What say you?"

The crowd responded in unison. "Yes, Head Fault Finder."

All righty then.

Suddenly, the woman who'd looked at Devin and me, rushes toward the Fault Finder like she's going to attack him. "Set my husband free! Set him free! It's not fair —"

The man recoils and steps back as masked guards tackle the woman to the ground, restrain her, and lead her away. She struggles against them, continuing to shout about setting her husband free. I look at Devin. "Will she be all right?"

"No."

I see his muscles tense and his jaw tighten.

The crowd grows restless, yet no one steps forward, no one takes up her chant for freedom. I thought I understood intimidation. Regalia was good at it, but this is different. To forcibly remove her . . .

Suddenly I hear a gasp from the crowd. Everyone looks up at the loft. An enormous creature stares down at us. It's taller than the tallest man, and is entirely black. Its arms end in horrific black hands with long, pointy fingers that look as sharp as knives. There is no hair, no nose, no mouth, no ears, just an ominous shroud of blackness, with mirrored eyes, reflecting back at us.

It spreads its arms wide, its fingers splayed as if ready to slash. It stares down at us, taking the Sanctuary captive.

The Judge.

Everyone kneels and bows their heads, not out of reverence, but out of fear. I do the same. I have no choice. And my fear is real.

The Head Notable declares, "Go forth, subjects of the Judge!

I suffer a shiver. I don't want to be its subject. I don't even know what it is. I especially don't want its ominous presence hanging over me. I have so many questions, yet I'm fearful of the answers.

When it withdraws people stand and start to leave, a hoard of bodies not touching one another, yet sharing a desire to distance themselves from something evil. Their fear and tension is palpable. We follow the crowd.

No one lingers outside. Everyone hurries away.

As do we.

As we get out of sight of the Sanctuary, Helsa says, "That was creepy."

"What is that thing?" Oria asks.

"Shh!" Devin says. "Nothing until we get home."

I've never seen my son afraid before. In Regalia, he was fearless.

Here in Legalis? His fear spurs my own.

**

Once home, Devin closes the door behind us and lingers there. His eyes avoid ours, and his body is on edge.

"That Judge is really scary," Lieb says.

"Yes, it is."

"Do they worship that thing?" Helsa asks.

"They fear that thing," Devin says. "I suppose fear is a sort of worship."

"It has claws," Lieb says. "Knife-y fingers."

"Yes, it does."

"Does it physically hurt people?" I ask. "You said people go to jail, but is there more punishment? From . . . *it?*"

"There are stories of it swooping down and killing people, but —"

"It can fly?" Liebs eyes are wide.

Devin shrugs. "The stories say it can."

"Do you know the woman they took away?" I ask.

He draws in a breath as though it's painful to do so. "I do."

This makes sense. The way she looked at him . . . "Is she part of the Exiled?"

"She is." With a spurt of motion he moves to the table. "Sit. I have a lot to tell you."

His jaw is tight, his forehead furrowed. Once we're seated he begins. "The woman who rushed forward is one of the Exiled. Her name is Coli. Her husband has been in jail for two weeks."

"Did you know she was going to do what she did?" Oria asks.

Devin hesitates, then shrugs. "She talked about wanting to do it. I tried to talk her out of it. She just wants to be with him."

"In jail?" Helsa asks.

When he hesitates, my mind goes to more permanent consequences. "Or worse?" I ask.

"The worse is called Judging Day."

"What's that?"

He bites his lip. "I don't want to go into it. You have enough to absorb."

"But it's bad?" Helsa asks.

"That, it is." He takes a deep breath as if to rid himself of the subject. "I'll visit Coli at work tomorrow."

"You work at the jail?" Oria asks.

"My job is to clean out the cells, and deliver food and buckets of fresh water."

My son, who is highly skilled in leatherwork, cleans cells.

He continues. "You've been in Legalis one day. You don't understand how the laws weigh on us. Confine us. Even though most of us aren't in jail, we're all prisoners."

I touch his hand. "I apologize. You're right, son, we don't fully understand."

"The only way I've survived is by keeping my head down and not drawing attention to myself."

"You blend in," Helsa says.

"Exactly." He glances at Elum. "I thank the Keeper that I was assigned to share a unit with Elum, who also believes."

I wait for Elum to speak, but he only nods.

"Were you born here?" Oria asks him.

Again, a nod.

"Can you talk?" Lieb asks.

The boy's too blunt, but it's a good question—that is also answered with a nod.

"Elum *can* be a man of few words," Devin says. "Though when he does speak . . ."

Elum shrugs away the compliment.

What an interesting man. A handsome one too with his graying hair and beard. His eyes show a kind intelligence.

Suddenly Devin stands. "Enough doom and gloom. Since there is no Count today, it's the best day to show you around."

I'm disappointed when Elum stays behind.

Chapter Three

Helsa

I don't want to be here.

I love seeing Papa again and I'm glad to be with Nana and Lieb—I'm glad I wasn't left behind in Regalia—but this place. This absurd, nasty place…

Papa takes us on a tour of Legalis. There's not that much to see. Where the Imp Ring back home was bland and gray, at least there were other Rings that offered variety. Each of the seven Rings was different. In Legalis, everything looks the same: white stucco buildings and white clad people—neither has any embellishment, except for the stupid Fault studs on people's shoulders. I find myself judging people by how many Faults I see. That can't be a good thing. And *we* stand out because our robes are new. Everyone else's are dirty from the dusty streets. Ours will be soon enough.

"How many people live in Legalis?" Oria asks.

"I'd be guessing, but maybe there are three hundred in the Masses."

"The Masses?"

He waves his hand to encompass the whole. "Us."

Nana says, "It looked like there were about a hundred Notables up front in the Sanctuary."

"That sounds about right," Papa says.

"There were 135 Faults last week," Oria says. "Which means nearly half of the Masses got a Fault?"

"Probably."

"How depressing," I say. "Doesn't it make you want to just get a ton of 'em all at once and be done with it?"

"No, it does not!" Papa flashes me a hard look. "Don't even think such a thing."

Nana gives me a look too. Don't they see how ridiculous this whole thing is?

Lieb points at a line of people. "What are they waiting for?"

"Lamp oil, linens, pots. But that longest line is for food allotments."

"What's the currency?" Oria asks.

"There isn't any. Everybody gets the same."

"Then what's the incentive to work?" Nana asks.

He shakes his head in disgust. "There isn't any of that either."

The idea of not having tokens or anything to use to buy stuff is weird. "We didn't have a lot of choices in Regalia, but at least we could spend our tokens however we wanted to."

"What does Legalis produce?" Oria asks.

"Discontent," Papa says.

Yes, yes, we get it. "No, Papa, really. Regalia produces fashion. What do people make here?"

"Whatever is needed for them to survive. Pottery, furniture, cooking utensils, lamps . . ."

"All very useful things," Nana says.

"At least fashion was pretty," Oria says.

Papa faces us and steps close. "There's no commerce here, no creativity. Remember in the Sanctuary this morning where twelve people got Faults for the 'adaptation of proscribed design'?"

"I remember that," I say. "What does it mean?"

"It means twelve people got tired of making the same pots or chairs or pottery that are prescribed by the authorities and did something different. They were creative."

"And they were punished for it?"

"They were. There are shops where we can get the essentials, but everything is doled out; every pot matches the next pot, and so on."

"Where's the fun in that?" I say.

Papa scoffs. "Fun? Surely you jest."

Oria keeps shaking her head, obviously disgusted. "In Regalia the Creatives were constantly coming up with new fashion."

"Sometimes outrageous fashion," Nana says. "Remember your snake outfit?"

Oria flips her hand at the memory. "Don't mention it. It was ghastly."

"Yeah, it was," I say. "But at least it was allowed to be ghastly. It was something different."

Papa continues our tour and sweeps his hand to the right. "On the outskirts is farmland for crops and animal breeding which is our food supply. But around here?" He points at a few straggly trees that sparingly spot the street. "This is all the green we get."

"How do people spend their days?" Nana asks.

"Working jobs they didn't choose and being bored to death. The citizens are called the Masses because that's what they are: a mass of people who share tedium and an oppressive case of the blahs."

"Yuck, Papa. It sounds horrible," I say. "Even though I didn't always like my work at the factory, I *did* like creating something. And work gave me friends."

"Community," Nana adds.

Lieb looks at the other lines of people as we walk past. "I liked delivering messages. I could do that here."

"People aren't supposed to write," Papa says. "They *can* write, and once in a while someone will bring a note to one of the prisoners in jail, but about a year ago the Masses were told that writing and reading were nonessential. They had to turn in all books and paper." He spreads his hands. "The absence of which, adds to their boredom."

I've never read much—I didn't have much free time *to* read, but to not have that option makes me sad. And I remember Mama reading to me when I was little.

We move along the narrow, winding streets. I'm lost and have to trust Papa to get us home.

He stops and points at a large arch. "Down there is where the Notables live."

I peer through the arch but don't see any buildings. The street dips downward and disappears beyond an iron gate. I point. "They live *down* there?"

"They do. It's cool there—or so I've heard. They basically have their own town beneath the town."

"Do they have to wear white robes?" Oria asks.

Papa shakes his head. "When they're out among us they wear black—like you saw them wearing in the Sanctuary. But I expect amongst themselves they wear pretty things. At least that's what I've heard."

I gaze at the brilliant blue sky. "I get why they prefer the cool of being underground. It's hot out here, and a few trees don't offer much shade."

Nana looks ahead. "Where's the jail where you work?"

"Follow me."

We come to a one-story building with five high horizontal openings, all in a row.

"That's the jail. Those are the prisoner's light and air slits. There are a few other jails around town, but this is where I work."

I stare at the openings that have no glass. At least the prisoners would be able to hear street noise—not that there'd be much comfort in it.

"Is there real crime here?" Oria asks. "Like stealing and such?"

"What are people going to steal? A bowl that's like the bowl you already have? We own nothing. We can't earn anything. We have no tokens to spend."

"Then why do you work at all?" Nana asks him.

"Because we're told to, and it's something to do. I'm still in the job I was assigned when I got here."

"Supposedly we get *our* job assignments tomorrow," I say.

"Whatever they are, make the best of them."

"You're depressing me, son," Nana says.

"It is what it is. You need to know the truth—even if you don't like it."

I don't like it at all. Can we go home now? Home home? Regalia?

Chapter Four

Oria

Why am I here?

Though my heart and mind are open, walking through Legalis offers me zero insight. As Devin said, the oppressiveness of the laws makes everyone a prisoner—physically, mentally, emotionally, and spiritually. Freedom is nonexistent and hope is dead. Providing both to the Masses needs to be my goal, but I have no idea how to go about it when people have been so beat down by the laws and the Judge.

When we return to Devin's unit after our tour, I ask, "When can we meet some of the Exiled?"

"Tonight," he says as we go inside.

"Where?"

"Here."

Elum has set out bread and cheese. We sit and eat. The rest of them seem used to this simple fare, but I miss the flavors of home and the delicious meals Irwin used to cook for me. Will I ever eat roast beef, sugar cookies, or cherry tarts again? I imagine the faces of Devin and Elum at their first taste.

I shake the image away. Food is the least of our problems.

**

That evening the Exiled begin to arrive.

Devin's unit is small—barely holding Elum and our group of four, yet there are already five additional people here.

Devin opens the door to one more. Now we are twelve.

"Welcome," he says. "Find a place to sit." Space is made on the benches for two, but the rest sit on the floor.

Introductions are made, though I doubt I'll remember names. They are friendly and I see an eagerness in their expressions that I have not seen anywhere else in Legalis. Dare it be hope?

The first man to arrive eagerly asks a question. "Tell us what's been going on in . . . you know where." He glances at the others. "Most of us have been gone a long—"

A woman interrupts and looks right at me. "Devin said you were a Patron, and you do look familiar. But Oria? I don't remember that name."

"I went by Cashlin."

Her eyes light up. "Patron Cashlin?"

"That's me—or was me."

"You were exiled?"

"I was."

"For what? You were high up . . . I didn't think the Council ever exiled Patrons."

"I was the first. Let's just say I pushed the boundaries until they had no choice."

Solana raises her hand. "She boldly spoke about the Keeper in public."

Devin nods. "Many of us are here because of that, yes?"

Most nod.

"I admire your courage," a man says.

A woman addresses Solana. "How did you three end up here? Were you exiled too?"

Solana shakes her head. "When the sands parted, we followed Oria through."

"You were taking quite a risk. We all had the sands part, but since you weren't the one exiled . . ."

"The path could have closed in on us." Solana looks at me. "But it didn't. And we're glad we came."

I glance at Helsa and can easily see she is *less* glad.

"Do you three believe?" another asks.

"We do," Solana says. "Though we never spoke in public, we believe in the Keeper."

A woman sighs. "If only the Keeper were here right now."

Isn't he?

"What can you tell us about the Judge?" Solana asks.

"Yeah," Helsa says. "What *is* it?"

"We don't know for sure," a woman says. "But it has everyone afraid."

A man who's sitting on the floor says, "We've heard that it's killed people who go out at night."

Devin raises a cautionary hand. "We've *heard*. We have no proof."

The man tosses his hands in the air. "What do we need? Bodies?"

Solana waves her hands. "The Judge scares me too, but haven't we gathered here tonight to learn more about the Keeper?"

"We have," I say. "We need to learn and figure out ways to win people over to him." I remember one of the Keeper's messages that helped me more than once. "One of the Relics we collected said, 'Fear not, for I am with you always.'"

I wait for the words to sink in, but instead of finding comfort a man says, "Relics? What are you talking about?"

I'm shocked. I thought Relics had been around for years, long before us. "They are slips of paper that have ancient wisdom about the Keeper written on them," I say.

"We collected quite a few back home," Solana says.

"And copied them, and handed them out," I add.

Lieb jumps to his feet. "I'll be right back." He rushes out of the house.

Solana turns to her son. "Didn't you see Relics before you were exiled?"

"I'd heard of them, and people quoted them to me, but I've never seen any."

"I never saw any either," a woman says.

"Who wrote them?" a man asks.

I exchange a look with Solana. She shakes her head and says, "Originally? I have no idea."

"Maybe they aren't authentic," a man says. "Maybe somebody wrote down what *they* wanted the Devoted to hear about the Keeper."

There's no way for us to prove otherwise.

Suddenly Lieb bursts through the door. He's carrying his messenger bag. "I've got them!"

My heart skips. Of course! Lieb has the proof we need.

"How did you get that bag here?" Devin asks.

"I carried it."

"But why didn't they take it away from you?"

He shrugs. "I dunno."

Devin points at it. "You've been lucky. Keep it out of sight and don't wear it outside."

"I know why no one took it," Solana says. "Because there were Relics inside and the Keeper was protecting them. Empty it, Lieb."

He turns the bag over above the table and dozens of Relics fall free. The Exiled just stare at them, but Solana picks one up and reads it. 'He is your protector, there at your right side to shade you from the sun. You won't be harmed by the sun during the day or by the moon at night.'" She smiles at Lieb. "You read this one to us in the desert."

"It was just what we needed to hear," he says.

I scan their faces. They're open, but wary.

"Pick one and read it aloud."

A man hesitates. "We're not supposed to read. What if the one of the Fault Finders find out?"

"Or worse, the Judge?" another says.

A woman scoffs. "Be brave, people. I'm willing to take a chance." She picks one. "'A cord of three strands is not quickly broken.'" She looks up. "Like a rope?"

I've never heard that one before. From her expression, neither has Solana, but she attempts an answer. "Yes, I think like a rope. Two strands—two people—are weaker than three."

"I believe that," a man says. "We're stronger together than we are alone."

Devin chooses a Relic. He reads it, then reads it again. "This is the one I'd heard about, and here it is, in my hands: '"There's a man who has a hundred sheep, but one of them wanders away. He left the ninety-nine and went off to look for the one. Recovering the one made him happier than the ninety-nine that didn't wander off. To the Keeper each one is precious.'"

People are silent, taking it in. Finally, a woman says, "I'm precious? To him?"

"You are," Devin says. "We all are."

We take turns reading the Relics. I pick the last one and after reading the first four words silently, I know it's special.

"What's it say?" Helsa asks.

"It says, 'Be strong and courageous! Do not be afraid or discouraged. For the Lord your God is with you wherever you go.'" Everyone nods. We all need these words. "My maid told me to 'be strong and courageous' when I first went before the Council."

"You went before the Council?" a man asks.

"Twice. I had two trials. I won one, and obviously, lost the other."

"Were you afraid?" a woman asks.

"Very."

"With good reason," a man says. "They exiled you."

"Maybe so, but I like the words," says a man. "I'm tired of being afraid all the time."

"As if we have much choice?" a woman says.

"Apparently we do." I shake the Relic in front of them. "This says we have a choice."

Solana doesn't say a word but extends her hands, summoning us to stand and form a circle.

"To being strong and courageous," she says.

**

When the Exiled leave, I know it's time for us to go too. Lieb packs up the Relics in his messenger bag and starts to fling it over his head and shoulder.

Devin stops him. "Lieb, give the bag to me for safekeeping."

He puts a protective hand on it. "I'll keep the Relics safe."

Devin is adamant. "I know you'll try, but if you're stopped and searched, you'll get more than a few Faults." He glances at Elum. "We have a place we can hide them."

Elum nods.

"Give them up, Lieb," Solana says. "It's sacred cargo you're carrying. They need a special hiding place."

Reluctantly, Lieb hands over his bag.

"Where are you going to hide them?" Helsa asks.

Elum goes into the sleeping area and moves a cot away from the stone wall. There, he pries loose a white stone to reveal a large space behind it. He puts the bag with the Relics inside, replaces the stone, brushes off his hands, and moves the bed back into place.

"I know you'll keep them safe," I say. I hope.

"We promise," Devin says.

Good. Because it feels like our lives depend on it.

Chapter Five

Solana

"Up! Everybody up!"

Oria and I stumble out of bed.

Durth walks in front of the cells, yelling and clapping. "Come on. I ain't got all day."

Have we inadvertently done something wrong? Oria looks wary. Helsa and Lieb are up too. Lieb's hair reminds me of Devin's when he was young, all tousled and wild.

"Work assignments today!" Durth shouts. "Eat, then go where I send you. Someone will meet you and explain what yer supposed to do."

Now I'm nervous. I'm not feeble by any means, but as a petite sixty-year-old I do have limitations.

Durth points at me. "Clock winder. Report to the first clock on your left."

"Yes, ma'am." I can do that. Except all the clocks are high . . .

Oria is next. "Food distribution booth two, to the right."

"Yes, ma'am."

The woman moves to Helsa and Lieb. "Both of you: whitewashing walls. Meet at the Sanctuary."

"Painting? I get to paint?" Lieb says happily.

"Shush boy. Get some breakfast, then be on yer way."

We put on our sandals, use the privy, then quickly eat our allotted bread and cheese before Durth shoos us out the door.

"Well then," I say. "I guess . . . let's all have a nice day?"

"Yeah, well . . ." Helsa says.

"Try not to break any laws," Oria says with a smile. But I know she's serious. This whole place is serious.

Oria heads to the right, while the rest of us turn left. I stop at the first clock. I reach out to embrace Helsa, but she steps back. "No touching, Nana."

I almost break a law only ten minutes in. It's going to be a long day. A long life?

Lieb and Helsa say their goodbyes and walk toward the Sanctuary. I'm glad they've been assigned a job together.

I stand beneath the clock and wait for someone to approach. People walk by, but no one pays any attention to me. That's not all bad. Devin said the best way to survive Legalis is to blend in. Durth told us that was *the* most important thing to do.

But then I see Elum walking toward me. Is he...? Could he be...?

"Good morning," I say.

"Good morning, Solana," he says.

It takes me a moment. "You talked."

He gives me a quick nod. "So I did."

"Why haven't you talked before now?"

"No reason to." He glances at the clock that's hung on the building behind us. "You ready to work?"

"I am. I'm waiting for—"

"For me. You're working with me."

I feel my face light up. "I'm glad it's you," I say simply. I turn to look at the clock. It's so high. "How do we do this?"

"One at a time."

"How many clocks are there?"

"Sixty."

It's a daunting number. "How often do they have to be wound?"

"Every three days."

I wish he'd just explain all at once. "How many do we wind in a day?"

"Twenty."

Duh. "What do we do during the Count?"

"We take cover at the nearest home or shop and are counted from there."

"It's hard to believe they just let us in."

"It's the law."

Of course it is.

**

I quickly realize Elum is a gentleman. All the clocks require a ladder to reach them, which he won't let me climb. My job is to hold it steady for him. I can do this job. Especially with him. Actually, anyone could do it.

The Count is a constant disruption every hour. As Elum said, we are welcomed into every home or shop we enter. There is always a bowl of pebbles near the door, and we place two black ones on the ledge outside. Sometimes we talk to people. Sometimes we don't. Since I'm not good at small talk the lack of it is fine with me.

I notice all the units are the same, with the same table with benches in the middle. The same pottery pots and cups and bowls. Occasionally there is more than one bedroom. The shops have their wares on open shelves. Oh, how I'd like to paint one of those pots. Color is so lacking here.

We return to Elum's unit for a midday meal. Again, we share bread and cheese.

"Do you ever get fruit and vegetables? Or meat?" I ask as we sit at the table.

"Occasionally."

"Do you get to choose what food you receive at the booths?"

"We do not." He tears apart a loaf and hands some to me. "Tell me about your old life in . . ." He shrugs.

The question surprises me. "As part of the Exiled I thought you were from there too."

He shakes his head. "I was born in Legalis."

"But now you believe in the Keeper."

"Now, I believe."

"Did Devin tell you about him?"

"That, he did. Your son is a good man."

"So there *is* hope we can reach people?"

"Some." He slices the cheese.

"How much do you know about Regalia?" I ask.

Elum flashes me a look. I'd said the forbidden word.

"Sorry," I say.

"I only know what Devin has told me. Its focus is fashion?" He gestures toward our white robes. "Obviously there's no such thing in Legalis."

I chuckle. "You wouldn't believe the wild and wonderful fashion that's there. Helsa and I worked in a garment factory. Oria was one of the Patrons—the influential people who wear new outfits that are voted on."

"By the Favored."

"So you do know about it."

He shrugs. "Pardon me saying so, but it sounds rather frivolous."

No more frivolous than the laws of Legalis. "Did Devin tell you about the Rings?"

"He did. Other than Oria you were Imps. Implementors?"

"Helsa and I were, but Lieb was a Serv."

"You were like the Masses here."

I take offense. "Not at all. Despite the walled Rings we were happy. There wasn't a Count. Most people had jobs that involved creativity and if we did them well, we were pretty much left alone to live our lives."

"That's not completely true," Elum says.

I'm confused. "Why do you say that?"

"Because faith was banned."

Even though I feel defensive I can't argue with him. "At least we don't have to wear symbols of our sins on our shoulders."

Elum eats a bite of cheese.

I regret the tone of my words. "I shouldn't have made our discussion a contest of which society is better. I'm sure there are some parts of Legalis that are good." That still sounds negative. "You are good."

"I assure you I am not."

"But you have no studs."

He touches his left shoulder. "I've had my share. Just haven't been caught since Zero Day. Basically, I choose to behave. You get used to it." He pours water and offers me some. "Tell me about your family. Where is your husband?"

"He died years ago, when Helsa was little. I lived with Devin and his wife after that."

"He didn't know his wife had died," he says.

"He didn't. She mourned him to her own death."

"It happens."

The way he said it . . . "Has it happened to you?"

He shakes his head. "I've never been married."

I'm surprised. Elum is a kind, handsome man. "Why not?"

"It's complicated." He glances at the clock. "We need to get back to work."

**

As we walk through Legalis, winding the clocks, I notice an absence. Something very lacking.

And Elum notices. "You seem troubled."

"There doesn't seem to be any laughter here."

"I don't even know what that is."

I stop walking and face him. "You're kidding." I rephrase it. "You're not serious."

"I'm serious. Explain what laughter is."

For a moment I'm stumped. It's like having to define air. "It's a sound people make when they're happy or joyful or find something funny."

He shakes his head. "I've heard Devin say the word *happy*, but I'm unfamiliar with the other two words."

"You've never been happy enough to feel joy or have fun?"

Elum thinks a few seconds. "I've been happy before. Very happy. But I've never heard the word joy. Or fun."

I think of ways we had fun in Regalia. "Do people ever dance or sing?"

"I'm not sure what those are."

I'm surprised and start singing. "'I'll sing you one O, green grow the rushes O.'" I move my body to the song. "'What is your one O? One is one, and all alone, and ever more shall—'"

He raises his hand. "Stop! You must stop."

People *are* looking at me. Suddenly a Fault Finder storms over. I freeze.

"No frivolity!"

"Sorry. I—"

"Maintain decorum at all times!"

"Yes, sir."

"She's new here," Elum says. "She won't do it again."

The Fault Finder glares at him, then me, then pulls out a stud. "A law of Legalis has been broken. Someone must pay! Wear your Fault for all to see."

He hands it to me. My hands shake as I pin it on my shoulder. It feels heavy in consequence, if not weight.

"Off with you," he says, and strides away.

I touch the stud. "I can't believe I got a Fault for a tune and a jig."

"You have to be more careful."

I look at the people on the street. No one is smiling. "It's hard to fathom that joy and fun are against the law."

"Not specifically," he says. "We're just not aware of them."

I sigh deeply. "That makes me sad."

He raises a finger. "Sad, we know."

Which makes me sadder still.

At least I'll have a good story to tell the others.

Chapter Six

Helsa

Me? A painter? I've never painted anything in my life.

Lieb and I meet a man at the Sanctuary who shows us how to make the whitewash with powdered chalk and water. He points at a ladder and says, "Go to it."

Lieb scans the tall interior. "Where?"

"Wherever it needs it." He leaves.

I look around. We're alone. It's weird to think that yesterday the Sanctuary was filled with hundreds of people. I look up at the hole in the ceiling. The sun blazes in, but the building is blessedly cool. It even smells cool.

Lieb stares at the loft.

"He's not here today, Lieb," I tell him. "You can relax."

"How do we know he won't come?"

A good point. "I guess we don't. But surely he has better things to do than watch us paint some walls."

When I accidentally drop a brush, the sound echoes. I doubt anything good ever happens in this place. "Judge or no Judge we'd better get to work."

**

During the hourly Counts people come in the Sanctuary but they stay close to the door, never venturing deeper into the main space. No one even looks in our direction. It's like we're invisible. Actually, that might be good. We were ordered to blend in.

Our work is busywork. When I look around for places that need whitewashed, I don't see any. So we start in one corner and just keep going as high up as we can reach. Surprisingly, I don't mind the work, especially because it's inside, out of the heat.

Up on the ladder, Lieb begins to sing. "'My Keeper, you supply my need, most holy is your name; in pastures —"

"Shush!" I say.

He looks shocked. "I like that song. Oria taught it to us."

I look around the Sanctuary. "Like it or not, you can't sing it here. You can't say . . ."

I see understanding wash over his face. He lowers his voice. "Oh. No Keeper."

"Exactly."

We go back to work, but he still hums the song. I shush him again. I'm afraid for him, here in Legalis. He's utterly sincere but naïve. In Regalia he thrived because everyone loved him. He was a messenger of letters, but also of goodwill. Here where he is a stranger, where laws rule, he is bound to get in trouble. I vow to do my best to keep him safe, to be *his* keeper.

Repeatedly, we have to go outside and mix more paint. Every time we do so I notice a man sitting in the shade, leaning against the outer wall of the Sanctuary. He has a makeshift crutch nearby, his dark dirty hair hangs over his forehead, veiling his eyes. He always holds out his hand, "Food please?" Everybody hurries by without looking at him. As do I. We ate our lunch already. We don't have anything left to give.

"Here."

I turn around and see Lieb handing the man a hunk of bread he must have had left over.

The man's face brightens. "Thank you, sir. A good man is hard to find."

Lieb beams. "I'm no *sir*."

"But you are." The man raises the bread like a toast and smiles.

I think it's the first time I've seen anyone smile here.

We move on to mix more paint. "He called me 'sir,'" Lieb says. "He called me a good man."

"You are a good man," I say.

Lieb's definitely a better person than me.

Chapter Seven

Oria

I don't mind working in a food booth, handing out allotments. But I do mind that no one — absolutely no one — smiles. They barely look up when I hand them their food. They don't say hello or thank you. I start out being polite by sharing a greeting, but it quickly seems hopeless.

"Next."

The only thing they do say is a number, which I quickly figure out is how many people are in their family. I'm glad we get our food from Durth. Having to stand in line every day seems tedious.

When the line empties, I'm ready for the lull. The woman manning the booth with me draws a deep breath. "Finally."

Other than exchanging names, it's the first time we've spoken. Her name is Trina.

"Is it always this busy?" I ask.

"People need to eat, don't they?"

"Can't they get enough for a few days at a time?"

She gives me a dirty look. "You think you know better than the Law Commission?"

"No, no. Of course not. I'm just trying to understand."

She counts on her fingers. "Three meals times the people in their family. It's easy math." She glares at me over smarmy eyes. "You can count, can't ya?"

I've been counting all morning. "What's to stop someone from saying they have five people in their family when they have two?"

Her eyes widen. "You lookin' fer ways to get some Faults?"

"No, no." Forget I asked.

Trina sneaks a slice of cheese and talks while she's chewing — not a pretty sight. "Durth says you're new. Where are you from?"

I remember Durth's warning. "The desert."

"I don't believe you. There are monsters in the desert."

I remember Durth's other suggested answer. "I was saved from the desert."

"Lucky you. Did you see monsters out there?"

I think of the scaled creatures and the howling animals. "A few."

She points at me. "That's why Legalis is good. It saved you from those monsters."

I'm not going to argue with her.

I nibble on a hunk of bread. The daily allotment of food according to household makes me think of the food Devin and Elum have shared with us. They've been very generous.

We sit on stools behind the canopied counter. Trina drinks from a water skin—which in the heat is much needed.

She does not offer me any. I've seen water pumps in the street. I'll have to bring my own tomorrow.

"Do you have family?" I ask.

"I have a husband, Aury—but don't get me started. And a son. Pan is six. And you? You married?"

Does it count that I was nearly engaged? "I'm not."

"Good for you."

How negative. "What job does your husband have?"

"One that thankfully keeps him as far from me as possible. He works at the dairy. He makes cheese."

"It's good cheese." We've eaten it at every meal. I think of her boy. "I don't see many children around. Do they go to school?"

"Indoctrination."

We've been through some of that. "It's an ominous term."

She shrugs. "Pan was just starting to learn how to read and write, but then they took that away from us."

"Without those skills, how can children learn?"

"They memorize stuff. He can recite the first twenty Laws of Legalis word for word."

"How many laws are there?"

"The current count is 227."

Now *my* eyebrows rise. "That sounds horribly harsh."

"It is what it is." She stretches and yawns loudly.

The clocks begin to chime, and our booth is soon filled with people getting off the streets. They cram under the awning—which apparently counts as "inside." Trina sets out the right number of pebbles.

Again. And again.

The whole thing is ridiculous.

As imperfect as Regalia may be, I want to go home.

**

Our first workday is over and I'm back at our cells. I get out the food Durth provided and sit at the table to wait for my friends.

Helsa and Lieb come in first. They have white paint on their hands.

Lieb sits down. "We had fun painting."

Helsa rolls her eyes.

"What did you do today?" he asks me.

"I worked at a booth, handing out food."

"That sounds *so* exciting," Helsa says sarcastically.

"I met a woman named Trina."

"We met a nice man," Lieb says. "He can't walk good and sits outside the Sanctuary."

"He's a beggar," Helsa says. "I told Lieb to ignore him like everyone else."

"He was hungry," Lieb says. "I gave him some bread."

"That was very nice of you," I tell him.

His smile returns. "He called me *sir* and said I was a good man."

"You are good."

Helsa shakes her head. "I told Lieb he needs to watch who he talks to or else he'll break some law."

She isn't wrong. "Just be careful."

"I will," he says. "I promise."

Solana comes in. Helsa gasps. "Nana, you have a stud!"

She touches it. "I sang and did a little dance. Apparently, frivolity is against the law."

"Was it scary?" Lieb asks.

"Kind of. But otherwise it was a good day." She sits at the table with a moan. "I'm glad to be sitting. I'm not used to being on my feet all day."

"Winding clocks?" Helsa asks.

"Winding clocks with Elum." She grins again.

"It must've been hard to be around him all day, with him not talking," I say.

"He can talk. He *did* talk," Solana says.

"Then why hasn't he?"

She shrugs.

"Tell us about him," I say.

"He's from Legalis."

"Why didn't he say something last night?" Helsa says. "I assumed since he knew the Exiled, he was one of them."

"I'm sure he had his reasons. Devin told him about the Keeper — which is encouraging, don't you — ?"

"Can we eat now?" Lieb asks.

Priorities.

**

Devin comes to visit us, but we all retire early. None of us — save Lieb — are used to standing all day.

But I can't sleep. The thought of working in the food booth day after day is discouraging. Trina rubs me the wrong way — and I think she feels the same about me. I doubt we'll ever be friends.

My only friends are Solana and her family. Maybe, eventually I can include the Exiled, but so far I feel pretty much alone.

And worthless.

Sudden tears threaten. I don't want to wake Solana so I slip outside. I duck into the shadows, hiding from the moonlight. I make myself as small as possible by sitting on the ground, pulling my knees to my chest.

One huge truth weighs on me: No one knows me here. And worse, no one cares.

I feel arrogant for letting this bother me, but in Regalia I was important. I had status, perks, attention, and applause. Here, I'm one of the unsmiling masses who spend their day surviving.

I hear movement and suck in a breath. My heart skips when someone comes around the corner.

"Helsa!" I whisper, as I breathe again.

"I saw you leave," Helsa says.

"Go back in," I say.

"Nah. Move over."

I scoot to the left, giving her space to sit beside me in the shadows.

"What's wrong with you anyway?" she whispers. "You don't seem yourself."

I decide not to share my snobbish feelings of lost rank and privilege and focus on something else. "I feel useless."

"You're the one who led us here."

Harsh, but true. "Actually, the Keeper did the leading."

"Whatever."

"Why are you so against him?" I ask.

She shrugs. "It was hard enough believing in him back home, but here? With that Judge looming over us it's hard to believe in much of anything."

"Don't stop believing because of him. Or life here. I know it will get better."

"We'll see about that."

I wish I had something more encouraging to say.

She extends her legs out straight. "If the Keeper has something for us to do here, it *would* be nice if he showed us what it is."

"I agree."

"What do you know? We agree on something."

Small steps. I stand and hold out my hand to help her up. But as soon as I do, I hear movement.

Fault Finders? I press her against the wall. "Shh!"

She protests for the briefest moment, then is still. Though my heart is pounding I don't dare move. I don't dare breathe. Then out of the corner of my eye I see the glint of light flashing and immediately think of the mirrored eyes of the Judge.

I brace myself against what will surely come. *Keeper, protect us, please protect us.*

I sense something black and ominous pass by, a disruption of the air around us. I hear the faint sound of breath going in and out.

The Judge's. Not ours.

Even after I sense that it's passed by, I remain still. Finally I have to breathe, so without saying a word, we both rush back inside. Where it's safe.

Actually, we don't know that for sure. But inside is all we have.

"Did you see that?" Helsa whispers from the safe side of the door.

"I saw the eyes and then a black mass passing by."

"I did too." She shudders.

"It was evil," I say. "I felt it."

"I did too." She sighs deeply. "And I do know one thing."

"What's that?"

"I never, ever want to see it again."

Helsa and I agree for a second time.

Chapter Eight

Oria

At breakfast the next day I'm eager to tell Solana and Lieb about the Judge.

Helsa beats me to it. "Don't go out at night," she says. "Ever."

"I know," Solana says. "We could get a Fault."

Helsa shakes her head. "That would be the least of your worries. Right, Oria?"

Solana looks at each of us in turn. "What happened?"

"Helsa and I couldn't sleep and went outside. We sat completely out of sight in the shadows, but then we saw flashes of light. Mirrored eyes."

Lieb's eyes grow large. "The Judge's eyes?"

I nod.

"Did it see you?" Solana asks.

"I don't know," Helsa says.

"I don't think so," I add. "Because this black presence moved past us. It didn't stop. It felt like evil passing by."

"When we hurried inside it felt like the boogeyman was nipping at our heels," Helsa says.

"What would have happened if it had seen you?" Lieb asks. "Would it eat you?"

"It doesn't eat people, Lieb."

"You don't know that for sure." He pushes his food away. "It could. Or it could claw at you with its long nails." He shivers. "Don't go out in the dark again! Ever. Promise me, Sa-Sa. Promise me, Oria."

We both promise. I hope I'll be able to keep that promise.

**

Approaching the food booth I balk when I spot Trina talking to one of those masked Fault Finders. She's pointing to the right, clearly explaining something. Is she in trouble?

As soon as they leave in the direction she'd been pointing I approach. "Are you all right?" I ask her.

She blinks as though she has no idea what I'm referring to. "Of course. Why do you ask?"

"I saw you talking to a Fault Finder. Are you in trouble?"

She grins and touches her shoulder where there used to be three Faults. Now there are two. "Not at all."

"What happened to one of your studs?"

"I got one cancelled."

"How did you do that?"

"By tipping off the Fault Finders to violations."

I'm shocked. "You tell on people?"

"Why shouldn't I?" She counts off on her fingers. "Duty, Deference, Dedication, Dependability. Without those we have chaos."

Or freedom.

"Speaking of faults, a few days ago I saw you with people who were hugging each other, right on the street."

"It was a family reunion."

She shrugs. "It's against the law."

"We didn't know that. We'd just arrived from . . . the desert. I hope you don't—"

She shrugs again. "You being ignorant isn't my fault." She grins. "Ha. Fault."

I make a connection that I hope is wrong. "Did you just turn us in?"

"No. I let that slide because you *were* new. This time."

I feel a shield of wariness come between us. Trina can't be trusted.

She sorts through a basket of apples, tossing a few rotten ones aside. "If you must know, I turned in Aury."

"Your husband?"

She smiles, yet her smile is wicked. "He took a walk after dark last night."

I think of my middle-of-the-night experience with Helsa, and the Judge slinking by. "Isn't that dangerous?"

"It certainly can be. And now it is." She wipes her hands on her robe. "That'll teach him."

"Teach him?"

She sighs as if his offenses are too many to mention. "He's a horrible man who constantly tries to control me. I, for one, refuse to be controlled by the likes of him."

I think of my mother and brother who tried to control *me*. "I'm sad he's doing that to you."

"Don't feel sad for me cuz I'm handling it. By the time I'm done with him, he won't know what hit him."

I shiver at the thought.

**

We run out of food and there's still a line.

"Now what?" I ask Trina.

She shoos the people away. "We're all out! Go on now. Check back later."

"Is another delivery coming from the farms?" I ask.

"Eventually."

"So what are we supposed to do until it gets here?"

Trina moves her stool against the wall, leans back, and gets comfortable. "You can do whatever you want. I, for one, am going to take a nap. Come back after lunch. We should have food then."

I suddenly have time on my hands? I'm certainly not going to spend it watching Trina sleep.

I decide to check out the Sanctuary where Helsa and Lieb work. They said there weren't many people there except during the Count. Will I feel something there? The presence of the Keeper? Or the Judge?

I long for contact with the Keeper. I need to talk to him. Of course I pray, but I long for physical interaction. Will I ever get it again?

As I approach the Sanctuary, I see Helsa and Lieb painting outside.

"Hello there," I call out.

Lieb is up on a ladder and nearly topples when he turns to greet me. Helsa steadies the ladder just in time.

"See what we're doing?" he says.

"I do." I look upward at the towering building. "Do you have to paint way up there too?"

Helsa shakes her head. "If they tell us to, I'm saying no."

Lieb climbs down, and his forehead furrows. "We can't say no."

"Wanna bet?"

Helsa the rebel.

"What are you doing here?" she asks me.

"The booth ran out of food so I thought I'd come see the Sanctuary again."

"No one's in there," Helsa says.

Good.

"Actually, someone is," Lieb says. "Come meet our friend, Rand."

I follow the two of them inside and see a man seated against the wall. He has a beard and long dirty hair that nearly covers his eyes. I wonder how long he's been living like this.

"Good day to you, Lieb," he says. "Helsa."

"Good day right back," Lieb says. "I want you to meet a friend of ours."

His smile is genuine as he looks at me. "I would love to. I'm Rand. And you are?"

"Oria."

He blinks multiple times, then cocks his head. "It's you." Then he claps his hands in glee. "It's you!"

I'm so shocked at his words that I take a step back.

Helsa points at me. "What do you mean, 'it's you'? You don't know her."

"Do you know her?" Lieb asks.

"Do you know me?" I ask.

"I know *of* her," Rand says. He grabs his crutch and struggles to his feet. Under his robe I spot a leg that's deformed. I reach out to help him, but he waves my hand away. "No touching."

It's hard to stand by and watch him work so hard, but he eventually stands with the crutch under one arm.

It's winded him. "It's so nice to meet you, Oria. I've been waiting for you for a long time."

Helsa shakes her head. "This doesn't makes sense."

"It makes complete sense," Rand says, "when you consider our mutual friend."

"Who's that?" I ask.

"Someone who loves gardens?" he says.

I suck in a breath. The Keeper said those very words when he visited me in my garden. "You saw him too?"

"Not in a garden, as gardens are quite lacking in Legalis, but yes, I *was* in his presence."

I want to hug him and ask a thousand questions. "Can we talk here? Safely?"

A man comes in the door of the Sanctuary and points at Helsa and Lieb. "What are you doing in here? Back to work!" Then he glares at Rand and says, "Out, Marked Man!"

Marked man?

Rand raises his hand in acknowledgment, and we all go outside. Helsa and Lieb go back to work, but Rand walks toward the shady side of the building, then stops and leans against it. I want to talk more about his experience with the Keeper, ask about his condition, or the indignity of being shooed out of the Sanctuary, but he has another subject in mind.

"How do we stop the Judge?" he asks.

I'm taken aback and look up and down the street. I wish we'd stayed in the Sanctuary and yet . . . that's where *he* reigns. "Stop him?"

"Show everyone in Legalis the truth about the Judge — and in turn, get them to understand the truth about the Keeper."

He says it so simply. But there it is; my purpose for being here. I clasp my hands against my chest. "Thank you."

"For what?"

"I was having a hard time pinpointing why I was sent here. But now I know." I take a deep breath, letting a new certainty and assurance fuel me.

"It's what he told me to share with you. I heard him in here." Rand thumps his chest. "Sure as I can hear you, I heard him."

"Isn't he amazing? To have you mention gardens . . . to repeat something so personal . . ."

"He told me to watch for someone who would help me. Oria. You."

Our connection is an honor, but it's also weighty and overwhelming. "But how can we, I mean you . . . and me . . .?"

"Me, a middle-aged cripple, and you, a stunningly beautiful newcomer?"

I smile at him. "How can we possibly do as he asks? Neither one of us has any power here."

"Perhaps our lack of power *is* our power."

"Explain what you mean, please."

"Without status, without extraordinary talents or abilities—" He pauses. "I shouldn't speak for you. Perhaps you have many talents and abilities."

"I can honestly say I have none whatsoever."

"And so . . . we two blend in. We can work secretively without drawing attention to ourselves and our plan."

I've spent my entire life drawing attention to myself. But I ignore that fact and ask, "Our plan? You have a plan? My thoughts are too jumbled to come up with one idea, much less create a plan."

He looks at the people walking by, then at a nearby clock. It's nearly time for the next Count. "We need to find someplace we can talk in private until that's over."

I briefly think about Devin's but it's not close. Then another place comes to mind. "We can go to the cells where my friends and I are staying because we're newcomers. There's no one else there right now."

"It sounds perfect."

**

We make it back to the cells just as the hourly chimes mark the beginning of the Count. Unfortunately, Durth already has one white pebble on the ledge—meaning she's inside. I add one white stone for me and a black stone for Rand, then check to see where she is, but don't see her. I lead Rand to the table where we eat.

Speaking of food . . .

"Would you like something to eat?" I ask.

"If it wouldn't be too much trouble . . ."

I offer him some food, leftover from breakfast. And a cup of water. He eats everything voraciously, which makes me wonder how long it's been. Does he depend on the kindness of strangers? Kindness doesn't seem to be a Legalian trait.

He washes it down with the water, then says, "Now. To the plan."

I'm so relieved he has one. "Tell me everything."

He shrugs. "There's not that much to tell—yet. But I do think the plan has two parts: firstly, we get rid of the Judge."

"Get rid of it?"

"As long as it presides over Legalis—looms over Legalis—people will be too afraid to listen to any news about a kind and loving Keeper."

I agree—in theory. "Can you tell me exactly what *it* is? Is it a man? Or something else? Those eyes and sharp fingers . . ." I shudder.

"I'm not sure what it is." He picks up his mug to drink and finds it empty, so I refill it. "Not knowing is a big problem because we need to know what we're dealing with."

"No one's going to volunteer to find out."

"Maybe they will—if they're on the inside."

"Of . . .?"

"The inner circle of the Notables, or maybe the Fault Finders.

"Do you know anyone in such a position?" I ask. "Anyone friendly?"

"Not yet. But I'm hoping there's at least one person inside who questions the system."

His words make me think of my past. "I questioned the system in… where we lived. No other Patron had ever rebelled."

"You're from Regalia, aren't you?"

"Shh! We were told not to say its name."

"Being invisible has its advantages. I hear things. I've heard of . . . it." He waves the subject away. "Rebelling . . . it's always hard to be first. What made you see the truth?"

There was only one answer. "The Keeper."

"Of course. He is the spark of all sparks, the fire of all fires."

"That, he is," I say, for he certainly sparked a fire in me. I pour water for myself. "How do we infiltrate the inner circle? The masked Fault Finders don't seem to be the sort who would ever talk with citizens."

"We're not citizens," Rand says. "We're called the Masses."

"That's right."

He continues. "The Notables are inaccessible in their underground world. I've never met anyone who's been down there."

The fact there is a "down there" is discouraging. "Concerning the second part of the plan?"

He presses his hands flat against the table "With the Judge's influence out of commission, we tell everyone about the Keeper."

"And how do we do that? The Notables will still be around. And the Fault Finders."

He tucks his hands in his sleeves. "I'm counting on the Keeper to show us a way."

I admire his faith. Is mine as strong? Our two-fold mission is daunting. I hope it's not impossible.

We hear the single chime giving us the signal that we can leave. I stand. "I should get back to the booth. We'll be in touch. We can do this."

"Thank you for the food."

"Of course." I receive an inner nudge — an idea — so move close to him, speaking low. "I'd like you to meet with a group of believers — my friends. Can you come here tonight after the six Count and I'll take you there?"

"I'd love that."

He leaves the cells, and I begin to clean the table.

When I turn around I see Durth standing near the privy with a broom.

How much did she hear? I cover my panic by saying, "You scared me."

"*You* scare *me*."

I'm not sure exactly what she means but need to find out — without giving everything away. "How do I scare you?"

Her eyebrows rise and she leans against the door jamb. "Getting rid of the Judge? Really?"

If she heard that she heard everything. "What you heard . . . can you unhear it?"

"No."

"Whatever we're discussing is for the good of the Masses. We mean no harm to anyone except—"

"The Judge."

"It's such a negative force. It prevents us from feeling free and hopeful about life."

Durth crosses her arms and is silent for a moment. But then, "Who is the Keeper?"

In an instant I realize this is the first time I've been asked that question. I'm not sure how to describe what he *is* as much as what he does for us. "He's our protector and our provider. He loves us and cares for us. He's the opposite of the Judge."

"Is he something you invented back home?"

I think of Rand. "My friend who was here is from Legalis and he knows about him. Believes in him."

"Believes *in* him? So he's a god or something?"

My ignorance is disconcerting, but I say, "Yes. He is."

"Where can I find him?"

I scoff. "My, my, Durth. You're putting me on the spot."

"Shouldn't you know where he is?"

"I don't think it's that simple. He's not like the Judge who people can see." Though *I* saw him. I place my hand on my heart. "He lives in here."

"In yer innards?"

Sigh. "In our hearts. In our minds. It's like we're inextricably connected to him."

"If you can't see him and he's this . . . thing inside you, how do you really know he exists? Maybe it's just indigestion."

I remember feeling the Keeper's presence by seeing a slice of sky open up among the clouds. "Have you ever seen a sunrise or sunset that's so beautiful you feel full inside? As if something has stirred within you?"

Durth shifts from one foot to the other. "I suppose. When there's nothin' to do I sometimes go outside and look at the sky — seen some pretty sun ups and downs out there."

"I believe that feeling is the Keeper stirring inside us."

"*He* didn't make the sunset."

"Are you sure?" I ask. Even though I'm not sure myself.

"I don't know how he could."

"I don't either, which makes him even more special and amazing. He does things we can't do. He's full of miracles."

"Like what?"

She's put me on the spot again. "I was doomed to die in the Swirling Desert that surrounds where I came from. He parted the sands so I could walk through safely. Then he got me here."

Her left eyebrow rises. "I woulda liked to see that parting-stuff."

"I *lived* it," I say. "He saved me. And my friends."

She reaches inside the neckline of her tunic and scratches her shoulder. "The others from there, the ones who've been here a while? Did that happen to them too?"

"It did."

Durth shifts from one foot to the others. "I wouldn't mind a miracle or two."

"Stick around. Wouldn't you agree that being rid of the Judge would be a miracle?"

"Wouldn't hurt my feelings," she says.

"Then don't tell anyone what you overheard."

"Not even the Keeper part?"

Hmm. "You can share about *him*. You should share about him," I say. "But you need to be discreet about it. At least for now."

"Until you get rid of . . . the other one?"

I nod.

"Good luck," she says as we both go back to work.

What an amazing day.

Chapter Nine

Solana

After dinner we gather at Devin's. The four of us, plus a new addition, a crippled man, Rand, who Oria and Lieb seem excited about.

Helsa doesn't let on if she knows Rand or not. Or if she cares.

I'm worried about my granddaughter. She's going to be twenty soon. Shouldn't she be over the moodiness and angst of her teenage years?

Yet she *has* been through more than most people her age. She lost her father to exile, lost her mother to grief, was assaulted by her boss — who later killed a dear coworker, and she had to deal with me becoming full-out Devoted. Not to mention seeing me run after Cashlin when the sands parted, and Lieb pulling her with him, after me. If not for me she would be living a constant — if ordinary — life in Regalia.

Life in Legalis is neither.

When I was her age I was engaged with dreams of creating a home and having children. What are Helsa's dreams? She's never shown interest in boys her age — though none of the ones working at the factory would've been my pick for her either. And now? Here? In a strange land with strange rules, and people devoid of dreams because they're consumed with not getting in trouble? Where can she find love, hope, and happiness in this twisted, cruel place that has no laughter?

I glance at Elum standing across the room and instantly smile. He smiles back. I don't have romantic feelings toward the man. I barely know him. Yet Elum has reignited feelings I thought were long dead. I expect nothing to come of it beyond friendship, but I do plan to enjoy the journey.

Devin interrupts my musings when he invites us to sit around the table. Rand sits beside me and leans his crutch against the table. His left leg is twisted oddly, as if some broken bones didn't heal right. Age-wise he looks to be fifty or so; his hair and beard have streaks of gray. His skin is leathery like someone who's spent a lot of time in the sun. He's a small man but other than his leg, he looks strong. And his expression vibrates with infectious emotion, which makes me more interested in the source of his positive attitude than the cause of his negative handicap.

"Welcome, Rand," Devin says. "Tell us about yourself."

He scans our faces, then says, "I am who I am."

That's a bit cryptic. "Oria and Lieb said they met you at the Sanctuary?" I say.

He looks at Helsa. "I met Helsa there too."

She shrugs.

"He said I was a good man," Lieb says.

"Because you are," Rand says.

"How did you hurt your leg?" Helsa asks.

My granddaughter has no filter. But Rand graciously answers. "I had an accident and broke it. It didn't heal well so I couldn't work." Curiously, he exchanges a look with Elum.

"Couldn't they find you something for you to do?" I ask.

He hesitates. "They could, but they didn't. Besides, I like to move around Legalis and see what I can see, and my lack of a job allows me to do just that."

"You're an observer," I say.

"That, I am."

"What have you seen?" Devin asks.

Rand exchanges a glance with Oria. "All my life I have seen cruelty and tyranny. And a complete absence of freedom and hope."

Oria taps the table twice. "Tell them your plan, Rand."

"For . . .?" Devin asks.

Oria answers. "For ridding Legalis of the Judge and sharing the good news about the Keeper."

More than one set of eyebrows rise.

"We've talked about sharing news of the Keeper before," Devin says. "I mean, when I first met Elum I talked to him about the Keeper."

Elum nods. "That's why I believe."

"But have any of you talked about getting rid of the Judge?" Oria asks.

He hesitates. "We have not. And I don't think it's a good idea at all."

"Why not?" Rand looks at each one of us. "The people won't listen to the good news until they rid their lives of the bad news."

"You may be right," I say. "But it's also a huge problem. "How do *we* rid Legalis of anything? Except for you and Elum, we're new. We're in the dark."

"There are the Exiled," Oria says.

"Who are they?" Rand asks.

"Others from . . . where we're from. Others who believe."

"We know of six," Devin says.

"They were here the other night," I say.

"How often do you meet?" Rand asks.

We all look to Devin. "We've met three times."

I interrupt. "Three times? In all the months you've been here?"

My son's face reddens like it's always done when he feels like he's in trouble. "Well, yeah."

Something isn't right here. "You made it seem like you've been active with them a long time."

He squirms in his seat. "I didn't mean to imply that."

Yes, he did. What has Devin been doing for the Keeper since he got to Legalis?

I hate seeing Rand's expression cloud with doubt. "Will the Exiled help us?" he asks.

"I don't know." Devin sighs. "What I do know is that Masses are so beaten down that they can't even imagine a loving Keeper."

"Which is exactly why they need him," Oria says.

I stand and begin to pace, hoping to jar my thoughts into an answer. Finally I stop and speak. "How is it possible to get rid of the Judge?"

"I'm not sure it *is* possible," Elum says. "Or wise."

"Is *it* even real?" Lieb asks.

"Of course it's real," Helsa says. "You saw it in the loft on Sanctuary Day. And Oria and I . . . we saw its eyes and saw its blackness go by, almost like a cloud."

Devin shakes his head. "A cloud doesn't sound real." He looks at Oria. "Did you actually *see* it?"

"We saw something physical."

"Back to the question . . ." I look at Rand. "Is it a person or something else?"

"I vote something else," Lieb says. "It gives me the creeps."

"Something else is a possibility," Helsa says.

Lieb's eyebrows rise. "Really?"

"We just don't know," Rand says.

I return to my seat. "We can't stop it if we don't know who or what it is."

Elum raises his hand. "Let me stop this discussion. The Judge is very real, as tangible as you and I."

"How do you know?" I ask.

"I just know."

I can tell he's hedging. "Can you give us something more to go on?"

He looks uneasy, as if he wishes he hadn't said anything. "I've heard about people talking to it. Meeting with it."

"Now there's a change in direction," Oria says.

"If people talk to it," Rand says, "it might mean we can get someone on the inside to scout around. Someone who can help us bring it down."

"Inside?" Elum asks.

"Get close to one of the Notables or Fault Finders, someone within the system."

"Do you know someone who'd be approachable?" I ask him.

Rand shakes his head. "Not at the moment."

Devin sighs. "I don't think we should press the system. At all."

I don't understand. "What happened to Devin the dynamo I knew back home?"

"He's encountered a hard dose of reality."

"What does that mean?" Oria asks.

Devin crosses his arms as if he's protecting himself.

"Devin?" I say. "Tell us why you're so hesitant."

He uncrosses his arms and takes a cleansing breath. "When I first got here I was full of fire, encouraged from being saved from the Swirling Desert. I happened to meet one of the Exiled who was passionate about the Keeper. One day he was preaching on the street, and I was set to go next. Things were going well, and people were listening."

"That's wonderful," I say. "We need to do that again."

He shakes his head adamantly. "No, we don't. Two Fault Finders saw us and started to give us Faults, but my friend threw his Fault on the ground. They hit him and he hit back and . . . " He looks right at me. "They beat him to death, right there in the street. I got away but . . . he was a really good man."

No one says anything. But this does explain why Devin is reluctant to take a risk, and why the Exiled seem kind of meek.

Helsa rubs her hand across his back. "I'm so sorry, Papa."

"Yeah. Well. Now you see why this might be something we shouldn't do."

Unmasking the Judge does sounds impossible. "To be a spy would be dangerous. Even deadly," I say.

"It could be," Rand says.

Suddenly Lieb lifts his hand high and waves. "Ooh, ooh!"

I call on him. "Lieb?"

"Sa-Sa and I are painting the Sanctuary. Nobody but Rand is ever inside. We could sneak up to the loft where the monster stood and see if there are any clues about what it is."

Helsa shakes her head. "Count me out." When we all look at her, she adds, "I mean, what if *it's* there?"

"I doubt it hides up there," Rand says. "I never see it."

Devin crosses his arms again. "I've heard of it swooping down and slashing people. Children grow up being warned about it."

"*Swooping down* doesn't sound like it's human," Rand says.

Oria nods. "There's definitely something evil about it."

Helsa waves her hands in front of her face. "I want nothing to do with it. I definitely don't want to stir it up by going where we shouldn't go."

I understand her reluctance, yet we need a place to begin. "I'll go to the loft with you, Lieb."

"Thank you, Nana."

I wait for someone to object to me — the oldest person here — going on this mission, but no one does. What's wrong with them?

Oria looks at Elum. "Where do the Fault Finders live?"

"There's a compound."

"And the Judge, where does it live?" I ask.

"Underground." Elum says.

"Have you seen the Judge up close?" I ask.

"I have not." He sighs deeply. "The truth is, whatever the Judge is, is a mixture of myths and stories. And the Notables like it that way. People fear the unknown more than the known."

Lieb nods. "It *is* the boogeyman."

No one says anything. Round and round we go.

Oria interrupts. "So where did we leave all this?"

I raise my hand. "Lieb and I will try to get up to the loft to see what's there."

I wish someone had a better plan.

Devin stands behind me and puts one hand on my shoulder and one on Lieb's. "Keeper, our protector and provider, we need your help..."

We need a miracle. And an invisible shield would be nice.

CHAPTER TEN

HELSA

When Lieb and I head to work at the Sanctuary the next day, Nana tags along.

"You're not really going to sneak up to the loft, are you, Nana?"

"Someone has to do it."

"Do they?"

"Our mission can't move forward if you-know-who is still in power."

I stop walking. "You-know-who *has* all the power. We have nada. We're not even from here. We're supposed to blend in. If this was the right thing to do, why didn't Papa and the others do it way before we showed up?"

She blinks, which means I've asked a good question.

I begin to walk again. "I rest my case."

This time Nana stops *me.* "Rand is a local and Oria trusts him. They know what they're doing. They're behind the push to get this started."

"What if *it* gets mad?" I shake my head. "I do not want to get a zillion Faults on my shoulder, or be arrested, or . . . I don't know, maybe even die. We don't know what it's capable of."

Lieb shakes his head adamantly, his face worried. "I don't want to die either."

Nana thrusts a finger toward my face. "Stop it, Helsa."

"What did I do?"

"You made us doubt."

"Maybe doubt is wise instead of blindly following Oria's whims. Which begs the question: why isn't *she* here?"

"Because Lieb and I volunteered. As you just said, we don't know what it's capable of because we don't know enough about it. It's always wise to know our enemy. You can either help us or get out of our way. This *is* happening."

I raise my hands in surrender. "Go for it, Nana. But don't come running to me if something dark and gruesome swoops down and eats you."

"Eats us?" Lieb says, looking considerably more nervous.

Nana touches his arm. "Ignore her. We can do this."

I follow them inside the Sanctuary to get my painting supplies. The echoes of our footfalls swirl around us before fading to silence. We stand still as if making a noise will bring us to a bad end.

No one is here—that we can see. I wish Nana wasn't so stubborn. I hate Oria for goading her on. She's—

"You coming or going?" Nana asks me.

"Going. I'm going." I grab the supplies and head outside, letting the huge doors bang shut behind me. I walk to the shady side of the building.

"Good morning, Helsa," Rand says from his usual spot.

"Morning." I stir the leftover paint from yesterday.

"Where's Lieb?" he asks.

"Inside with Nana. They're hunting for ghosts like everybody told them to do."

Rand fumbles to his feet. "They're doing it now?"

"When Nana gets something in her head . . ."

"We should be in there with them, as lookouts." He heads toward the door.

Which leaves me in an awkward position: be a part of something I don't agree with, or leave them to it. Good or bad.

Seeing a man with a crutch go into harm's way is more than even I can handle. "Wait. I'll go with you."

I open the heavy door for him and we go inside. I wait until the reverberation of the closed door stops echoing.

"Nana?" I whisper loudly.

"Over here."

I see movement up front to the right—*not* in the loft that spans the Sanctuary from side to side. Rand and I hurry forward.

"Did you go up there already?" I whisper.

"We couldn't. There aren't any stairs on this side," Nana explains.

"I'll check the other side." Lieb comes back, shaking his head. "There's nothing there either. No stairs. Not even a ladder."

"Maybe it flies up there," I say, only partly kidding.

"Really?" Lieb says.

I shouldn't provoke him like that. "No. Don't be ridiculous." Though maybe . . .

We all turn toward a sound and hold our breaths. When we hear footsteps, we quickly exit the way we came. I'm glad to be outside again.

"That was unproductive," Nana says.

"At least we didn't see it," I say.

Lieb shakes his head vehemently. "I was so afraid it would appear, that'd it'd be mad and do something yucky awful to us."

"But it didn't," Rand says.

"So what's your plan B since plan A was a bust?" I ask.

"It wasn't a bust," Nana says. "We know more than we did, but it did create more questions."

I'm tired of questions without answers. Yet I'm not sure I want to know what we don't know. Ignorance is bliss, and at the moment it's all we have.

**

"This is so boring," I say as I whitewash yet another wall.

Lieb doesn't respond.

"You have to admit I'm right," I say.

He shrugs. "I did like delivering messages back home better. I got to see everything and everybody."

I look up and down the street. "Not much to see here. White on white on white. Everything's white except for the . . ." I kick up some sandy dirt, then get an idea. I throw a few handfuls into the bucket of paint and stir.

"What are you doing? It's making it tan."

"I know." I dip a brush in the new color and paint the trunk of a tree on the wall. Then some branches.

"Helsa, stop!" Lieb says. "We'll get in trouble."

"It's just color. This place could use some color—even if it's only tan." I look at my design. "I wish I had green so I could paint proper leaves."

Lieb looks around frantically. People have stopped and are staring. He panics. "I'm going to mix more white. We need to cover that up, Sa-Sa." He hurries toward the Sanctuary entrance.

Probably. I stand back to admire my work. I've never painted anything before. The tree isn't half bad. I feel the eyes of our audience.

A young woman wearing a black robe stops nearby.

My breath hitches. People in power wear black.

Now I've done it. My courage leaves me and I retreat toward the Sanctuary door.

"Wait!" the young woman says.

My heart beats double-time as I turn around. "Yes. Ma'am?"

"Did you paint that tree?"

"I did. But I'll paint over it."

She shakes her head. "You shouldn't."

"I shouldn't?"

She bites a fingernail as if she's thinking hard. Then she says, "Come here, girl."

I move closer. She's a few years older than I am, pretty, with dark brown hair that nearly reaches her waist. Although she clearly has authority, there's a softness to her.

"Would you be interested in painting something on the walls in my home?" she asks.

I'm shocked by her offer. "Wouldn't that be against some law?"

"Not if they're painted on the inside," she says. "My mother has been sick and I think a colorful mural might cheer her up."

It might cheer me up too. But a mural? My repertoire consists of a single tan tree. Yet I'd be stupid to turn her down. "If you can arrange it, I'd be happy to." I see Lieb come out of the Sanctuary carrying a pail of white paint. "When? And can my friend come with me?"

"Now. And no, just you."

Lieb returns and gives me a questioning look. I start to answer his unasked question. "This lady — what's your name, ma'am?"

"Nixi. And yours?"

"Helsa." I turn to Lieb. "Nixi wants —"

"It's Mistress Nixi."

"I apologize. I didn't know."

"Now you do."

"Anyway," I say to Lieb. "Mistress Nixi wants me to paint pictures on the walls of her mother's room."

"To cheer her up," Nixi says.

His eyes widen. "You need to do it, Sa-Sa. That wouldn't be boring at all."

"You'll be all right painting here by yourself?" I ask.

"I have Rand to talk to."

I have another thought. "Are you sure this is legal?" I ask Nixi.

"I am a Notable."

She implies that's enough.

"Can you come with me now?" she asks.

"Of course, mistress."

"Follow me then." But as she's walking away, she pauses and turns back to Lieb, glancing at the tree. "I'd paint over that quickly if I were you."

**

Mistress Nixi and I arrive at the arch I'd seen on Papa's tour of Legalis. The street heads downward, underground. I'm going where few have ever gone. My stomach tightens.

At the bottom of the street there is a guarded iron gate which is opened immediately for Nixi. It leads to another guarded door of wood that is also opened without a word being said. I immediately notice how much cooler it is down here.

The street turns from sand to intricately laid stones in tan, gray, and white. It widens to a good twenty feet. There are single-story white homes set back on both sides, but they aren't like the buildings in the rest of Legalis. They are embellished with intricate carved moldings around the doors and windows, with decorated columns marking each entrance.

Although we are underground there's a lot of light. I look up and see circular tubes.

Nixi sees the direction of my gaze. "Those are solar tubes. They intensify the sunlight from above without bringing the heat."

"What a good idea."

Around the tubes the ceiling has been painted blue with puffy clouds. Nixi glances at the fake sky. "At night they change it to show stars and the moon."

"How do they do that?"

She cocks her head. "I'm not sure. It's not my job to know anything beyond the fact that it happens." She pauses and faces me. "Do you know how the actual sky turns from day to night?"

"No."

She flicks her hand at me. "As I said."

Before we start walking again I address another observation. The street is empty. "Where is everyone?"

She smiles. "By everyone I assume you mean the other Notables?"

"I guess I do."

"We have our ways of getting around without being seen."

"How's that?"

"Tunnels." She starts walking again. "We visit each other and go to gathering areas and shops via tunnels. We prefer not to make a show of it. Our world is self-contained and exclusive, and we like it that way."

She turns to a door on the right between two columns carved with stars. "This is me."

As I walk inside I gasp—which makes Nixi smile.

"I know," she says. "It's a lot."

"That, it is. But it's wonderful—and very unexpected for being underground."

She scans the expansive foyer. "I suppose it is."

The walls are white but adorned with moldings of gold at the ceiling and floor—floors which consist of tiny tiles of every color imaginable. The foyer opens to a huge parlor with lush chairs, upholstered in brocades. There are cabinets and tables made of dark wood, decorated with carvings of animals, flowers, and stars. Vases, flowers, and statues populate every surface.

"Come with me. I'll introduce you to my mother."

We walk toward a hallway that leads to bedrooms.

"That is my chamber," Nixi says as she motions to the right. "That is my father's," she says to the left. "At the end of the hall is my mother's room."

She knocks on its door and says, "It's me, Mama."

I hear a faint, "Come in."

The room drips elegance. The furniture is massive, its carving intricate. The brocades on the chairs and bed include metallic threads of gold and silver, but the underlying colors are muted browns and gray.

The woman in the bed sits up when she sees me. The bodice and sleeves of her bed gown are a floral of blues and greens.

"Who is this?" she asks.

"This is Helsa, Mama."

The woman pulls the covers higher over her torso. "Why did you bring her here?"

Nixi moves to her mother's bedside and smooths the covers. "She's a painter. She was painting a tree on the side of the Sanctuary and —"

"Painting a tree? That is not allowed."

I fight the urge to flee.

"I know, Mama. And it's being painted over, but her talent . . . I thought she could paint a mural on the wall over here." She sweeps her hand toward the wall opposite the bed. "Something with bright colors to cheer you up."

"I appreciate the effort, but I'll be fine."

"I know you will. But I also know how much you hate this room and how masculine it is." Nixi turns to me. "The Notables weren't used to a woman becoming the Head Notable."

Head Notable? With difficulty I contain my shock. On Sanctuary Day we'd seen the Head Notable up front, but he was a man. Confused or not, I can only imagine the power she has.

Yet she doesn't look powerful. Beyond the pretty gown she looks like a weak middle-aged woman, her skin a little ashy, her graying hair unkempt. But her dark eyes are pretty, yet tired.

"Are you an artist, girl?" she asks me.

Uh . . . "No. No ma'am."

"You address her as, Head Notable," Nixi says.

"Of course, I apologize. No, Head Notable. I am not an artist."

"So what makes you think you can paint a mural?"

I don't want to say I *can't* paint a mural, yet I don't want to lie either. "Mistress Nixi thinks I can. And so I'm willing to try."

"You're willing to risk the splendor of this room by simply trying?"

Nixi intercedes. "I'm willing to risk it, Mama. It will all be on me. You need some color in here."

The mother runs her hands over her face. "I'm too tired to argue with you. I put it in your hands, daughter."

Nixi kisses her cheek. "You won't be sorry."

The mother waves her hand. "Go on then. Let me sleep." She sinks down into the covers.

Nixi hurries me out to the hallway. "When can you start?"

I put my hands on my cheeks—which are hot. I try to understand this new reality. "I think you're overestimating my skills. I have no idea what to paint or where to get paints and supplies."

"I'll get you everything you need. You come up with the idea. Can you start tomorrow?"

I shake my head. "I need a day to draw something up, mistress." I think of a glitch in my idea. "I need paper and pens. Since writing isn't allowed . . ."

"Correct. But drawing is totally fine." She detours into her room and I hear her rustling with something. She comes out carrying a drawstring bag. "Will this do?"

I look inside and see a roll of papers and drawing supplies. "It will." But then I see something else, something out of place. I pull out an orange.

"I added a few of those. For your time."

Lieb will be so excited. We haven't had oranges since we got here.

"What about my job?"

"I'll take care of that."

"But—"

"If you'd rather go back to whitewashing walls, that's your choice."

"No, no. I appreciate the opportunity. I'll come up with something."

"Good." She sees me out to the stone street. "Can you make your way up-top from here?"

Up-top? What an interesting term. "I can."

"I'll meet you tomorrow after the five Count, where I first met you. You can show me your design and tell me what you need. Yes?"

"Yes."

She gives me a look.

"Yes, mistress."

As I walk home I have the feeling this "yes" is the biggest yes of my life.

**

After leaving Nixi and her mother, I know I should go back to the Sanctuary and help Lieb paint, but I don't want to.

The Head Notable of all Legalis has ordered me to paint a mural. I will have special supplies. But first, I need inspiration.

As I walk, I get discouraged. There is nothing inspiring in Legalis, at least not "up-top." Only white buildings and white-clad people, with an occasional sickly tree thrown in. Their leaves aren't even bright green.

When the Counts happen, I take refuge with others and add my black pebble to theirs. But even in those close quarters no one talks to each other. As Papa said, they're just a mass of people who share tedium and an oppressive case of the blahs. Doing the same thing, every hour, every day. Looking the same, acting the same.

What I'd seen today — down below — was the opposite of blah.

As the workday ends, I head to our cells, but see Nana coming out. She's carrying an armload of food. "From now on we're going to eat at your father's. Help me carry our food over to share."

I take a loaf of bread from her. At least we'll have oranges tonight. I can't wait to surprise them.

We go inside, and Papa, Oria, Rand and Lieb enter in quick succession. Apparently Rand is now a member of our family?

They chatter about their day and when they are all seated I say, "I have a present for all of you." I set four oranges on the table.

As expected, Lieb gasps with delight. "Oranges!"

Papa picks one up, taking in its scent. "Where did you get these?"

"From the daughter of the Head Notable."

He fumbles the orange and it rolls to the edge of the table where Elum saves it from the floor. "Notable Glynis?" Elum asks.

"She didn't give me her name, just her title. But I spoke with her in her bedroom."

His eyes grow large. "Her bedroom?"

It's nice to have something exciting to share. "Her bedroom. She's been sick and needs cheering up."

"I know," he says.

"How do you know?" Nana asks.

"I've heard. That's why Ivar is the acting Head Notable. So why were you in there?"

I tell them the story of the tree, Nixi, and the underground homes of the Notables.

"I can't believe you were there," Rand says. "None of the Masses ever get down there."

This is *very* enjoyable. "But now I have the problem of designing a mural—and painting it. I have no idea if I can even do such a thing."

Nana puts her hand on mine. "You can do it. You must do it. This is a marvelous opportunity."

"It will be nice to do something creative again," I say.

"Beyond that," Papa says.

"What do you mean?"

Oria takes over. "You've gone where none of the Masses has gone before, and you're going to spend time there. It's a chance to find out more about the Judge."

Papa asks Nana, "Did you get into the loft this morning?"

She shakes her head. "There weren't any stairs."

"The Judge must fly up there," Lieb says.

"It can't fly," Papa says.

"How do you know?" Lieb asks.

"I don't, but—"

I slap both hands on the table, getting their attention. "Hello? I was telling you about my amazing experience?"

After a beat of silence, Nana says, "It *was* amazing, child. We're excited for you."

"And it just might lead to so much more," Oria says.

They annoy me. "You all have one track minds. Judge this. Judge that. I have an immediate problem here. I have to come up with an idea by tomorrow. Something colorful. Something I can paint. Help me."

They all nod and seem apologetic. Which they should be.

"Why not paint the sky and clouds?" Lieb says. "They're pretty."

"They already have that on the ceilings of the street. I need something different."

"They have the sky and clouds on their ceilings?" Lieb asks.

"Can you just paint shapes of color?" Rand asks.

"I think it needs to look like something. If not totally realistic, based on something real."

"You painted a tree on the Sanctuary wall," Lieb says. "Why not a tree?"

"My garden!" Oria says. "You were in my garden. Paint that."

"That's a wonderful idea," Nana says. "Trees, flowers, a path…"

"You had a garden?" Papa asks.

"All the Patrons did. It's where the Keeper visited me."

"You told us he likes gardens," Lieb says.

Rand taps a finger on the table. "Which makes it very appropriate. We want to spread news of the Keeper throughout all Legalis? Then you paint him a garden."

"And he'll appear?" Elum asks.

Oria holds up her hands. "I don't think that's the way he works, but it would be nice to paint something *he* likes."

I get out the paper and pencils. I begin to sketch simple leaves.

"Put more details in it than that," Papa says. "Like an oak leaf."

I try again, and Lieb takes up the pencil and draws a flower. Soon everyone offers their ideas — which I'm grateful for. As they help, I feel a mural coming together in my head. "I think I've got it. Now I just have to make it happen."

"You can do it, child," Nana says.

I have to do it.

Chapter Eleven

Oria

Durth comes into the cell area just as we're about to leave for breakfast at Devin's. "Home assignments today."

"We get a real house?" Lieb asks.

Her shrug speaks volumes. "A unit."

The word sounds institutional.

"Was it hard getting a unit for four?" Solana asks.

"Impossible. Which is why you three are together, and you're not." She points at me.

I'm the *not.* "I have to be alone?"

"You'll have a roommate."

"Why can't she be with us?" Solana asks. "We'd make room. We've gone through too much to be separated now."

I notice Helsa isn't giving an opinion, though I think I know where she stands.

Durth puts her hands on her hips. "This isn't a negotiation," she says. "Yer time's up here. Follow me."

Lieb stuffs some bread into the pockets of his robe, and Helsa grabs a few apples we were lucky enough to get. We have no possessions other than Lieb's messenger bag which is hidden away at Devin's. I start to fold up the blanket but Durth says, "Leave it. You'll have one at yer new place. And, you don't have to go back to work the rest of the day."

"How unreasonably kind of them," Helsa says.

"Shh," Solana says.

Durth points at Helsa. "You'd be wise to mind yer mouth, girlie."

As we are ready to leave, Lieb gives me some of his bread. "Since we're not going to Papa's."

Solana tells Helsa, "Give Oria one of the apples."

She does so, but only reluctantly. Will she ever like me?

Durth leads the way and we head to the right. She points at a building two past where Devin and Elum live. "In there. Second floor."

"Yay!" Helsa says. "Papa's close."

I'm happy for them. Or I try to be.

Durth and I start walking again.

We walk. And walk.

"Is it much farther?" I ask.

"Does it matter?"

"I suppose not." But it does bother me that we're walking in an area that I haven't been to since Devin first gave us a tour.

She finally stops and points. "There. Top floor."

"What's my roommate's name?"

"How should I know?" She leaves me there.

I go up narrow exterior stairs and knock on the door.

A blonde young woman answers. "Yes?"

"I've been assigned to live here."

"I heard someone was coming." She opens the door wide and I enter. "This is it."

It is one room. There are a few shelves with food and bowls on them, a fire grate with a pot, a table with three chairs, and two cots along opposite walls with a single window between them.

"Privy's down the stairs in the alley to the right."

There was no need to ask about baths. I should have enjoyed them more back home. I've seen a few water pumps in the streets, but hauling it to bathe? As if we have a choice.

"Have a seat," she says.

I pull out a chair. The table is tiny. It's awkward to face a stranger with such a small space between us. She appears younger than me, younger than Helsa too. Her eyes are a deep blue.

"I'm Berit."

I start to extend my hand to shake hers but return it to my lap.

I'm learning.

"I'm Oria."

"They say you're new?"

"I came here from the desert."

"No, you didn't."

"I didn't?"

"You came from Regalia, didn't you?"

Her voice isn't confrontational. I take a chance. "Yes, I did."

Her eyes widen with interest. "I've heard of it. Is it a nice place?"

Better than this. "It's a nice place."

"Then why are you here?"

"I broke some rules and was exiled."

"Rules like our laws?"

"Not exactly. Legalis has a *lot* of laws."

"I hate laws." She gives one long sigh. "I'm going to die soon."

I'm taken aback. "What?"

She shrugs. "My father is in jail awaiting his punishment from the Judge."

"I'm so sorry. What kind of punishment?"

Berit leans back and crosses her arms as if protecting herself. She looks like she needs protection. She's as tiny as Solana, her skin pale, her blonde hair dull and lifeless.

"Da was arrested for having too many Faults. He was put in jail a month ago and is waiting for the Judge to announce his Judging Day."

"So he's already had a trial?"

Her eyebrows touch. "Trial?"

"A trial, where he gets to defend himself — or have a solicitor defend him?"

"I've never heard of such a thing. So no, there are no trials. Every so often the Judge declares a Judging Day."

"My friend, Devin, mentioned Judging Day as something bad, but he didn't explain it."

"It *is* bad, and it's pretty straightforward. People are chosen from the jail and are brought to the square in front of the Sanctuary. Then the Head Notable calls for the final punishment."

"The final punishment?" It sounds very ominous.

She nods once. "Judging Day is it. The end."

"As in death?"

She shrugs.

Shrugs at the possibility of death?

"Does anyone speak for the accused?"

"No."

"Do *they* get to say anything?" I ask.

"Not that I've ever witnessed." She sits forward. "It would be nice if Da *could* say something. He didn't do anything really wrong. When he was arrested he was going through the dump pile of unclaimed food, gathering up extra to give to our neighbor who was sick." She points downstairs.

"So he lived here with you?"

"He did."

"And your mother . . .?"

"She died when I was born. It's always been just me and Da."

"He was helping someone. He shouldn't be punished for it."

"He'd gathered food before, got caught, and earned studs for it, but this time someone turned him in and he was arrested."

I think of Trina's glee at being a tattletale. "I don't understand a system that encourages people to tattle on each other — for no good reason."

"Getting Faults removed is a good reason."

"I mean, for no real crime. Certainly it's not a crime to be charitable."

Berit bites her lip.

"When will he be sentenced or punished or whatever it's called?"

She breathes in, then lets it out slowly. "All we know is 'soon.'"

Her sadness lingers in the air between us.

I remember what started this conversation. "But if he's the one who's going to be punished, why did you say *you're* going to die?"

She hugs herself. "Because the most severe punishment is the Cudgeling Circle."

"I don't understand."

"Twelve people are called to Cudgel Duty. They stand in a circle and one at a time, they step forward and hit the person who stands in the middle with a club."

"That's horrible. But that doesn't mean certain death, does it?"

"Most people die."

"But surely those on Cudgel duty don't have to hit hard."

She looks aghast. "Of course they do. They're Beaters. If they don't they'll have to go in the Circle themselves."

Once again, I think of our first subject. "So your father might be . . . cudgeled?"

Berit shakes her head and points at herself. "Not him. Me. A relative of the accused is cudgeled. I'm Da's only relative."

I gape at her. It's too cruel to possibly be true. "That's inhuman."

"It's the law."

I'm bowled over by the insanity of it. "Berit . . . isn't there something we can do to stop it? Is there someone we can talk to?"

"Talk to?"

"Appeal to. Petition. Or plead to if necessary."

She looks appalled, not at her fate but at my reaction to it. "I've never heard of such a thing."

Her unfamiliarity hits me like a punch to the gut. I know Legalis is overly zealous about controlling its people but I hadn't realized it was brutal and merciless. And devious. They've made an atrocity normal.

Berit pushes back from the table. "I need to get to work. They allowed me time off to be here when you arrived, but they'll be expecting me."

"I wouldn't want you to get in trouble on my account."

She points at a cot. "That one is yours. I'm working late at the farm tonight. I'll see you then." She leaves.

I look around, needing my friends. I have so much to tell them about the Judge and his punishments. But they're not here. I feel fully alone for the first time since coming to Legalis.

But my aloneness is nothing compared to what Berit is going to go through — alone.

Chapter Twelve

Solana

Everyone but Helsa meet at Devin's to share dinner, and I bring along some of the food we've been allotted for our unit. Elum and Rand set out bowls and we begin to eat.

After passing the bread Devin asks, "I wish Helsa would get back from her meeting with the Notable."

"I do too," I say. "I hope something bad hasn't—"

The door opens and Helsa comes in. She's beaming.

"It went well?" I ask.

"Very. Nixi liked the idea of a garden and is getting paints mixed up for me. I start tomorrow morning."

"What about painting with *me*?" Lieb asks.

"You'll have to do it alone for a while," Helsa says. "You'll be okay. I'll see you every night in our new unit."

He seems appeased.

"How do you like your new space?" Rand asks.

Lieb's eyes brighten. "Nana and Sa-Sa share a room." He points to the room Devin and Elum share. "Like here. And I sleep near the door so I can protect them."

I don't think we need protecting, but say, "Thank you for being so brave."

Oria sits at the end of a bench, her hands in her lap, her forehead furrowed. "Tell us about your place, Oria," I ask.

She shakes her head.

Considering the three of us have our own unit, I know she must feel left out and lonely. She's not used to being alone.

"Do you have a roommate?" Rand asks.

"I do."

She still won't look at us.

It must be something serious. "What's going on?" I ask.

Oria sits up straighter in her chair. "My roommate is a girl who's going to be killed because her father is in jail."

"What?" I ask.

She tells us about some strange Cudgeling Circle that's too bizarre to even fathom.

"So the man in jail isn't punished, his daughter is?" I ask.

Oria looks to my son for confirmation. "It's true. Right, Devin?"

"That *is* the truth of it. He's in my jail. His name is Yair."

Oria looks at Rand and Elum. "How did this happen? How can a society be so cruel?"

Rand's shoulders are slumped, as if he feels ashamed for the whole of Legalis. "I have no explanation for it. That's just the way it's always been. People accept it."

Elum interjects. "They have no choice. If they don't go along, they risk the Circle themselves."

"Accept it?" Oria asks loudly. "Accept transferring punishment to an innocent? Where's the accountability?"

Elum pours water. "There is none. In Legalis it's every person for themself.

"That's not quite true," I say. "You have to behave or else your family will suffer for it."

"And you also risk people turning you in to get rid of their own Faults," Oria says. "Like Trina did."

"There's danger from the Judge, the Fault Finders, the Notables, and each other," Rand says. "Actually, the latter is why I'm living on the streets."

A silence falls over the room as we look at him. "Did someone turn you in?"

He fingers his crutch, clearly uncomfortable with our attention. "It's a long story and we're not talking about me here, we're talking about that girl."

Oria says, "But maybe your story will help us understand. I want to understand."

"I do too," I say. "Please tell us your story."

Lieb raises his hand. "Can we eat while he talks? I'm hungry."

That boy is always hungry.

"We need truth, Rand," Oria says. "Say whatever it is you have to say."

Rand breaks a chunk off a loaf of bread and passes the loaf around. "I guess the best way to start the story is to say I was lazy, mouthy, and violent."

"You? Violent?" Lieb asks, shaking his head. "Not you."

"Not me, now. But I was." He tears his bread into smaller pieces, sets them in a row on the table, but doesn't eat any. "I broke three Directives. Numbers four, five, and six."

We look at each other. "I don't remember what those are," I say.

He counts them off on his fingers. "Never miss Sanctuary Day. I missed because my mother was sick. The two of us missed three times."

"You had good reason," Devin says.

"The Judge doesn't listen to reason," Rand says.

"What's Directive number five?" Helsa asks.

"'Never speak against those who have authority over you.'" He raises his hand. "Guilty again. "I publicly argued against Directive Four."

"And Six?" Oria asks.

"'All lives belong to Legalis. No violence allowed.'" He sighs. "Again, I am guilty. When the Fault Finders came to arrest me, I was with my mother — who was just on the mend — and I lost my temper and slugged one of them. Both of them."

"Good for you," Helsa says.

"Not good for me. They chased me and I fell off a wall." He reaches down and touches his crippled leg. "My leg was broken, but they still dragged me to jail. I was in there a long time and it didn't heal right."

"I'm so sorry," I tell him.

"It doesn't hurt much anymore. I've learned to manage."

"But how did you get out of jail?" Oria asks.

He glances at Elum. But then he says, "That's a story for another day." He looks at Oria. "Your new friend . . . what's her name?"

"Berit."

Rand addresses Devin. "When will her father be sentenced?"

"Judging Days are announced on Sanctuary Day. There's no particular order over who gets judged first, but Yair has been there the longest. I've heard the guards talking . . ."

"What about the woman from last Sanctuary Day?" Oria asks. "The one who stepped forward demanding her husband be released. Is she still in there?"

"Is *he*?" I add.

"He is. They are," Devin says. "Though I expect her punishment might be worse than his because she made a scene in public."

"The clock is ticking for all of them," Rand says.

"Can't we speak out on their behalf?" Helsa asks.

"There's no trial. No defense allowed," Oria says. "No solicitor to speak for the accused, and the accused can't say anything either."

I'm stunned. "So the Judge will punish them according to what? How it feels that morning?"

"The Judge lives underground, but where?" Oria asks. "How do I get an audience with it?"

Elum scoffs. "You don't."

"As far as living somewhere?" Rand says. "It's rumored it has a compound somewhere, but no one knows where."

Helsa raises her hand. "Nixi told me there are tunnels down below. It's how the Notables get around so they don't have to be seen."

Oria taps a finger on the table. "Helsa, you have to see what you can find out when you're down with the Notables. If they have tunnels, maybe one of them leads to the Judge's compound."

She shakes her head vigorously. "I am not exploring any tunnels. Especially if that *thing* might be at the end of one."

"I heard someone say it slices people up and eats them," Lieb says.

Here we go again . . .

Devin shakes his head. "My daughter is not exploring any tunnels. I forbid it."

I press my hands on the table. "This is getting out of hand. We need direction—divine direction. Let's pray."

We bow our heads and I ask the Keeper to help us find the Judge, save the accused, and keep us all safe.

It makes me nervous that all three of the asks are intertwined.

Chapter Thirteen

Helsa

Today's the day.

I walk toward the arch leading down to the Notable homes. My stomach spins. Not only am I in a foreign place like Legalis, I'm going to interact with people far above my station. I did something similar when I got involved with Oria in Regalia, so I *can* do it successfully. It's not like Nixi and Glynis are gods or anything. They're just women.

Somehow that doesn't calm my nerves.

Glynis is the Head Notable, which means she has power beyond all the others I might come in contact with. But it's not even her position that makes me nervous. I'm nervous because I have no idea if I can paint the garden I've been asked to paint. Plus, my family and friends want—and need—me to find out more about the Judge. And tunnels.

I'm no spy. I'm not even twenty years old. Despite the fact I often act like I know it all, I'm don't. I'm clueless about most everything. I shouldn't be responsible for gathering such important info.

And now Oria's all stirred up about her roommate who's going to be beaten to death—I assume that's what "cudgel" means—and I'm upset about that too. That is *not* justice. Yet was Oria being exiled into the Swirling Desert justice?

I'm glad I'm not in charge of such decisions. It's above my pay grade. Which as far as I know is zero, as I was told nobody gets paid in Legalis. Nixi never mentioned getting paid—other than giving me four oranges.

I wish I could go home—home-home—back to Regalia. I'd never complain about my factory work again if I could quietly live in the cottage I shared with Nana. Although I didn't realize it at the time, I was happy there. Content.

Will I ever be content again?

At least with this job, I *have* moved up. I no longer whitewash walls that don't need whitewashing, and I'm getting to spend the day in a home that isn't hot and dusty. Plus, I'm getting to do something creative. I used to embroider and do hand work all day—and I liked most of the sewing I did. But unlike this mural, *I* didn't design the projects. I was just the hands that did the work.

I spot one of the women from the Exiled. She taps her chest with her fingers—a sign *we* taught them. I do it back, but we don't stop and talk. She glances up at a clock.

Ah. The Count is minutes away.

It always seems to be minutes away.

It's strange my family hasn't become better friends with the Exiled. We've met and talked a little about *him,* but that's as far as it's gone. They seem passive; lukewarm. When we left Regalia the Devoted were growing in numbers in exciting ways. Here? They seem stagnant.

Is it because they're afraid of the Judge? They were exiled from Regalia for their faith, I'm sure they don't want to be punished again, like that one street preacher was, the one killed near Papa.

I don't either. And with the rumors—myth or true—about the Judge's wrath, the Cudgeling Circle is real enough to keep everybody in their own little circle, unwilling to venture a toe beyond lest it be tread upon.

Or cut off.

Hey, I wouldn't put it past the Judge.

Now I've been assigned to be a big part of bringing it down?

Good luck with that.

I reach the arch just as the hour begins to chime. There's no time for second thoughts. I hurry down the street to the first gate.

The guard stands at attention. "Where do you think you're going? They'll be no Count crashing here."

"I have a job here. I'm working for the Head Notable." Surely Nixi arranged for me to get through.

He takes out a list. "Name?"

"Helsa."

The chimes are nearly ending. If I don't make it through in time, or if he sends me back to the street, will he call a Fault Finder? But as the last chime ends, he opens the gate. I look around for pebbles. "Do I need to put a black one—?"

He scoffs. "No Counts down here, missy. You know where yer going?"

I remember columns carved with stars. "I do."

"Good, because I can't leave my post."

I make it past the second guard with merely a nod, and am truly on my own. It's eerie walking on the cobblestone street alone. Which brings to mind the tunnel system I'm supposed to explore. If all the tunnels look like this I'm okay with it, but if they're dark and dank and scary?

I'll pass.

But I can't pass. People are depending on me.

I look up and see the fake sky and clouds. I would like to be here at night and see the stars and moon.

Of course, being out at night is forbidden. That's when the Judge comes out. Then again, it *would* be one way to draw him into the open.

No way. Stop thinking like that, Helsa!

None of the columns I pass have stars on them, so when I come to two that do, I assume it's the right door.

I don't like the way my knocking breaks the silence.

I'm about to knock again when the door is opened by a young woman wearing a white robe. There is not a single Fault on either shoulder.

"You must be Helsa," she says.

"I am. I—"

She opens the door wide to let me enter. "I know why you're here. Follow me."

We walk through the grand foyer, then down the hall to the Head Notable's bedroom. She's lying on her side, snoring softly.

"Should I come back?" I whisper.

The servant seems uncertain and whispers back, "She told me to bring you here and—"

Head Notable Glynis suddenly wakes up. "So I did." She pushes herself to sitting and the maid adjusts her pillows. "Thank you, Kal. You can go."

Before she leaves, Kal flashes me a look that either says *behave yourself* or *beware*. Just to be on the safe side, I'll do both.

"So then," Glynis says as she smooths the covers over her legs. "I saw the drawing you made of a garden. The real question is, can you bring that drawing to life?"

"Yes, Head Notable." I say, though I quickly realize it sounds like I'm yelling in such a small space. "I mean, I hope so."

She nods. "Honesty. In a land of lies, I appreciate honesty more and more." She points to the wall directly in front of her, which has had all the furniture moved aside. "I assume Nixi gathered what you need?"

I see jars of paint, rags, and many brushes. And my drawing. "I think so." But then I see that something *is* missing. "I do need a pencil to sketch on the wall."

"Of course." She rings a bell that sits on the bedside table.

Kal comes in, then leaves to get a pencil. When she returns with it she notices the full breakfast tray. "Can I get you anything different, mistress? You didn't eat your breakfast."

"Unfortunately, nothing sounds good to me," the Head Notable says. "But maybe—if you insist—some broth."

"I'll get some right away." Kal hands me the pencil.

"Don't mind me," the Head Notable says. "Pretend I'm not here."

That's unlikely. But I start to work, folding my drawing in half and finding what should be the approximate center point of the wall. I begin to sketch.

"That's a very logical way to approach the work," she says.

"I'm a logical sort, Head Notable." I'd thought about it last night. Since I'm pretending to be an artist, I should act like one.

I begin to sketch, and repeatedly consult the drawing. I'm nervous having her there, which makes me drop the pencil more than once.

After a short time she says, "We could use more of your kind."

"My kind, Head Notable?"

"Creative people."

This is the second disparaging thing she's said about Legalis. As the Head Notable I expect her to sing its praises.

The door opens and Nixi comes in carrying a bowl of broth. "Here you go, Mother. And I'm not leaving until you eat all of it."

"Don't be a bully, daughter. I deal with enough bullies."

Make that three negative things. Somehow it gives me hope for Legalis—and the chance for change.

While her mother eats, Nixi checks on my minimal progress. She pulls a chair close.

Great. I have another spectator. Yet, I'm more comfortable with Nixi than her mother.

After a couple of minutes of sketching, Nixi interrupts. "So Helsa. You're not from here, are you?"

I remember what we're supposed to say. "I came from the desert."

"Regalia?" she asks.

It makes sense she knows the truth. "Yes. Regalia."

"Does that mean you were exiled? I've heard that's the only way people leave."

"It is, and I was. Or rather a friend was, and the rest of us ran after her."

"Whyever would you do that?"

I snicker. "Great question, mistress. I'm not really sure."

"It was a pretty big choice to make without being sure. I mean, did you know about the desert?"

"We knew there was a Swirling Desert surrounding Regalia. But we didn't know what was beyond."

"You were either very foolish or very brave," she says.

I finish sketching a palm leaf and face her. "Probably both."

"Who are the 'rest' of you?"

"My grandmother, my best friend, and one more."

"One more?"

It *was* an odd way to say it. "The woman who was actually exiled. Oria is her name."

"What did she do to merit expulsion like that?"

I'm not sure what to say. Do I mention the Keeper? Or keep it more simple. I choose the latter. "She broke a lot of rules."

"Ah. Rules. We understand rules."

Do they?

"Where are your parents?" she asks.

They know I'm from Regalia, but don't know that Papa's here? I'll make my answer generic. "My parents were gone within a few months of each other so I was left with just Nana. I was shocked when she bolted after Oria, running toward the opening in the sand, and then Lieb grabbed my hand and we ran in."

"You're a risk taker."

"Not usually. Not even then. I just didn't want to be left behind. Honestly, there wasn't time to think about it."

"You mentioned there was an opening?"

Unexpectedly, Nixi's mother speaks. "You know about the opening, Nixi. I told you about the interviews I've had with a few Regalians. They all said the Swirling Desert parted for them, allowing them to pass through unscathed."

"But why would it do that?" Nixi looks at me. "It's not much of a deterrent if people get through safely."

"Not all do," I say. "It's an shocking sight to see them swept away, screaming."

"So why are some people saved?"

Oh my. I hesitate as I think of a way to tactfully share the truth. I'm not sure how they will react.

"You know why, Helsa. I can see you do," Nixi says.

I stop sketching and face her. "Those who believe in the Keeper get through. Those who don't, die. At least that's what we've figured out."

Her mother points a spoon at me. "Now *that* is new information. I've asked a few survivors why they were saved but they wouldn't answer me. Actually, they said they didn't know."

I return to sketching, panicked by the Keeper questions that will surely follow. *Help me!*

My mind pulls up short when I realize I just prayed. I usually leave prayers to the others.

But still, I hope the Keeper heard me.

"Tell us about the Keeper," Nixi asks.

And so it begins. I've never had to define him. "He protects and provides for us." I think of an example. "Out in the desert, we were dying of thirst and exposure, and he provided us with a place that had trees, blankets, water, and food."

"And oranges," Nixi says simply.

She knows? "Yes, oranges. My friend Lieb loved the oranges."

"I'm glad," Nixi says. "We try to keep the oasis well-supplied."

I drop my pencil. "Oasis? That's what it's called?"

She nods.

"*You* put the supplies there?"

"Indirectly we still do. Mama instructs a man to keep it stocked."

I remember the man we met before we reached Legalis. "Is his name Jass?"

Her eyes brighten. "Yes! You met him?"

"Briefly. But yes."

Nixi motions toward her mother. "It was Mama's idea. About ten years back we were getting an influx of people from the desert and some were in bad shape, and—"

"Now now, I'll tell it, daughter." The Head Notable sets the soup bowl aside and adjusts her blankets. "I became aware of their plight soon after I was appointed to the Law Commission. At first I brought the supplies there myself—"

"With my help."

"With Nixi's help. But others on the Commission were against it, as was my husband, so I had to find another way. So I hired someone to do it."

"We're glad you did, Head Notable. We would have died without the supplies there." I'm surprised by her compassion. "We did see skeletons in the desert."

"Skeletons?" Nixi shudders. "I'm glad I never saw any of those."

"My reason for supplying the oasis was not completely unselfish," her mother says. "If people were coming to Legalis it was to our benefit if they could work."

Still . . .

Nixi picks up my dropped pencil and hands it to me. "Where do Lieb and your grandmother work?"

"You met Lieb. He was working with me, whitewashing the Sanctuary. Nana helps a man named Elum wind clocks."

I hear a slight gasp, but when I look at Glynis I can't tell if she made the sound or I imagined it.

"We're thankful for jobs," I say. "You provided for us just like the Keeper did." Kind of.

"With parting sands it sounds like his ways are a bit more . . . magical," Nixi says.

"Not magical, but definitely not natural, mistress. Nana often has dreams where she sees something special about him and then it comes true."

"She's a prophet?" Glynis asks.

"No, not that. At least I don't think she's a prophet."

"How else does he provide for you?" Nixi asks.

I thought of the desert again. "After Oria asked the Keeper how to get into Legalis, he made a light shine on the right side—which was the right side."

Glynis's voice drips with doubt. "He made a light . . .?"

"It was weird when it happened and it sounds weird now. But a sunbeam sliced through the clouds and shone to the right. We followed the light and found the entrance."

"Uh huh," Nixi says.

"It's the kind of thing he does."

"So all of Regalia believes in him?" Glynis asks.

It's another glitch in my story. "Actually, believing in him is forbidden. And speaking about him in public is why a lot of people are exiled."

"Sounds like a high price to pay," Glynis says.

It does. But then I think about Sanctuary Day. "I don't mean to offend, Head Notable, but I think worshipping the Judge like you do… and the restrictions and laws, are a high price to pay here."

"We do *not* worship the Judge." Her voice is adamant.

"I just thought since everyone *has* to attend on Sanctuary Day, and since the Judge has the final say in everything . . ."

"The Judge works in conjunction with the Commission," Glynis says. "It enforces the laws that *we* create."

I don't want her angry or she might kick me out. "Forgive me. I'm just trying to figure things out. It's all new to me. To us."

"What do you mean 'forgive' me? What is that word?"

I don't understand the question. "Forgive?"

"Yes." She flips her hand toward Nixi. "Are you familiar with the word?"

"I'm not. Helsa? Please explain."

I'm stunned and confused. "It means letting something go. Not holding a grudge against another person. Forgive and forget?"

The Head Notable shakes her head adamantly. "If such a thing was encouraged, then the rules of judgment that are the hallmark of Legalis would be worthless."

"Would that be a bad thing?"

Their silence makes me nervous. Clearly, I have gone too far.

She points to her bowl, her face returning to its uninterested state. "Nixi, I'm done eating. Leave Helsa alone so she can work and I can rest."

Nixi takes the bowl and leaves us.

The Head Notable turns on her side to sleep.

I go back to sketching, feeling very relieved I'm still here.

**

Suddenly the Head Notable moans and bolts up in bed. "Bowl!"

She fumbles for a bowl sitting near the foot of the bed, and I run to get it for her. She gets it just in time and throws up violently.

I don't know what to do. We're not allowed to touch. Yet she's miserable.

Her hair hangs down dangerously close to . . . I reach out and hold it back for her.

She finishes and makes a motion for a towel—which I find nearby.

As she wipes her mouth I take the bowl. My own stomach threatens to do something nasty.

"In there," she says, pointing.

I take the bowl to a room that has a covered privy, a bathtub, and a sink with its own water supply. I empty the ick and rinse out the bowl, drying it so I can return it to her.

She shakes her head and nods for me to put it back in its original position.

"Do you want me to get Kal? Or Nixi?" I pour a glass of water from a carafe.

"I'll be all right." She adjusts her covers carefully, attempting to regain control. "And thank you."

"Of course. Would you like me to leave so you can rest better?"

"That's not necessary. Usually once will do it."

Does this happen often?

I go back to work, my mind swimming with everything I've learned.

Chapter Fourteen

Oria

I am weary of listening to Trina complain about her husband and all the laws she hopes to catch him breaking.

"Thanks to me he's nearly running out of shoulder space to put all his Fault studs," she brags.

"If he has so many, why isn't he in jail?" I ask.

"That, I don't know. But I'm doing my best to get him there."

I think of my conversation with Berit. "But if he ends up in jail and gets sentenced to the Cudgeling Circle . . ."

Shockingly, Trina is quiet a moment.

I complete my point. "*He* doesn't get punished, you or Pan does."

Her eyebrows rise. "Hmm. I need to think this through."

You do that.

As the morning wears on, Trina has absolutely no interest in anything I have to say, so I stop even trying to talk. I've never seen someone say so many words without a break. She even takes breaths at lightning speed.

I'm learning to block her out as I distribute food. She doesn't even stop talking about her husband when we have customers.

I move to refill the bread stock and suddenly notice something different. Silence. I look up and see Trina smiling at something. Someone.

"Pan, my boy," she says, beaming.

So she *does* stop jabbering occasionally? At least for her son.

Pan is five or six and has his mother's light brown hair. He smiles back at her, which implies she's not as bad a person as I think she is.

Trina hands Pan an apple, which he immediately bites. He comes behind the counter and sits on the ground behind us.

"What did you learn at indoctrination today?" she asks.

He considers this as he chews. "We learned that if we break laws and go out at night and stuff like that, the Judge will dive down from the sky and slice our throats with its knife-fingers." He mimics scary fingers. "Stuff like that."

"That's a horrible thing to teach children," I say.

Trina glares at me, aghast. "The truth is never horrible. And when the Judge does such a thing we can be assured it has a good reason."

"But it can't fly," I say.

Her eyebrows rise. "And you know this how?"

Pan balances the apple on an upraised knee. "Teacher says it can. It does it all the time, flying all over Legalis, looking for people breaking laws. It can even make itself invisible. It knows everything and sees everything." Pan nods once as a period.

I hand a customer a loaf of bread, then ask mother and son, "Where does it live?"

Trina scoffs. "Where does it *not* live? I've heard stories of it being in two or three places at once."

Pan nods. "Teacher says it lives underground, real deep in a scary cave with killer bats that attack when it wants them to."

A cave? Or maybe the tunnels Helsa spoke about? "But if it lives down there, how can it know everything everyone is doing up here?"

"Because it can," Trina says.

"Teacher says there are desert monsters too." Pan takes another bite of apple. "But we're safe as long as we stay *in* Legalis."

It's an interesting way to keep people from leaving. "Have you ever had contact with the Judge?" I ask. "Seen it up close?"

She shakes her head so violently that her jowls jiggle. "Never! People die if they get too close."

Pan nods as if that's what he's learned too.

"Its eyes are mirrored," I say. "Why —?"

"That's so we can see ourselves in the reflection. Its eyes can bore right into a person. Burn them." Trina points at Pan. "Which is why you have to be a very good boy, all the time."

He nods.

More customers demand our attention. Separating fact from fiction regarding the Judge is going to be difficult.

**

After work I'm eager to talk to Berit to see if she's heard anything about the timing of her father's Judging Day.

She's inside our unit, setting fresh lettuce and carrots on the counter. "Are you hungry?" she asks.

"I am. This looks wonderful. Better than what we hand out in the booth."

"Because I picked it all myself." She's brought in a bucket of water and carefully cleans the vegetables. She points at a knife. "Want to cut some carrots?"

Of course.

I'm curious about her looming situation. "How often do you get to visit your father?"

"Visit?" She glances at me. "They don't ever let me see him—which is incredibly hard." She cuts up the lettuce and brings a bowl to the table. "For my entire life it's just been him and me. We're everything to each other. Not talking to him . . ."

"Can you send letters? Or a note?"

She smiles and wipes her hands on a towel. "Just a minute."

I put the cut carrots on the table and sit.

Berit retrieves a small wood box from under her cot. She sets it on the table and begins to open it. "These are from . . ." Her expression changes and she quickly shuts the box. "Wait. I'm not sure . . ."

Why is she hesitant?

Yet she's only known me two days. "If you're not comfortable sharing with me, I understand. But please know I'm on your side. I will never do anything to hurt you or your father."

She pauses, then opens the box. Inside are small pieces of paper folded in fourths. "A friend of mine at the farm delivers the food to the jail. Papa has been able to get a few notes out to me, and me a few to him. He's an amazing man; so good and giving." She hands me the box. "I have to trust you. Please don't make me regret it. There are a few personal notes, but some . . ." She takes two notes out. "See for yourself."

I unfold one. I read it silently and feel my heart overflowing. "You believe in the Keeper!"

"I do." She whispers. "Do you?"

"I do. We do." I'm filled with relief and joy. I pull her into an awkward embrace, then remember it's not allowed and let her go. "I apologize. I'm just excited."

Berit's face is flushed but she doesn't seem angry. "It's all right. I liked it. And touching is allowed because we're in private."

Gladly noted.

I read the message out loud: "'Don't conform to the world. Transform from the inside out, letting the Keeper show you his will.' This is a Relic!"

"A Relic?" she says. "We call them Pages, but I like your term better."

"We assume they're Relics from the Before Times." I let my thoughts take a detour. "Do you know anything about the Before Times?"

"I've heard people mention 'The Before.' It's probably the same thing. But nobody talks about it."

"They don't talk about it in Regalia either. It's forbidden."

"I wonder why."

"Me too. We're not allowed to talk about our history at all."

"Same here. I'd like to know our history; to know how Legalis came to be. And Regalia." She fingers the box. "Something happened to separate us from each other."

"Why is it a secret?" I ask.

"I don't like secrets," she says.

"Neither do I. So who *does* know about it?"

She shakes her head. "People far more powerful than us, that's for sure." She takes the Relic from me. "I really like this one. It gives me hope that there's something better."

Something better beyond jail and Cudgeling Circles. "Read another one," I say.

She unfolds one. "'The Keeper has set us free! Don't be slaves of the laws.'"

"That's pretty pertinent," I say. "Legalis has laws for everything."

"They just posted another one today."

"They post them?"

"Near the clocks."

"How often does this happen?"

She shrugs. "Once in a while."

"What's the new one say?"

"It is now against the law to wear any head covering."

"But I haven't seen any."

"It will mostly affect people working the farms. The sun can be vicious."

"So is that law. It doesn't make sense."

Berit holds up the Relic she read. "That's why I like these. They make sense. They help me find hope when there is no hope."

"Where did your father get them?"

"All over. He'd come home with one that he found in a basket of bread, and another time say he found one under a rock near our door."

"It sounds like people put them there to be found."

"That's what he thought." She gets up to put bowls out for eating, adding a loaf of bread. "He memorized them and left them for other people." She glances over her shoulder at me. "Do you have any?"

"We do."

"I'd love to see them."

"I'll copy them for you. And I'd like to copy these. Do you have some paper and a pencil?"

She hesitates. "I'm not supposed to have either, but . . ." Berit gets up and gets both, hidden away in a basket on a high shelf. "Here."

I copy the Relics. I'm excited to show the others. In fact, I'm excited to introduce Berit to the others. And to meet her friends who also believe.

"How many others believers are there?" I ask her.

"I have no idea. Da knows more than me. We don't get together, but the Pages have to come from somewhere." Her face clouds over. "Everyone is hesitant to speak about the Keeper because of all the Fault Finders."

"And the tattlers."

"Them too. We have to be suspicious of everyone."

"That's not a relaxing way to live," I say. "Or a productive one. It pits neighbor against neighbor."

I see the weight of it settle across her face.

"But there *are* other believers," I say. "The ones we know call themselves the Exiled. They're all from Regalia."

Her eyes brighten. "How many?"

"Only a handful, but I'm sure there *are* more. Like you say, the laws silence people."

"I'd like to meet them," she says. "Or at least meet your friends."

I push back my chair. "Then let's go now. We usually gather at Devin and Elum's unit and eat together."

She beams as she picks up the bowl of vegetables. "At least we won't come empty handed."

My heart is lighter as we go to Devin's. We knock on the door lightly before walking inside.

I look behind me. "This is my new friend, Berit," I say to the group. "She's my roommate."

They welcome her and gladly accept the vegetables.

"I know you," Devin says. "You're Yair's daughter."

"I am." She sits on the bench where Lieb has scooted over to make room. Lieb's eyes get big. "You're the girl who's going to die for him?"

"Lieb!" Solana says. "Manners."

"Oh. Sorry."

Berit is kind. "You're partially right. *If* the Judge condemns him to the Cudgeling Circle, I'll be the one to endure it."

"That's disgusting," Helsa says as she pours water for everyone.

"I'm certainly not looking forward to it," Berit says simply.

Rand's eyes are full of compassion. "A good woman is hard to find."

"Hey," Lieb says. "That's what you said to me!"

"Man or woman, it applies," Rand says.

"Berit believes in the Keeper," I blurt out. I take two Relics out of my pocket. "Some of the notes she's gotten from her father are Relics. Look."

They pass them around and I watch their faces light up. Rand reads them intently.

"I told Berit I would share ours." I look to Elum as he's the one who hid them.

He hesitates, but then retrieves Lieb's bag from its hiding place behind his cot. He hands the Relics to Berit.

Her face brightens as she reads them. "It's like finding treasure."

"I'll copy them for you after dinner," I say.

Helsa brings bread to the table and sits. She doesn't look happy, as if our conversation offends her. Maybe it does because it's not about her.

I chide myself for my rude thoughts — true or not.

She rips off a chunk of bread then says, "If anyone's interested, today I talked to the Head Notable about the Keeper."

"That's wonderful," I say.

"How did the subject of him come up?" her father asks.

"While I was sketching the mural on the wall of her bedroom." She glances at Berit as if wondering if she's impressed. "She asked about Regalia and how we got here — she knows we're from there. *She* said 'Regalia', not me. I mentioned people getting exiled, which led her to ask why. I had to mention the Keeper. She said exile was a high price to pay for believing. And I said worshiping the Judge and having all its cruel laws is a high price to pay here."

"We don't worship the Judge," Berit says.

"That's what Glynis said."

"Glynis?" Elum asks. "You called her Glynis?"

"Not to her face. You told me her name. I call her Head Notable."

Helsa's words to the Notable seem risky. "How did she respond?"

"Ok, I guess." Helsa shrugs. "She wasn't feeling well, so I just went back to work."

"Is she sick?" Berit asks.

"She is. Her daughter made her eat some soup, but then she threw it up."

Berit nods. "She hasn't presided over Sanctuary Day in weeks. Ivar has taken her place."

"How many weeks?" Solana asks.

"Four or five?" Berit says.

"Five," Elum says.

"Obviously she's not getting better considering her daughter hired me to paint the mural to cheer her up."

Elum suddenly stands. "I need to go."

"Go where?" Devin asks.

"I'll be back before dark." He leaves, letting the door slam shut behind him.

"What's all that about?" I ask.

"I have no idea," Solana says. But then she asks Berit, "Are there doctors in Legalis?"

"Healers, we call them. A few."

"You need to ask Nixi to send for one," Solana says.

"I don't think that's my place," says Helsa.

Her father points at her. "Your place would be in trouble if she died while you're in the room. You ask Nixi. Tomorrow."

"I will," she says. She chews a slice of carrot, then adds. "There's one more weird thing. I said, 'forgive me' and neither of them knew what the word meant."

"How can they not know?" Devin asks.

"*I* don't know," Berit says. "What does it mean?"

We're all shocked and do our best to share.

Without forgiveness, Legalis is in trouble.

Chapter Fifteen

Solana

Elum and I have a steady routine. I know exactly which clocks will be wound during the three days it takes us to work the circuit.

I am even used to the hourly Counts, repeatedly finding refuge without hesitation.

As we walk toward our fifth clock of the day I share a thought with him. "Isn't it interesting how we seek routine, as if finding it gives us peace and a sense of security? It was that way working at the factory, and it's that way now, winding clocks. It always comes back to routine. It's not a bad thing. Just an observation."

"Maybe it reflects our need for order."

"Maybe."

"I've never thought the Counts are all bad," Elum says. "They help regulate the order of our days."

I scoff. "I could do without *that* particular regulation."

We walk past a decrepit door that I'd noticed the first day. There are small rocks scattered haphazardly around it, and the sandy soil has blown upward at the bottom, showing that it's not been opened in a very long time. It looks inaccessible and uninviting.

But it also piques my curiosity. "Where does that door lead?" I ask Elum.

With only a glance he says, "Nowhere. It's been like that forever. I think the unit behind it is in bad shape so it's not used anymore."

"Why don't they repair the unit and use it?"

"How am I supposed to know?"

"I mean, couldn't someone make a request? Surely the unit could be put to good use."

His expression turns stern and I see a vein in his neck tighten. "I don't know, and I don't care. It's none of our business, Solana. There's a law that states quite plainly, 'Don't go where you don't belong.' I suggest you adhere to that."

I'm taken aback by his tone, so much so that I make light of it. "I'm just curious. No harm intended and no harm done."

His shoulders shuffle as if signaling he's moved from the stern Elum to the one I know. "Ready for number five?"

**

I *have* to get through that door.

It's a stupid thought that won't leave me. And it's an impossible thought because I am never alone. Elum and I are together all day, every day. We spend the Counts together, eat lunch together, then spend the evening together with everybody else in his unit.

It's not that I don't enjoy his company—I do. Very much. He reminds me how much I miss my husband and having someone near to my own age to talk to. Helsa, Devin, and the others fill one part of my need for companionship, but Elum fills another.

Yet there's something about the way he forbade me from exploring that door that rankles me. I don't like being told what *not* to do. I can be a stubborn old woman when I want to be.

So as we complete clock number fifteen I utilize a ploy I used back in Regalia when I was dealing with our horrible boss, Bru.

I lean against a wall, put my hands on my thighs, and breathe heavily.

"Are you all right?" he asks.

"I . . . I just don't feel very well." I put the back of a hand to my forehead and sigh deeply.

"Would you like some water?"

I shake my head and take another deep breath. "This happens from time to time. It's usually best if I lay down. I think I need to go home early. Would that be all right?"

"Of course. I'll take you."

"No. Thank you. I'll be fine. Someone needs to finish our work. I'll see you this evening."

He gives me a worried wave and I begin to weakly walk back the way we'd come. As I glance over my shoulder he takes the ladder and moves on.

As soon as he's out of sight I make a beeline for the door. But before I approach, I scope it out. Since Elum was so quick to squelch my interest, would others care if I walked up to it, or went inside?

I wait until the street is clear. Then I walk straight to the door and without a pause, open it. It's a good thing there are no locks in Legalis.

I'm surprised that it's not a unit at all, but a landing at the top of spiral stairs heading downward. Thankfully it's open to the sky so I can see the steps as I descend.

I hear the clocks chime in the distance. Another Count has begun. I can't go back right now. But will people come through the door, seeking shelter during the Count? I hold my breath and don't move.

But when the chimes finish and no one comes in, I continue walking downward. And downward.

I finally reach the bottom of the stairs and follow a narrow, dark corridor. The air is refreshingly cool compared to the heat of the street above. The walls are stone and I use them to guide me forward. Who—or what—lives in the depths of Legalis like this?

I stop walking when I hear a familiar sound—the sound of a treadle sewing machine. Someone's sewing up ahead? I make a silly assumption that anyone who sews can't be dangerous and keep walking. Then I see a lit opening. It's a door with a small window in it. I peer in and see a workroom where a few dozen people sew brightly colored garments. Some are dying fabric in vats. Some are cutting the fabric. It reminds me of the factories in Regalia.

The familiarity erases my fear. I open the door and step inside.

One of the workers sees me and points. Which makes everyone stop what they're doing.

"You're not supposed to be down here," the pointer says.

"I didn't know that," I say. "I was just curious about a door on the street that looked abandoned."

"As we are abandoned," the man says.

What an odd statement. "My name is Solana. I'm not from around here and—"

"Solana?" A woman at a sewing machine stands. "From Regalia?"

I take a closer look at her and remember a woman who was known for her speed on the machines. "Miri?"

She runs to me and we embrace. "What a happy reunion this is," I say. "You've been gone a long time."

"Three years." She sweeps her hand to include the others. "We've all been here a long time. We're all from Regalia."

"Did you all work in the factories?" I ask.

"We did," says the pointer. "I'm Zir. I worked in the shoe factory."

"I was in the headdress factory," says a man.

"And I worked in the jewelry factory," says a woman.

Others chime in. I notice that the clothing they're making is striking, with fabrics woven in bright patterns and colors. They would fit in well in Regalia, but here? in the land of white robes?

"Who do you sew for?" I ask.

"The Notables," Miri says.

"But they wear black."

Zir shakes his head. "In public they wear black. In their own community they wear color."

Miri nods toward the room. "They wear what we sew."

"That doesn't seem very fair."

A woman scoffs. "Since when should we expect fairness in Legalis?"

The others murmur their agreement.

"It's so exciting to find others from home. My family and friends recently arrived and we've been homesick." I start to think of all the questions Oria and the others would ask, when another thought comes to mind. "Were all of you exiled?"

"We were," Zir says.

"Why?" I ask.

They look wary. "Why were *you* exiled?"

I don't want to get into the details of only Oria being exiled and all the rest of it, so I simplify my answer. "For our faith."

Their expressions show relief. "Us too."

"Praise to the Keeper!" one says.

"So the sands parted for you too?" I ask.

"It did." Miri looks around at all her friends and smiles. "We were all part of the Devoted in Regalia."

I'm thrilled and clap my hands. "We were too!" To feel a part of something good in this awful place fills me up. "There are more of us here. They call themselves the Exiled. I know they'd love to meet you."

Miri's eyes grow big. "They're safe?"

"I'm not sure what you mean."

"We were a part of the Exiled until there was a raid where we were meeting, and everyone ran into the streets." She makes a circling movement over the workers. "We were arrested and taken down here. We never knew what happened to the rest."

"I don't know if the people I've met are from your group, but there *are* some Exiled out there."

"We assumed more would be assigned her after we were shut in, but we haven't had contact with anyone," Miri says.

I zero in on two key words. "Shut in?"

"We aren't allowed to leave. Ever."

"You can't go . . . up-top?" I ask.

"We can't," Zir says. "We were rejected by Regalia, hidden away by the Notables, and abandoned by the Keeper."

"Don't say that," I say. "He's still with you."

His eyebrows rise. "You coulda fooled me."

"Don't mind him," Miri says. "Not all of us have lost our faith."

Another woman steps forward. "But it *is* hard to keep believing when we're stuck down here, out of sight. We survive exile and the desert, only to become slaves?"

Slaves? My thoughts swim. "What happens if you leave? If you just use the stairs like I did and step out, into the open?"

"Me and a couple men tried that," Zir says. "I made it back, but they didn't. All I heard was a lot of screaming."

"The Judge got 'em," says a younger woman.

"Got them? As in killed them?" I ask.

She shrugs. "We never saw them again."

Zir threads a needle. "If they weren't killed, we assume they were arrested and probably sent to the Cudgeling Circle." He shrugs as if that's that.

"I'm so sorry. Did you witness many Circles before you were sent down here?"

"More than our share."

"How often did they happen?"

"There's no schedule to it," Zir says. "Which is how they keep people afraid."

Miri shakes her head, as if shaking the subject away. "You're skilled, Solana. Why didn't they put you down here with us?"

"Stop it, Miri," a woman says. "I don't wish *this* on anyone."

"Where *do* you work?" a man asks.

"I wind clocks. All the clocks."

Zir scoffs. "No need for clocks down here. No Counts either."

As much as I dislike the Counts, at least I have some semblance of freedom.

"Where do you live?" I ask.

The girl points to a door across the room. "There are two big rooms, one for men, one for women."

Which means no privacy. Ever.

"Do you have enough to eat? I could probably get—"

Miri brushes my words away. "They feed us well enough."

Zir disagrees. "Enough, but not well."

"I don't understand why you can't do what you do out in the open."

Miri answers. "Because if everyone else knew that nice clothes—"

"Really beautiful clothes," the girl adds.

"Knew that really nice and beautiful clothes are available, and there are people skilled enough to make them, then they might rebel and want something beyond the white sacks we're all forced to wear."

"And people would look different from each other," a man says. "Legalis survives by making everyone look the same, and have the same."

"When everyone has the same, no one wants anything more," Miri says. "When you're in a rut it's hard to find that first foothold out."

Her words bring an image to mind. "Do you want to be free?"

"Of course we do," Zir says. "Don't you?"

I'm surprised by the question. "But I'm not being held captive."

"Can you leave Legalis?"

It's a complicated question. "There's nowhere else to go," I say. "We can't get into Regalia. And I spent enough time in the desert."

"So you *are* a captive," Zir says. "You may have sunlight and fresh air, but you're a captive just the same. At least down here we're safe from arrest and the Circle."

"They need us," Miri says.

I suddenly think about Elum. I'd told him I didn't feel well and was going home. *I* need to leave.

"I'm going to go now," I say. "But I'll come back. I'll even help you with the work if you want me to."

"Visit as you like," Miri says. "But we're good with the work."

"Can I bring you anything?"

A few of them look at each other, as if only now thinking about their needs.

Finally a girl says, "News. Come back and bring us news of everything that's happened in the past three years."

That, I can do.

**

As I approach the door to my unit, I see Elum, standing in front of it. Knocking.

I turn around to walk out of sight, but it's too late.

"Solana?"

I'm sure my smile does *not* cover up my panic. "Hi there," I say stupidly.

"I came by to check on you," he says.

"I'm feeling better, thank you."

"You weren't sick long."

I am faced with a choice. Lie or tell the truth.

The truth sets you free.

"I wasn't sick."

He cocks his head and I can see him thinking. "You wanted time away from me."

"Not you exactly." I give him a genuine smile. "I enjoy spending time with you."

"But you needed time alone."

"I did." I open the door of the unit I share with Lieb and Helsa. "Come in and I'll explain."

We sit at the table. In a way I feel like a child admitting I skipped school. Yet I would like his take on what I found.

"Remember the door I asked you about? The one that looked abandoned?"

He only hesitates for a moment. "You opened it."

"I did. And you'll never believe—"

"You found the Workers."

My eyebrows rise. "You know about them?"

He shrugs. "I am aware."

His nonchalance skirts the edge of upsetting. "They're being held captive there. They can't leave."

"Don't act like they're being tortured. They have simply been made aware of the repercussions to society if the Masses know what they're making for the Notables."

"That no one else gets."

"Exactly."

"Surely you don't approve."

"Legalis is filled with particulars that aren't ideal but must be accepted."

My eyebrows rise higher. "Particulars? I hardly think imprisoning…" I raise my hand. "I'll soften the word… I hardly think *restraining* a segment of people and forcing them to use their skills for only an extremely small group is at the very least selfish, and at the most, disturbing."

"You're overreacting."

"I don't think I am. I'm also a skilled worker—in fact I know one of the women they have hidden away. Why didn't Helsa and I get assigned there?"

"I don't know." Elum seems oddly nervous. "But I'm glad you weren't."

I won't let him deflect the conversation. "Does everybody know about the Workers?"

He shakes his head adamantly. "Of course not. As I said, if everyone knew then—"

"So how do you know about them?"

He is taken aback. "I . . . I don't know when I found out about them. I was born in Legalis. At some point, I just knew."

He's lying. No one could find out about enslaved people and not remember their first impression.

He pushes his chair back, ending the conversation. "Shall we join the others for dinner?"

I agree, but I'm not finished with the subject. At all.

**

At dinner we share the events of our day. Helsa has nothing more to report about the Judge or Head Notable Glynis. She says she asked

Nixi about calling a Healer, and was assured that one had already come.

Devin has nothing more to report about Berit's father, though he's heard that Judging Day is soon.

Oria brings Berit along again, and I find her sweet and unassuming.

Lieb happily reports about the people he talked to while whitewashing.

Elum and Rand observe more than talk.

Finally, it's my turn, I tell them about the Workers.

"They're prisoners?" Oria asks.

"They are. And they're believers too. They were a part of the Exiled but got arrested and were put to work for the Notables."

Rand's eyes widen. "I remember a contingent of people arriving from the desert a few years back, talking about the Keeper and getting arrested. I think a few went to the Circle."

I spread my hands. "I found the rest of them."

"And you'll leave them where they are," Elum says.

"But they want out."

"They told you that?" he asks.

"Well . . ." I change my tack. "They deserve to be out. We need them out so they can add to our numbers. We need believing bodies out *here*."

"Believing, active bodies," Oria says.

Exactly. My frustration demands release. "We've been here a week, but what have we accomplished? We've shared a few Relics, and we're on a quest to find out about the Judge. But we need to do more."

"I don't know about that, Nana," Helsa says. "We're doing what we can."

"Are we?"

Devin spreads his hands flat on the table. "We can't be too bold or we'll get arrested too. What do you suggest?"

Confronted with the question, I feel panic. "I don't know exactly."

"That's helpful," Helsa says.

I point at myself. "I am not a leader. Oria is. Devin is." Or he was. "All my life I've worked in a factory and let others tell me what to do."

"But you're strong, Solana," Oria says. "You ran into the desert after me. That's not the action of a follower, but of a leader."

In that one moment, I was strong — or foolhardy.

"Think of one specific thing you'd like us to do right now," Rand says.

Only one comes to mind. "I want us to free the Workers."

Elum shakes his head. "That's not possible. We talked about this. If news gets out then everything gets off-kilter." He looks at the others.

"If the Masses find out that the Notables are keeping something good from them . . ."

"Like color?" Helsa says.

"Or beautiful clothes?" Oria says.

"Maybe throwing everything off-kilter isn't a bad thing," I say.

Elum keeps shaking his head no. "Leave it be, Solana. Please. I beg you."

His resistance doesn't make sense. He must know more than he's letting on.

"Fine," I say. "For the moment. But can we at least talk to them about the Keeper? Their faith is waning, if not gone. They were Devoted in Regalia, but their circumstances have made some of them doubt. Maybe we can change that."

"Bring them Relics," Rand says.

"We have seven of them now," Oria says.

"And I have two more," Berit says.

Rand rubs his crippled leg as if it's aching. "There will be more."

"When?" Lieb asks.

"I don't know exactly," Rand says. "But we should all be on the lookout." He smiles at me. "Is that a start, Solana?"

I feel only the slightest bit appeased, and even less encouraged.

Chapter Sixteen

Oria

Once again we're walking toward the Sanctuary on Sanctuary Day. It's hard to believe we've been here over a week. In some respects it seems like a flash, and in others, a lifetime. Either way, my life in Regalia seems eons away.

I wonder about my friends left behind. Marli and Dom. Pinno and Ladi. Even my mother and brother. Have they missed me even a smidgen?

Have I missed them?

And then there's Xian . . . I don't let myself think of him often because I miss him a lot. Although we didn't know each other long, I know the Keeper brought us together. It was not a coincidence that Xian walked into my waiting room at my trial. Or that we bonded in mere minutes. He was my rock, my comfort, and my wisdom. When I was with him I felt *more*. How I wish he had run through the parting sands with me.

I don't have to wonder if he misses me. I know in my heart he does. Maybe someday he'll get himself exiled and come find me. Yet it's a long shot, for I can't imagine the Council exiling one of their own Enforcers.

What's going on back home? Are the Devoted able to express their faith? I don't want my exile to be for nothing. Have more Relics been found and shared?

Berit walks with us to the Sanctuary. She and I have grown close, though I have the feeling she gains the affection of everyone who spends more than two moments with her. She has a sweet sensibility of spirit that I've never seen in anyone else. Again, I know the Keeper brought us together, and honestly, I'd rather room with her than with Solana and her family. Although I love Solana and Lieb, Helsa dislikes me so there's always tension between us. Legalis makes me tense enough. I don't need to add more during my few off hours.

As with the last Sanctuary Day, the mood going into the building is subdued. Also like last time, we make our way toward the front so Solana can see.

I look up to the loft where the Judge appeared. Will it come again today and loom over the crowd?

I glance at Berit. She seems nervous. Understandably so. Will her father's fate be announced today? *Her* fate?

The two men in black walk to the front and the people repeat, "Duty, Deference, Dedication, Dependability. All hail, Legalis!"

There's the recitation of the Directives, and once again, Devin, Elum, and Rand repeat them. Berit does not—though she moves her lips.

It bothers me that Devin seems to waffle about Legalis. I know just because you repeat some words doesn't mean you agree with them, but being fairly new and a Regalian . . . shouldn't he hold back a little? Stay strong against this insanity?

Hooded Fault Finders walk up and down the outer edge of the crowd. They pause at our row, so like Berit, I move my lips as if listing the Directives. There *I* am, giving in.

Suddenly, the masked men stop at the end of our row. Then they stride toward us, and grab Berit by the arm, pulling her up front.

"What are you doing?" I call out.

Everyone looks at me.

"Shh," Devin says. "Don't get involved."

Don't get involved? She's my roommate.

Yet with the murmur of voices quieting amid the commotion caused by the Fault Finders, my moment to act slips away.

Berit is brought to a place near the leaders up front, and forced to face the Masses. I expect her to look petrified.

But she doesn't. She appears calm with her hands clasped in front of her in the same casual manner as if she was standing with a friend, listening to a conversation. Yet I sense some nerves as her jaw tightens and loosens.

All at once, I hear a communal gasp. Everyone looks toward the loft.

And there it is. The Judge, in all its horrifying power. Its mirrored eyes reflect off the sunlight pouring in through the roof opening. It points down at Berit, its long, sharp nail a warning in itself.

Everyone kneels in fear.

The Notable unfolds a scroll and reads. "As of this day, Criminal Yair has been sentenced for his crimes against Legalis. The Judge hereby proclaims that his daughter, Berit, will be punished in the Cudgeling Circle on Judging Day, this Wednesday at noon. So sayeth the Judge."

Berit does not react except to swallow slowly.

But more surprising than her calm is the silence of the crowd. The initial murmurs that occurred when she was plucked away were driven by surprise. Now fear has silenced everyone. Me included.

The Judge spreads its arms wide as if showcasing the breadth of its power over us. I shudder.

I hate that the sight of such a being elicits such a visceral reaction in me. I should be stronger. Act stronger. I glance away, but when I look back at the loft it is gone. How did it do that?

Surprisingly, Berit is led back to us. Once again she stands beside me. If only I could hug her and offer comfort. She offers me a wry smile.

I mouth, *I'm so sorry.*

She nods once.

The service moves on to the part when the Head Fault Finder lists the number and detail of Faults that occurred during the past week.

I'd like to give them a Fault to list. I'd like to call out, "This is wrong! Berit is an innocent! Stop this madness!"

But I don't.

My cowardice shames me.

That is a Fault.

**

On the way home from the Sanctuary, we gather Rand and as many of the Exiled as we can and invite them to Devin's. A few beg off, but three come home with us.

Once inside, Berit accepts their condolences graciously. Humbly.

I want her to cry, to shout, to resist. I want somebody — anybody — to cry, shout, or resist.

Eventually I can't take their compliance any longer. I get up from the table. "What's wrong with all of you? With us?" I say. "Most of the laws of Legalis are annoying or idiotic, but this Circle? This is barbaric. Are we going to let an innocent woman die without a fight?"

"How can we fight?" Rand says. "There's nothing we can do. It's the way it's always been."

"The duration of its absurdity does not make it right."

One of the Exiled says, "But we're visitors here. We have no power."

Another says, "Visitors who can't go anywhere else, meaning we're part of the Masses — like it or not."

Their faces show a communal absence of outrage "We have no power because we *take* no power!" I say.

Devin presses his hands down, trying to calm me. "Shush, Oria. There may be no Counts on Sanctuary Day, but the Fault Finders still roam about."

"I don't want anyone to get arrested on my account," Berit says.

"But your punishment isn't fair," I say.

She smiles at me. "Fair or not, it's the law."

"But how can you—?"

She lifts her hand to stop my tirade. "I am at peace with my fate."

"How *can* you be?" Solana asks.

"Because I won't fully die. I will have everlasting life."

It takes me a second to let the words sink in. "The Keeper mentioned those same words to me."

"He what?" one of the Exiled asks.

I've never told them the story of his personal visits. I'm not sure I should now. Today is about Berit.

But Solana's eyes are full of encouragement. "Tell them."

I look at Helsa, but she doesn't give me any support. But Lieb nods enthusiastically. "You're going to love this story."

It is what it is.

"As you know, I was a Patron in Regalia. I had a big house with a beautiful garden."

"It was stunning," Solana says.

It was. "After witnessing an exile where the sands parted, I was in a state of awe and confusion. I went back to my garden to think about all I had seen, when suddenly *he* shows up."

"He?" a woman asks.

"The Keeper!" Lieb says. "She saw the Keeper, in her very own garden!"

"Twice," Solana says. "She saw him twice."

Devin puts a finger to his lips. "It's Oria's story. Let her tell it."

My mind quickly gleans through the experience, choosing the most important points. "He was as real as you are to me here," I say. "But more than how he looked, was how he made me feel." I take a deep breath and let it out slowly. "I felt fully at peace. Fully loved. Fully . . . known."

"Known?" Elum asks.

How to explain . . .? "He already knew me, knew the kind of person I was, my faults, my strengths. He knew who I *was* and more than that, he knew who I was supposed to be."

"Oria," Solana says. She looks at her son who gives her another warning with his eyes. "Sorry to interrupt."

He shrugs.

"He said my name would be Oria."

Solana interjects again. "Which means a person who is humble in spirit and manner."

"Nana," Helsa says.

"I had to tell you, because she won't. Because even though Oria *was* arrogant and prideful, she isn't anymore. He changed her."

I smile. "I don't like remembering my lesser qualities, but Solana is right. I even argued with the Keeper when he mentioned the new name. And the humble part, that's new, because as a Patron I was all about drawing attention to myself."

"What did he look like?" Rand asks.

"He was handsome, with long hair and a beard. The kindest face I've ever seen."

Rand bites the nail on his thumb. "What else did he say?"

"He told me to tell people about him. And to open my eyes to see and my ears to hear."

Rand suddenly stands, nearly falling over as his bad leg isn't in the right place to hold him. "That's what my man said!"

"What are you talking about?" Elum asks. "Your man?"

He puts a finger to his lips and hobbles away from the table, leaning on his crutch. "This is Oria's story. I shouldn't have interrupted."

I'm excited to hear about his experience. "Tell us. Did you see him too?"

His excitement overrides his hesitation. "I didn't know it was him, but now that I hear what he said to you . . ." His eyes are bright. "It *was* him!"

"Did he come to you in a garden?" a woman asks.

"Not at all. I was living outside the Sanctuary like I do now. I was trying to stand and bobbled myself. A man rushed forward and said, 'Let me help you, Rand.'"

"He knew you?" I say.

Rand nods. "He did, but *I* didn't know *him*." He runs his hand over the top of his crutch. "I knew we had never met, but I also knew that he *did* know me, and . . . I felt something stir deep inside. Now I know it was him. The Keeper." He nods at me. "The peace. That inner knowing . . . I felt the same thing as you did."

"Wow," Lieb says. "Both of you. That's amazing."

"I wish he'd come talk to me," a man says.

I feared telling my story might elicit envy. It's one reason I'd kept the story to myself.

Rand shakes his head. "I don't know why he decided to show himself to Oria and I, but the message he gave us applies to everyone."

The man scoffs. "I'd accept the message better if he showed himself to *me*."

"Doesn't it take more faith to believe without seeing?" I ask.

He considers this for a moment. "I suppose."

"You have an advantage over me," I say. "You've trusted in him longer than I have. Because I was on the wrong road I *had* to see him to believe."

"Me too," Rand says. "That you follow without seeing is to your credit."

The man seems to take the compliment to heart—and it's not an idle one. I do admire those who believe without concrete evidence. *That* is true faith.

"Your stories are good stories," Helsa says, "but I still don't know how we can reach people. We can share a few Relics like we did in Regalia, but what good does it really do?"

While her point is valid, and I don't want her tone to bring the others down, I have to admit, "I don't know the answer to that."

Berit raises her hand. "I do."

I'm ashamed that the discussion has moved on from her plight. "I'm so sorry. Today is about you. I shouldn't have—"

"You should have," she says. "You've both encouraged me with your testimony about visits from the Keeper. I too have one to share. Though my encounter is of a different sort."

Lieb claps his hands. "Oh good! Another story!"

I'm as excited as he is. "Tell us, Berit."

She looks around the room, and I expect her to be a bit timid around so many strangers.

But she's not.

"In the month that my Da has been in jail, through secret notes, he and I discussed what might happen. His punishment."

"Your punishment," I say.

"The threat of it became very real. I was just getting used to living without him, but to wrap my head around the Cudgeling Circle and its pain? The most certain death—all by myself?" She shudders. "I felt like curling up in a corner to wait for the end."

My heart hurts for her. "I'm so sorry. I can't imagine."

"Thank you." Then her expression changes. She actually smiles. "One day at work on the farm, I was weeding a field of beans, bent over, yanking weeds out and tossing them in a basket.

When the basket was full, I took it to the burn pile, where all the weeds are gathered. My basket was the first to be discarded there after a recent burn. And yet, there, in the middle of the blackened ground was a bright green weed, growing strong amid the ashes. That's when it hit me: death is not the end, but a new beginning. A new start. Life cannot be totally diminished." She sighs deeply and looks upward "That's when I knew my death would not be something final, but a new beginning. I would rise out of the ashes. From that point on, I felt at peace. Somehow I knew that everything would be all right."

"Even though it won't be," Helsa says. "Because you'll be . . . you know. Dead."

We all stare at Helsa, shocked by her brazenness.

Berit's forehead furrows. "I know it's hard to grasp, but I believe it *will* be all right."

"You have such a great faith," I say, trying to undo the harshness of Helsa's comment.

"I do now. And on a day soon after that, two new words came to me as I was weeding: everlasting life."

"The words he gave to me," I say.

She nods. "I wasn't sure what it meant so I wrote to Papa and he sent me a Relic he'd found in his cell."

"How'd it get there?" Elum asks. He looks at Devin. "Have you seen Relics in the jail?"

"I have not."

For a moment I feel bad for him. As a man of faith, working amongst the prisoners, shouldn't he have been involved?

Berit continues. "Papa didn't know where the Relic came from, but it helped both of us."

"What did it say?" I ask.

"It's quite simple really. 'If you follow the Keeper you will harvest everlasting life.'" Her smile is radiant. "Since I work on the farm, the word *harvest* spoke to me. I see new life blooming every day."

"That *is* simple," I say. "Faith in him . . ."

"Has the power to give us new life forever and ever."

Elum shakes his head. "That's far too easy. There have to be laws and rules and —"

"Hoops to jump through?" Solana asks.

"Order," he says.

"But faith can't be honed down to a to-do list," I say. "It can't be measured."

A woman holds up her hand. "How do we know if we have enough faith to get this everlasting life?"

When no one answers, Helsa crosses her arms. "She tripped you up on that one, didn't she, Oria?"

I've had enough of her. "Why do you always choose to be negative, Helsa? Why do you try to make people doubt? Where is *your* faith?"

Devin speaks up, his face serious, his voice gruff. "Watch your tone, Oria."

I regret my tone, but not my words. "I don't think it's right for any of us to question anyone else's experiences regarding the Keeper and their faith."

Helsa grins wickedly. "So if I said the Keeper told me to run through Legalis naked, you'd believe me?"

"Helsa!" Nana says. "Respect your elders."

Helsa scoffs. "She's my *elder* by three years."

Her father points at her. "I don't care what age anyone is. In this unit we will treat each other with respect."

Helsa sighs dramatically and nods.

Once again, we've gotten off track. I smile at Berit. "Thank you for explaining more about everlasting life. And I'm very glad he's given you such comfort. In turn, you've given comfort to us."

Helsa takes a breath to say something, but catches her father's look, and falls silent.

All and all, I'm relieved.

Chapter Seventeen

Rand

The next day I enter the Sanctuary in the early morning, before Legalis begins to stir.

I walk to the right, hugging the wall. I stop in front of a specific place, then pause to look around. I *have* to be alone to do this.

I even hold my breath to listen. There's a bird fluttering in the high rafters, but other than that, the vast room is silent.

I take a small knife from my pocket and carefully pull up one particular stone from the floor. There are two folded pieces of paper inside. I'm thrilled. Sometimes the space is empty. Other times there is a single paper. But to get two?

I take them out and return the stone to its place, brushing sand over its joints. I open them, absorb their wisdom, then slip them into my pocket.

These are good ones. These should help.

**

I hurry to Solana's unit, needing to get there before the three of them leave for work. I pause outside the door and put a note beneath an apple I place there. Then I rush to the place where she and Elum store their ladder and put another under one of its feet.

I return to my spot outside the Sanctuary and sit on the ground waiting for Legalis to awaken around me.

Chapter Eighteen

Solana

It's time for work. Another day in an endless stream of days.

As I open the door, I see an apple sitting on the ground.

That's odd. Food is scarce, so to have such a perfect apple sitting outside is unusual.

As I pick it up, I see a piece of paper beneath it.

"What's that?" Lieb asks.

I unfold it. My heart leaps. "It's another Relic!"

Helsa is the last one out the door. "What's going on?"

"A Relic," I say before reading it aloud. "'If you don't speak up now, then when? Perhaps you were made for such a time as this.'" I press the page to my chest. "Oh my. This is huge."

Lieb leans toward me, speaking low. "We're supposed to speak up about him?"

"Yes," I say. "And the time is now."

Helsa slings a bag of paint brushes over her shoulder. "I don't like feeling pressured like this. I'm doing the best I can."

"I know you are." I don't want her to be discouraged. What I take as a call to action, she takes as pressure. And the pressure *is* real. Yet it excites me. It's an affirmation that the stirring in my gut to do something has merit and comes from him.

Speaking of time, the clocks won't wind themselves. I fold the Relic and put it in my pocket. "Have a good day at work. I'll see you this evening."

**

I'm excited to show Elum the new Relic, but as we walk together to pick up the ladder, I sense now is not the time. We usually talk easily, but today there is a silent barrier between us. Things *have* been chaotic lately. From me lying to him about being sick and discovering the Workers, to my recent outburst in front of everyone when I scolded them for not doing enough. I've definitely added to the chaos instead of making things calmer.

The silence on a normal day wouldn't bother me, but today I wonder if I've lost him.

I don't want to lose him.

Finally, I can't take it anymore and stop walking. Thankfully, he stops too.

"Why did you stop?" he asks.

"Are you angry with me?" I blurt out.

I expect him to ask, 'What for?' but he doesn't. Instead he says "A little." He looks away.

I usually appreciate the truth, but this time it hurts. "I didn't mean to upset you with the lie about being sick or finding the Workers. Or being so blunt about doing more."

"I know you didn't." He scratches an eyebrow. "I guess I'm concerned."

"About . . .?"

"About you, all of you. All of *it*. None of you have blended in like they told you to do. You've inserted yourself into the workings of Legalis in a way that's . . . intrusive."

The term surprises me.

His expression shows genuine concern. He lowers his voice. "What would you think if I arrived in Regalia and suddenly wanted to change the justice system and unmask the leaders like Oria is trying to do; or upend the system like you're wanting to do with the Workers; or infiltrate the inner workings of the upper class to use it for your own purposes — as Helsa is doing?"

"Wow," I say. "We're doing all that?"

"Aren't you?"

Maybe we're doing more than I thought we were. "We're trying to help. We're trying to give the people of Legalis some indication that there's a better future, and —"

"According to you."

The words are a slap. "Yes, according to me. And Oria. And Helsa and Lieb. And Devin. You've known Devin a long time. You share a unit with him. Do you feel the same animosity about him as you feel about the rest of us?"

"No."

"Why not?"

"Because he knows his place. He's not trying to upend our society."

I'm shocked we're so far apart on this. I thought Elum was as passionate about his faith as we are. "You prefer the status quo."

"I prefer order, and don't — won't — condone anarchy."

I'm taken aback by the word. "Isn't that a little harsh?"

A man walks by and gets Elum's attention. Elum heads over to him, waving me off. "Go on ahead. I'll catch up."

I walk to the ladder, feeling the weight of his opinion pressing down on me. I don't like conflict. I don't like when people are mad at me. It makes me feel tight inside, and more than a little panicked.

Have we gone too far? Are we too pushy? Does Elum have a right to be upset?

I reach the ladder and bow my head. *Keeper, help us do the right thing. Give us courage.*

When I open my eyes I see a scrap of paper beneath one of the legs of the ladder. I slip it out. It's folded the same as the other Relic.

I'm just about to read it when I see Elum walking toward me.

I slip it into my pocket, my desire to share any Relic with Elum completely gone.

**

The morning has been grueling. Not the work of winding clocks, but the tension between Elum and me lies heavy in the air.

He's never been a chatty man, but he's usually friendly. I don't want to lose our friendship. I need to find a way to open the lines of communication again.

Then there's the other problem: I want to bring the Workers more Relics. Before leaving this morning, I'd put one copied Relic in my pocket. And now, after finding the hidden ones, I have two more.

But how can I get them to the people who need them? Elum all but told me to leave it be — leave *them* be.

When we pass the door — their door — Elum stops walking.

"Don't do it," he says, looking defeated

I force my gaze away though I'm relieved he knows what I've been thinking. "What's the harm in sharing some Relics?"

Elum puts his hands on his hips. "Why do you feel the need to do this? I don't understand."

"Back home they were Devoted. I'm not corrupting them. I'm simply encouraging them."

"I suppose." He looks up and down the street, his face neutral and discreet. "When we're through for the day, you can go back. But don't let anyone see you."

I'm so happy I want to hug him.

If only I could.

**

The day crawls along. It's odd how time goes slowly when I have something to be excited about.

Finally, we wind the last clock. I hurry back to the door, taking Elum's advice to be discreet while sneaking inside. I walk down the spiral stairs, the long corridor, and peer in the door before I walk in.

"Solana!" Miri says upon seeing me. "You came back."

"I said I would."

The Workers stop their tasks and give me their attention. I pull out the Relics. "I've brought good news from the Keeper."

"We could use a little of that," says a girl.

I give her a Relic.

The girl reads it aloud. "'Ask for my help. I will answer and give you courage.'" She hands it back. "Courage for what?"

Miri scoffs. "It doesn't take a lot of courage to do as we're told."

"Then maybe we shouldn't do as we're told," Zir says. "Maybe it's time to—"

In an attempt to stop his words and keep my vow to Elum not to stir things up, I hand him another Relic. "Read this one."

He unfolds it. "'Fear not, for I am with you always.'" This is the one I'd brought from home. Again, the note is returned to me and Zir says, "If the Keeper's here, I sure wish he'd do something to help."

This is not going as I'd hoped. How can I convince them the Keeper loves them when they feel unloved, used—and used up?

I spot a young woman with long black hair coming into the workroom from the far end. She wears a caftan of golds and blue, reminding me of one I'd seen Oria wear when she was still Cashlin.

The woman looks at me and blinks. "Who are you?"

"Solana," I say simply.

"You don't belong here," she says.

Miri steps forward. "Solana and I used to work in the factory together, Mistress Nixi."

Nixi? Helsa mentioned a Nixi.

"How did you get down here?"

"I got lost and opened the wrong door."

She glances at the door I'd come through.

Zir comes to the rescue. "Out, woman! Like we told you! We don't want you down here." He bows to Nixi. "Sorry, Mistress. She appeared out of nowhere. She will never come again."

Nixi considers this a moment, then says "Make sure you don't. Now leave these people alone and from now on, stay where you belong or suffer the consequences."

"Yes, mistress," I say. I hurry out the way I'd come.

Maybe Elum was right. Maybe I need to leave the Workers alone.

Chapter Nineteen

Helsa

I stand back and look at the mural. It's coming along nicely, and I've perfected the art of painting leaves. I've even managed to add shadows. I had no idea I had any artistic talent.

"It's looking quite nice," Glynis says. She sits in a chair near her bed, reading some papers.

"Thank you, Head Notable," I say. I move to my stock of paint at the far end of the mural to get a different color of green. I squat down to stir it, and look up when the door opens.

"Glynis, my darling wife."

A stocky man with slicked back hair sweeps in and leans down to kiss her cheek.

She cringes slightly. "Hello, Varo. Long time no see."

He sits on the bed, then falls back upon it, spreading his arms wide. "Yeah. Well. I've been busy too, dearest."

"Doing what?" she asks.

He bolts upright. "Don't get high and mighty with me, wife," he says. "You may be Head Notable to everyone else, but never to me. *Never* to me," he repeats.

"I appreciate your support."

Awkwardness washes over me as I realize that Varo hasn't noticed me yet. I don't move, and look at the floor trying to be invisible. But then an extra brush topples off the top of a jar.

I'm found out.

He stands swiftly and comes closer. "Well look what we have here."

I notice he says *what* and not *who*.

I stand. "Hello. Sir."

His eyes sweep over me. "You're a pretty thing, aren't you now?"

"Leave her alone, Varo," his wife says.

He flips his hand at her. "Don't get your pride in a panic, darling. I'm just making an observation."

"I'd prefer you go observe something else. Somewhere else. We're busy here."

He sighs dramatically. "See how she treats me, girl? I come to see how she's feeling and get tossed out." He studies the last leaf I painted. "Needs more detail."

Then, with a sweep of negative energy, he leaves, letting the door slam behind him.

I have no idea what to say — or if I should say anything.

Glynis speaks first. "I apologize for the lack of manners and crass nature of my husband. I'd say he means no harm, but that would be a lie." Her eyes roam over the emerging garden, yet I'm not sure she's really seeing it. "Please watch yourself around him."

Great. Another Bru situation.

I must have made a face because Glynis says, "Perhaps you know another cretin like him?"

"I did, Head Notable. And yes, cretin is an apt word for such a man."

"I'm sorry you had to endure such a thing."

"I'm sorry *you* have to endure such a thing," I say. I realize how presumptuous my words are. "I spoke out of turn, mistress. I don't know what I'm saying. I've only met him this once."

She snickers. "Once is more than enough."

Nixi comes in, and assesses the tone of the room with a glance. "I saw Father come out. Did he upset you?"

"No more than usual," her mother says. "Though he did make a pest of himself to Helsa."

By her intake of breath I know his actions are not to be taken lightly.

"Do be wary of him, Helsa," Nixi tells me. "My father is not a man of honor. He leaves a wake of stolen virtue wherever he goes." She looks at her mother, then takes the papers from her lap. "Enough work. If you ever want to return to your full duties you must rest." Nixi helps Glynis to bed.

Glynis slips her feet under the covers. "Your father would love to see me fail, wouldn't he?"

"That, he would." She glances at me. "He's always been jealous of Mama's position. He thinks he would be better suited as Head Notable."

Glynis snuggles into the pillows. "As if he could do half of it."

"He could never. You deserve every ounce of your position." Nixi tucks her in, then comes to check my work. "Moving along well, I see."

"It's slow work."

"Take whatever time you need." She lowers her voice to a whisper. "My mother enjoys your company."

"I heard that," Glynis says.

"Well, you do."

"Hmm."

Nixi mouths the next words, just to me. "She does."

The truth is, I like her company too.

**

On my way home, I swing by the Sanctuary to pick up Lieb so we can walk together. But instead of finding him cleaning out brushes, I find him sitting on the ground next to Rand, sobbing.

I run to him. "What's wrong?"

He shakes his head, unable to speak.

Rand speaks for him. "He got a notice calling him to the Cudgeling Circle."

"To be beaten?"

"To beat."

I suck in a breath. It's almost worse. For Lieb it *is* worse, for there is no gentler soul.

I sink down beside him and put my arm around his shoulders — if I get a Fault for it, so be it.

"I'm so sorry Lieb." I squeeze his shoulders as he leans in. We've always protected each other.

Suddenly a Fault Finder walks by. He does a double take, then points at us. We separate immediately and he studies us a moment, before moving on.

I'm relieved, but nervous. I don't want him to change his mind.

"Let's get you home. Surely Papa or Nana will know what to do."

People look at us as we walk home. The sight of a young man crying with his head hung low seems to surprise the dour citizens of Legalis. If they feel compassion, I don't seen evidence of it.

Of course Nana rushes to Lieb's side as soon as he gets in the door. "What's wrong?"

"I have to beat Berit."

"What are you talking about?"

He starts to sob again, so I answer for him. "He was chosen to be part of the Cudgeling Circle."

"That's impossible," Papa says.

"It's not," Lieb says. "A man told me I'm a Beater." He shakes his head adamantly. "I can't hit anybody. I just can't."

"Is there someone we can talk to?" Oria asks, looking at Devin and Elum.

"Not that I know of," Devin says.

"No one," Elum says.

Lieb wraps his arms around himself. "I don't feel too good."

"Do you want to lie down?" Nana asks.

He nods. As I take him back to our unit, he's hunched over as if the assignment is beyond bearing. He falls on his cot and curls onto his side, facing the wall.

"Can I get you something to eat?" I ask.

"No. I just want to be alone. Okay, Sa-Sa?"

I don't know whether I should abide by his wishes or not. But I lean down, kiss the top of his head, and go back to Papa's.

**

There isn't much conversation at dinner. What can anyone say? The most innocent, pure person in all Legalis had been ordered to be a part of the most despicable, evil act in all Legalis.

I only have one idea—and it's a bad one. "Could Lieb hide somewhere until it's over?"

Elum shakes his head. "There's nowhere *to* hide, and when they found him he'd be punished severely."

"I'm afraid he has to do it," Devin says.

I've never felt so helpless.

After dinner no one sticks around long. Nana and I are eager to check on Lieb. As we open the door to our unit I put a finger to my lips to remind Nana that he might be sleeping.

But he isn't there.

Nana sees a note on the table and reads it out loud. "'I can't do this. They can't make me. I'm leaving. I love you both.'"

"Leaving?" I ask.

Nana presses a palm to her forehead. "Leaving where? Where can he go? As Elum said, there's nowhere in Legalis where someone wouldn't find him, or turn him in."

In Legalis. But what about—? "He wouldn't leave Legalis completely, would he?"

Nana's eyes grow large. "The desert? Surely not."

"We have to go after him."

We virtually run to Papa's unit and quickly share the dreadful news with him and Elum.

"I'm coming with you," Papa says. He puts food and a skin of water in the middle of a blanket and ties it up.

Supplies. I never even thought of that.

We hurry to the entrance where we'd first entered Legalis. Durth is in her office, cleaning her fingernails with a knife. She doesn't seem surprised to see us.

"If yer lookin' fer the boy, he left 'bout a half hour ago."

"Why did you let him leave?" I ask.

"It's not my job to keep 'im here."

We rush outside and thankfully spot footsteps in the sand, going off to the right. We hurry in that direction.

Nana's short legs make her lag behind Papa and me. "Go on, you two. Run ahead. I think I'll go home in case he comes back."

I hate leaving her behind, but it is the best choice.

Papa and I run up and down multiple hills. The sun is going down. The air is already cooler. It gets hard to see where we're going. More than once we narrowly avoid prickly plants and rocks.

"Lieb?" we call out. "Lieb, answer us!"

Our voices are absorbed into the never-ending sand, yet that doesn't stop us from calling out to him.

I trip on something and fall down. And stay down, totally out of breath. "Papa, what if we can't find him?"

He shifts the blanket bag to his other shoulder. "We *will* find him." He gazes upward, "Keeper, protect Lieb. Show us where he is. Let him be safe."

I suddenly hear, "Sa-Sa?" called from a distance.

"Lieb! I'm here." I look right and left but can't see him. "Call out again!"

He does and we hurry toward his voice. We find him sitting with his back against a rock, his head down.

"Thank you, Keeper!" Papa says.

I run to his side.

"You came after me," he says pitifully.

"Of course we did, son," Papa says. "Are you all right?"

His head shakes back and forth vigorously. "I'm really scared."

I kneel and pull him into a hug. "I'm scared too."

He looks up at me with eyes that beg me to do something to make it all go away. If only I could.

"Let's go back and be scared together, all right?" As soon as I say the words I realize they're not exactly encouraging.

"You can't stay out here, Lieb," Papa says.

"I know. I was just trying to get to the orange place but I think it might be too far."

"You and your oranges." I laugh softly and stand, pulling him to his feet. "Let's go home and I'll see if I can find you some oranges tomorrow."

He stands, but shakes his head. "Tomorrow I have to do that awful thing."

I still can't imagine it. Or him being part of it.

The three of us go home, the reality of that awful thing hovering around us like an oppressive shroud.

Chapter Twenty

Oria

On Judging Day, everyone gets the day off. A day off to rest? No. A day off so they can attend the public beating of an innocent.

That's beyond wrong. It's sickening. Barbaric.

Speaking of innocent . . . I sit at the table with Berit. I suggested we go to Devin and Elum's this morning so she'd have people around her, but she declined.

"Just you is enough."

I don't feel like enough. I have no experience comforting people who are facing death. I don't have much experience comforting people, period. For years, my life as a Patron was happily and obliviously detached from discomfort other than the stress of competition. Sometimes I long for that oblivion. But other times I realize it's good to fully *feel* like I do here. What an odd thought, to embrace pain.

Berit moves a piece of bread from one side of her bowl to another. Then back again.

"What can I do to help?" I ask.

Berit shakes her head and pushes her bowl away. For the first time I see her forehead crumple with emotion.

I touch her hand. I almost say *It will be all right* but stop the trite truism before it comes out. The fact is, it will *not* be all right, a fact which is the true source of our anguish. Soon Berit will be beaten by her fellow citizens. She will be forced to suffer excruciating pain. She might even die.

Her hands trace the rim of her bowl. "I'm trying to be strong, to remember the Keeper's promise of life everlasting. This is *not* the end." Her voice weakens as if she's trying to convince herself.

"Of course it isn't the end." I say, though I still don't fully understand what comes . . . next.

"I wish I understood what comes next."

It's comforting that our thoughts mirror each other. "It has to be better," I say. "He wouldn't promise something that was worse."

She nods once. "The Keeper doesn't lie. He'll take care of me."

"Exactly," I say. But my mind wonders as to what "care" might look like as she suffers physical pain.

My stomach jumps when there's a knock on the door. Berit's hands turn into fists.

Deliberately, she stands and opens the door. Two Fault Finders loom over her. I realize how advantageous and intimidating it is for them to have their faces covered. It's easier to do evil work anonymously.

But I see their eyes. I will remember their cruel eyes.

"Citizen Berit. Come with us."

She turns toward me, her face panicked. She pulls me into a full embrace. "Thank you for your friendship, Oria. The Keeper brought us together for a reason."

So I can witness her death?

She walks away with one Fault Finder on either side. At least they aren't touching her.

I hurry after them and am glad to see the rest of my friends already in the street. We walk together toward the Sanctuary.

Lieb isn't sobbing anymore, but he walks like a dead man. Him being chosen as one of the Beaters is as much a horrifying travesty as the beating itself.

We reach the public square outside the Sanctuary. People crowd in front of the buildings but leave a large area open in front of the Sanctuary steps. I'm appalled to see children in the crowd.

Berit is led into the center of that area. She is so jarringly alone. The white of her robe stands out against the dirty, sandy ground, reinforcing her innocence. She sees us and turns her gaze in our direction. I can see her struggle to stand tall. I would be cowering in a heap on the ground. *I* want to do that now so I don't have to see this ghastly thing that's about to happen. But if Berit can stand tall, I have to stand tall with her.

Her eyes lock with mine and I tap my chest. She taps hers. The family around us does the same. She is not alone.

The crowd settles as if a show is about to begin.

There is commotion as a man is led to stand on the edge of the clearing opposite the Sanctuary entrance, facing it. His hands are tied in front of him.

"Is that Yair?" I whisper to Devin.

"It is."

How cruel to have him here. Not only is he forced to have his daughter pay for his supposed crimes, but now he has to watch her death. He raises his bound hands to acknowledge Berit as she stands alone, not twenty feet in front of him. She presses her hand to her heart. He does the same. The love between them is palpable.

I want to run into the Circle and grab them both, pull them away. Save them. But I'm as helpless as everyone else. *Keeper? Where are you?*

I watch as Notables, all dressed in black, gather on the steps on both sides of the Sanctuary entrance, two undulating black swarms of complicit people, guilty of crimes far worse than Yair. I want to scream at them: *You did this! You are responsible!*

Then Ivar steps out of the Sanctuary. Without preamble he raises his arms. "Those who have been chosen for the Circle come forward."

Lieb hesitates, but takes one step forward, his rule-following nature leading him toward this horrible act. He looks as though he's collapsing in on himself.

Eleven other people step up with a disturbing certainty — almost a pride — in their chosen status. Ivar motions for the Fault Finders to hand out clubs, and the Beaters form a wide circle around Berit.

It's surreal. My body tenses and I want to do something, but I don't know —

Suddenly the Judge appears on the front balcony. As usual, the crowd startles at its ominous presence. It looms like a black omen against the whiteness of the building. Its mirrored eyes gleam like fire in the hot sun.

It points at the accused and then, the condemned. But it doesn't speak. The Head Notable speaks for it. "Yair and Berit, accept your punishment! Hail Legalis!"

Berit nervously looks around the circle. Left. Right. Behind.

Ivar points at a man, choosing who will be first. He steps toward Berit, his club raised. Berit raises her hands to defend herself. But there is no defense. His blow comes down on her right shoulder.

She falls to her knees just as the second Beater steps forward. This one is a woman, but her blow against the upper arm of the same side makes Berit scream in agony.

I see her father fall to his knees, his head to the ground, stricken. Broken in his own way. A Fault Finder yanks him to his feet, forcing him to watch.

A third blow. A fourth. Each meeting of wood to flesh and bone makes Berit's body fall further downward, pulling in on itself. I want to cover my ears against the horrific sound.

Our attention is drawn to Lieb. He is number six. He holds the club limply in his hand, his other hand at his mouth. His head shakes back and forth.

The fifth blow is taken, straight across Berit's back.

It's Lieb's turn.

He doesn't step forward. When a Fault Finder steps up behind him and yells, "Go!", Lieb takes one meek step.

Suddenly Helsa rushes toward him. "Leave him alone! I'll do it!" She pushes past the Fault Finder, grabs Lieb's club, and walks toward Berit. Berit looks up at her and their eyes meet.

"I'm sorry," Helsa says. Then she hits Berit hard, on her thigh. She returns to Lieb, takes his arm, and leads him toward our family.

She cries. Lieb cries. We're all crying at the inhumanity. People should not be forced to do this, to see this, to hear . . .

As the clubbing continues, I see others in the crowd crying. Maybe compassion does live somewhere in the hearts of the Masses.

But then I spot Trina. She's taking it all in, an avid witness.

I see her son, Pan, standing in front of a man with four studs on his shoulder. The boy keeps looking up at him, his eyes pleading as if needing comfort. Not being able to touch each other is crazy. That boy clearly needs a hug. And is this the evil husband? He doesn't look evil to me. His face is strained with emotion and disgust.

After the next blow, Trina smiles, as if Berit's pain brings her joy. Who is the monster here? It's not the husband. From now on I will not believe anything Trina says.

As the eleventh person clubs Berit, she goes motionless.

The twelfth blow elicits no reaction at all, the only sound being the thud of the club against muscle and bone.

Is she dead?

My friends and I look at each other, tears running freely.

But then Lieb gasps and points at Berit. "Look!"

Diaphanous streams of light rise from Berit's body, weaving their way skyward.

"Look at what the Keeper's doing!" Lieb says.

The bands of light dance higher and higher until they disappear into the wisps of clouds above us.

I look around the crowd. Others see it too. They're all pointing, their jaws slack, their eyes wide.

"Everyone sees it!" I say.

Even the Fault Finders are looking up. And Ivar.

And the Judge! It stares as the rest of us stare. It was clearly caught off guard. It's surprised. An all-powerful being shouldn't be surprised.

Which spurs me to action. I step out of the crowd and begin singing the song a Devoted woman taught me in jail. "'When through the shades of death I walk, your presence is my stay; one word of your supporting breath drives all my fears away.'"

Solana and Lieb step forward, singing with me. "'Your hand in sight of all my foes, does still my table spread; my cup with blessings overflows, your oil anoints my head.'"

No one speaks. Everyone stares at us. With utter certainty I know this moment is why the Keeper brought us to Legalis.

I raise my hands to include the crowd. "Listen to me! The Keeper lives as our protector and provider. Berit's body died in this miscarriage of supposed justice, but her spirit lives on with the Keeper in life everlasting. You saw her spirit rise above the pain that was so dishonorably inflicted. Stop believing in a system that brings you sorrow. Believe in the Keeper! He is yours as much as he is mine. Only he will bring you peace and freedom!"

I make eye contact with the Judge. I try not to look away from its evil eyes.

Shockingly, it looks away first and turns, retreating out of sight. The evidence of the Keeper is so blatant, this monster has no choice but to run.

We spooked it!

The crowd surrounds me. At first I'm afraid they'll hurt me, but their faces reveal another intention: excitement and hope.

"Tell me about the Keeper."

"I've heard of him."

"Can he help me?"

So many voices. So many questions.

I see Fault Finders barging through the crowd to get to me.

Elum appears at my side. "Come with me! We need to get you out of here."

With him on one side and Devin on the other, all of us run back to their unit. Once inside, Elum guards the door.

"You did it!" Solana says jubilantly. "You spoke about him to everyone!"

"Was that really Berit's spirit?" Lieb says. "Cuz I saw it!"

"Everyone saw it," Devin says.

Helsa sits at the table. "You are in so much trouble."

"I don't care," I say. "It was worth it." I press my hand against my innards which are trembling as much as my hands are. "This is what the Keeper wanted me to do. I know it."

Elum peeks out the window. "Not only did you speak out, you sang." He swallows hard. "Music is not allowed."

"Of course it's not allowed," Solana says. "Because it's joyful."

Elum shakes his head. "You put us all in danger, Oria."

I understand Helsa's pessimism, but not Elum's. "Isn't this what we've been wanting?" I ask. "I didn't plan it, but when I saw that everyone could see the white tendrils . . ."

Solana sits beside me. "Unlike the parting sands back in Regalia, which only the Devoted could see, everyone saw this miracle. I wonder why?"

Reality starts to sink in. "Am I really going to be arrested?"

"They arrested Coli for causing a scene on Sanctuary Day," Elum says. "You did more than that. You stirred up the crowd. Directive

Three: 'Never speak against Legalis or the Judge.'"

I try to rationalize it. "Everyone saw the miracle. I simply addressed it. Did you see how hopeful they all looked? The Keeper just created a crowd of believers in one fell swoop." Excitement overrides the fear. "This is just the beginning."

"The beginning of the end," Elum says.

I turn on him. "Stop it! Something good happened out there. Something miraculous. The Keeper didn't do it as a side show, he did it to attract hearts and minds. He did it to get their attention."

Helsa scoffs. "He certainly did that."

"I say again, stop it!" I stand and separate myself from them. I can't believe their cynicism. "This is why we were brought to Legalis. This is our purpose."

I hear the shouts of a crowd outside. "That doesn't sound good," Elum says.

"It's fantastic," I say. "I need to go out and talk to them."

Devin shakes his head. "I'm not so sure—"

Suddenly, we hear the clocks chime. "I thought there weren't any Counts today," I say.

"There weren't supposed to be," Elum says. "I bet they want to clear the streets."

People knock on the door wanting in.

"Then clear the streets. Let the people in," I say.

Both Devin and Elum look at each other.

"Let them in so I can talk to them."

They look out the window, then exchange a glance. "There are too many," Devin says.

"It's not safe," Elum says. "If you let the crowd in, there's no stopping them. The commotion will draw attention, the Fault Finders will come, and then . . ."

I get the picture. "Then I'm a goner."

"All of us are," he says.

The sounds outside grow silent. Elum peeks out, sets out the correct number of pebbles, and closes the door.

"All of you are staying here until further notice," Devin says.

Solana motions for me to sit beside her. She links her arm through mine. "It will be all right."

As fear takes root I'm not so sure.

"You really rattled them, Oria," Devin says.

"That wasn't my intent."

"Wasn't it?" Helsa asks as she takes up playing cards to shuffle.

As usual, Solana comes to my defense. "Stop being so confrontational, child. Oria did a good thing."

Helsa starts dealing the cards to herself and Lieb. "She stirred things up just like she did in Regalia."

She's right of course. "I'm just doing what he asked me to do."

Helsa doesn't look convinced.

Solana snatches the cards out of Helsa's hands. "Moving on from Oria's brave act . . ." She touches Helsa's shoulder. "Helsa, my dear girl. You taking over for Lieb was a very courageous, magnanimous act."

Lieb reaches across the table and takes her hand. "I *really* thank you for that."

"I'm proud of you, daughter," Devin says.

Helsa pushes some of the cards away and shudders. "I still had to hit her. I wish I hadn't had to hit her."

"You did more than anyone else by stepping in for Lieb," I say.

"Maybe I should've refused to hit her," she says. "What happens if people refuse?" she asks Elum.

Elum stands. "I don't even want to think about that."

I want to focus on the good in it. "Your sacrifice was a beautiful thing, Helsa. Berit's death was evil, yet the Keeper turned it into something awe-inspiring by letting us see her spirit rise from her broken body."

"Where did it go?" Lieb asks. "Where did *she* go?"

It's a good question.

Solana answers. "To life everlasting. With him."

"He lives in the sky?" Lieb asks.

I chuckle. "You ask good questions, Lieb. I don't know exactly where the Keeper lives. But I've always felt like he's everywhere, and the biggest everywhere there is, is the sky."

Lieb nods once. "Berit's spirit went up to the sky, so she's with him."

"Very aptly said," Devin says.

When the all-clear chime rings Elum says, "I'm going out to see what's going on. I'll be back as soon as I can."

"I appreciate that." I stand. "I want to go home."

"Do you want company?" Solana says.

"No, thank you. I need time alone."

Elum and I leave together but he goes one way and I go another. I'm relieved there's no crowd outside our door, but I'm wary as I walk back to the unit I shared with Berit. Passersby *do* look at me as if they recognize me, and a few even nod. And more than a few look at me then look away as if they're scared.

Truth is, I'm scared too.

Once inside my unit, the silence flows around me like water engulfing a pebble thrown into a pond. I look at the table where Berit and I sat a few hours ago. I see her bowl of uneaten bread, pushed to the center. I think of her last words to me: "The Keeper doesn't lie. He'll take care of me."

Did he take care of her? For as miraculous as today was, the pain had been major. He didn't save her from that. She felt every blow.

But then it was over. Only it wasn't over. The Keeper drew her spirit upward in a tantalizing exhibit of redemption and peace.

I draw in a cleansing breath, feeling scraped out inside, as if every emotion and every thought has been exposed.

I need to rest. I go to my cot and lay on my side. But as I slip one hand under my pillow I feel a piece of paper. I pull it out. It's a note from Berit: *To my new friend, Oria. I feel the Keeper at work in me. He has a message for you: Fear not, he is with you always, as he will be with me. Be strong and do the work — no matter what.*

I take a deep breath of renewal. I know the Keeper was with Berit in her time of need and I know he is with me now as I march forward to my destiny.

I don't need to see him again like I did in my garden.

I see him in my mind.

I see him in my heart.

And I see him in my soul.

Chapter Twenty-One

Rand

After the events in Sanctuary square, I didn't follow my new friends home— I couldn't keep up with their running even if I'd wanted to. Plus, I was too caught up in the wonder of it all. Despite the Fault Finders making their presence known, people lingered, unwilling to leave the place where the spectacle happened.

But now, as the clocks chime for an unexpected Count, I take refuge in the Sanctuary with many others. Everyone talks excitedly about the vapor, the smoke, the fog—and a dozen other terms—that arose from Berit's body. The general consensus is everyone wants to know what "that" was.

I want to share, even though I'm not sure they'll listen to me as a Marked Man. "I think it was Berit's spirit rising up to join the Keeper. For life everlasting."

Their curiosity overcomes their disgust at my presence. "The lady with the red hair said that. Who's the Keeper?"

I draw in a breath hoping a clear answer comes to me. "The Keeper is . . . God." I can't be much clearer than that.

"He can't be god," a man says. "The Judge is god."

"No!" I say strongly. "It is not. God helps people. The Keeper loves us, protects and provides for us. He does not oppress us. Name one thing the Judge does to help Legalis."

When the silence settles, I continue. "The Keeper offers peace, reconciliation, strength, courage—"

"Why did that girl take the place of the young man in the Circle?" someone asks.

"Because that man is a tender soul who wouldn't hurt a fly. She knew violence was against who he is, so she stepped in so he wouldn't have to beat Berit. She did it because she loves him. It was a very self-sacrificing thing to do."

"I didn't know we had a choice when we're called," a man says. "I had to be a Beater once. It was horrible. I hated it."

"I'm glad you hated it," Rand says. "You should have hated it. Killing another person is wrong."

"I knew Berit," a woman says. "She was the nicest, sweet-tempered woman. She didn't deserve to die like that."

"No one deserves to die like that."

"But her father was guilty."

I see a few nods around the crowd. "Was he?" I ask. "I question the severity of his crimes, as I question the severity of the punishment. Guilty or not, the punishment is unnecessarily cruel. And shouldn't *he* be the one to be punished rather than his innocent daughter?"

A man cocks his head, staring at me. "You're a Marked Man. You were guilty of something."

"I was." I need them to move beyond that. "The point is, things need to change. Do any of you want to witness another Circle?"

Everyone shakes their head.

"How can I learn more about the Keeper?" a woman asks.

At that moment I see the acting Head Notable come out of a room at the front of the Sanctuary—a room that I've peeked in before. It's a very small storeroom with a few pieces of furniture inside. What an odd place for the Head Notable to be.

He makes a beeline toward us. He does not look happy.

I take a Relic from my pocket and hand it to the woman. "Copy this and pass it on. These are the words of the Keeper. Be on the lookout for more of them. Learn and share." I nod toward the Head Notable who's closing in fast.

He arrives just as the all-clear chime begins. He sweeps the crowd outside. "Out with you! Move along!"

In the commotion of their leaving, I begin to leave with them, but at the last moment I feel the need to stay inside. I slip behind a column. Ivar closes the door with an echoing thud.

I hear a voice coming from the storeroom. "Come back in here," a man says. Demands.

Ivar returns to the storeroom and shuts the door. As quickly as I can, I hobble toward it and stand outside. I need to hear what they have to say.

"Who was that despicable woman who spoke?" asks a voice I don't recognize.

Oria?

"I heard murmurings she's a newcomer. From Regalia."

Oria.

"She's one of the Exiled?"

"It seems so," the Head Notable says.

"I thought they were under control."

"The most vocal are where we put them, working underground. There are a handful of others, but they're relatively passive. We assumed Berit's death would quash what little influence they had."

"She was one of them. As was her father," the man says.

"Very true. But now he'll be released as a Marked Man. The Masses will be forced to shun him."

"Or admire him. Turn to him."

"That's never happened before," Ivar says. "Marked Men are ostracized. They have no power."

"Neither does a random woman in the crowd, until they do. No one has ever spoken out like she did. And singing? There can be no more of that."

"Agreed. Should we have her arrested?" Ivar asks.

There is a pause. "I don't think so. We might risk stirring up the Masses even more. But we do need to know more about her. We need a name."

"I'll see what I can find out."

"Actually, I have someone who can help us . . ."

"Excellent."

When there is silence, I hurry away from the door.

But no one comes out.

Where did they go?

I want to find out, but it could be dangerous.

I argue with myself as to whether I should pursue it, or leave well enough alone. I'm a cripple. I'm not brave like Helsa or Oria.

And yet . . . I've just been given information no one else knows. If it can help the group and help the Keeper I have to be brave.

But I wait longer than necessary to ensure the two men are gone.

After putting my ear against the door and hearing nothing, I carefully enter the small storeroom. The walls are made of stone, and there's nothing in it but a few chairs. I'd discovered the room previously when I'd had the whole Sanctuary to myself. I know there is absolutely no other way out.

So where did they go?

I look upward. The small room is lit by a tall, inaccessible window. But then . . . . I notice sunlight streaming across the floor and see a disturbance in the dust, like people have walked from the door toward the back wall.

I give the wall my full attention, touching it, studying it. The grout looks solid. But then, on a whim, I push on it.

It swings inward! It's a door!

My heart pounds. The mystery is solved. But do I dare go through it?

Do I dare not?

I push the stone-faced door wider and find myself on a large landing. There is a lit sconce on the wall, and stone stairs spiraling downward to the right — and others stairs winding upward to the left. I can't see where either lead. I pause and listen. If there are voices . . .

When I don't hear anyone I head down the stairs. I hold my crutch as a cane to steady myself and slide my hand down the curved wall for support. I move slowly and try to calm my breathing so no one hears me. I stop when I hear a woman's voice. I realize there's no place to hide. If someone wants to come up the stairs I will be seen.

And then what?

Luckily, the voice trails off. Do I go farther?

I have no clue how far down these stairs will go, but I have to see more.

The landing at the bottom leads to a corridor, with light beyond. I hug the wall and step toward the light.

I'm stunned when the corridor opens up to an enormous rock cavern with a cobblestone street and buildings on either side. There are tables and chairs outside one building, and a group of four people are eating a meal there. Another building has a window that showcases brightly colored shoes and dresses. A woman comes out of the shop, carrying a purchase. All of them wear lovely clothes. Urns of flowers spot the street, and holes in the ceiling let in sunlight. The ceiling is painted with blue sky and clouds. I remember Helsa's description of the Notable area, and Nixi telling her that tunnels connect their underground world.

But why would the Notables have a back way into the Sanctuary through a storeroom? They are free to come and go as they please. Why use dark stairs and a hidden door?

A man comes out of the nearest building. I retreat, climbing up the stairs as quickly as I can.

But when I reach the landing, the steps leading further upward entice me. Would they lead me to the loft? Is this the way the Judge gets up there?

I've come too far not to see.

With great effort and increasing pain in my leg, I climb the spiral stairs. There are far fewer than the ones going down. Light shines in from above. At the top, the area is brightly lit with the sunlight from the hole in the roof. . . I see the rafters of the Sanctuary. I must be in the loft!

I'm relieved no one's there, and I walk a few tentative steps toward the middle. But then I notice scuff marks where the Judge usually stands. Scuff marks. As in shoes. As in a person wearing shoes.

I'm excited to tell Lieb that the Judge does *not* fly. In fact, the Judge may not be an *it* at all.

I peek over the solid railing. The view is impressive. A person would feel powerful standing up here, looking down on the rest of Legalis.

Which is, of course, the point.

But since *I* am not powerful, I need to leave. I hurry down the stairs and through the hidden stone door to the storeroom. I crack open the door to the Sanctuary. No one is there, so I walk calmly outside, once again becoming invisible and insignificant.

But not insignificant. For I know a *lot* more than others do. Not just about the underground town and the loft, but about two Notables who are plotting to silence Oria.

Information she needs to know as soon as possible.

**

I head to the general location of Oria and Berit's unit. I'm not sure exactly which one it is, but I assume I'll find it one way or another. The Keeper will lead me there.

I consider stopping by Devin's. Oria might be there with the others. But I don't want to tell everyone my news yet. Just Oria. So I try to find her unit, and hope to find her there.

I knock on a door. A woman peers out, gives me a good once-over, and says, "What do you want, Marked Man?"

"Can you tell me which unit Oria lives in?"

"Who?"

"The woman who spoke out at the Circle?"

Her eyes widen. "That one? Never knew her name. She lives — lived — with Berit. Poor girl. Upstairs."

I start to leave, but she opens the door wider. "Is what she said, true?"

"Yes, it's true. All of it." I pull a Relic out of my pocket. "Read these words of the Keeper's. Copy it and pass it on. And if you want to learn more, talk to Oria or myself. My name is Rand and I'm usually around the Sanctuary."

She eyes my crutch and my slovenly appearance, and I know she's doubting I have anything worthwhile to share. But she palms the Relic as if we're passing secret notes.

"What's your name?" I ask.

"Frin."

"Nice to meet you, Frin." I nod and she closes the door.

I peer at the steps leading to Oria's unit. My day has been full of steps to climb. My leg throbs with pain. But I make it upstairs and knock.

No one answers. I'm sorely disappointed. The thought of walking all the way back to the Sanctuary or Devin's makes me cringe with anticipated pain. I simply can't do it right now.

Needing to rest, I knock again and quietly open the door. No one is there so I go inside. I know Oria won't mind. And Berit... It's hard to grasp that this morning she was alive and well in this very place.

I sit at the table and use my waiting time to send prayers to the Keeper. I imagine he's keeping Berit company right now.

**

"Rand?"

In a split second I realize I've dozed off in Oria's unit, leaning forward on the table. I sit upright. "Oria."

"What are you doing here?"

"I needed to rest, I'm sorry to have fallen asleep."

"You can stay here anytime, but what are you doing here?"

"I have important news for you."

She slumps into the chair across from me, but rubs her hands roughly over her face. "I've had a hard day, Rand. Can it wait?"

"It can't. It's related to your very hard day."

She sighs. "Then tell me."

Her exhaustion makes me get to the point faster than I'd planned. "Two things. First, I found a secret door in the Sanctuary that leads to stairs heading down to an underground passageway to the Notable area, and other stairs that lead *up* to the loft."

Her expression comes to life. "So that's how the Judge gets up there without being seen."

"Exactly. And I'm guessing there are other passageways leading who-knows-where."

"So as Helsa has said, the Masses live up-top where it's hot and dusty, and the Notables live down below where it's cool and clean."

"Pretty much."

She gets up and pours two cups of water, then returns to her chair. "That was the first news. What's the second?"

"I overheard the Head Notable and another man talking about you. They're worried about the impact your talk had on the Masses."

"Sounds like what happened in Regalia. That's one reason I was exiled."

"You're very brave," I say. "I can speak about the Keeper to a few, but I'd never be able to speak to so many like you did."

"I hope some of them listened."

"I know they did."

She sighs deeply. "I'm glad of that. But . . . am I going to be arrested?"

"They said no because it might stir up the Masses."

"That's a relief."

"They don't even know your name."

"Another relief."

I remember something else. "Actually, there was a third thing they talked about. They are aware of the Exiled and said they aren't a threat because they're passive."

"That's a horrible label to bear. Yet it fits with what I've seen. They are followers. I haven't met anyone who's a leader."

"Which is why *we* need to be leaders."

"Exactly." She stares at a bowl of uneaten bread. "Berit can't have died for nothing. Her faith was so unwavering, even in the face of—" She stops, then changes direction. "What happens to her father now?"

"He's released."

"It can't be that simple."

"It's not," I say. "He has to wear the Mark of the Guilty so everyone knows he caused his daughter's death."

"What's the Mark?"

"He has a G branded on his forehead."

"That's atrocious. What's the purpose of that?"

"So people shun him." It's time I let my new friends know of my shame. "As they've shunned me." I move my hair off my forehead.

She gasps. "You've been branded?"

"I am a Marked Man." I let my hair fall over the G, hiding it.

I watch her eyes put two and two together. "I heard a man call you that, but I didn't know what it meant. So you were like Yair? Arrested?"

"I was. And a family member died in my place."

"Oh my. Who?"

It still pains me to remember. "My mother."

Oria puts her hand on mine. Instinctively I pull my hand away. "I'm not used to being touched." But I return my hand where it was and she touches it again. It's a wonderful feeling to have skin touch skin.

Her eyebrows dip. "I'm so sorry, Rand."

"As am I." Fully and totally.

"Can we help Yair somehow?" she asks.

"Not really. He'll be joining me on the streets and people will shun him. He'll probably be sent to another area besides the Sanctuary to camp in."

"Maybe they won't shun him. Maybe they'll be kind."

I scoff. "They can't be kind. If they offer him aid, they'll get in trouble. He's an outcast. All of you are in danger of punishment for being kind to me." I feel ashamed. "I should've told you that the first time I joined you at Devin's. I'm sure he and Elum know of the risk, but to be with people again . . . it was selfish of me."

Oria pushes away from the table, stands, and tosses her hands in the air. "What is it with this sickening place? Condemnation, punishment, never-ending guilt . . . it's a horrendous way to live."

"It is," I say. "But that's why the Keeper sent you here. Legalis needs you."

She runs her hand over her copper hair. "I don't know if I'm up to causing another revolution. I was a Patron of fashion. This is far beyond my talents."

"It may be beyond your talents." I say. "But it is your calling."

She lets out a breath. "That's a heady word."

"It is. But the Keeper will never take away the gifts or the calling he's given you." He smiles. "You're stuck with them."

Oria presses her hands against her eyes. "It's a lot of responsibility."

"It is. But he and I know you're up to it."

She chuckles. "You two are definitely more sure than I am."

I don't want her to laugh it off. She needs to understand. "The Keeper wouldn't have sent you here if he didn't know you could do it. He doesn't give us more than we can handle. Look at me. When my mother was killed and I was marked, I thought my life was over. But the Keeper had other plans."

"Yes, he did," she says to me. "You're an amazing man, Rand."

This shouldn't be about me. "The point is, as the Keeper equipped me, he has equipped you." I sweep an arm in the direction of the Sanctuary. "You didn't have to say what you said after Berit's death, but you did—and very eloquently too. More words are inside you, just waiting to get out."

She holds a fist against her midsection. "Maybe that's what keeps my stomach churning all the time. Those dratted words."

"Fateful, important words that can change the whole of Legalis."

She scoffs. "Don't let the Judge hear you say that."

"He already knows. He was right there. He heard you."

"He? Not *it?*"

"I saw shoe scuff marks in the loft. He's a man."

"Wow. That's huge."

"*I* thought so."

She sits and leans forward, hiding her head in her arms. "I'm so tired. I have no idea what to do next."

I want to comfort her, and I even hold my hand near her hair. But I'm unfamiliar with the notion of comfort, having last experienced it when I was a child being comforted by my mother.

My mother, who died for me.

But I'm here now. And Oria needs me.

I force myself to touch her copper hair. Tentatively at first. But then I gently stroke stray pieces behind her ear. "It will be all right, Oria. I promise."

With *my* act of comfort, *I* am comforted.

Chapter Twenty-Two

Oria

My first thought when I awaken is crushing. *Berit is dead.*

It's hard to fathom that the Cudgeling Circle happened yesterday. It seems like a lifetime ago.

There are so many lifetimes ago . . . And now, here in this unit, I am alone. I vacillate between grief and anger. Yet saying a few words at the square yesterday stirred things up in a way that may have big consequences. Rand warned me of those consequences. The powers that be know me now, maybe not by name, but they're on the alert. And with my red hair I can hardly blend in.

I splash tepid water on my face. I run a damp cloth over my teeth. What I wouldn't give for a long, luxurious bath scented with lavender and rosemary. I've noticed a general aroma in public that indicates everyone could use a bath. I suppose I'll get used to the smell. Not exactly something to aspire to, but it is what it is.

I get dressed—which involves throwing a robe over my head and belting it. Gone are the days of perusing my filled-to-the-brim closet and discussing shoes and accessories with Marli. She'd fix my crowning mane of hair and help me apply just the right makeup to make me look like *the* Premier Patron of Regalia.

I peer in a small mirror on the wall—which has a diagonal crack running through it. I have no make-up here. Not even a hairbrush. Berit let me use her hair comb—I suppose it's mine now—but before then, my fingers were all I had to contain my unruly hair. Most days, I tie it back with a piece of string I found on the ground.

As for my skin, Berit showed me how to use candle tallow for some semblance of moisture, but I miss the creams and lotions from home. I lean forward and look into my eyes. I look older than my twenty-two years. I do *not* look like a Premier anything.

I used to walk down the street and people would notice me for my beauty and style, but now they notice me for being the crazy woman who disrupted Judging Day. It's hard not to wallow in the good old days.

I cut up an apple—which is a nice addition to the usual bread and cheese. I could eat with my friends, but I'm not up to it. And so I sit at the table meant for two and wonder if someone else will be assigned to live with me. I'm not sure how I feel about that. I'd like the company, yet the thought of meeting someone new and the chit chat it entails wears me out before I've even started.

I'm such a hypocrite. I'm lonely, yet I'm hesitant about a new roommate; I want change, but I'm close to giving in and accepting the way things are.

I find it impossible to name one good thing in Legalis. No one is happy. No one has dreams or aspirations. I see a few isolated smiles, but hear very little laughter. People seem stuck, with no way out.

Yet who am I to unstick them? It's a pretentious notion; arrogant, stupid, and risky.

I slice a piece of bread. I wish they had butter here.

"Enough, Oria. Stop it."

I stand and eat at the window — which I always keep open unless the wind makes the air too dusty. I especially like it open at night when the heat relaxes its stranglehold on the day.

My view is nonexistent. The stucco wall of another building is four feet away. If I weren't a story off the ground I'd ask Helsa to paint something pretty there.

Which is probably against the law. Beauty is against the law. It's absurd.

I peer down at a narrow alley that extends from the street to the shared privy. I'm as far from my lovely garden in Regalia as I can get.

And there's nothing I can do about it.

**

When I arrive at the food booth Trina is already there stocking the bins.

"I didn't expect to see you today," she says.

"I need to get my mind off things."

She scoffs. "That's not what I meant. Why haven't they arrested you already?"

A few snarky responses come to mind. And go. Then I decide to be bold. "I guess the Keeper has plans for me. He's protecting me."

"Whoooo, you think a lot of yerself, doncha?"

"I think a lot of *him*."

A bunch of carrots falls to the ground. She picks them up, swipes the sand off them with her sleeve, and puts them in a bin. "You sure added to the show yesterday. You and those friends of yours. That boy was a complete wimp letting a girl stand in for him. Being called to the Circle is an honor."

"You don't know him. He's the kindest, most loving —"

"Yeah, yeah. Kind and loving will get you nothing in Legalis. It's best to learn that up front."

"I think it was very honorable that Helsa stepped in so he didn't have to do something that was totally against his nature."

She cocks her head. "I suppose that *was* kinda interesting. Never seen that happen before."

"Maybe it should happen more often."

"You can be sure the Judge won't let *that* catch on."

"Have you ever been called to the Circle?"

"No, but I'd like to be."

"I'm not surprised. You seemed to enjoy it."

She does a double-take, as if checking to see if I mean the words for or against her. "I'm not the only one. In case you haven't noticed, life in Legalis is pretty boring. So what if we enjoy Judging Days?"

"So what if you enjoy killing innocent people?"

She shrugs.

She actually shrugs.

I feel the heat as blood rushes to my face. I'm so angry I want to upend all the bins and have a good scream at her. If she likes drama so much . . .

But I don't scream. I don't upend the bins. I have another idea.

"I saw your son and husband there."

"Of course."

"Pan was upset by everything that was happening. Your husband was very kind and sensitive toward him. Unlike you, he did *not* relish the violence. He tried to shield Pan from it."

She stares at me, her eyes cold. "My husband's as much of a wimp as that friend of yours. As for Pan, he'll get used to it. I'll make sure of that."

"May the Keeper protect them both from your influence."

Trina draws in a deep breath and lets out a bellow. "How dare you!"

Then she punches me in the face.

I fall to the ground, the pain exploding from my jaw toward my eye.

She sits on top of me and pummels me, screaming with each blow.

"Stop it! Stop it!" I yell. "Get off me!"

A crowd gathers but no one steps in to help.

Until . . .

"Enough!" a man pulls her off and shoves her back. He points at her. "Stop! Now."

"You shoulda heard what she said to me," Trina whines. "She's the woman who caused a scene yesterday. All that blather about the Keeper."

He ignores her and helps me to my feet. But my legs won't hold me. Blood pours out of my mouth and down my chin. I've never felt such pain.

"Get a towel for her," he tells someone, pointing at the food booth.

A towel appears, and I press it to my mouth. My entire face aches and throbs.

"I'll get you cleaned up," he says. "Let's get you home."

I'm glad for the help. "It's not far." I point ahead.

When we reach the steps going up to my unit, I say, "I can make it from here. Thank you for your help . . .?"

"Wyan."

The clocks begin to chime for the Count. Great timing.

He nods at my unit. "Since we need to get inside I might as well help you the rest of the way." He follows me into the unit, but doesn't bother with the pebbles.

"Two pebbles?" I say.

Wyan looks at the ledge where I'm pointing and sets out one black and one white. Then he pulls out a chair for me. He gets me a cup of water, and wets a clean cloth.

He pulls the other chair close. "Let's see what we have here."

I hand him the bloodied towel.

"Show me your teeth," he says.

It feels odd, but I bare my teeth, though it feels weird because my lip is swollen.

He makes a face as he studies them. "It doesn't look like any are broken, but you bit your lip."

"My jaw hurts bad."

"Trina whopped you good." He uses the damp cloth to clean off my bloodied face. He has a gentle touch.

"Do you know her?" I ask.

"Not really." He concentrates as he works.

He's got an interesting face. Not handsome, but pleasing. His dark eyes focus on what he's doing as if cleaning my face is the most important thing in the world.

I wish my face was bloodier.

In mere seconds, he's sitting back, looking at me. "There," he says. "Face cleaned. Are you hurt anywhere else?"

My entire torso hurts but I'll deal with that later. I shrug and say, "She sat on me."

He chuckles. "That was indeed a hefty punishment. Why was she so angry?"

"We had a difference of opinion."

"Obviously. About what?"

I'm not sure how much to say. Yet I feel he deserves my honesty for all his trouble. "The Cudgeling Circle. She relishes it while I think it's barbaric."

"It's supposed to be. To keep people in line."

I'm appalled by his rationale. "Berit was an innocent. And her father's crimes were insignificant."

"No crime against Legalis is insignificant."

I need room for my words, so I stand and step away. "Only because most of the laws are insignificant. Taking food from a rubbish heap to feed people in need? The law should submit itself to logic and compassion."

"Submit? The word 'submit' and 'laws' don't belong in the same sentence."

"There may be a few people like Trina who relish the pain of others, but I'm betting there are more who detest it as much as I do."

"You have a lot of opinions for a newcomer."

He says it like it's a bad thing. "How do you know I'm a newcomer?"

He points to my shoulders. "You have no Faults."

I see he has two. But I scoff at him. "I have many faults, but they're not visible for the whole world to see. Which is another thing I'd like to ask the authorities. Why do they think shaming people is the way to create a satisfied public?"

"Maybe they don't want them satisfied."

I'm taken aback. "Why wouldn't they? When people are miserable they look for ways out. I'm sure the Notables don't want a rebellion on their hands."

When he doesn't respond, I realize I've said far too much. "Forgive me. I'm still upset about yesterday, and Trina's attitude, and . . ."

"Tell me about the Keeper."

I'm taken aback. "You recognized me?"

He gestures toward my red hair. "You're hard to miss. So tell me about this Keeper who prompted you to make a scene. In public."

Oh my.

He points at the chair. "Sit and tell me. I truly want to know."

Although part of me wants him to leave, I know I can't throw away this opportunity. I pray for the right words.

"The Keeper is . . ." I'm at a loss.

"Yes . . . ? Finish the sentence."

I don't trust this man. What if he takes what I say and turns me in?

"You can't tell me?" he asks. He has a challenging smile on his face. As if daring me.

And then I know what to say. "It's simple. The Keeper is love."

Wyan makes a face. "That's it?"

His sarcasm annoys me. "That's the core of him. The Keeper offers peace, courage, trust, joy, and never-ending hope." I add something else. "And freedom. From ridiculous laws."

"He has no laws of his own?"

I'm not sure how to answer. "I'm new in my faith, but the laws I imagine coming from the Keeper involve being against anything that detracts from all the qualities I just listed. If we all work with him toward those innate, deepest desire goals, then there is no need for laws that suppress and oppress."

He claps his hands. "Bravo! You are quite the orator, Oria."

I blink. I don't remember giving him my name. Yet I'm sure word has gotten around.

"I'm no orator. I speak from the heart."

"Isn't that dangerous? Without logic and critical reasoning, the power of emotions and the insipid sincerity of the heart is limited."

I gawk at him. "Insipid sincerity?"

He lifts his hand to stop my objection. "I admit that's harsh. But I'm a man of facts. Laws appeal to me, emotional sentiments do not."

"Then I think we're done here." I push my chair back. "Thank you for your assistance, Wyan, but I—"

His eyebrows rise. "I've insulted you," he says.

"Greatly."

"I didn't mean to do that."

"I'm not sure I believe you."

He stands. "You're a very intriguing woman, Oria. I'd like to hear more of your views. Perhaps at another time? Would that be possible?"

The thought of arguing with him again appealed to me as much as seeing Trina again.

And yet . . .

"I would be open to that. But I'm afraid I need to be fully rested. Talking with you takes a lot of energy."

He laughs. "Perhaps tomorrow at noon, meet at the Sanctuary?"

I nod and see him out.

I go to the window of the bedroom and look down at the street to watch him go.

He stops and looks up at me. And waves.

What have I gotten myself into?

Chapter Twenty-Three

Solana

It's odd—and almost disconcerting—to go to work the day after Berit's death, the day after seeing her spirit rise, and hearing Oria's bold words. *I am changed.* As for everyone else?

I hold the ladder for Elum and watch people go by. No one is upset. There aren't even many people talking to each other. When Elum comes down I have to express it. "How can everything be back to normal so quickly? Everybody was there. They saw. They heard."

"They most certainly did." He hooks the ladder on his shoulder to move to the next clock.

"You make it sound like the experience wasn't moving."

He shrugs.

I scramble to block his way so he has to stop. "Elum. What's going on with you lately? I know I pushed you by talking to the Workers, but you and I are friends. All of us have the same goal."

He adjusts the ladder and looks to the sky. "I am with you regarding the goal, but the methods? Oria's extremely lucky she didn't get arrested—or get the rest of us arrested."

"I think the Keeper protected her."

"Hmph." He actually rolls his eyes.

I swat his arm. "Elum! Why are you suddenly a skeptic?"

He starts walking. "I'm not a skeptic. I'm a realist. And I really don't want to see my friends die for talking about him in public."

"No one does. But the Keeper *has* to be talked about."

"Does he?"

I have to stop him again. "Is your involvement with my family and the Exiled a farce?"

He pushes past me. "Don't question my faith, Solana."

"Then don't question mine!" My voice is too loud, and people look at me.

"Let's concentrate on our work, all right?" He sets the ladder in place and steps up.

No, it's not all right. But what choice do I have?

**

At lunchtime Elum says he has an errand to do. I begin to sit against a wall to eat my bread and cheese when two words come to me: *Follow him.*

I've learned to obey inner nudges, so I walk after him.

Once I catch sight of Elum I hang back. I'm surprised when I see him enter the Sanctuary. What errand would bring him there? From what I've noticed, no one goes in there other than on Sanctuary Day and during a Count.

I wait outside. *I* don't want to go inside that place. The memories of the Judge on the balcony yesterday are enough to keep me outside.

Rand is leaning against the building and waves me over. "Are you working?" he asks.

I lift up my tied towel of food. "Lunch break. You want some? He nods and I hand him some cheese.

"Where's Elum?" he asks.

"He went inside."

Rand's eyebrow rises. "He seems to make a lot of visits there, three or four times a week, usually in the early morning."

I try to hide my surprise. "Do you know why?"

"I don't. He's never in there long." Rand looks toward the door and I can tell he's thinking hard about something. "I have some other news that—"

I hand Rand some bread. "How long have you known Elum?"

"A year or so. I don't remember exactly when we met."

"Do you trust him?"

He seems surprised by the question. "He's part of your group. He lives with Devin."

"I know, but . . ."I shake away my vague and unsubstantiated concerns. "I'm sure it's fine. He's fine. I'm sorry to make you doubt."

"Make who doubt?"

We turn toward the voice. It's Elum, standing not a dozen feet from us.

My stomach flips and I begin to talk way too fast. "I'm sorry I made Rand doubt that we'll ever get something other than one kind of cheese." My heart races. "Do you think we ever will? I mean this kind is all right, but back home we had many flavors, and—"

"This place is not that place," he says. He glances at a clock. "Let's get back to work."

I give Rand the rest of my lunch and scurry after Elum.

This isn't good. Not good at all.

**

After work, we gather at my son's unit.

Devin does a double take when I come in alone. "Where's Elum?" he asks.

"He walked off after work and said to eat without him. He had somewhere he needed to be."

Rand comes in and we exchange a glance.

"Elum won't be here tonight," I say again — to Rand.

His eyebrows rise. "Really."

I nod.

Helsa looks at me oddly. "Elum's not going to be here. Got it. You act like there's something fishy about it."

I quickly cover. "Not at all. I'm just telling Rand."

"Hmmm," Helsa says.

Oria shows up and we gasp when we see her.

I hurry to her side. "How did you get a black eye?" I ask. "And a cut lip?"

"Did the Fault Finders get you?" Lieb asks.

She sits at the table. "Trina beat me up."

"Who's Trina?" Devin asks.

"I work with her at the food booth."

"Why did she hurt you?" he asks.

"We had a disagreement about Judging Day. She's the type who enjoys it."

"She beat you up for that?" Devin asks.

Oria shrugs. "I mentioned that her son and husband seemed disturbed by it, and also said something to the effect of 'May the Keeper protect them both from your influence.'"

"Good one," Rand says.

"I thought so." Oria puts her hand against her ribs. "She also sat on me. If it weren't for Wyan pulling her off who knows — ?"

"Wyan?"

"A new friend. He saved me, got me home, and cleaned my wounds. I've been resting all afternoon."

"As you should," I say.

"Who is this Wyan?" Devin asks. He looks at Rand. "Do you know him?"

"I don't."

Oria winces as she tries to get comfortable on the bench. "He's just a helpful man who was in the right place at the right time."

"I'm glad he was there," I say.

"Me too. Though afterward we had a rather pointed discussion about the ways of Legalis. I mentioned the Keeper and he was interested. But it's hard to tell if he was sincere or just fishing. He has a way of steering the conversation in ways that challenge me. But he does want to talk again. Considering he's willing to listen I can't *not* talk to him."

Helsa grabs an apple and sits across from Oria. "Actually I'm surprised you're here," she says. "I thought you'd be arrested by now."

"Don't say that, Sa-Sa," Lieb says. "Don't ever say that."

Helsa shrugs and bites the apple with a loud crunch.

Rand scratches at a dried piece of food on the table. "Speaking of being arrested . . . right after the Circle I was in the Sanctuary and I saw the Head Notable go into the storeroom and not come out. I heard a discussion between him and another man about Oria. About the Exiled. They disapprove of her, and they want to investigate her."

Oria nods.

"You know about this?" Devin asks her.

"Rand told me last night."

She doesn't seem very worried. "I don't like the term *investigate*. Are they going to arrest her?"

Rand shakes his head. "Not right now. They're afraid it would upset the Masses."

"It certainly would upset me." I put my hand on her shoulder. "You've had a hard day."

"Very."

"But there's more," Rand says. "Yesterday I did some exploring in the Sanctuary and found stairs that led underground to the Notable area. And another stair . . ." he points upward, "led to the loft."

"So that's how the Judge gets up there?" I ask. "We looked but couldn't find stairs."

"There are stairs, all right. Hidden stairs," Rand says. "I assume there are others leading to the front balcony where he was yesterday." He looks at Lieb. "Which proves the Judge doesn't fly."

Lieb lets out a puff of air. "That's good. That's really good. I've been worried about that."

Helsa touches his arm. "At least we have *that* mystery solved."

Oria touches her cheek and winces, but then says, "Tell them about the scuff marks."

Rand's eyes light up. "Yes! There were scuff marks on the dusty floor where the Judge always stands. From shoes."

It only takes us a moment. "Meaning he's a man, not an 'it.'"

Rand shrugs. "I think that's a fair assumption."

The repercussions sink in. "Which means he can be bested."

Devin shakes his head. "I don't know about 'bested' but it does lower the fear factor."

"I agree," Rand says. "And after seeing the underground area of the Notables—they were eating a meal at a restaurant and shopping. It was all very normal down there."

"I wish we could dine out and shop up here," Oria says.

Rand shakes his head, discounting her response. "Helsa. you've mentioned there are tunnels down there."

"I haven't seen them. But that's what Nixi says." She turns the apple over, readying it for another bite. "If there are tunnels, they aren't for us."

"Not *for* us," Rand says. "But maybe we could use them to find the Judge."

She makes a face. "After the Cudgeling Circle I've seen enough. I've *done* enough. I *never* want to risk getting in trouble again. I never want to hit another person again. Ever."

I put my hand on her shoulder. "You were very courageous to step in for Lieb."

Lieb nods enthusiastically and leans his head toward hers. "I just couldn't do it, Sa-Sa. Thank you so much."

In recognition she leans her head to touch his. I know how much they love each other. The siblings they never had.

Helsa takes a fresh breath. "The point is, man or monster, the Judge is super powerful. I don't want any of us to get arrested and have to go to the Circle. Ever." She nods at Oria. "After your public speech and Trina beating you up? Maybe we all need to lay low awhile. Remember blending in?"

I'm not against the idea. Yet . . . "The door has been opened. We know more about the Judge. Oria's spoken about the Keeper. We can't stop now."

"I agree with Nana," Devin says. "People *are* talking about Oria's speech, and some are interested in knowing more. I had a guard ask me about the Keeper—all very hush-hush, but that's okay. We can't backtrack. His name is out there now. I'm confident we *will* see results." He hands Helsa a bowl of carrots and a vegetable I don't recognize.

She holds it to her nose. "What *are* these purply things?"

"Eggplant," Devin says. "It's rare we get them. Have a taste. They're good."

And just like that the subject is changed.

It's probably best.

CHAPTER TWENTY-FOUR

HELSA

For the second day in a row, people stare at me when I walk to and from work. Oria was the rebel on Judging Day, not me. All I did was step in when Lieb needed help. People's expressions don't tell me whether they're against me, or for me. It's like they're studying me as some oddity.

I guess I am.

When I knock at Nixi's home, *she* answers—which surprises me. Where is Kal? "Good morning," I say.

"We need to talk." She steps aside so I can enter. "Come with me."

We walk into the lush parlor. I've walked past the room, but have never stepped into it. The luxurious furniture reminds me of Oria's parlor back in Regalia—though this is that times ten.

"Sit," Nixi says bluntly.

I set aside my admiration of the room. She is not pleased. I mentally brace myself.

"I should have addressed this yesterday," Nixi says, "but the full details had not yet come to light."

"Full details of what, mistress?"

Nixi paces, the red and gold of her dress billowing like a flag in the wind. She stops in front of me. "I might as well get it over with. My mother wonders if you are close with this Oria-person, the one who made such absurd proclamations in the square."

What should I say? "Uh . . . not close. No."

"Didn't you arrive in Legalis with her?"

"Yes, but that doesn't mean I know her that well."

"Don't you see her every evening, at your father's home?"

My stomach suffers at being caught in a lie, and for the fact they know who my father is. "How do you know that?"

"So do you?"

I try to sound confident. "Yes, I do. She's a friend of my grandmother. But that doesn't mean I agree with her actions."

"She spoke out against the Judge, against the system." She points toward the floor twice. "You work here; my mother is the Head Notable. I'm sure you can understand the delicate implications." She presses two fingers above her eyebrows. "That woman's actions will not be tolerated. You and your people coming to Legalis, stirring up our carefully balanced society . . . we will not put up with it. Again, I ask: do you understand?"

I stifle a shiver. "Completely, mistress," I say. "I would never disrupt your system." *I* wouldn't. But the rest of them?

"You would never?" Nixi pauses and cocks her head to the side. "Yet didn't you just do that very thing?"

I know it's dumb to act ignorant, but I do it anyway. "How so?"

"Did you, or did you not, interfere in the Cudgeling Circle by taking the place of one of the Beaters?"

I feel a sudden urge to flee. "I did . . . but not because I was going against your traditions, but because my best friend Lieb had been chosen. He doesn't have a violent bone in his body. I knew it would kill *him* to hit Berit. That's why I did it."

"You do realize you could be punished. I could give you a dozen Faults, right this minute."

"I . . . I understand that now. But at the time I didn't consider consequences. I just knew what I had to do, and did it. I love Lieb like a brother. I'd do anything for him."

Nixi sighs, looks at the floor, then flicks a hand at me. "Go on then. Get to work. Mother's waiting."

As I leave the room I risk a glance back. Nixi stands where I left her, her head down, her hand to her mouth.

I'm not sure what it means, but I take hope from it.

After all, I'm still here.

******

I paint slower than I need to. I like spending my days with Glynis and Nixi. I like being away from the Masses. I feel special here. Useful. And after being taken to task by Nixi, I'm extra diligent. I don't want to give the Head Notable any reason—any more reason—to punish me. Or dismiss me.

As I work I expect her to speak to me about the Circle. But as one minute passes to the next I start to feel more secure. Maybe Nixi's scolding was from both of them.

I'm painting an orange lily when Nixi comes in.

"There was a note, Mother. I'm sorry for not checking yesterday."

Note?

Nixi hands her mother a tiny piece of paper. Glynis sits up straighter in bed to read it. She immediately throws off her covers and says, "I have to go. Now."

"What did the note say?" Nixi asks.

She glances in my direction, but I look away, pretending not to hear.

"A new problem needs to be discussed immediately."

"What problem?" Nixi asks, but Glynis gives her a harsh look. Nixi immediately says, "I know. It's none of my business."

"Help me get dressed."

"Do you feel well enough to go out?"

"It doesn't matter how I feel." She glances at me.

"Would you like me to leave?" I ask.

Nixi pauses, then says, "For a short while."

Glynis nods. "Actually, I think it would be best if you call it a day, Helsa. We'll see you tomorrow."

I wrap my wet brush in a towel, close the jar of paint, and head to the front door.

What problem would get Glynis out of bed? Is this about Oria? Or me?

When I exit their home there's no one around. On impulse, I turn right instead of left. My family wants me to check for tunnels. Here's my chance.

I shove the paintbrush in my pocket and walk like I know where I'm going, passing house after house with their carved columns. But then the homes end and I'm in a corridor carved out of stone. A tunnel. There are sconces for light, so it seems obvious this is a way many people take—though not people like me.

I come to an intersection of two additional tunnels veering to the left and the right. Which way to go?

It's a tossup.

I turn left.

The tunnel gets narrower, with sconces fewer and farther between. I'm ready to turn back when I hear footsteps ahead.

I freeze. There is no place to hide, so I turn around and walk back the way I'd come. Calmly. Or as calm as possible.

The footsteps get closer. I feel like running, but that might make things worse. If the person catches up to me I can plead ignorance.

I won't be lying.

And then . . . "Hey you. Stop!" a man yells.

I stop but don't turn around. My chest feels like it's going to explode.

The man catches up to me and whips me around to face him.

I gawk at him—a tall, bald man I've seen before. "You're him! You were in Regalia!" He's the mysterious man who kept turning up, first on the day of my mother's funeral, then always in the background, watching us.

"Shush, girl! Quiet."

He takes my arm and pulls me deeper into the tunnel. I try to yank my arm away, but his grip is too strong. "Let me go! Where are you taking me?"

He stops me, and points in my face. "I said quiet! Do what I say, or else."

I know he could fell me with a single blow. I stay quiet.

"Wise girl. Now come on."

His grip is less painful, but he doesn't let go. We keep walking down a long, curving tunnel. Occasionally there are other tunnels veering away from ours. How many are there?

We finally reach a door—which he opens.

The light is blinding and I raise an arm to shield my eyes. The temperature is hot compared to the coolness of the tunnel. I look down and see sand.

He lets go. My eyes adjust and I look around. We're in the desert. The exterior of the buildings of Legalis stretch in either direction.

"You're not going to leave me out here, are you?"

"I should. You have no business snooping around the tunnels."

"I work for the Head Notable. I simply turned the wrong direction when I left her house."

He gives me the look I deserve.

"Why are *you* here?" I ask. "Why are you wearing the white robe of Legalis? When I last saw you, you were wearing the brown tunic of a Serv—in Regalia."

He squints up at the sky. "I go where I'm needed."

"According to who?"

"Whom."

He's correcting my grammar?

He walks a few steps away from me, then back. "There are some things you need to know, and some . . . you don't."

Any information would be helpful. "Can I ask you a question?"

"You can ask . . ."

"Should I be afraid of you? Should my family be afraid?"

He considers this a moment. "If you behave yourselves, no."

"What does behave ourselves mean?"

He runs his hand over his bald head. He's not a bad-looking man. He doesn't look evil. Yet in Regalia I saw him in scary situations like the dark woods near the Pile, and skulking around in the shadows. And today is no different.

He finally says, "Don't move too fast."

"Move?"

"Take action. I know what Oria did."

"You know her name?"

"I know all of your names, Helsa."

It's unnerving for him to know about us while we know nothing about him.

"Don't look so worried," he says. "I approve of what she did. And what you did, sacrificing yourself for Lieb."

All fear leaves me. "Then you're on our side."

He raises his hand. "In theory, but perhaps not in implementation. Not completely anyway."

"If you have any ideas about how to do . . ." I'm not sure whether I should share our goal.

"How to unmask the Judge and tell people about the Keeper?"

"Yes!" I'm completely relieved. "How did you know all that? We've tried to be discreet."

"I just know." He studies me a moment and must see the questions on my mind, because he says, "Don't try to analyze it, Helsa. Everything will go much smoother if you just accept what I tell you without needing to know the whys."

I'm usually skeptical and always defensive, but for some reason I trust him. "Do you have any ideas about how to do what we're trying to do? We're open to suggestions."

"Let's just say this isn't a single-prong project. The goal of unmasking the Judge is valid, but there is work to do along the way to prepare the people."

"The people, as in the Exiled?"

"Far more people than them."

He reminds me of Oria. "The Masses?"

"As many as possible."

He *does* remind me of Oria. "How do we do that?"

"Keep talking about the Keeper. Keep showing people that your life is different—better—because of him." He bites his lip, then adds. "And keep showing them what mercy, self-sacrifice, and forgiveness looks like."

"Forgiveness . . . Glynis didn't even know what the word meant."

"Which illustrates how daunting our assignment is."

His last word catches my interest. "Assignment?"

"The one given to Oria. The one shared by all of you."

"And you?"

"And me." He taps his fingers against his chest.

I return the gesture. "Would you come to our house and talk to everybody? They could use a pep talk."

He shakes his head adamantly. "It's best I stay incognito."

I scoff. "You're tall, bald, and muscular. You do *not* blend in."

He shrugs. "I am what I am. People see what they need to see."

I'm not sure what he means, but he told me not to ask questions.

He looks toward Legalis. "Let's get you home."

The thought of winding my way through the tunnels is daunting and more than a little scary. "Will you walk with me? I'm not sure how I could explain myself if I run into someone."

"I'll show you another way. It will take you to an exit near your unit."

We walk through the desert door into the tunnel, and at one of the offshoots he tells me to turn. "Follow it to the end."

"Will I see you again?" I ask.

"Perhaps."

"Is there a way to get a hold of you?"

He just smiles. "May the Keeper be with you."

**

The tunnel ends with a rickety door that opens inward. Actually, it barely opens, because one hinge is on its last leg. Once outside I squint at the sunlight.

I'm in an alley that's so narrow I can hold out my arms and touch both sides. It's littered with broken pottery, rotting apple cores, and things I don't ever want to smell again. How many people know about this door? I remember Nana telling us about a law that basically says don't go where you're not supposed to go. Sounds rather pathetic — and generic — but I suppose it could keep people out of the tunnels. From what I've seen, most of the Masses are passive. They're followers. A go-along-to-get-along bunch.

I slip out to the street and close the door. No one pays any attention to me. I'm very relieved to be safely back.

But then I realize I have nothing to do for the rest of the day. Everyone else is at work.

So I wander. Legalis isn't very interesting, though I suppose Regalia wasn't either unless you lived in an upper class Ring like Oria did. Yet in Regalia Papa, Mama, Nana and I were happy in our cozy home in the Imp Ring. I wonder who lives there now? Have they found my box of childhood treasures that I hid under my bed? They were simple mementos of no value to anyone but myself, but they were more than I have now.

Suddenly, two masked Fault Finders look in my direction. I step against a wall to take myself out of their path. But they turn toward me. They walk toward me.

"Are you Helsa?"

"Yes . . ." Did they spot me in the tunnels? Or outside with . . . I realize I don't know the tunnel man's name.

It's disconcerting to only see their eyes — which are not kind.

One of them hands me a Fault. "A law of Legalis has been broken. Someone must pay. Wear your Fault for all to see."

"What's it for?" Even though I know…

"For interfering in a Cudgeling Circle."

"I didn't interfere, I participated."

"You were not called."

"I volunteered. Why is that a crime?"

"You sassing us, girl?"

"No, but—"

"Directive number Five: Never speak against those who have authority over you.'" He turns to the other Fault Finder. "Perhaps we should give her two."

"No, no," I say. I fumble with the black stud. It has a pin in the bottom of it, and a metal back. I attach it to the left shoulder of my robe.

"Satisfied?" I ask.

One of them points at me. "You deaf, girl? Didn't you hear what we said? Shut yer mouth!"

The venom in his words rattles me and I stay quiet.

They walk away, and I notice people have stopped to watch. "Go on!" I tell them with a swat of my hands. "The show's over."

I keep walking, trying to look confident. But I'm not. I have a Fault on my shoulder. I'm not a newcomer anymore. I'm one of *them* — and I don't like it.

And it's worse than that. The Fault is proof that I'm no longer anonymous.

They know my name.

**

As I wander, the clocks chime. I follow a man and woman into a nearby unit and are joined by two others. No residents are at home. A man places five black pebbles on the ledge outside. Two women lean against a wall, and the men sit on the floor and close their eyes until it's safe to go out again. The whole thing is tedious and boring, besides being a total waste of time.

A woman stares at me. So much so that I eventually ask, "What?"

"Are you the one who interfered in the Circle?"

This is getting old. "I did not interfere, I helped a friend."

A young man points at my Fault. "Did they give you that for interfering? You didn't have it in the Circle."

I touch the Fault which feels heavy on my shoulder. The man has four Faults. "Want to tell me how you got yours?"

"No."

"Then mind your own business."

He stands up, glances in a pitcher on the table, then drinks from it.

"That's not yours," I say.

He wipes his mouth with his sleeve. "Is it yours?"

"Of course not."

"Then mind your own business."

Such lovely people.

**

I walk around a while longer, then head home. The clocks say it's nearly quitting time. I can't wait to tell everyone about the tunnels, ending up in the desert, and talking to the Tunnel Man. Nana saw him in Regalia too. She'll be relieved to know he's not someone to fear.

But as I turn around, I spot Varo. The husband of Glynis is a dozen yards away. He sticks out because he's wearing all black—a far cry from the colorful clothes he wore in his home.

He's speaking to a man who wears a white robe. Their heads are close, their words obviously meant for their ears alone.

The man hands Varo a small, brown, drawstring bag. Varo palms it and pulls his sleeve over it. Then he walks away.

What's in the bag that's so secret?

Without making a conscious decision, I find myself following him.

Not surprisingly, he walks in the direction of the Notable area.

I want to follow him inside but I've been sent home. Yet if Glynis is away at her meeting . . .

I decide to risk it. Varo's secrecy has piqued my curiosity to the max and reinforces my dislike and distrust of him.

After Varo goes through the Notable gate, I follow. The guard waves me through. I hang back and watch Varo enter the residential area.

He's going home.

Do I dare follow him inside?

I've come this far . . .

I see his front door close, and hesitate. I can't knock, so I wait a moment and slip inside. I don't see him in the foyer. I spot him in the parlor, and immediately hide behind an urn. Varo is talking to the maid, Kal. He hands her the brown bag, and she nods, slipping it in her pocket. Again, the secrecy is telling.

But then Varo looks in my direction. "Helsa!"

My heart skips a beat.

He comes out to the foyer. "Why aren't you at work?"

His tone is combative — very different from the flirtatious attitude of our first meeting. "I was, but then your wife sent me home because she was called to an important meeting."

His expression shows he knows nothing about the meeting, and he's *not* pleased about it. "Why wasn't I told?"

"I don't know, sir." I remember the toweled brush I've been carrying around and pull it out. "I mistakenly left a brush without cleaning it."

"Whatever. You got it? Now go. You might work in our home and be in good graces with Glynis and Nixi but you do not belong here. Remember that, girl."

"Yes, sir."

I don't like the idea of having Varo as an enemy.

Chapter Twenty-Five

Rand

Helsa had a momentous day.

I'm the first to notice she has a Fault on her shoulder. "When did you get that?"

She touches it. "Today. Two Fault Finders blindsided me, and forced me to put it on."

"How scary," Lieb says.

"It was."

"Did they hurt you?" Solana asks.

"Not physically. But they're bullies and they enjoy being bullies."

"That they are," I say. I still remember them coming to arrest me at my mother's house.

"You got that stud thingy because you saved me, didn't you?" Lieb asks.

Helsa touches his arm. Their affection is so tender. "I got it for interfering with the Circle."

Devin shakes his head in disgust. "You do something good and get punished for it."

"Forget the stud. I'll probably get more."

"No you won't," Solana says. "You can't." She touches her own stud, earned for "frivolity."

"I'm not going to try to get them, Nana."

Solana shakes her head to close the subject.

"I had two more strange things happen today." Helsa sits at the table and shines an apple against her robe. I saw Varo, the Head Notable's husband. He was acting really suspicious. He had this secret transaction and walked away with a little bag he tried to hide in his sleeve. I followed him back to his house—pretending I'd left a brush behind—and he gave it to the maid, but not in the open. Very secretive."

Elum looks concerned. "The maid, Kal?"

"Yes, their maid." Helsa says, giving Elum a once-over look

Elum knows the name of the Head Notable's maid?

"What made it look secretive?" Oria asks. "If he lives there, certainly he has daily contact with the maid."

"It's the way they did it," Helsa explains. "Quickly. Standing close together. And she hid it immediately."

"We have to do something," Elum says.

His words surprise everyone. "Do something?" Devin asks. "Like what? About what?"

He blinks. "If something's amiss . . . she's our Head Notable, and if her husband is sneaking around in some way . . ."

Lieb shakes his head. "I don't like Notables. They put me in the Circle. I didn't like the Circle."

Elum gets up to pour himself more water.

Helsa has more to share. "Thirdly . . . I have even bigger news. I met this weird man." She looks at her grandmother. "Remember the guy who kept turning up in Regalia? The man we first saw in the woods, then always alone, watching us?"

Solana's eyes grow large. "The loner who was always taking notes?"

"That's the one."

"How did he get here?"

"We didn't talk about that," Helsa says. "I ran into him when I was in the tunnels."

That gets our interest. "Tunnels?" I ask.

Helsa sits up very straight to tell the story. "Glynis got a note that called her away to a meeting, so they sent me home early. She's still not well, but she was adamant about going."

"What sort of meeting would get her out of her sickbed?" Oria asks.

"I'm thinking it had something to do with what you and I did in the square."

"Oria puts her hand to her mouth. "I don't like the sound of that."

"*I* just got a Fault. And Nixi got mad at me for the Circle thing. I think you're next."

Oria wraps her arms around herself. "I don't like waiting around for consequences. If you got a Fault for helping Lieb, I should get a hundred."

"Anyway . . ." Helsa says, clearly annoyed the attention had been diverted from herself. "You wanted me to explore so I explored. I found a whole slew of tunnels leading from the Notable homes to who-knows-where. Even outside to the desert. That's where the Tunnel Man talked to me."

"Does he have a name?" I ask.

"He never told me and I never asked," Helsa says.

"I don't want you going outside," Devin says. "What if you couldn't get back in?"

"Maybe being out there is better than in here," she says.

"*We're* in here," Devin says. "Don't go out again."

She shrugs. "Exploring the tunnels was really risky. If I was seen I had no excuse for being there. And then I nearly freaked out when I heard footsteps, but it turned out to be the Tunnel Man."

"What was he doing down there?" I ask.

"I don't know, but he recognized me. He knew my name."

"That's unnerving," Solana says.

"And he's a believer."

Oria says, "And *that's* encouraging."

Helsa looks at each of us. "He knows our names. He knows what Oria did. What I did. And he knows what we're trying to do."

"How does he know all that?" Oria asks.

"I asked him that, but he told me to trust him."

"Him knowing our plans isn't good," Devin says. "We have to be more discreet."

"He told me we shouldn't move too fast," Helsa says. "Don't push."

She looks at Oria — who points at herself. "Am I pushing?"

"I think you were very brave," I say.

"I wasn't trying to be. But is speaking out 'pushing'?"

"Maybe a little," Solana says.

I don't want Oria to doubt herself. "I disagree. We *have* to speak out. You didn't plan what you said. The Keeper nudged you to say it."

She raises her hand as if taking an oath. "That's true."

Helsa shrugs. "I asked if he wanted to meet all of you and he said no. He wants to remain incognito."

"Incog-what?" Lieb asks.

"Undercover." Helsa slices the apple into fourths. "Though I doubt he can do that, being a tall bald guy, with lots of muscles."

I stop with a piece of bread halfway to my mouth.

"Rand? What's wrong?" Solana asks.

Nothing. Not really. "I've seen a man like that around the Sanctuary. I know exactly who you mean."

"Has he talked to you?" Oria asks.

"Sometimes he nods when he passes by. He goes into the Sanctuary a lot." I suddenly make a connection. "Your Tunnel Man . . . if he's in the Sanctuary *and* the tunnels, does he get from one to the other via the storeroom? If he's on our side, then what's he doing down there?"

No one has an answer.

"Has anyone else seen him?" Helsa asks.

No one has.

"I'll keep an eye out for him," I say. "I'll try to speak with him."

We eat in silence for a while, then Solana says, "Oria? Helsa? May I speak with you for a moment?"

They slip into the bedroom. When they return, Solana stands across from me. "We ladies have a proposition for you, Rand. I'm going to move in with Oria since she has an empty space in her unit. And so, you can move into my space with Helsa and Lieb."

Lieb jumps out of his chair and rushes to hug me. "We get to be roommates!"

I'm shocked and deeply moved. "You don't have to do that. I'm used to sleeping in the street — that's my lot as a Marked Man." I brush aside my hair to show my mark.

Solana shakes her head. "I refuse to recognize any such mark. You are a good man. And you are our friend."

"You might get in trouble," I say. "It's a law that no one's supposed to help my kind."

"Too late," Solana says.

"That's very nice of you, Mother," Devin says. "Isn't it, Helsa?"

"It will be fun, Sa-Sa," Lieb says.

I can tell she isn't thrilled with the idea, but to her credit Helsa agrees. "It'll work. I'll sleep in the main room on Lieb's cot, and you two men can have the room."

"You don't have to—" I say.

"Those are my terms," she says.

It *does* make sense. "Thank you, Helsa," I say. "And thank you, Solana and Oria. May the Keeper send many blessings your way."

**

Lieb chats happily while he and Helsa rearrange the bedding on the cots. Their unit is smaller than Devin and Elum's, but it's a roof over my head. I haven't had that in years. Truthfully, I never expected to have it again.

"I hate to kick you out of the bedroom," I tell Helsa — not for the first time.

"Stop it, Rand. This is fine. A cot's a cot. Now if you two don't mind, I'm really tired."

Which means Lieb and I have to go into the bedroom and close the door, so she can sleep.

Lieb pours water into a low bowl and places it next to my cot. "Sit. Let me wash your feet for you."

Wash my feet?

Although I don't say anything, he sees my expression. "Nana says it's important to wash our feet every night so we don't dirty the covers. She says we wash away the filth of the day." He kneels in front of me. "Come on. Rules are rules."

I take off my well-worn sandals and slip my feet into the water — which immediately turns cloudy. Lieb takes a cloth and dunks it in the water, rubbing it over my feet and ankles. I'm embarrassed by his actions, and the extent of my griminess.

"I'm sorry," I say. "They're very dirty. I can't remember the last time they were clean."

He places a dry cloth on the floor next to the bowl. "Not anymore. Put them here."

I do, and he wipes them dry. "There," he says proudly. "As Nana would say, 'Your feet are cleansed and ready for rest.'"

I feel tears threaten. For this young man to humble himself, to do this. For me . . .

Lieb turns his head as he looks at me. "Are you sad? I didn't mean to make you sad. It's a good thing."

I smile and place my hand on his head. "It's a very good thing, Lieb. And as I said the first time I met you, you are a very good man."

He beams as if I've made his day.

He's certainly made mine.

CHAPTER TWENTY-SIX

ORIA

Yesterday Trina wasn't at the food booth—which was a huge blessing. I enjoyed running the booth by myself. People noticed my bruises but no one asked about them, or—heaven forbid—showed compassion.

I wondered if she wasn't there because she'd been arrested. If people can get a Fault for touching she certainly should've gotten a few for beating me up and sitting on me.

Yet maybe they looked the other way because she is one of their best informants. And since I'm in their sights for my speech at the Circle, maybe they approve of my beating.

Even if she's back today, I know she won't apologize for beating me up. She won't seek forgiveness.

There's that word again.

Forgiveness. I'm ready to apologize and ask her for forgiveness for my rude comments about her bad influence on Pan. She does love her son—even though I still believe I'm right.

As I approach the booth, I see the awning is open, but I don't see Trina. So who put up the awning?

Suddenly, Wyan pops up from behind the counter and sets a basket in place. He sees me and smiles. "Good morning, Oria."

"Good morning to you. What are you doing here?"

"I work here now."

I feel a surge of pleasure. "Where's Trina?"

"Jail."

Really? "Jail?"

"She broke Directive number Six: All lives belong to Legalis. No—"

"No violence is allowed," I say with him.

"Good for you."

I'm glad she's out of commission, but jail? I think of her husband and Pan. I don't want them getting punished for her offenses.

He studies my face. "Your bruises are getting colorful. Do they still hurt?"

I touch the most tender area under my left eye. "I'll survive."

"I believe that," he says. "You're stronger than you look."

What a curious thing to say. "Are you saying I don't *look* strong?"

He gives me a mischievous smile. "You look very feminine. Very beautiful. Add courage and strength to all that and . . ." He shakes his head. "You're a force to be reckoned with, Oria."

His compliment touches me deeply. How odd that the man who challenges me more than any other, compliments me more than any other.

A farm cart arrives and we fill the food baskets on the counter. People will be coming soon.

Wyan makes conversation as we work, "So what is the source of that strength of yours? Your family?"

My impulsive answer is not kind. "I'm afraid not."

"But I've seen you with them. You seem to be a tightly bound unit."

I realize the only 'family' he's seen me with is here in Legalis. "I have no blood family here, though I *am* close to the people I traveled with. My mother and brother are back in . . ." I realize I can't say "Regalia".

"In . . .?"

"I came from the desert."

He rolls his eyes. "I know the bunkum them want you to say. Be straight with me. You're from Regalia."

It's a relief to be able to say it. "Yes, I am."

He nods once, as if that issue is done with. "You were speaking about your family?"

"Yes. They . . . they were *not* supportive of my . . . change."

"Change from what?"

"Change from a self-centered, shallow girl who cared only about fashion and winning."

"Fashion?"

"I was a Patron there. Have you heard of them?"

"I have. Though Regalia sounds like a silly society, consumed with dressing up in absurd clothes and selling them."

He's not far off.

"So you changed from a frivolous woman into . . .?"

He's putting me on the spot to brag about myself. "To what you see before you."

He shakes his head. "That's not an acceptable answer. How do you see yourself now? You've obviously made yourself known in Legalis."

"I didn't plan to speak out at the Circle," I say. "It just happened because I knew Berit. She was a wonderful woman who didn't deserve to die."

"The Judge thought otherwise."

"The Judge is wrong." I suddenly realize what a dangerous statement that is. "I shouldn't have said that."

"But you did. And you believe it."

He's right, but I'm wary. I look at Wyan, trying to read his face. He's good at keeping his emotions in check. I see no hint of animosity in him. And yet . . . "I don't know you. Are you going to turn me in?"

His face grows serious. "I wouldn't do that. I simply want to get to know you better."

An odd question pops out. "Why?"

He grins. "Are you wanting me to give you more compliments?"

It *was* a leading question. "I don't. Really. Just forget I asked."

"But I *can't* forget. The answer to your question is simple: you, Oria, are a fascinating, perplexing woman, unlike any I have ever met."

"Perplexing?"

He chuckles. "You choose that word and ignore *fascinating?*"

I feel my cheeks turn red, yet I truly am curious. "Why do I perplex you?"

"Because you're a newcomer yet you risk everything to buck the system and make yourself stand out."

"Blend in. We were supposed to blend in."

He raises a finger, accepting the point. "That, you were. Then to top it off, you talk about this Keeper person who sounds like the antithesis of all things Legalis."

"You're right. He is." And he's not a person. Not exactly.

His eyebrows rise. "Generally, when someone is new they *do* try to blend in, to adapt to the customs and laws here. Not insert totally new ideas."

"The Keeper isn't totally new. People know about him. Locals know about him."

His head jerks back. "They do? I can't imagine how."

I realize I'm treading on dangerous ground. Elum and Rand's stories are not mine to tell. Nor is any information about the Workers or the Exiled. "Let's just say the Keeper makes himself known."

Wyan scoffs. "Where is this Keeper? I want to meet him."

"It doesn't work like that."

"Then *you* arrange a meeting for me."

It's my turn to scoff. "It doesn't work like that either."

"Then how — ?"

Two people approach the booth and others get in line. Our discussion is put on hold.

Which is for the best because I don't know how to answer him.

**

The morning passes quickly as the line has been constant.

Wyan lets out a deep sigh. "Well then. So that's how it's done."

"That's how it's done," I say. "Are you hungry?"

"After being around all this food? Absolutely. What do we do for lunch?"

I smile. "We eat. Grab what you want."

He takes carrots, bread, and cheese. I do the same. Then I lower the awning and sit on the ground behind the booth, leaning against a wall. "Sit with me," I say. "Unless you have someplace you need to go."

He sits.

"Tell me about you, Wyan. Do you have family here?"

"I do not. My parents died a few years ago, as did my sister."

"I'm so sorry." I want to ask how they died, but feel it's prying. "Where did you work before this?"

"Here and there. I go where they send me. I don't have any real skills so I'm a jack of all trades, a master of none."

"There's no skill in handing out food." I say, looking around at our scant surroundings.

"My point is taken."

Oops. Without family or jobs to talk about, I'm at a loss.

But maybe not. This is my chance to gain information. "Why do you trust the Judge?" I ask.

"Because he keeps order."

"Through fear."

"If fear begets order, it's a good fear. Under the Judge the Masses know their roles. There's no gray area."

I shake my head. "Life is full of gray areas."

"Gray areas get people in trouble. Things work more smoothly when everything is black and white."

"You're for the Judge, no matter what."

His eyebrows rise. "Of course."

I take a bite of cheese. "Such attitudes ignore free will and logical thinking."

He scoffs. "My my, you *are* full of opinions."

I *was* the one who started all this by asking about the Judge. "What is Legalis so afraid of? Not allowing people to touch, not allowing them to sing and express themselves? Discouraging people from reading and writing? They're creating frustrated people who are a shell of who they were created to be."

He tears off a chunk of bread and eats it. "When left to their own devices, people are evil. They turn on each other, they argue, steal, and kill."

What a horrible point of view. "The capability for all that is in us, but we can rise above it and do good. Be good."

"We can't count on that. The Laws of Legalis keep the peace."

I'm astounded by the lie. "The laws keep people brow-beaten and oppressed."

"In line. Legalis is rooted in regularity and order."

"Legalis is rooted in brutality."

"That's harsh, Oria."

It is. But at this point I see Berit's father, Yair, lean on the building to our right. His eyes are down, his shoulders slumped. His forehead tattoo—his Mark—is raw and fresh. I point at him. "You don't think branding someone, condemning them to life as an outcast is brutal? Or making citizens beat his daughter to death? Wyan, please tell me you don't condone such evil."

He's silent, but I see his jaw clench. I've been too brash. I reach out my hand to touch his arm, but stop short. "I know the ways of Legalis are not your fault."

He still doesn't say anything, which makes me wish our lunch was over. He takes a bite of a carrot, and I do the same. Other than our chewing we share an awkward silence.

But then he says, "I know I'll regret asking, but how would your Keeper handle crime and punishment?"

I inwardly smile at his word choice. "You say he's 'my Keeper', which is the core of who he is. We are his. He keeps those who believe in him close."

"You said Berit believed. Why didn't he keep her close? She's dead."

"But we who believe trust that there's everlasting life after this one. A better life. With him. So while her death fills us with sadness and anger, he did keep her close, and everyone saw her soul rising to heaven."

"Is that what it was?"

"Prove otherwise."

"So how would the Keeper deal with her father over there?"

I look at Yair again. He's a shell of a man and wears his grief like a heavy yoke. He slides down the wall to the ground, a sorrowful lump of a man. But then Rand walks up to him. Rand—another Marked Man. He gives Yair a chunk of bread.

"Like that," I say. "The Keeper doesn't approve of law-breaking, but he is merciful and wants us to be merciful too."

Then Rand hands Yair a piece of paper. A Relic?

Panic rushes over me. Instinctively I know Wyan isn't ready to know about Relics—if he ever will be.

Yair opens the note and reads it. He nods at Rand before touching his chest. Rand returns the gesture.

"Writing is against the law," Wyan says. "Passing notes is too."

I fear he's going to turn Rand in.

"The note seems like it was encouraging," I say. "Surely that can't be against any law."

"What did the note say?"

"I obviously don't know," I reply truthfully. "But it made Yair feel better. That's also what the Keeper does for us. He spurs us to encourage each other. He's always there for us, even in the darkest times. Can the same be said of the Judge?"

Wyan hesitates. "That's not his job."

"No," I say. "You're right. The Judge *creates* the darkest times." I stand and brush off the back of my robe. "We need to get back to work."

I wish I could go home. I'm exhausted.

**

Wyan and I don't talk much the rest of the workday — which is fine with me. I know the Keeper asked me to tell people about him, but I feel like I've done it all wrong. I've antagonized Wyan. He's never going to believe anything beyond what Legalis has taught him.

We close up the booth and I turn toward home. "See you tomorrow."

"Tomorrow is Sanctuary Day," he says.

"I'll see you there then. Have a nice evening."

Wyan calls after me. "You never answered my question."

I turn back to him, totally done in. "I answered a lot of your questions. Probably too many for your liking."

"Let me be the judge of that."

"Judge. How appropriate."

"My question was, how do I meet the Keeper? Can you arrange it?"

I'm not sure I'm up for this. "As I said, it doesn't work like that. But I *can* say that once you're open to him, he'll find a way to reach you. *You* don't arrange it. He does."

He cocks his head. "That's an interesting answer."

"Glad you like it." I raise my hand to wave goodbye. "See you tomorrow."

"Yes, you will."

I'm not sure if that makes me happy or nervous.

Chapter Twenty-Seven

Oria

Solana and I leave our unit to join the others for Sanctuary Day.

"We haven't had much chance to talk since I moved in," she says.

"I know. I feel bad about that." Solana has been with me for two nights. The first night we were both exhausted after Helsa's adventure in the tunnels and meeting the mysterious Tunnel Man. And last evening I was exhausted from my discussions with Wyan. Hopefully today we'll have some quality time.

We join the others and walk on.

"Do you realize this is the first Sanctuary Day since Berit's death?" Solana says.

No. But yes, it hits me now. "I wonder if people will act differently."

"I've thought about that. I also thought you might be worried about what the Head Notable might say about your . . . outburst."

My stomach tightens at the thought.

Helsa overhears and taps the Fault on her shoulder. "If I got one of these for helping Lieb, you should get more than one."

It does feel like I've been living on borrowed time.

We follow the Masses inside. Rand separates from us and stands in the back. I keep an eye out for Wyan but I don't see him anywhere. Then again, I know I could've missed him among the hundreds here, but still...

"Who are you looking for?" Solana asks.

"Wyan. The man who took Trina's place at the booth."

"The one who took care of you after she beat you up?"

"The same." Up front I see the acting Head Notable and the Head Fault Finder step forward. The Ten Directives are repeated — and I recite most of them, which bothers me a little. It's disturbing how quickly these words have permeated my mind; how quickly I've succumbed to their ways.

Outwardly, anyway.

The Judge comes onto the balcony. He stares down at us — which is surprisingly just as effective as threatening us with his creepy hands. People still cower every time they see him.

Him. Not it.

His appearance lets us know it's time for the Head Fault Finder to list the number of Faults from the past week. The first ones are negligible—people are behaving themselves, perhaps because of Judging Day. But then he says, "We have two grievous Faults this week in regard to interference in the Cudgeling Circle. The first has been handled, but the second—a more serious Fault—has not."

He's talking about me!

Suddenly two Fault Finders walk down the right side of the crowd, then push people aside to get to me.

I tense up, wanting to flee. But there's nowhere to go.

One hands me a stud and says, "A law of Legalis has been broken. Someone must pay. Wear your Fault for all to see."

Up front the Head Fault Finder booms, "For dire interference in the peace of Judging Day and for the lies told against Legalis."

"They weren't lies!" I call out.

Solana shushes me.

I see the faces of Elum, Devin, and Lieb. They all shake their heads no.

For once I take their advice and stop talking.

"Take your punishment!" the head man shouts.

With Solana's help I attach the stud to the shoulder of my robe. It feels heavy for reasons beyond its weight.

The Fault Finders withdraw, but I don't hear the rest of the service as my mind swims with the public condemnation. And relief that I wasn't arrested. During our first Sanctuary service a woman was arrested for speaking up for her husband. I know my crime is far worse.

I fill my thoughts with prayers of gratitude for the Keeper's protection.

When we leave, people give me a wide berth. I can't blame them. To be seen with someone who was singled out isn't wise.

"You're lucky they didn't arrest you," Devin says on the way home.

"I know. I don't understand why they didn't."

Rand walks beside me. "Like I told you. They don't want to rile the Masses."

"But it's not fair you get the same punishment as me and Nana," Helsa says. "You did way more than we did."

"I know."

I know all of it. I pull up short and tell my friends, "I'll see you at the house. I need to walk a while."

Solana looks worried, but they let me go. As I walk, the Fault feels hot on my shoulder. I am not a newcomer anymore. I have been fully initiated as one of the Masses.

That's one way to blend in.

I consider going back to my unit, but my body insists on movement. I walk with my head down, wandering.

Literally and figuratively.

With my punishment very real and very public, how can I reach more people for the Keeper? Making declarations about him may have planted the seed of him in people's minds, but now that they've witnessed the consequences . . . they're not going to eagerly become his followers. To them, it looks dangerous.

To me, it looks dangerous.

Is it dangerous? Surely the Keeper doesn't want to put me in danger.

Yet I did just that many times in Regalia. I suffered by losing my status and then being exiled, but the Keeper got me through all that. He led me to safety in Legalis.

And he led me to speak on Judging Day. No matter what happens next, I know he will be with me.

What I'd like most is to talk to him again. Get some guidance. I've prayed, but no concrete plan comes to mind. No door has opened wide.

"Oria!"

I turn around and see Wyan coming up behind me. I wait for him, glad for a familiar face.

He stops, panting. "You walk fast."

"I do." Which means he's made an effort to catch up to me. "I looked for you at the service."

"I was there."

"So you saw my humiliation?"

"I did. It proves you can run, but you can't hide."

"I wasn't trying to run or hide. But I thought . . . never mind what I thought."

"You thought you were free and clear since nothing had happened before today?"

I shrug. "I was hoping."

He looks around. "Where are your friends?"

"I told them to go home without me. I needed to be alone."

He grins. "But now you're not alone. Are you all right with that?"

I think of a stipulation. "As long as we don't talk about my Fault."

"Agreed. So what *would* you like to talk about?"

I try to think of something innocuous. "It's not as hot today . . ."

He rolls with it. "What was weather like where you came from?"

So we *are* going to talk about the weather. "The temperatures were mild. Never too cold. Never hot like it is here."

"Not hot in climate, but hot in regard to peculiar ideas?"

It's my turn to blink at him. "Believing in the Keeper is not peculiar. It's life-changing in all the best ways. You should consider believing in him." There. I'd said it plain.

"I thought you might give that up considering what happened at the Sanctuary."

"I thought we weren't going to talk about that."

"You brought him up."

I did. "Actually, I'm shocked that you think my faith could so easily be set aside."

"Weren't you exiled because of the Keeper?" he asks.

"I was exiled because those in power were afraid to let people hear the truth. As apparently, are those in power in Legalis."

"Those are dangerous words, Oria. You need to be careful."

I know they are, but I can't seem to stop myself. "I thought Legalis — as a society that tries so hard to get people to conform — might embrace truth. People will rally around truth; conform to truth."

"We have our own truth," he says.

"Which is based on oppression."

He gives me a double take, but then smiles. "You are passionate about your beliefs. I admire that."

He could have fooled me. "You're being very generous."

"I just want to be your friend, Oria. Is that all right?"

Despite our inability to *not* argue, it was. "I'd like to be your friend too."

"Excellent," he says. "And I am sorry about that very public Fault ceremony."

"I am too. Most people aren't given their Faults in front of all Legalis."

"No, they aren't . . ."

There was an unspoken "but" in his sentence. "But . . .?"

"Most people don't earn a Fault in front of all Legalis."

"Touché."

"There is one thing I'd like to know," he says.

"Only one?"

"Touché back at you. *Why* are you so passionate about the Keeper?"

My first impulse is to hedge my answer, but then I feel an inner nudge. "I'm passionate because the Keeper is mine."

"Yours?"

"And I am his — I'm one of his sheep."

"Are you sure you want to be associated with sheep? They're dumb animals that can't get anywhere on their own."

I smile. "Exactly."

He cocks his head. "You want to be deemed a follower? Weak?"

"A follower of him, yes. But not weak." I think a moment. "He's strong *for* us. He leads us to safety. We can trust him."

"You trust someone you can't see; who only exists in your imagination."

I can answer him by sharing my one-on-one experience, but I'm not sure I should.

He makes a figure-eight in front of my eyes. "You have an answer for me. I can see it in your eyes."

"The curse of a transparent face," I say.

"Then tell me. You can trust me."

"I'm not so sure about that."

He slaps his hand against his chest. "I'm crushed."

I shrug. "I have a question for *you*."

"Only one?"

"Is it possible for you to talk to me and *not* argue?"

Wyan laughs. "I'll give it a shot." He walks me home and we manage to talk of simple things beyond Faults, lies, and the Keeper. Thanks to him, the panic and pain of the morning are forgotten.

When we part, I'm sad to see him go. And instead of dissecting my feelings — as I am prone to do — I just let them *be*.

There's something very freeing in that.

Chapter Twenty-Eight

Solana

I awaken from a dream. I sit up in bed and let the images sink into my memory, for I've learned to quickly grab onto them, and never ever discount them. Sometimes they serve a purpose.

Today's dream feels purposeful. I saw a pretty woman in her fifties. She's in bed, groaning in pain. A man sneaks into her room but he doesn't help her.

And there's a second dream. I see myself being pushed into a tiny room with high windows. A grated door slams shut behind me. Am I in jail?

What does one dream have to do with the other?

I look across the room and see that Oria is already dressed for the day. She puts on her sandals. "Good morning, Solana. You tossed and turned a lot last night. I thought you needed the sleep. I tried not to wake you."

"You didn't. I need to get up."

"I'm going to Devin's for breakfast. You coming?"

"Of course." I swivel and put my feet on the floor. "I had a restless night because I had dreams. Vivid ones."

"You often have dreams, don't you?"

"I do. And it seemed like they could be special dreams. They might be important."

"Do you want to talk about them now, or tell everyone at breakfast?"

"At breakfast. I'll be there presently." Oria leaves and I dress in a hurry.

The person I want to tell most is Helsa. She's always been there to listen to my dreams. Not living in the same unit is hard. I mourn the closeness we shared in Regalia. We lived and worked together. We confided in each other. Now we only see each other in a group at Devin's. I feel like I'm losing her. I question giving up my unit with her and Lieb.

I run my fingers through my hair that's grown more gray, and tie it back. How many times did she brush my hair or I brush hers? How many times did she sit beside my rocker and lean her head against my leg?

Helsa is happy to see her dad. Seeing my son again is the Keeper's doing. Yet he's changed from the dynamic, charismatic man who charmed people with his stories, and inspired them with his talk about the Keeper. Legalis has dampened his fire, as if a wet blanket has been thrown over him. It's not as though his faith is weak, but his willingness to share has faded.

Which makes me think of someone who *has* the fire. Oria longs to share, but she's on a trajectory leading to trouble that scares me.

Scares me into silence? I'm not sure. I feel like I'm drifting from moment to moment with one day fading into the next, like I'm moving and talking, but not fully thinking or feeling. I'm living without purpose. An old woman with nothing to offer.

Except my dreams.

**

Once we're seated for breakfast I say, "I had two dreams."

"I have lots of dreams," Lieb says. "Sometimes I wake up laughing."

"This was not that kind of dream, Lieb," I say. And I know I've certainly never had that reaction to any of my dreams.

"Nana has important dreams," Helsa says. "They usually mean something."

"When was the last time you had one of these?" Devin asks.

"It's been a while." I look at Oria. "The last time led me to Oria — when she was still called Cashlin."

"So who is this one leading you to?" Rand asks.

"A woman, sick in bed."

"None of us are sick." Lieb says.

"I didn't recognize her."

Elum is suddenly interested. "Could she be Glynis, Helsa's mistress?"

"It could be. I don't know for sure since I've never met her."

"Did she have graying hair and pretty eyes?" Helsa asks. "Was her bed cover brown with metallic threads running through it?"

"This is where it gets hard. My dreams are fleeting. Details are often unclear."

"It still sounds like her," Helsa says.

"Anything else?" Elum asks.

"A man snuck into her room."

"A robber?" Oria asks.

"I didn't see him take anything. She was moaning in pain and he just stood there. He didn't help."

"Who is the man?" Oria asks.

"Her husband," Elum says.

"How do you know?" I ask.

He shakes the question away. "If the woman is Glynis, the man is Varo. I've heard he's not a nice man."

"I'll agree with that," Helsa says. "He makes me nervous. He doesn't seem to like her much."

It starts to make sense. "You said he bought a bag of something secretively. . . could it be poison? Would he poison her?"

Elum stands, clearly agitated. "I wouldn't put it past him."

"Do you know him?"

"I know *of* him."

"So what do we do about it?" Devin asks. "What *can* we do?"

"Can I tell Glynis about your dream?" Helsa asks.

"I wouldn't." Oria shakes her head. "She's the Head Notable. You're accusing her husband of a heinous crime."

"Oria's right," Devin says. "You need proof."

"How do we get that?" Helsa asks. "I'm just a worker, and I'm getting close to being done with the mural."

"Paint slower," I say.

Elum starts to pace.

Then I think of something. "Elum, do you know someone who could check into it? Check into Varo?"

He stops pacing and blinks. I see his mind working. "I think I might. I need to go." He heads toward the door.

"But what should *I* do today?" Helsa asks him.

"Act normal and keep your eyes open." He leaves us.

"This is serious," Rand says. "An assassination attempt against the Head Notable?"

My head swims. "I hope Elum can alert the right authorities."

I realize I never told any of them about the second part of my dream, where I'm put in a small room, like a cell.

I'll save it for later. One crisis at a time.

**

Me, Rand, and Lieb head to work. But when I reach the ladder I realize I have a problem. Without Elum I'm stuck. I'm not sure I can wind the clocks without him.

As Lieb walks on, Rand sees my predicament. "Want me to help with the ladder, Solana?"

I glance at his bum leg.

"*You'll* have to climb it," he says, "but between the two of us we can move it. And I can hold it steady."

It's a plan—that works. We quickly find a rhythm. I know I'm going to be sore later because of all the climbing, balancing, and stretching, but it will be pain caused by hard work. There's satisfaction in that. I'm sure Rand is hurting right now too. He's not used to walking so much, or standing so long.

Surprisingly, we reach the halfway point early. It's time to break for lunch and Elum is still not back. I notice Rand has no food with him. "We can share a lunch," I say.

"I'd like that," he says.

We sit on some steps in the shade, but since we're sharing, we're quickly done eating. I notice the door leading to the Workers nearby. I haven't visited them in nearly a week—since Nixi chased me off. Do they know what happened on Judging Day? Do they know Yair and Berit?

I feel guilty for not even thinking of them. I have good reasons with all that's been going on, yet I feel like I've abandoned them.

But now's my chance to be brave like Oria. With Elum gone it's the perfect time.

"Rand? How would you like to meet some special people?"

"Always."

"Come with me."

When we get to the decrepit door he balks. "It looks abandoned. Are you sure it's all right if we go in?"

"Probably not." Yet I feel driven to do *something*. To share *something*.

Rand follows me inside, manages the spiral stairs, and walks down the hallway to the door, with light beyond. He gasps when we enter the workroom. "Wow. Look at this."

Everyone looks up. "Solana!" Miri comes to greet me. "We were wondering if you'd come back. After Nixi . . ."

"I shouldn't have been gone so long." I nod at Rand. "This is my friend, Rand. Rand, this is Miri. We worked together in Regalia." I sweep my hand to include the others in the room. "Everyone here came from Regalia. They are all believers."

"That's wonderful," he says. "The Exiled can use more people."

"We were part of the Exiled," Miri says. "But we can't be anymore. We're stuck down here."

"I'm so sorry," Rand says.

Zir scowls at him. "You're a Marked Man. You—especially you— shouldn't be down here."

Rand takes a step back. "I mean no harm."

Zir is so rude. "Rand is more of a believer than you or I," I say. "Behave yourself."

Zir shrugs.

Miri tries to make amends. "Ignore him. It's good to see anyone new."

"Thank you," Rand says.

"Any news from up-top?" Miri asks.

"You haven't heard about Judging Day?" I ask.

"No," Miri says. "There was another Circle?"

I tell them about it, about Berit's horrendous death.

"We knew her!" a woman says. "She and her father were neighbors. How dare they kill that sweet girl!"

I'm about to tell them about the tendrils of light leaving Berit and weaving heavenward, but a young girl asks, "Would we be sent to the Circle if we try to leave?"

"Of course we would," Zir says. "There is no mercy here."

I hate his defeatist attitude. "Remember the Relics I gave you? 'Fear not for the Keeper is with you always.' Ask him for help and he'll make you courageous."

Zir harrumphs. "Easy for you to say. We'd pretty much forgotten about the Circles until you brought them up again."

"Sorry," I say. "But you wanted news from up-top."

"Not that kind of news," a girl says.

"We have a decent life down here," a man says. "So what if we can't go anywhere? What's known is safer than the unknown."

A few others imply they won't risk leaving. They'd rather stay and work; stay and be prisoners.

Rand shakes his head. "Your situation isn't right."

"It is what it is," Zir says.

Rand pulls a few papers from his pocket and sorts through them. "Here. Maybe this Relic will help." He hands it to Miri.

She reads it aloud: "'The Keeper has set us free! Don't be slaves of the laws.'"

A powerful Relic, but Rand is treading on dangerous ground.

Miri hands it back to Rand. "These may be good words, but we have no choice but to be slaves to the laws. The Keeper saying we're free doesn't really mean much."

"Unless he comes down here and leads us out," Zir says.

Their expressions show people mired in the throes of survival. I can't argue the intangible with those living in a very real tangible.

I realize a lot of time has passed. I need to get back to work before Elum comes back and can't find me. "We're sorry to have interrupted your day."

Rand nods, and says, "I'll be back."

"I'm not sure either of you should come again," Zir says. "No offense, but you being here might get *us* in trouble."

Rand takes this in a moment, then repeats, "I'll be careful. But I'll be back."

We go out the same way we came in. "We need to get them out of there," he says. "We need to set them free."

"Now *there's* a way to get us both arrested," I say. "I'm an old woman and you're a cripple. We're hardly the Keeper's first choice to spark a revolution."

He grins at me. "I have nothing else to do."

**

When Rand and I get back to work Elum is nowhere to be found. It isn't until I'm winding the last clock that he shows up.

"Good timing," I say. "Pun intended. Did you find out anything about Varo?"

"I tried, but no. I couldn't talk to who I wanted to talk to." He notices Rand. "You've been helping Solana all day?"

"I have."

"I owe you. I owe you both."

I'm glad he acknowledges that his absence was a hardship. "Did you find anyone who can help the Head Notable in case what we think will happen actually happens?"

He runs his hands through his hair. "No one. Our access is limited."

"We still need proof Varo is poisoning her," Rand says.

"Isn't it proof enough that she's sick all the time and doesn't get well?" I say.

Rand points his crutch toward the Notable area. "Varo needs to be caught in the act. Like you saw in your dream."

Technically, I didn't see him get caught. I just saw a man sneak into her room.

"I think Helsa is our best bet at being our eyes and ears," Elum says.

"I don't like the idea of my granddaughter being put in harm's way."

"She's the only one who's in the room with Glynis."

"But she's almost done with the mural."

"As Glynis is almost done."

We head home.

I wish someone had a solid plan

**

Devin comes in with some slices of ham the guards at the jail were throwing away.

Meat is such a rarity. We carefully divide it equally between the seven of us. Everyone takes small bites, savoring it.

"I could eat a thousand bites of this," Lieb says.

He'll have to settle for three.

There's very little chitchat. Elum takes the lead. "Did you see anything today, Helsa?"

"Nothing unusual. Kal brought her lunch but Glynis didn't eat much of it. She was feeling real poorly today. Didn't even talk much."

"Kal," Elum says. "You saw her and Varo talking the other day, yes?"

"I did."

Devin eats his last bite of ham. "Could Kal be putting it in her food?"

"She has access," Helsa says. "I haven't seen her putting anything in her food in the room, but maybe she does it in the kitchen?"

"Have you ever been to the kitchen?" Oria asks.

Helsa shakes her head. "When Kal brings it in, I eat *my* lunch."

"In the room with her?" Rand asks.

"Usually. Except when her husband comes in. Then I go up-top to eat outside." She shudders. "He gives me the creeps."

"If he's a murderer, rightfully so," I say.

"I don't want you in the room with him," Devin says. "Whenever Varo comes in, you leave. You understand, daughter?"

Helsa nods.

Elum shakes his head. "I'm afraid I have to contradict you, Devin. Helsa *has* to be in the room as much as possible. She's our witness, and in a way, Glynis's protector. The Head Notable shouldn't be left alone."

Helsa doesn't look enthused. "Elum's probably right."

"Which keeps her safe for the moment, but not the long term," Elum says.

"And if Helsa's there and sees something," I say, "who's going to believe her word against a Notable?"

"That's a good point," Rand says.

"If I confront him, he might hurt me," Helsa says.

"Another good point," Rand says.

"Can't you get the Fault Finders to arrest Varo on suspicion?" Devin asks. "They seem to arrest everyone else without much cause."

"Can a Notable get a Fault?" Lieb asks.

"No to both," Elum says simply. "They are above the law. They *are* the law."

"Does that mean Varo can do whatever he wants?" Helsa asks.

Elum thinks about this for a moment. "In the end I think the Judge has the final say."

"So no Notable has ever broken a law?" Oria asks.

"If they did, they wouldn't tell us," Elum says.

"They make the laws," I say.

"For the Masses," Devin says. "But not for themselves?"

Elum shrugs. "Not for themselves."

Helsa pokes around at her last bite of ham, then puts it in Lieb's bowl. He happily eats it. "I just thought of something. If the food is already poisoned when Kal brings it in, then it's too late for me to catch anyone. I need to find a way into the kitchen. Maybe I'll see something suspicious."

"That's a very good idea," Elum says.

"Can you do that?" I ask.

She hesitates, as if she's having second thoughts. "I . . . I can try."

I'm so proud of my granddaughter. She's braver than I'll ever be.

Chapter Twenty-Nine

Helsa

I'm nervous.

I'm comfortable coming and going in the Notable area, and I feel at ease spending my days in Glynis's room. But today . . . knowing that my family and friends want me to sneak around, get into the kitchen, and look for evidence of poison?

I'm no spy. I'm not at all brave. I'm too young for this.

A few short months ago I was doing embroidery in a clothing factory and living under Nana's care. I'm a follower, not an adventurer.

Or am I?

The other day, I *did* venture into the tunnels by myself. That was kind of brave. Even a bit dangerous. I met the Tunnel Man all by myself.

Which means I can do this. I have to do this. Glynis can't die. And I'd love to see a brute like Varo be held accountable. I'd volunteer to take a swing at him in the Cudgeling Circle.

Kal opens the door for me. She's never warmed up to me, even though we're about the same age.

Without exchanging a word I go to Glynis's bedroom. I knock and wait to hear "Come in."

Glynis is always the first to say, "Good morning." Sometimes she's sitting up in bed, and sometimes she's lying down. I can usually tell by the tone of her voice how I will find her today.

Today I hear nothing. I put an ear to the door and still hear nothing. I knock again, and when there's no answer I crack open the door and find her cocooned in the covers.

"Good morning, mistress," I say.

When she doesn't respond, I think the worst.

"Mistress?" I say again.

Again, no answer.

I am just about to tap her shoulder, when she moves. At least she's alive.

She turns on her side, and opens an eye. "Helsa."

"Morning, mistress. Are you all right?"

She nods weakly and closes her eyes to go back to sleep. Has she been poisoned this morning? I step away when Kal comes in with breakfast, a gruel of some sort. I pretend to stir paint, but I watch her to see if she adds anything to the bowl.

She doesn't, but that doesn't vindicate her. It only increases my need to get into the kitchen.

Glynis refuses the food. "I'm not hungry," she says, waving it away.

"You have to eat, mistress. You need to keep up your strength."

Glynis sighs, sits up in bed, and eats a bite. Kal prods her to eat more. She makes it through three more bites, making a face every time.

It makes sense that poison would taste bad.

Glynis refuses any more and Kal finally takes the tray away. Glynis falls back on her pillows with a groan. I feel so bad for her. We have to stop whatever evil is hurting her.

And then she suddenly lurches for the bowl that's never far away. She wretches into it. I bring her a towel. She pats her mouth and moans. "I'm getting very tired of this."

"I'm sure you are. I . . . could it be the food, or something in the food that disagrees with you?"

She eyes me a moment. "It's the same food I've eaten all my life. I don't see how it could hurt me now."

I see an opening. "I'll get you some broth. Or tea."

"Just call Kal."

"Maybe it's something in the way they prepare it. I'll go get it myself." I leave before she tells me not to.

Though I've never been to the kitchen, I know its general location. I nearly run into Kal as I turn a corner. I see the kitchen ahead.

"What are you doing back here?" she asks.

"The mistress threw up her breakfast. She wants some broth and tea."

She waves her hand at me. "I'll get it."

"She asked *me* to get it."

Kal cocks her head and looks at me warily. "Why would she do that?"

"Because I was there. Because she trusts me."

It's the wrong thing to say. "Are you implying she doesn't trust me?"

I quickly backtrack. "Not at all. I was simply there. I helped her . . . clean up. You're so busy, it only makes sense that I should help more."

Her face softens. "I suppose. I do have other things to do."

I follow her into the kitchen where an extremely fat man sits with his feet up, napping.

"Bog. Wake up!" she says none too gently.

He opens one eye, then slowly shifts to wakefulness, obviously feeling no need to impress me. "Whatcha want now?"

With a flip of her hand, Kal passes the question to me. "Apparently, the mistress wants broth and tea."

He groans as he stands. "It's always something."

Perhaps Nixi and Varo are demanding, but I know Glynis is not. Or maybe Bog just likes to complain. I'm guessing the latter.

I smell chicken in a pot on the fire. I haven't had chicken since Regalia, and even there, it was a rare treat.

But then Varo steps into the room and does a double-take at seeing me. "Well, well. Who do we have here?"

I look down. I don't want any interaction with him, not even the exchange of a look.

When I don't respond he says, "No matter," and looks at Kal. "Come with me, girl. I need you."

Although I detest his presence, him calling Kal away is well-timed, for that gives me a chance to talk to Bog.

He points to a cup and saucer. "Make yerself useful," he says. "There's tea in the tin. Water's in the kettle."

I get out a cup and saucer, and take the lid off the tea tin. The crushed leaves could easily mask poison herbs. How would anyone know?

"Have yerself a cup if ya want," Bog says.

"No thank you."

"Suit yerself." He stirs the chicken in the pot, then sits again. He's a ponderous man, obviously used to eating freely.

"I hear yer painting somethin' on a wall."

"A garden," I say. "To cheer up the mistress."

"Yeah," he says, picking at his teeth. "Even beyond being sick, she could use some cheerin'."

"Why do you say that?"

He studies my face a moment. "Not sure I should say. I don't knows you from squat."

"I understand," I say. "But you can be assured I've grown to care about the mistress. I want her to be well and happy. All of Legalis needs her back in her position as Head Notable."

"I'd prefers it. I like how she does things more than how her stand-in does." He shudders.

"What's his name again?" I ask.

"Ivar. Between him and Varo they don't give the mistress a stitch of relief."

I'm glad he brought up Varo. "Her husband . . . I've only had contact with him a few times, but . . . he makes me nervous."

"With intent and good reason." Bog moves to the fire and stirs the chicken pot again, then glances past me to the doorway and lowers his voice. "What he and Kal have on the side makes me cringe in my capers," he says.

"Really?" I try to keep my face neutral.

"Fer some reason she's totally smitten with 'im, like she's his beck 'n call girl. In fact, if truth be a boiling bubble, it wasn't until he took a fancy to her that the mistress started to get sick."

I keep my voice low. "That sounds suspicious."

His bushy eyebrows rise. "Are youse sayin' what I think yer saying?"

I have no reason to trust Bog, yet my gut says he's an upright guy. I keep my answer vague, just in case. "I think I am," I say.

He runs a towel over his sweaty forehead. "Mighty soup and crackers. I've had a sliver of a slice of a notion about that, but I wouldn't let meself think it. But that could explain why she's been sick so long."

"Yes, it would." My time alone with him might be short. I have to risk confiding in him. "The other day I saw Varo and Kal talking secretly and he gave her a small, drawstring bag of something."

His eyes widen. "A tan bag?"

My heart skips a beat. "Have you seen it?"

He goes to a cupboard and pulls out a large sugar bowl with a lid. Inside is the bag. "Kal said it was special medicine."

I carefully remove the bag and take a whiff of it. It smells pungent. "So you've seen her put this in the food of the mistress?"

He cocks his head, thinking. "Of course. Didn't think two spoons about it. But thinking now . . . it's the second bag she's brought in."

"So she ran out of the first one?"

His scratches his forehead. "Peas a plenty, she did!"

I get an idea. I grab a napkin and empty the entire bag onto it.

"Let me see it," Bog makes a point not to touch it. "It looks like tea."

It does. And so . . . I fold the napkin of poison as tightly as I can, and put it in my pocket. Then I spoon tea into the drawstring bag, stuff the bag in the sugar bowl, and return the bowl to the cupboard.

"Yer a smart one," Bog says. "If the mistress feels better after this then we'll know."

Speaking of . . . "I need to bring her that broth and tea."

He serves it up for me and puts it on a tray. "What's yer name, girl?"

"Helsa."

He winks at me. "Tis very nice to meet ya, Helsa. Very nice for the mistress too."

I pass Kal in the hall as I walk back to the bedroom. "I'll take that," she says.

"I've got it," I say.

And I do.

**

I don't know much about how the body works, but I do know that Glynis didn't get any sicker during the day—even after eating lunch brought in by Kal. When I start to clean up the paint to head home she even sits up in bed.

"Are you feeling better, mistress?" I ask.

"I am." She seems surprised. "I'm eager to get back to work." She tries to reach a box on her bedside table. "Hand that to me, Helsa. I asked Nixi to bring me something to read but I haven't felt up to it until now."

I hand her the box and she removes the lid. "Essays from past Head Notables is not light reading but it will make me feel useful. Maybe I'll learn something."

As I finish with the supplies, she says, "Hmm. This is interesting."

"What, mistress?"

She glances at me, as if only then remembering I'm there. "I just learned something completely new. And rather surprising."

I'd like to ask her what, but it's not my place. "That's always satisfying," I say.

"Actually, it is. Very."

I gather my brushes and bid her good night. I'm so glad she's feeling better, and her change of health emphasizes the significance of the poison in my pocket.

I hurry home to share my evidence with the others.

**

As soon as everyone is assembled at Papa's, I carefully place the folded napkin in the middle of the table.

"What's that?" Papa asks.

"Poison."

Lieb touches the napkin to unfold it and I bat his hand away. "Don't touch it!"

"How did you get this, child?" Nana asks.

I tell them about going to the kitchen and hitting it off with Bog. "He's no fan of Varo—or Kal either. I mentioned seeing Varo secretly hand her a bag of something and he showed me where it was." I point at the napkin. "*That* was inside. Kal called it medicine—and it's the second bag she's used."

Elum pokes at it with the tip of the fire poker and unwraps it enough to see. "Could it be dried foxglove?"

"Or oleander?" Rand asks.

"Whatever it is, that's very good work, daughter," Papa says. "But what will happen when Kal and Varo find it missing?"

This is the good part. "We substituted tea leaves for the poison. Kal can keep poisoning her, but it won't hurt her anymore. In fact, by the end of the day Glynis was feeling better."

"That's excellent," Elum says. "Very well done."

"Thank you." It feels fantastic to be the hero.

Oria stares at the pile of poison. "You've stopped the poisoning—which is admirable—but how do we officially connect Varo and Kal to it?"

Leave it to Oria to bring me down.

I cross my arms. "I did my part. Let someone else handle the rest."

Nana runs her hand along my back. "We are very appreciative, child. You went above and beyond."

"Thank you, Nana."

Elum reaches between us and folds the napkin over the poison. "I'll take it from here," he says.

"What are you going to do?" I don't like the idea of him taking our evidence.

"I'm not sure—exactly. But . . ." He looks at me. "Helsa, I need you to get a note to the Head Notable. Secretly. Can you do that?"

"I can."

"What's the note going to say?" Rand asks.

"I don't know yet," Elum says. "If you'll excuse me, I'll work on it."

He takes the poison with him into the bedroom and closes the door.

"Can we eat now?" Lieb says.

Leave it to Lieb to help us find normal again.

Chapter Thirty

Helsa

When it's time to leave for work the next morning Elum hands me his note for Glynis. "Remember," he says. "Don't let anyone see you give it to her."

"I promise." I turn it over in my hands. I'm disappointed it's sealed with wax. What could someone like Elum have to say to the Head Notable that would make any difference? Yet at the moment it's our only plan.

A short time later, when I knock on the door to Glynis's bedroom, I hear a chipper, "Come in."

She sits on the edge of the bed, her bare feet dangling. "Good morning, Helsa," she says.

"Obviously, it is," I say. "Are you feeling better, Head Notable?"

"Very much so. I don't know what happened, but I'm thankful for it. And I am ready to get back to work. I'm sure Ivar won't be pleased, but so be it."

Instead of immediately going to paint, I remain standing near the door, which causes her to say, "Is there something else?"

I hand her the note. "Please read this."

"Who's it from?"

"A friend."

She breaks the seal and reads. Her forehead wrinkles. I wish I knew what it said.

"If there's anything I can do . . ." I say.

She rests the note on her leg. "This says to ask you for verification as to what he says. Is it true?"

"I don't know what he said."

Glynis shakes the note. "He says that Varo and Kal are poisoning me."

I'm surprised by how forthright Elum was, but I am glad to confirm. "It's true."

"It also says that you substituted tea for the poison."

"That's also true."

"When did you do this?"

"Yesterday morning when you asked for broth and tea."

She considers this a moment. "So my lunch and dinner contained no poison."

"Which is why you feel better, mistress."

She lets out a huff of air. "That was very brave of you, Helsa."

I fill in some details. "When I saw your husband buying a bag of something, and then secretively give it to Kal, I knew it had to be something bad. I couldn't stand by and watch them kill you."

She scoffs. "I'm very glad you didn't. Was my cook involved?"

"Not at all. Bog wasn't aware, though he was concerned with what else your husband and Kal are do—" I stop myself. This is beyond the scope of the current issue.

She raises her hand as if to say there's no need for me to continue. "I suspected as much. Kal is not his first dalliance, nor his last. As for the poison . . . ever since I achieved my Head position, Varo has been jealous that I usurped him."

"I don't know the process, but was he up for your position?" And is he in line to succeed her?

She scoffs. "He was a contender only in his own mind." She stands. "Since I don't want Kal anywhere near me, please help me get dressed. I have people to see."

I feel honored that she's confided in me. And for her to dress in front of me reveals a large measure of trust.

As soon as she's dressed she asks, "How do I look?"

"Healthy and strong, Head Notable," I say.

"And very, very angry." She goes to the door, then turns back to me. "You saved my life, Helsa. I will never forget you, or what you did."

I will never forget it either. Or *her*. She's amazing.

**

Glynis does not come back the rest of the day. Separately, Varo and Kal stop in her room, looking for her.

I can honestly tell them I don't know where she is, but find immense satisfaction knowing that Glynis will make things right.

Near the end of the workday, Nixi stops in for a second time. "My mother still isn't back?"

"No, mistress."

She looks a bit panicked. "Being gone all day . . . is she all right? I don't want her doing too much."

"She's quite all right," I say. "She's feeling much better."

Her eyes brighten. "I noticed she was feeling better last night. I'm glad her strength remained. Will she be at dinner? I miss sharing meals with her."

"I don't know. I—"

We hear commotion and loud voices coming from the main rooms. We go to see what it is.

Four masked Fault Finders have stormed into the house. Two of them have grabbed Varo.

"Father?" Nixi says.

He ignores her and tries to pull away from them. "Let me go, you idiots! You'll be sorry you ever . . ."

The third Fault Finder looks at Nixi and says, "Where is the maid named Kal?"

At just that moment, Kal comes out of the kitchen. When she sees the Fault Finders, she runs back. Two Fault Finders follow her and she's dragged into the foyer, screaming.

"Varo, do something!" she yells.

"What's going on here?" Nixi asks. "I demand you let them go!"

Varo squirms against their grip. "Do you know who I am? Do you know who my wife is?"

Suddenly, Glynis walks into the house like a queen entering her castle. "Do *you* know who your wife is, Varo?" She stops in front of him and roughly pinches his cheek. "I am the Head Notable, and I order you under arrest." She lets go. "Take them to jail! Up-top, through the streets so everyone can see."

"No!" Nixi yells, running toward her father.

"You won't get away with this!" Varo screams.

Glynis grabs Nixi's upper arm. "You don't know the full story, daughter. Let them go."

"But what did they do?"

Glynis closes the door behind them and glances at me. "They poisoned me."

"What?"

She links her arm with Nixi's. "Come to my room and I'll explain everything." She smiles at me. "Again, you have my deepest thanks, Helsa. You can head home now so you can watch all the excitement from the street."

I hurry out to do just that.

**

I follow the screams of Varo. If he would stop shouting, his arrest would have far less impact. With him yelling, everyone stops what they're doing. Everyone sees.

A contrast to Varo is Kal, who walks between two Fault Finders in silence with her head down. I almost feel sorry for her; a stupid girl who

191

let herself dabble where she shouldn't. What did she hope to gain by taking up with Varo?

But maybe Varo didn't give her a choice.

One more reason to hate him.

If they're heading to Devin's jail, they're taking the long way around. I suspect Glynis ordered the route for maximum exposure.

It surprises me that people aren't jeering. It appears that even in his shame Varo is a Notable of power. I understand why the Masses would be foolhardy to celebrate his arrest. Yet they're not silent either, as they talk amongst themselves. The Legalis grapevine has been lit on fire.

I spot Nana and Elum and join them. "I don't know what you said in your note, Elum, but it worked."

"Glynis did all this?" he asks.

"After reading your note she immediately left and was gone all day. When she returned she brought Fault Finders with her." I motion toward the scene playing out. "And so, this."

When he smiles I realize how seldom I've seen him happy. "Now Varo will finally get what he deserves," he says.

"What else has Varo done?" Nana asks.

"He exists. That's bad enough."

I can tell there's more he's not telling us.

"Come on," Elum says. "I want to see him enter the jail."

He leads the way and Nana and I follow. "You did good, child," she says. "Justice is being done."

I'm just glad my part is over.

**

At dinner everyone is eager to ask Papa about Varo.

"Is he in a cell like everyone else?" Rand asks.

"He is. They're all the same. There is no good or better cell." He pours water for all of us. "He's very loud. He won't stop ranting about how he's been done wrong. I heard the guards talking about knocking him out to get him to shut up, but they wouldn't dare."

"What happens next?" Oria asks.

"I have no idea. No Notable has ever been in jail."

"Glynis won't go easy on him," I say. "She was practically gleeful when he was arrested."

"You say she arranged it?" Nana asks.

I look at Elum to share his part in it — the note — but he doesn't say anything. I wonder why not. "She did arrange it. She was strong today without the poison in her system. Once she got evidence that Varo and Kal were guilty . . . she was gone all day arranging the arrest."

"I wonder who she went to?" Papa asks. "The Judge?"

Lieb shudders. "Can people actually talk to him? I wouldn't ever do that. I don't want to ever, ever see him—especially up close."

"Varo is where he belongs," Elum says.

"I wish I could see Glynis right now," I say. "I'd like to know how she feels."

"Me too," Elum says. "Definitely me too."

His enthusiasm seems a bit over the top. "You act like you know her."

He's flustered, but quickly recovers. "Of course not. I just wish you could see her too. She obviously trusts you and owes you a great debt."

I know there's a lot he's not telling us.

Chapter Thirty-One

Glynis

I'm glad for time alone with my daughter.

I hate that I've upset Nixi with her father's arrest. She used to be a daddy's girl, and in his defense Varo has been good to her — all things considered.

Nixi and I sit beside each other in my bedroom, my arm around her shoulders. Her crying has stopped, and I know her tears are rooted in shock, fear, panic . . . and shame.

When she speaks, it's shame that's on her mind. "Why did you have him paraded through the streets, Mama? Couldn't you have used one of the tunnels?"

"I could have," I admit. "But the members of the Law Commission know your father well. Although they were shocked by my claims and the evidence Helsa provided, they quickly accepted his actions as fact." I tap her arm. "Your father's arrogance is well-known."

"I know," Nixi says. "I also know it's kept him from rising up through the ranks."

I'm relieved she sees it.

"Did you ask them to be merciful?" she asks.

I did not. "How many weeks have I been in this bed? Did your father show *me* mercy?"

She shakes her head, conceding the point.

"He wanted me dead."

She sighs deeply. "And Kal . . . why would she be part of his plot?"

"I expect she had no choice," I say. "He's the one with the power. And it wasn't the first time he forced his wishes on vulnerable girls."

"So what now?" Nixi asks.

I lift my arm from her shoulders so I can fully see her face. "Unfortunately, I don't know. The Commission looked through records to find past precedent for such a crime by a Notable."

"And?"

"There is none. In fact, the only crime on record since the Before Time was some finagling of Commission benefits. It was handled privately without getting the Masses involved."

Nixi stares across the room at the mural — which is almost done and is already very lovely.

"If not for Helsa, I might have died."

Nixi nods. "I've often thought about the day I saw her painting a tree on a wall instead of just whitewashing it. I can't believe I asked her to paint a mural so randomly. I have no idea where that idea came from."

"I'm glad you thought of it."

"Without Helsa being here, you'd be dying. Or worse, be dead."

It's a sobering thought that I'm still trying to wrap my head around.

Nixi puts her hand on my knee. "Why did Father want you dead?"

I have no definitive answer for her. "Pride?"

She nods. "He does hate that you rose above him. He hates that you have regular meetings with the Judge, and that you achieved something he could never hope to achieve."

I put my hand atop hers. I'm relieved she understands. How could I have been so blind?

"What are you thinking?" she asks.

"I'm thinking that my husband of twenty-four years hated me enough to try and kill me."

Nixi lets silence float between us. Then she says, "Did you two ever really love each other? I mean deeply love each other?"

The truth will hurt her, so I lie. "We did, at first. As much as we could in an arranged marriage." I touch her cheek. "And we both love you."

"I hate to say it, but Father's a little hard to love."

I'm glad she sees it too. "I'm not without blame," I say. "I'm ambitious. I could have been more empathetic to his disappointment."

Nixi shakes her head adamantly. "No amount of disappointment or hurt pride excuses him for poisoning you." She rubs her hands over her face as if trying to awaken from a bad dream. "Have you spoken with the Judge about all this?"

"I have not." I was afraid he'd object to Varo's arrest.

"So *he* didn't order Father's arrest?"

"He did not."

"Are you going to talk to him?"

"I've arranged to meet him in a couple of days."

"That's a long time to wait."

"Let's just say I'm not his first priority."

"I don't envy you that conversation."

"Neither do I."

"Can I visit him? Father?" Nixi asks.

I'm a little hurt. "Do you want to?"

She shrugs. "I think it's the right thing to do."

I can't deny her. "You do what you need to do, dear girl."

We will both do what we need to do.

**

I'm restless.

But our house offers the wrong kind of solitude. I'd sent Helsa home, arranged for Varo and Kal to be in jail, and Nixi is visiting her father. I pace in my bedroom. I sit. I pace again.

Then I realize I need a different kind of solitude.

And so I leave the house, turn right, and enter the tunnels. A few Notables are out and about. They look nervous when they greet me. There's pity in their eyes, and a slight look of condemnation. How dare I allow a Notable to be arrested? How dare I allow this to happen? Or in a few cases, some might be upset that Varo failed.

I know I'm not universally loved by my peers. No one is. But as a person who's risen to the highest position in the land — besides the Judge — I'm not considered one of *them* anymore. I'm set apart. Ostracized by rank and power.

I shouldn't complain. I sought the position, but it wasn't because I craved power as much as I craved purpose. Merely being a Notable wasn't enough. The society of privilege began to grate on me, as did the forced camaraderie and inane chitchat of our gatherings. I know for a fact that many of my set never go up-top to mingle with the Masses. They are content to wallow in idle pleasures at the detriment and waste of their lives. Yet not to be a hypocrite, I admit I don't go up-top often either.

My, I'm testy today.

I turn into a narrow tunnel I know is rarely used. In fact, in my periodic visits, I've never seen anyone there.

Which is perfect.

I discovered the tunnel by accident when I was Nixi's age. Although I could have shared it with friends, I never did, preferring to have a secret from everyone else. I always felt adventurous going someplace so mysterious, and known only to me.

After assorted jigs and jogs I see *the* door ahead. I remember the strange tightness in my stomach as I opened the door for the first time. But when I stepped into the blinding light there was something thrilling about being fully *outside* that appealed to me. I never stayed out long, but the act of defiance and courage always helped me feel better about whatever I needed to feel better about.

I'm hoping to get the same results today.

I open the door and step into the desert, raising my hand to block the sunlight. The heat greedily enshrouds me, and I draw a deep breath to counter its oppressiveness.

So be it. Better to be out here in the light and heat than in the shadows and chill of home.

I start to walk the perimeter of Legalis, heading toward the shady side first. I have to veer around sand drifts that block a direct path. I see occasional small holes in the dunes, the work of snakes and rodents, and who knows what else. I don't begrudge their existence. This is their territory, not mine.

I lift up the skirt of my green silk caftan, and wish I wasn't wearing sandals. The feel of grit and sand under my feet is unpleasant. I should have thought this through better.

I see a boulder up ahead and sit in order to empty out my shoes — which will surely get filled as soon as I start walking again. Maybe the walking part is the problem. I'd best do my thinking sitting down.

I lean my head back and breathe deeply. My innards are still not back to normal. I'm so thankful Helsa saved me.

I'm saved, but my life is a mess. I'm not looking forward to talking to the Judge. Varo betrayed me and is a disgrace to all Notables. I'm not sure whether I should approach it as a domestic problem or with a wider scope. There's a good chance the Judge will choose to make an example of Varo. After all, we can't have Notables poisoning each other, can we?

But that might involve a Judging Day. And since the accused doesn't endure the punishment, but rather a member of their family . . .

"Would I volunteer?" I say aloud.

"You shouldn't do that."

I bolt to standing and turn toward the voice. A very tall, bald man stands ten feet behind me. "Who are you?"

"A friend. It appears you need a friend right now."

"You don't know me, or what I need."

"I don't, but I represent someone who does. Someone who knows you well and cares for you very much."

"Who's that?"

He pauses, looks toward the sky as he takes a deep breath, then looks back at me. "The Keeper."

Him again. "I don't believe in him."

The man shrugs. "That is *your* choice, Glynis. The Keeper believes in free will and doesn't force himself on anyone. But I promise you he's quite real."

"You know my name. How?"

"He shared it with me. Doesn't that prove he is real?"

"Not really. I'm well known in Legalis. You need to find another way to prove it."

He smiles and wags his finger at me. "Skepticism is allowed and your challenge doesn't surprise him. You got where you are by being a pragmatist and a problem solver."

"Yes, I did. I deal in facts, not . . ." I wave my hand in the air, unable to come up with the right word.

"Spiritual deities who created the entire universe?"

My eyebrows rise. "That's a big declaration."

"It's a big truth."

"Again, I ask you to prove it."

The man nods and sweeps an arm to encompass the desert. "This did not come to exist by accident."

I scoff. "If the Keeper *is* the creator, I hardly think a hot, dry, and worthless expanse of nothingness is anything to be proud of."

"It has its uses," he says.

"I can't imagine what."

"You'll understand. One day." He looks up. "How about the sky with its sun, moon, clouds, and stars? The beauty of the sunrise and sunset? Do those suit your vision of something worthy of creation?"

"I've never seen an actual sunrise or sunset."

"Ah," he says. "The disadvantage of living underground. You need to come out here to see it sometime. Venture beyond your *known*." He looks past me, then points. "In fact, I think you're here just in time. Come with me."

We return the way I'd come, and walk past the door. I see pink along the horizon—which is shocking. Such color when I'm only used to gray and blue is impressive. But I keep my pleasure to myself. "I see it. It's very beautiful."

"Not that," he says, waving at the color. "That's nothing. Come a little further. We're nearly there."

We turn a corner. I stop. I gasp. The colors overwhelm me. Not just pink or blue, but orange and gold and purple and violet and cobalt and and and . . .

He laughs at me. "I knew you'd like it. The Keeper enjoys painting the sky. He makes it different every day. No two have ever been the same—nor will they be throughout eternity. He loves variety."

The colors radiate through my soul, warming me, stirring something deep within me.

I don't want to be emotional about what I see, but I press my hand against my chest, trying to keep my reaction at bay. Logically, I know this man hasn't proven the existence of the Keeper with a few pretty colors, and yet . . . "It can't be random," I whisper.

He leans toward me and whispers back. "Because it's not. Nothing is random. All things were created by the Keeper with deliberate intention and care."

"We are creative because he is creative?" I'm surprised by my own words. I don't remember thinking them before saying them.

"That's quite insightful, Glynis. Creativity is one way we connect with him and him to us."

I shake the idea away. "But I'm not creative. People like Helsa are creative with her painting, but I'm —"

"Creativity goes beyond art. You are creative with ideas, large concepts, musings beyond what is set before you."

I shake my head. "You've got the wrong Notable. I don't deal in musings."

"Didn't you come out here to muse; to think?"

He's got me there. "I simply suffered a temporary moment of weakness."

"You are not weak for seeking solitude and help."

"I am not seeking help. I need to deal with this on my own."

"That's one way to do it. But the Keeper *will* help you. All you have to do is ask."

I shake my head adamantly. I need to turn the conversation toward something else. "A creative person would be someone who could imagine what doesn't exist. I'm pragmatic and practical. As the Head Notable I'm part of the Law Commission and work to make Legalis run smoothly."

"Even if the laws you help create are wrong and destructive?"

I'm shocked by his words. "Now you're talking insurrection, which certainly contradicts a Keeper who protects and provides."

"So Helsa's words stuck with you."

Another shock. "How do you know what — ?"

He points skyward.

I wave him off. "What you're saying has no bearing in my life. It's too out of the ordinary, too . . ."

"Extraordinary?"

He's turned my own words against me. And he's not wrong. If it's true.

He pulls a piece of paper from his pocket. "A gift for you. One to share."

I unfold the page and read aloud: "'The Keeper is the King. His kingdom isn't something you can see. His kingdom is here within you.'"

The man presses his hand to his heart. "In here."

I shake my head. "This makes no sense. If the Keeper is a King then why doesn't he act like one and show himself?"

"He does. In both cases."

"I haven't seen him."

He nods toward the sunset. "Are you sure about that? When you looked at the majesty of the sunset, didn't you feel him in your heart? Didn't you feel *his* majesty?"

Maybe. "But these words say his *kingdom* is in my heart. That doesn't make sense. I need to see walls and borders and —"

"Does your heart have walls and borders?"

He's getting tricky. "No, but —"

"Does your mind have walls and borders?"

I raise my hand to stop him. "No, but my mind and heart are not a kingdom."

"But they are. And if you believe in the Keeper, they are a part of *his* kingdom. His limitless, eternal kingdom."

My mind feels ready to explode. "I need to get back."

"Nixi's not home from seeing Varo yet."

I'm stunned. "You like to shock me with what you know, don't you?"

He grins. "It is rather enjoyable."

I make my own concession. "I will admit that our talk has been interesting."

He does a by-your-leave bow. "All for you, milady."

"I enjoy talking to people who stretch my thinking. Maybe we can speak again?"

"Who knows? Maybe we will."

"Maybe? You don't know?"

"I do not."

"I assumed you could tell the future."

"Only the Keeper is all-knowing. He shares what he wants us to know — when he wants us to know it."

I scoff. "Sounds like the Judge."

The man's face tightens and his voice deepens in anger. "The Keeper is nothing like the Judge! Nothing. It's like comparing a diamond to a piece of dust in the wind."

I raise my hands in surrender. "Understood. I meant no offense."

He nods once.

"But speaking of the Judge . . . I need to go home and figure out what I'm going to say to him to save my husband and my family."

He smiles. "As I mentioned, if you ask, the Keeper can help you with that."

"I'll consider it." I turn in the direction of the door. "Are you coming back in?"

"Not yet." He touches two fingers to his chest. "May the Keeper be with you and guide you."

I don't object to either notion.

Chapter Thirty-Two

Rand

Although I enjoy sleeping on a cot instead of the ground, I miss sleeping under the stars. Or sometimes I'd slip into the Sanctuary at night. It was dark and eerily quiet, but it's also majestic—in a domineering, exhilarating sort of way.

There's so much going on with my family—I feel I can call them family now. For them to take me in, feed me, and now house me? It's more than my own family would've done. More than they did. For when my mother was killed in the Cudgeling Circle for my crime, the few relatives I had wanted nothing to do with me.

Nor I with them. Their lack of support during my time in jail revealed that their loyalty was to the Judge. Perhaps not loyalty, but fear.

I get it. Everyone's afraid. But what a horrible way to live.

I think of the Workers, toiling underground, slaves to the Notables. They won't come up-top because of fear. They won't feel sunshine and breathe fresh air because of fear. They won't rebel because of fear. They won't break free because of fear. They aren't fully living, all because of fear.

Yet, who is?

I've accepted my lot as a Marked Man. At first it was hard to live on the streets, to be shunned by all who saw me, to hear their taunts. I learned to live with it, and as time passed, the Masses did something that was to my benefit: they ignored me. I became invisible. It was a lonely way to live, but I learned to replace my need for human interaction with the spiritual. The more I got to know the Keeper the less I cared about the opinions of the Masses.

Yet ever since I met the Workers, I want more for them—and for me. Actually, I think the way to get more for me is to help them. The more I give the more I get.

I need Relics to share. I haven't received one in a while—though I check the hiding place daily. Which I'm about to do right now.

As soon as I reach the Sanctuary, I slip inside and turn right to check the hiding place. But I immediately stop when I see a man walking away.

I step into the shadows and watch him. Since the sun is just starting to peek through the hole in the ceiling, I can't see his features other than noting his height and build. He's far taller than me and invokes a strength of presence even though his frame is slender. He moves with a determined purpose. To my surprise, he walks into the storeroom.

Down into the land of the Notables he goes? Is he sneaking through the tunnels or is he one of *them*?

Does the provider of the Relics interact with Notables and Fault Finders and who-knows-who in the tunnels of Legalis? I didn't expect that. I always assumed whoever was giving me Relics was one of the Masses. Someone outside authority, someone . . . separate. Special.

I guess there *are* special people among the Notables. The Head Notable and her daughter sound like good people. I shouldn't lump them all together.

Enough pondering. I need to see the Relic he left me.

I look around casually before going to the hiding space and removing the stone. I gasp. Inside isn't one Relic but four. It's like finding treasure.

It's too dark to read in the Sanctuary, so I slip the Relics in my pocket, put the stone back, and go outside. I walk to *my* spot where I exist as a meaningless piece of the landscape. No one has noticed me before and they won't notice me now. But I still have to be careful about reading anything lest the Fault Finders catch me.

I wobble my way to sitting, stealthily put a Relic in my lap, and arrange the fabric of my robe to hide it. I read it: *Don't worry about your life. Can worry make your life a day longer?*

The message is perfect for all of us.

I unfold another one: *You will know the truth, and the truth will set you free.*

This one confuses me. For truth isn't enough to set the Workers free. They need action. They need courage. Neither of which they possess.

I read the other two Relics and marvel at how appropriate they are. I glance up at a clock. I have ten minutes until the first Count. I need to act now.

I put all the Relics in my pocket and hurry off to see the Workers.

**

When I step inside the workroom, I find the Workers arriving for the day.

Zir does a double-take. "Where's Solana?"

"It's just me today."

Miri steps forward. "Is Solana all right?"

"She's fine." I pull out the Relics. "I come bearing messages."

Zir scoffs. "I have work to do." He walks away.

I'm taken aback. Maybe I shouldn't have come here alone.

"I'll listen," Miri says.

"So will we," says an older couple.

The rest ignore me and start to work.

I take out the first Relic and read it aloud — hoping a few of the other Workers will hear the words. "It says, 'Don't worry about your life. Can worry make your life a day longer?'"

"Might not make our life longer but worry keeps us from doing stupid things," Zir says.

And I thought he didn't want to listen.

"Shush, you," the older man says to him. "Don't you ever get weary of being negative all the time?"

"Not really."

"I like the words," the man says. "They make sense."

"They are the Keeper's words. *He* makes sense," I say. "The opposite of worry is hope."

The old woman says, "I gave up on hope a long time ago."

"Hope is here," I say, shaking the Relic. "The Keeper embodies hope." I read another one, "'The Keeper is there to rescue all who are discouraged and have given up hope.'" I marvel at its perfection.

"It does not say that." Miri snatches the Relic from me and reads it to herself. "It does." She looks toward her friends. "It does say that."

The wife wants to read it for herself. "How did the Keeper do that? How did he give us exactly what we needed to hear?"

"Because he knows each of us by name," I say.

The group around me has grown larger. A young woman asks, "Even if he knows our name, no one else does. Everybody's forgotten about us."

"I haven't. Solana hasn't. And the Keeper hasn't. Here. Read another one."

She unfolds it and reads, "'I will give you treasures hidden in dark and secret places. Then you will know that I, the Keeper, have called you by name.'" She lets out a long sigh. "How did you know which ones to give us? That's perfect."

"I didn't know. He did. He provides us what we need."

Zir scoffs. He seems to live to scoff. "This is *not* what we need." He sweeps his hand across their workroom. "There are no treasures here."

"He is the treasure. And he offers a way out." I give him the last Relic, but he flips his hand at it.

The old man takes it from me and reads. "'You will know the truth, and the truth will set you free.'" He hands it to his wife. "Who is this truth?"

"The Keeper is the truth," I say. "He is the keeper of the truth."

"I don't get it," the young girl says.

I've thrown a lot at them this morning. "It's not complicated. The Keeper created you, loves you, and wants to save you."

"Then why doesn't he show himself and do it?" Zir asks. "Right now would be good."

One step forward and two steps back.

"Where's your convenient answer now, Marked Man?" he asks.

"I don't know all the details, I just know that he doesn't want any of his people to be prisoners. He wants you to be free—in body, mind, and heart."

"I'll believe it when I see it." Zir motions to the listeners. "Back to work before a Notable comes in and we're in trouble again."

While the Workers seem reluctant, they all return to their stations. The old man and his wife lag behind. "Don't listen to Zir. Please come as often as you can."

"We like what you bring us," she says.

At least two hearts are open.

I turn to leave and bump into Solana as she walks through the door. "What are you doing here?" she asks me.

"I had some new Relics to share and—"

"These are not your people, Rand. *I* found them!"

I'm confused by her reaction. "I'm not trying to take over, I—"

"But you are! I bring you with me one time and now, here you are, coming without me. It's not right."

"I meant no harm, Solana."

"But you *did* harm! To me!"

Miri rushes toward us. "Quiet, you two. Our supervisor should be here any minute and—"

"What's going on here?"

We all look toward the inner entrance. A man in black has entered the space.

"Who are you?" He strides toward us.

"I'm Rand and—"

"You don't belong here!"

"We mean no harm," Solana says—repeating my words to her.

"This is a restricted area," he says.

I see venom in his eyes and back away toward our exit.

"Guard!" he yells.

Guard?

A guard rushes into the workroom. "Arrest them!"

The guard grabs Solana's arm. But as she resists, I'm still free. She looks at me. "Go, Rand! Go!"

I scramble out the workroom door and manage the spiral stairs as fast as my crippled leg will let me. I don't stop until I slip into an alley.

What just happened? How did my good intentions turn into this catastrophe?

I try to catch my breath. *Think, Rand, think.*

Solana was arrested. Which means they will take her to jail.

Where her son works.

That's where I have to go.

**

By the time I hobble to the jail and ask to see Devin, his mother has already arrived.

I hear commotion down a corridor to the right. I hear Solana yelling, "Let go of me! You have no right . . ."

Her words are muffled by a door closing and a lock latching.

I spot Devin, who stares in the direction of his mother's voice. "Devin!"

He rushes toward me, his face distraught. "Rand, what happened? How did my mother get arrested?"

There are guards around, so I nod toward the street. Devin follows me. "She mentioned your name . . . were you with her?" he asks.

"I was." I lean against my crutch. "It all happened so fast."

"Tell me everything."

The truth isn't pretty. "You know she and I have been helping the Workers, sharing Relics. I went alone today. She came in later and was upset I was there. I guess she considers the Workers her discovery. I didn't mean to upset her."

He waves my apology away. "But why was she arrested?"

"She was mad at me and raised her voice. A supervisor came in and said it was a restricted area. He called a guard to arrest us. He grabbed her but couldn't get us both. She told me to run. So I ran. Then I came here. What will they do to her?"

He stares back at the high slits of the jail cells. "I don't know."

I think through consequences. "Maybe they'll just give her a Fault and let her go. Yet . . . she already has one Fault."

"And being in a restricted area is a serious offense."

Especially for a Marked Man. I'm very lucky I wasn't arrested too.

"What can I do to help?" I ask.

Devin looks at the air between us, shaking his head. "I don't know."

"Maybe if I find Elum? Maybe he'd know what to do?"

He nods. "Please do that. I need to go."

"Tell Solana I'm sorry."

"It's not your fault. She chose to go where she shouldn't have been."

"But if I hadn't been there, she wouldn't have yelled and drawn attention and—"

"We don't have time for blame, Rand. Go find Elum."

I move through the streets with surprising speed considering the events of the day. The need to hurry makes my muscles work better than they should.

I spot Elum coming down a ladder after winding a clock. He flags me down and asks, "Oh no. What's wrong?"

"Solana's been arrested." I tell him everything I know. His anger intensifies the more I say. By the end of my story he's breathing heavily.

"When she wanted to visit the Workers today I told her she was obsessed. I warned her to be discreet. She never should have gone through that door. And now you're involved. They could still arrest you too."

Honestly, I'd never thought of that. "If they do, so be it. I already have a Mark. What more can they do to me?"

"They can do whatever they want to do, Rand."

I know. I *know*. "Devin's with her," I say. "But what can we do? What will happen to her?"

"I'm not sure."

"You sent a note to the Head Notable about Varo and it got him arrested. Can you send one about Solana? To get her out?"

Elum stares up at the clock. "The clocks need winding. I can't just leave."

"I'll help you get the work done. I held the ladder for Solana."

He nods once. "Time is wasting. Let's do it."

Chapter Thirty-Three

Oria

"It's true, Oria," Wyan says as we work the food booth. "I really enjoy working with you."

"And I with you," I say. "You're a big improvement over Trina."

"Such high praise!"

I enjoy our banter, which has evolved from ultra-serious discussions to friendship. I've never really had a friend. As a Patron I socialized with other Patrons—who were my rivals. True friendship didn't thrive in competition. I became friends with Solana, Helsa, and Lieb where we have our faith as our bond. And I was friends with Xian, the Enforcer who helped me in so many ways. I wanted that friendship to grow deeper, but my exile put an end to that option. Actually the restrictions of the Rings of Regalia put an end to it. Patrons weren't allowed romantic relationships. Our marriages were arranged for the good of Regalia. I was set to marry Rowan . . . odd how I haven't thought of him for more than a second since I entered the desert.

"Hello? Oria?" Wyan snaps his fingers in front of my face.

"Sorry. I was lost in thought."

"Good thoughts, I hope."

The way he smiles . . . "Good thoughts of past friends." I smile back at him. "And new ones."

"Are you flirting with me?"

I put my hands on my cheeks—which are hot. "I believe I am."

"Your flirtation is willingly accepted," he says. He points at a man coming toward the booth. "Here's your next victim. I believe the score is four to three in my favor."

"The morning is far from over." I smile at a little girl as she approaches the booth with her mother. "Hello," I say to her especially.

The girl blinks as if I've said something shocking, but says, "Hello."

Ha! We are now tied.

As soon as they leave, Wyan concedes. "Kids shouldn't count."

"Of course they count. And as I told you, kindness begets kindness."

"And as I told *you*, we don't do kindness in Legalis."

"Until now," I say.

He bows like a gallant. "Until the kind and beneficent Oria graced us with her presence."

I'm happy for this second compliment, but also know he's teasing. Still, it's kind of nice.

**

We lower the awning to break for lunch. I start to sit on the ground behind the booth, but Wyan says, "Nope. Stand up. I have something to show you."

"What?"

"It's not a what, as much as it's a where. Come with me."

He leads me down streets and alleys that I've never traveled before. He finally tells me to turn onto one particular alley. "You go first," he says.

Halfway down I realize it's a dead end. I face him. If he wasn't my friend I might be afraid. "We must have taken a wrong turn."

"Not at all." He turns toward a wall and pushes on it. A door that *was* virtually invisible opens inward. "After you," he says.

I step inside warily. Sunlight shines on narrow spiral steps leading upward. I steady myself with my hand on the wall as I hold up my robe so I don't trip. The stairs keep going up, far beyond another story.

"How far does this go?" I ask.

"Far enough."

With each step I get more nervous. This is obviously a place unknown by the Masses. Should I be there with Wyan? With anyone?

Finally we reach the top. My gaze is immediately drawn to the dome of sky overhead. I take a deep breath, as if only now can I fully breathe.

Wyan motions me over to a chest-high wall. I go to its edge and marvel at the impressive view of the desert. "Oh my," I say, then feel dumb for my meager reaction, for the view deserves so much more. "It's spectacular."

"That, it is."

I look away from the view and see that we're standing on a narrow walkway, leading in both directions. While the outer wall is chest-high, the inner wall is taller than me. "What purpose does this pathway serve?" I ask. "Who uses it?"

"No one."

I raise my eyebrows. "Except you?"

He shrugs. "I imagine it *had* a use, but it's long forgotten."

"So how do you know about it?"

He rests his forearms on the outer wall. "Just lucky I guess."

Which doesn't answer my question, but I'm too exhilarated by the view to press him. "How far does it go?"

"All the way around Legalis. It rims the perimeter."

"I don't remember seeing such a walkway from the street."

"From there it just looks like a wall. Except . . ." He walks ahead ten feet, and points at the inner wall. "Look."

There's a narrow, horizontal slit that I look through. "You can see the street." I think of the ramifications of this. "Are there slits like this all the way around? So people can be watched?"

"There are."

I look ahead and behind. "Do the authorities use these to spy on the Masses? Are there watchers up here now?"

"You're missing the point." He seems annoyed. "I brought you up here to look at the desert. Feel a breeze."

I turn around and do just that and try to make amends. "The desert stretches to the horizon. It's intimidating."

"You know that better than most."

I remember the journey from Regalia: the heat, the sun, the slithery creatures—and the howling ones. My body aches reactively, as I recall sleeping on the ground.

"Did you bring food and water with you when you left?" he asks.

"We did not. I was exiled. I expected to die. It was a total surprise to end up alive."

He looks at me oddly. "You truly expected to die?"

"I did. I'd seen the Swirling Desert suck people away in a second. No one could survive that."

"But you did."

I realize I've never explained my miracle to him. My heart skips with excitement with this chance to share. But will he accept the miracle? Or discount it?

Wyan laughs softly. "Come on, Oria. I showed you this secret walkway. Now it's your turn to share *your* secret."

It *is* nice he showed me this place. It does show he trusts me.

So I must trust him. "Here's how I got through the Swirling Desert. The sands parted for me." I make an upward motion with my hands. "I walked through unscathed. My friends ran in after me. Then the sands swept the path away behind us. There was no going back."

"Why were you saved and others weren't?"

"My faith in the Keeper saved me."

He studies my face and seems sincerely interested. "And how did he do that?"

"I . . . I don't know. He just did."

"So he has magical powers?"

The word 'magic' is offensive. "He has power, yes."

"It's too bad you left him behind in Regalia."

Wyan truly doesn't understand. "He doesn't live there. Or anywhere." I sweep my hand across the expanse of desert. "He's everywhere. And he *is* here too."

He scoffs. "Do you see him here?"

Currently, no. But I need to start small with Wyan.

"I don't have to see him to know he exists and that he's available to me."

Wyan snaps his fingers. "Can you conjure him up on demand?"

As his doubts pour out of him, he cheapens my faith. "I can speak with him at any time and know he hears me."

"Does he answer back?"

I start to get flustered. I search for the right words. "He does answer, though not like you or I speak. And not always in ways I understand, or in ways I want him to."

"That sounds random, unpredictable, and a little chaotic." He shakes his head and rests his arms on the wall. "I wouldn't like that. That's why Legalis works. People trust the structure of the system. Everyone knows what's what."

"No, they don't," I say. "New laws go into effect all the time which means we're afraid we'll break one without meaning to."

He makes a face. "It's more concrete than you talking to an abstract being and getting answers in obscure ways — if you get answers at all."

"You misunderstand," I say. "The Keeper is as real as you and I. And he does answer. Always. I'm just new at this, so it's my fault if I don't always understand his answers."

"He's real?"

"He is."

"I told you I want to meet him. Arrange it."

I've talked myself into a corner. "It's not that simple."

He flips his hand at me. "Apparently not. As I said, at least with the Judge people know where they stand."

"Yes, they do. They stand in fear or in punishment. There's nothing in between."

"That's harsh."

"So is the Judge. So is your system."

He sighs deeply, as if our conversation has exhausted him. It's certainly exhausted me. "We need to get back to the booth."

We leave the walkway but our discussion is not over.

"Since you're stuck here," he says. "What are your plans? You and your friends have faith in the Keeper. That doesn't fit well within the laws of Legalis."

"We're not alone," I say. "There are others who've come before."

"Others who believe in him? In Legalis?"

Oops. Maybe I shouldn't have said anything. "There are a few."

"I doubt the Judge would approve."

"We want to do good. For everyone."

"I heard what you said on Judging Day. I saw your friend cause a commotion in the Cudgeling Circle. I understand your high emotions. It was too bad about your roommate. But you must understand that disruptions are harmful. If you and your friends plan to interfere—"

I stop walking. "So you think Legalis is perfect, as is?"

I expect him to say *no, of course not.*

Instead, he says without hesitation, "Yes, I do. It's perfect for us. Without the parameters set forth by the Notables and the Judge, we'd have chaos. How is chaos good for anyone?"

I'm stunned by his answer. "No one is happy here, Wyan. Surely you see that."

"There are always complainers."

"But if it works so well, few people would complain."

"The majority of the Masses live totally satisfactory lives. They have work, lodging, and food. What more could they want?"

I'm shocked he's boiled life down so simply. "How about feeling like their lives count for something, that they have purpose? No one in Legalis is excited when they get up in the morning. No one looks forward to their future, and no one uses their gifts—if they even know what their gifts are. No one even dares to hope for a better life. Your laws kill dreams."

He faces me, his left eyebrow raised. "Dreams, Oria? Dreams aren't real. Dreams lead to disappointment and do nothing but stir people up. Dreams disrupt the system." He shakes his head. "They do no good to anybody."

I'm frustrated by how close-minded he is. "If there isn't any change there's no progress and growth. Don't you want people to be *more?* Don't you want Legalis to be *more?*"

Wyan gazes up at the sky. "Ideas like yours will get you in trouble, Oria."

"My ideas are the Keeper's ideas. They could help Legalis be a better place, and make its people happier. Happy people are more productive people."

"We don't need more production. We need order and consistency."

We've circled back to the beginning again.

He sighs disgustedly. "I advise you and your Keeper to leave well enough alone. Legalis doesn't need to change. You do."

Instead of making me want to give in, his words reinforce my desire to stay the course.

Suddenly the sun disappears behind some clouds, leaving us in shadow. I look up at them, remembering how the Keeper got my attention by showing me a slice of sky. I revel in the shadow of the clouds, feeling my skin cool. If Wyan doesn't believe in the Keeper *yet*, that's ok. *I* believe.

The clouds part and the sun shines through.

I laugh aloud.

Wyan looks in the direction of my gaze. "What are you doing?"

"I'm laughing at the clouds because they inspired me when I needed to be inspired."

"What?"

"The Keeper just used them to remind me to remain strong in the message he assigned me to share."

He glances at the clouds again. "All that in the clouds?"

"All that."

"And what is this message?"

"That he created us, loves us, and wants to save us."

"From what?"

An answer eludes me, but only for a second. "From sin and from ourselves."

"Your Keeper is too strange for me."

"I'm sorry you feel that way. I guarantee he isn't strange at all once you get to know him." We arrive back at the booth, where a line has already formed.

I'm glad that I had a chance to talk with Wyan about the Keeper, but sad that the progress of our friendship seems to have been undone.

It was nice while it lasted.

**

As the afternoon wears on, Wyan tries to tease me, as if he regrets the seriousness of our walkway discussion.

I appreciate his efforts, and I smile and accept his kidding.

But my heart isn't in it.

I'm frustrated—at him, and at myself. At him, because no matter what I say he won't budge from his unrelenting defense of Legalis. And at myself because I haven't found the right words to break through those defenses. How can I make him understand what the Keeper has to offer?

I feel like a failure.

As I fill a woman's basket with her food allotment, Lieb runs up to the booth. His face is red and he's out of breath.

"What's wrong?" I ask him.

"Nana's been arrested!"

Wyan and I ask the same question together. "What for?"

His face screws up in a confused expression. "She was in a place she wasn't supposed to be, talking to people she wasn't supposed to talk to."

"Where?" Wyan asks.

I can guess where. I don't want Lieb to answer in front of Wyan.

"That doesn't matter," I say. "I'm coming." I hand a woman her basket of food.

"I'll come with you," Wyan says.

He's the last person I want with me in this situation. Luckily, the line for food is long. "You stay here and work for both of us. I'll see you in the morning."

I hurry off with Lieb before Wyan can argue with me.

CHAPTER THIRTY-FOUR

SOLANA

I pace up and back in my cell. Four steps in one direction, three in the other.

My thoughts flit wildly like flies unable to land.

How did I get here?

When I awakened this morning I went to work with Elum, as usual. But when we reached the clock near the Workers' door, I felt compelled to visit them.

Elum had rolled his eyes. "You're obsessed."

"I'm invested," I say. "They're from Regalia."

He waved me away.

I did *not* expect to see Rand there, handing out Relics.

I remember my first thought: these are *my* people, not yours!

It went downhill from there.

I knew I was talking too loud. I knew I should stop. I knew it might get us in trouble.

Yet consumed with pride, I did it anyway.

I stop pacing as I remember my dream where I was pushed into a tiny room with high windows.

I look up. There are the high windows. Slits for light, but no view.

In the dream an iron door was slammed shut.

I look at the iron door that keeps me a prisoner.

The Keeper had sent me a warning—or was it a premonition? He'd done that before with my dream about meeting Oria and the dream about the poisoning of Glynis. Actually, he'd done it many times, giving me little snippets of events to come.

And I'd walked right into this one. Had I purposely escalated the argument with Rand in order for the dream to come true?

"That's pretty dumb, Solana," I say to myself.

"What's dumb?" comes a gruff man's voice.

I grip the iron door. "I am. I'm Solana. Who are you?"

"None of your business."

I'm taken aback. He started this conversation. "That's not fair. I told you my name. Tell me yours."

"I don't need to tell you anything, woman."

Whatever. "Suit yourself. Do you want to tell me what you're jailed for?"

"None of your business."

I'm done with him. "Is anyone else here?" I call out.

"I am," a woman says. "I'm Coli."

"I'm here too," a man says. "I'm Sar, her husband."

I remember my first Sanctuary Day when Coli rushed forward demanding justice for her husband. Now they're both here. "I heard about you from my son, Devin," I say. "He brings water and cleans—"

"Out the cells," Coli says. "He's a nice man. He's one of . . . us." She nearly whispers the word.

"Who's us?" the rude man asks.

I answer for her. "None of your business."

I feel bad for being rude right back, but I'm not in the mood to deal with him.

I hear movement and then Devin appears at my cell. He reaches his hand through the bars and I grab onto it like a lifeline. "Are you all right?" he asks.

"Get me out of here and I will be."

He glances back the way he'd come. "I'm not sure what I can do. I have no power here."

"I do!" the rude man says. "I am Varo! I'm the husband of the Head Notable!"

I knew he'd been arrested, but until now I hadn't put two and two together. To be in a cell next to a bigwig like him . . . no wonder he's incensed.

"I don't belong here!" he yells

I can't let his statement go unchallenged. "I think *you* do." I say. "Didn't you poison your wife?"

"He did what?" Coli asks.

Her husband gives his two-cents, "For doing that, you belong here way more than we do."

"I demand to see the person in charge!" Varo yells.

Devin's face looks pained. "Try to ignore him."

"No one dares ignore me. I am Varo! I demand to see my family."

Devin rolls his eyes. "Your daughter came. Let that be enough."

"She came? Why didn't I get to see her?"

"Nobody gets visitors. You're no different."

"I'm *very* different. I'm a Notable! I'm—"

"Quiet, prisoner, or the guards will put a gag on you!" Devin says.

Varo doesn't respond—which is a huge relief.

Devin gives his attention to me. He points toward the outside. "Rand came, obviously very upset."

"I can imagine. I was so dumb to do what I did. All of this is my fault."

"Rand is trying to find Elum to see if he can get word to Helsa."

"Do Lieb and Oria know yet?"

"Lieb does. He's trying to get word to Oria. You're not alone, Mother. Take heart in that."

"The Keeper is with us too," Coli calls out.

"Hmph," says Varo. "A lot of good he's done any of you."

He has a point.

"I'll be back." Devin leaves and I hear another door shut.

It feels symbolic. Another door shuts for me here in Legalis as so many already have.

I sit on my cot to ponder closed doors and am both frightened by the sudden silence and relieved by it. At least Varo isn't going on and on anymore.

I have enough of my own on-and-on thoughts. Obviously things haven't worked out as I'd hoped. I feel depression poke at me, wanting in. How did I get here—to Legalis, and to this cell?

At first we were elated to find refuge from the desert. If a choice had been offered I would *not* have chosen this stifling, unnerving, and joyless place. If not for Devin being here, and being with my friends and family, I would have volunteered to be in jail just so I wouldn't have to deal with my pointless life. Four walls, a bed, food and water are about all I have now anyway.

I had a position as the matriarch of my family, supposedly a woman of some wisdom and authority, but what good am I here? Helsa has found purpose with her art and befriending the Head Notable and her daughter. And saving her. She saved a life! And she stepped into the Circle to help Lieb. She obviously doesn't need me like she used to.

Lieb has found purpose happily painting walls and charming everyone he meets.

Devin . . . I'm disappointed in my son. The firebrand who spoke passionately about the Keeper to anyone who would listen has gone silent. He's grown passive and is *not* a leader anymore.

But who is?

We desperately need a leader; someone to help us figure out why we've been brought to this dreadful place.

The Exiled are another disappointment. They are lambs waiting for someone to lead them.

Again I ask: who is that leader?

Which leaves Oria . . . since leaving Regalia she and I have lost the sisterhood of our daily learning sessions about the Keeper. What started as me teaching her, was ultimately flipped when she met the Keeper in person and took off on her mission to turn Regalia on its head. But other than the one outburst on Judging Day she hasn't made much progress here. I hate myself for being a little glad about that.

Talk about rude. "She's not my competition," I whisper, needing to hear the words that I'm thinking. I know I shouldn't feel that way, but lately . . . I've had all sorts of thoughts that don't sit well.

I feel aimless. Without purpose. Without merit. What good have I done since coming here? Why would the Keeper bring me here to wallow in this unthinkable nothingness?

In a cell.

Defeated, I stretch out on the cot and stare at the ceiling.

Chapter Thirty-Five

Helsa

I'm worried about Glynis. Not her health—for ever since Kal and Varo were arrested she's felt better and is stronger mentally too. I see why people trust her to be the Head Notable. But the stress she must be under, trying to deal with something personal while stepping back into her position as a leader . . . I wish there was something I could do to help. But I won't be around. My mural is done.

I start to clean up my supplies. Glynis and Nixi come in, and stop, surprised.

"You're finished?" Glynis asks.

"I am." I step back so they can see the full mural. The lush garden consumes the wall. "Does it please you?"

She's trying to keep her composure but I see it. Joy. It's the first time I've seen her smile. "It pleases me very much. Thank you, Helsa."

Nixi beams. "Yes indeed. Thank you, Helsa. You've made both of us very happy."

"Happy for the mural, as well as happy and grateful to you for saving my life," Glynis adds.

I feel myself blush. "I'm glad I could help—on both accounts." I pick up my bucket of paints and brushes. "I guess I'll be leaving you then."

Nixi is panicked. "No! You can't go. I mean you can, but . . . Mama? Can she stay somehow?" Nixi looks down, embarrassed by her outburst. "The house is better with Helsa in it."

What a nice compliment.

Glynis thinks a moment, then nods. "Since Kal is no longer with us, I do need a maid."

Without hesitation I say, "I accept." I give her a little bob as I saw Kal do. "Use me however you wish, Head Notable."

"Excellent."

Nixi quietly claps her hands as *I* clap inside.

"Nixi will fill you in on your duties." She retrieves a notebook from her desk and leaves.

"As you wish, mistress," I call after her.

Nixi grabs my upper arms and bobs up and down in excitement. She realizes her error and lets go. "I didn't mean to be improper. I'm just so glad you're staying."

"As am I, mistress." I can't help but beam as the good news sinks in.

"Let's go to the kitchen and tell Bog."

On the way there's a knock at the front door. Nixi defers to me. "Answer it, please."

I smooth my robe, change my posture, and open it. A man stands outside. "May I help you?" I ask.

"A message for Helsa?"

I blink. "That's me."

He hands it to me, then leaves. I close the door, then read it: *Solana has been arrested and is in jail. Come right away.*

My heart beats wildly. The thought of Fault Finders taking Nana away . . . she must be so scared. And what was she arrested for?

Nixi waits in the foyer. "What's wrong?"

"My grandmother has been arrested. I need to go." I realize manners are needed. "May I go see her, mistress?"

"Of course. Let us know if you need anything."

I hurry up-top. Elum stands outside the entrance to the Notable area, and we immediately walk in the direction of the jail.

"What happened?" I ask.

"She got caught talking to the Workers. I told her not to visit them, but you know your nana."

"I do."

"Rand was with her, but he got away. He hasn't been arrested. Yet."

"So Nana is in jail all alone." I hate the thought of that.

"Your father is there," he says.

It's one consolation. The only one.

**

As we approach the jail, we see Rand standing outside with Lieb and Oria.

"How is Nana?" I ask.

Oria points toward the door of the jail. "Your father came out and said there's not much to tell yet."

"How do we get her out?" I ask.

"We don't," Elum says.

"That doesn't make any sense. She doesn't deserve this."

"It is what it is. She'll be out when they say she will."

It is absurd. "So once someone's arrested, they're in jail for the rest of their lives?" I ask.

Rand shakes his head. "I was only released after my mother was killed in the Cudgeling Circle. I think that's the only way out."

The immensity of the situation is like a yoke across my shoulders. "So Nana only gets out if one of us is killed?"

He nods.

"And even then, *she'd* be Marked?"

He nods again.

I toss my hands in the air. "Why can't they just give her a Fault—give her five Faults. Why do they have to arrest her?"

Rand answers again. "Because we were stirring up the Workers, sharing Relics about the Keeper, and also talking to them about being free."

Elum shakes his head. "She promised me she wouldn't share Relics anymore."

"It was me," Rand says. "I handed them out. This morning Solana came in while I was there, which happened to be when a supervisor came in. He called a guard, and . . . it's all my fault."

"Yes, it is," I say.

The others look at me, shocked for my lack of empathy.

"That's not nice, Sa-Sa," Lieb says.

I'm well aware, but I don't know how to merge nice into this unimaginable situation. I look up at the high slits that Papa said were openings into the cells. I step closer. "Nana? Nana, can you hear me?"

Elum shushes me. "Stop that! You'll get all of us in trouble."

I ignore him. "Nana?"

"Helsa!" Her voice is soft and weak—but there. "I hear you."

"Are you all right?"

"I am now."

"We're all here," I say. "You're not alone."

"Don't get into trouble on my account."

Of course she thinks of us first.

Elum touches my arm. "Listen to her." He points at a clock. "The Count is in a few minutes. We need to go."

"We'll be back, Nana," I yell.

We walk down a street until I spot some Fault Finders nearby. They're staring at me.

"Let's get undercover *now*," Oria says.

We hurry into a nearby home. No one's there. We put five black pebbles on the sill.

"Who do we appeal to about Nana's case?" Oria asks.

"The Judge!" Lieb says. "Let's talk to the Judge." He shudders. "But you do it. He scares me."

I put my hand on his shoulder. "He scares me too. And he's unapproachable."

"Yes, he is," Elum says. "Remember that."

"This system is so off kilter," Oria says. "People are imprisoned without any hope of justice or even a defense."

Rand adjusts his crutch under his arm. "Helsa, I know you're getting close to being done with the mural, but is there a way to talk to the Head Notable? Elicit her help?"

With all the turmoil I hadn't had a chance to tell them about my new position. "Maybe. The mural is done, but she just hired me as her maid, to take the place of Kal, the one who poisoned her."

Elum's eyebrows rise. "She must really like you."

"She does," I say proudly. "So does her daughter, Nixi."

"Then, do it," Oria says. "Talk to them."

"I'll do my best." At least I'll be doing *something*.

**

Nixi answers the door. "Helsa! You're back. Is your grandmother all right?"

I go inside. "She's surviving." For the moment. "Can I speak with your mother about her?"

Nixi seems surprised by my question. "I'm not sure what she can do."

Now *I'm* surprised. "If not her, who?" I feel tears threaten. "There has to be a way to fix all this."

I see compassion in Nixi's eyes. "She just came back. Go sit in the parlor and I'll see if she can talk to you now."

I sit in a chair of blue velvet. I remember seeing Varo and Kal in this room when he handed her the bag of poison. Now both of them are gone. Are they being held near Nana? I hope not, for their crime is a true crime, not something trivial like—

I stand when Glynis and Nixi enter the room. "Head Notable."

Glynis motions for me to sit, then they share a settee nearby.

"Nixi filled me in, Helsa. I'm sorry for your grandmother's situation."

"She doesn't deserve to be in jail, mistress. She was simply talking to some people."

"What people?"

I know my answer won't help Nana's cause but I can't lie. "I believe they're called the Workers. They sew for you?"

Her eyes grow large. "Their area is restricted."

"I heard that, mistress. But Nana . . . the Workers came from Regalia like us." I point at myself. "Nana and I worked in a clothing factory and Nana knows a few of them."

"So both of you can sew?" Nixi asks.

I suddenly fear we'll become Workers. "A little."

She looks like she doesn't believe me. She most likely knows the reason I've downplayed our skills.

Yet would sewing be so bad? I think of the predicament we're in. "If it will get Nana out of jail, we'd sew for you, Head Notable. Anything to set her free."

"You're not supposed to know about the Workers," Glynis says. "No one is."

"Nana was just visiting with old friends."

Nixi raises her finger. "An older woman who sews . . . I think I met your grandmother when I visited the Workers once. She said she could sew and had a granddaughter who could sew too."

"That was Nana, mistress." I blush, feeling like I should have mentioned something earlier. "She mentioned meeting you."

Glynis blinks twice. "So it's official: the Workers have been infiltrated?"

"Apparently so," Nixi says.

"Pardon me, mistress, but I think *infiltrated* is too strong a word." I take another approach. "She's my grandmother, she's in her sixties. She has no power. She's harmless."

"She went into a forbidden area and spoke to forbidden people," Nixi says.

All true. "Is there someone I can talk to about her defense, mistress?"

"There is no defense," Glynis says. "Not even my husband or Kal get a defense."

Which raises an important point. "They were arrested for trying to kill you. Obviously that's a crime. But talking to old friends like Nana did . . . surely that's *not* a crime, mistress. Surely that doesn't deserve the same punishment."

Glynis sits up straighter. "You dare question our system?"

My heart sinks at the anger in her voice, but I can't back down now. "Yes. I guess I do, Head Notable." I sit forward in my chair. "Nana is honest, kind, giving, and is a woman of great faith and —" I stop there. I shouldn't have brought up faith.

"So she's one of *those?*" Glynis asks.

There's no going back now. "If by *those* you mean people who believe in the Keeper, then yes, mistress. She's one of those."

"As are you?" she asks.

I can't leave Nana alone in this. "As am I, mistress."

"Then ask *him* to solve your problem."

"I have," I say—even though I haven't. I feel bad that I haven't prayed. Why haven't I prayed?

Glynis stands and walks to a table where she runs her finger across its top as if checking it for dust. Then she faces me. "I am not ignorant, Helsa. The Notables and the Judge are well aware of the Exiled *and* the threat of their beliefs. Your beliefs."

"We are no threat to you, mistress. We only want to enrich the lives of the Masses."

"By turning them against their government?"

"No!" I lower my voice. "I'm sorry, Head Notable, but no. We want to help people feel more fulfilled so they can be of more use to Legalis."

"But your kind call our system harsh and cruel," Glynis says.

I point in the direction of jail. "Isn't it harsh to arrest an old woman for merely having a conversation?"

"She did more than that." It's the first time Nixi has spoken. She glances at her mother. "The Relics?"

Her mother nods. "I have no idea where these random pieces of paper come from or who's producing them, but we've confiscated a few and find them extremely incendiary."

I don't even know what that word means.

"Aggressive," she adds.

This shocks me. "I don't know what Relics you've read, mistress, but the ones we embrace talk about the Keeper watching over us and caring for us. They give assurances that he is with us all the time and we're not supposed to be afraid."

"But what about . . ." Glynis pulls a piece of paper from her pocket. "'The Keeper has set us free! Don't be slaves of the laws.' If that's not incendiary, I don't know what is."

"I've never heard that one," I say honestly.

"It's one the Workers had in their possession."

And it's damning. "I don't think it means what you think it means," I say.

"Then explain it to us." Glynis sits and crosses her arms.

My mind goes blank. "Can I see it, please?" She hands it over and I read it. The last part is the problem. And yet . . . I feel a flash of clarity. "The Keeper wants us to find our purpose and not be afraid. It doesn't say ignore laws, it says don't be slaves to them. Don't be held captive by them. Work *within* them, but don't let them become your focus."

The women are quiet and I wonder if I've said anything that will help Nana at all. "By the way, *I* didn't come up with that explanation, mistress," I add. "The Keeper just gave it to me. I guarantee you, I'm not that smart or good with words."

Glynis scoffs. "And how did he give it to you?"

I touch my heart. "In here." I sigh. "I know it sounds farfetched, but it's true. It's how we communicate with him. We feel things and think things, and communicate with him by appealing to him. Talking to him. Letting him know what's on our minds. It's give and take."

"It sounds made up," Nixi says. "You could say anything came from him."

I'm taken aback but only for a second. "I suppose I could. And it takes practice to realize when it's him talking and when it's me." I'm quick to add. "I don't always get it right either. But Nana has more practice. She's really close to him."

Glynis looks to the ceiling, then down again. "So if the Keeper believes your grandmother has been hurt or wronged, will he swoop down and wreak vengeance on us?"

"Like the Judge does?" I ask. "Mistress."

I immediately regret creating more tension between us. My heart pounds in my chest.

"The Judge does what must be done to maintain control and order," Glynis says.

"At the expense of free will and choice?"

She points at me. "If we allow free will and choice, Legalis will erupt in chaos."

"Maybe. I expect bad people will always act badly. But good people won't take advantage. If we let them, the Masses could use their free will to create better lives for themselves and for each other."

"You know this how?"

Good question. I put a fist to my gut. "Don't you ever just know something that you didn't know before, mistress? Something that is beyond your knowing?"

"It's called insight and trusting our own innate abilities," Glynis says.

"It's also called faith and trusting in the Keeper's love and care."

She shakes her head and stands. "I can offer no promises about your grandmother, Helsa, but I will take the situation under advisement."

I also stand. "Thank you for your time and consideration."

She leaves the room. Nixi lingers behind. "You're an interesting girl, Helsa. I'll give you that."

"I hope the two of you understand that I—"

She shakes her head. "I'm not sure what I understand right now. You need to get to work. This room needs dusting." She opens a cabinet, pulls out a dust rag, and tosses it to me.

As soon as she leaves I start dusting, but my hands are shaking. I turn to a wall and press my hands against it, trying to find strength and stability in something solid. Then I lean my forehead against the wall and pray, thanking the Keeper for giving me words beyond anything I could have said on my own, and asking him to help Nana in ways beyond anything I can *do* on my own.

He's the only one I trust.

Chapter Thirty-Six

Oria

Rand walks me home from the jail. "Do you want company? Because I sure would like yours."

His offer appeals to me. "I'd like that very much. Come up with me."

"You go first," he says. The stairs are hard for him, but he manages. I hold the door open for him.

"Thank you," he says as he comes inside. But then he stops and stares straight ahead.

I turn to see what he's—

"Keeper!" I say.

He's standing near the window. "Good day, Oria." He smiles at Rand. "Nice to see you, Rand. I've been waiting for both of you."

Rand stands there, staring. He looks to me for confirmation. "Is this really . . . him?"

"Yes," I say, laughing. "It's really him."

"Yes, it's really me," the Keeper says. "I thought it was time for another visit." He checks out my meager unit with his eyes. "Though I will say it's not as beautiful as your garden."

"I'm happy to see you anywhere you want to visit," I say. "Sit. Please sit." I pull out the third chair, and laugh.

"Why do you laugh?" he asks.

"I always wondered why this unit had three chairs when it was clearly meant for two people, but now I know why. The chair was meant for you—has always been meant for you."

"I had to have a place to sit, didn't I?"

Rand sits across from me and leans his crutch against the table. He hasn't taken his eyes off the Keeper. "Oria told me about meeting you, but I never dreamed I'd ever have the chance. I mean she's…and I'm…"

"She's my child and so are you."

Rand's forehead furrows. "I am?"

The Keeper puts his hand on Rand's. "You are. And a very special one at that."

Rand moves his hair to reveal his mark. "I know." For the first time he looks away.

The Keeper shakes his head. "That mark means nothing to me." He reaches over and touches Rand's chest. "'Blessed are the pure in heart, for they shall see God.'"

Rand's eyes fill with tears. "You must forget that my heart is *not* pure."

"Let me be the judge of that." Then the Keeper slaps his hands on the table. "Now then. Let's talk about what's *on* your hearts."

"Solana is in jail," I say.

"I put her there."

"What?" we both ask.

He lifts his hands to fend off our question. "My ways are not your ways. Just as I have put you where you need to be, I have put her where *she* needs to be."

"But she can't get out."

"At the moment," he says.

I sit back as relief settles in. "You have it under control?"

He gives me a sideways smile.

"Yes. Of course you do. Sorry," I say.

Rand raises his hand. "I was with the Workers too, I was the one handing out the Relics, yet only Solana was arrested. I should be in jail too."

"No, you shouldn't," the Keeper says. "I need you out here."

"Doing what?"

"Open your eyes to see and your ears to hear."

Rand's eyes get big. "Long ago that's what a man said to me outside the Sanctuary. I thought it might be you. And now I know it *was* you!"

The Keeper touches his shoulder. "You're doing a good job sharing Relics. I appreciate that."

"Thank you. I keep finding them hidden away in the Sanctuary. Is that your doing?"

"Indirectly, more or less."

"Send more, please. I promise to keep sharing them."

The Keeper laughs. "I'll see what I can do—and I appreciate your dedication."

I feel jealous for the attention Rand is getting and the fact they've met before. I thought I was special that way.

How self-centered is that?

Of course, he knows everything I'm thinking because he says, "Now then, my Oria."

My Oria? I melt.

"I know you're frustrated."

"I am. I thought I would have some impact here, but other than speaking the one time on Judging Day—"

"By the way, that was very well done. But I want you to know that your impact *is* materializing, even though you might not see it. Yet."

"But who's being reached? The Exiled are lukewarm. Solana and Rand have the Workers to help, Lieb is a light to everyone he meets, and Helsa has a relationship with the Head Notable and her daughter. I feel like I'm alone here." I glance at Rand. "I'm sorry, Rand. I don't mean to discount you, but—"

"Think again," the Keeper says. "Who have you befriended?"

There's only one answer. "Wyan. But he's totally against you and is a champion for everything Legalis. All we do is argue. And I don't even know if he fully hears anything I say, or if I'm even saying the right things, and . . ." I sigh deeply. "So yes, I'm frustrated."

"Do you like spending time with Wyan?" he asks.

It's a complicated question. "There's a connection between us, but then we argue and I want nothing to do with him."

"Did I ever imply your mission was going to be easy?" the Keeper asks.

"No. But in Regalia . . ."

His eyebrows rise. "In Regalia you were arrested for your words about me, put on trial, then exiled. Here, you are free." He smiles. "Frustrated, but free."

I feel bad for complaining. And yet . . . "When is the next time I'll be able to talk about you? I need an audience if I am going to spread your words."

"Do you need a big audience?"

Oh. Dear. "No. It's just that I want to reach a lot of people and that means a big audience."

"Hmm," he says, tapping his lips with a finger. "That's one way to do it."

I laugh. "You enjoy being cryptic, don't you?"

"Cryptic no. My truths are plain. But my methods can take unexpected turns."

"Then turn me," I say. "Please turn me."

"Me too," Rand says.

The Keeper stands, and I feel a swell of panic. Rand and I both stand too. "Please don't go," I say.

He puts his hand on my upper arm. "I've enjoyed our visit but I have work to do. As do both of you."

"Tell us how to help Solana," I say.

"Trust me," he says. "Can you do that?"

We both nod, but agreeing is hard.

Then he smiles at me. "Regarding your *other* friend . . ."

"Wyan?"

He shakes his head. "The one left behind in Regalia."

One handsome face comes to mind. "Xian?"

"He misses you. But don't worry, I have plans for him — plans that are playing out, even now."

"Here? Is he coming here?"

The Keeper doesn't answer, but when he reaches the door, he turns back to me. "Regarding the here and now, be aware that not everyone is who or what they seem, all right Oria?"

"Xian?"

He shakes his head.

"Then who?" I ask.

He sighs. "You people and your need for details. I will give you wisdom. You must do the rest." The Keeper puts his hand against our foreheads. "May blessings and courage abound in your hearts. Now, be strong and do the work."

When he leaves it takes all my self-control not to run after him.

"That was amazing," Rand says.

I lean back against the door. "I wish he would stay. I have a thousand questions."

"Who's Xian?" Rand asks.

"A good friend in Regalia who saved me more than once. He got left behind."

"Do you miss him?"

The mention of his name has stirred my memories and my feelings toward him — feelings I've buried to save myself from the pain of knowing I'd never see him.

"Oria?" Rand asks. "Do you miss him?"

"Very much. I expected never to see him again, but after what the Keeper said . . . maybe I will." I hope I will. I really, really hope I will.

"It doesn't sound like Xian is the person who isn't who or what they seem."

I can say this with full confidence. "He isn't. Xian is genuine in all ways. It can't be him. It's someone else."

Rand puts his hand to his chest. "It's not me. I'm an open book. I hope you trust me."

"I do," I say with all sincerity. "I trust you completely. And I'm glad to have you as an ally."

"And I, you. Do you think it's someone you've met already or someone you haven't met yet?" he asks.

I scoff. "The only people I've had dealings with are Trina — who is no longer in the picture. And Wyan. It can't be . . ." I let my sentence trail off. "Was the Keeper talking about Wyan?"

"If there's any chance it's him . . . be wary and wise around him," Rand says.

"I'll do my best."

Rand takes my hand. "Let us rest in the assurance that we're exactly where the Keeper wants us to be. Yes?"

He's completely right. "He's got us."

"He most certainly does."

I squeeze his hand. "I'm glad we shared this experience, Rand."

"It's one I'll cherish forever."

Amen to that.

Chapter Thirty-Seven

Solana

I doze.

"Mother?"

Devin.

I open my eyes but it takes me a moment to remember where I am. Devin stands on the other side of a barred door. Of my cell. In jail.

"Are you hungry?" He holds a tray of food.

Not really, but I know I need to eat. He opens the door and brings it in.

"Can you sit with me?" I ask.

"I can't." He nods toward the corridor where I see more trays of food.

"How is everyone?" I ask. "How is Helsa taking this?"

"She's doing all right." He lowers his voice. "She's asking the Head Notable for help."

A commotion erupts from the other cell to my right. "I heard that!" Varo yells. "How dare my wife help anyone but me!"

Devin and I don't respond. The man must be delusional to think the wife he poisoned would help him.

"I need to go," Devin says. He embraces me. "We're all praying, Mother. May the Keeper be with you." He lifts up the bowl on my tray and I see a folded piece of paper. He smiles and puts his finger to his lips.

"Thank you, son."

He leaves to deliver the rest of the meals. I immediately unfold the page. As hoped, it's a Relic: *The Keeper will rescue all who are discouraged and have given up hope.*

I press the tiny note to my heart. Once again, the Keeper has provided just what I need.

What we need.

I see Devin pass on his way out. "Son?"

He pauses to look at me. "Yes?"

"It's perfect."

He winks and leaves.

I ignore my meager meal and stand at the door. "Everyone? I'd like to share something with you—something that's given me hope. Maybe it can do the same for you."

"I'll take hope," Coli says.

"Fire away," Sar says.

"Sure," Varo says, "Why not?"

I begin to speak but am surprised to hear another voice.

"I'd like that too," a woman says.

I stammer for a second before asking back, "Who are you?"

"Kal."

Varo explodes. "Kal! You're here? Why didn't you say anything?"

I suddenly get the connection. Kal is the maid who helped Varo with the poisoning. And according to Helsa, his girl on the side.

"I don't want to talk to you, sir," Kal says. "I want to hear what the lady has to share."

Varo huffs. "Like it or not, we're in this together, girlie."

"I didn't want to do any of it. You made me!"

"Shut up!"

Her voice grows louder. "He threatened to sack me if I didn't put the poison in his wife's food. He —"

"Shut it! Now!" he roars.

A guard comes in. "What's going on?" He stops in front of Varo's cell. "You causing trouble again, Notable?"

"You have no right to talk to me like that!"

The guard laughs. "You're behind bars. I'm not. That dictates who's got the right. Now pipe down!" The door slams on his way out.

Nobody talks for a bit after he leaves. Although I enjoyed the guard's takedown of Varo, it reinforces that none of us are getting out of here. Helsa can talk to the Head Notable for days but she won't do anything. Whether she's *able* to do anything is another unanswered question.

Kal is the one to break the silence. "Can you share what you were going to share, ma'am? About hope. I need some of that."

"Of course." I read the Relic out loud. "'The Keeper will rescue all who are discouraged and have given up hope.'"

"That's me," Coli says.

"I'm counting on it," says her husband.

"I want to believe that," Kal says.

Once again, Varo ruins everything. "So where is he? Where is this precious Keeper of yours? I don't see him doing anything."

I think of another Relic. "He says, 'Fear not, for I am with you always.'"

"He's full of the big talk, isn't he?" Varo says. "If he's here, ready to rescue us, I demand he show himself. If not, shut it. I've had enough."

"I haven't," Kal says. "But . . . where *is* he?"

I'm not sure how to answer.

But Coli does. "He's everywhere."

"I don't understand," Kal says.

"Oh!" Varo says, "There he is! Hanging from the ceiling! Would you look at that!"

"Stop it," I say quietly.

"Then don't say he's everywhere. Not unless you can prove it."

I wish Oria was here. Maybe she'd know what to say.

"I tell *you* prove he's *not* here," Coli says.

"I suppose you want me to prove there's no air, too, right?" Varo says.

An image comes to mind. "You know there's air because you breathe in and out and need it to live, and you see what it does when air becomes wind. So it is with the Keeper," I say. "We need him to live, and we know he exists because of what we see him doing."

"How he moves in our lives," Sar says.

"Exactly."

"Those are meaningless, fancy words," Varo says. "If he's got power, then let him get us out of here."

"The way to do that is to pray to him," I say.

"Go ahead," he says.

"Nope," I say. "If you want his help, then you need to pray too."

"Nope back at you," Varo says. "But you go right ahead."

I start a prayer out loud, and Sar and Coli add to it. Even Kal adds a few words.

"Stop the words!" Varo says. "All of you."

He acts like they're hurting him. "No," I say, and we continue on.

Varo doesn't object after that.

Perhaps that's progress.

Chapter Thirty-Eight

Rand

I leave our unit early, being careful not to wake Helsa or Lieb. I'm eager to do what the Keeper has asked me to do—share more Relics. I feel a sense of urgency about it, as if time is short.

I am also up early because I'm nervous. The desire to share with the Workers remains, yet it's even more dangerous now.

I'd share elsewhere, but my options are limited. I'm a Marked Man, shunned by the Masses. I can't stand on a corner and start reading Relics. No one would listen, and surely I'd be arrested before I'd done anyone any good.

Dangerous or not, the Workers are my audience.

I enter the empty Sanctuary. It's odd how it always feels like coming home; a cavernous, echoing, impersonal home where people visit because they have to; a place of fear, Faults, and ferocity. A place they leave as soon as they can.

But for me, it's my place to be alone—with him.

After being given my Mark, the Sanctuary was just that, a safe place where I could sleep in the shadows, away from the heat and judgmental eyes.

It's also a place where I find inspiration. Not through any dramatic ceremony the Notables put on, but through the quiet contemplation of the Keeper's Relics.

I'm hoping for more than one this morning.

I'm disappointed when I look in the cubby hole and find it empty. Its emptiness causes *me* to feel empty. I need something to share. Maybe it's too early and the man will come later.

I head toward the door, to sit in my usual spot.

"Rand."

The voice is low but carries. I turn around and see the Relic man walking toward me from the storeroom. I meet him halfway. It's the first time I've met him face-to-face. His height is more impressive closer up. I see that he's bald.

"Good morning," I say.

"To you too." He pulls out two pieces of paper. "You're eager today."

"I am."

"Any special reason?"

I don't know this man. I only know him by his good work—supplying me with Relics.

"You can tell me," he says. "We are kept by the same Keeper."

I smile and take a deep breath, needing to share. "I talked with him last evening. In person."

The man smiles broadly. "Good."

Which implies he's spoken to him in person too. I immediately feel a bond.

"What did he tell you to do?" the man asks.

"Continue to hand out Relics. So I need as many as you can give me."

"I give as I receive."

I'm intrigued. "So he gives them to you—directly?"

"Is he not our provider?"

He's teasing me. "It's all right. You don't have to tell me."

"You know he works in mysterious ways."

"I'm proof of that." I look at the floor. "That he would come to *me*... use *me*..."

"Why not use you? People judge looks. The Keeper judges hearts."

"I am overwhelmed by the wonder of him," I say. "I have to trust he knows me better than I know myself."

"Which he does." He hands me two Relics. "Pass them on."

He turns to leave. "Wait!" He faces me again. "Solana got arrested for visiting the Workers. Will I be arrested?"

"You're asking *me*?"

"I thought you might know."

"I know only what the Keeper wants me to know. Did he ask you to share with them?"

"Not exactly. But they're my—his—best audience."

"Then be strong and do the work—whatever it entails."

"Those were his exact words."

The man smiles. "Where do you think I got them?" Before he leaves he asks, "Is there anything else?"

"Your name. What's your name?"

He hesitates, but then says, "Daymon."

I nod to him in deference, but he shakes his head. "There will be none of that. You and I both serve him in our own unique ways. Agreed?"

"Agreed."

"Go do your work, as I do mine." He walks toward the storeroom.

I call after him. "Where do you go in there? Where are you from?"

He turns and smiles. "Those are two different questions."

"I suppose they are."

He gazes upward to the high rafters of the Sanctuary. "I go where I'm needed."

I hate vague answers. "And where are you from?"

He nods. "Where we're all from: him."

"Can you just answer the question?"

His smile is patient. "Just because you don't understand my answer, doesn't mean I *didn't* answer." He heads toward the storeroom again.

"Can I come with you?"

He cocks his head as if considering. "Perhaps. One day. But not this day. Anything else?"

"Not at the moment."

"Then go where *you're* needed, Rand."

Message received. I watch him go, eager to know everything I can about this man called Daymon.

But I'm also eager to read what he's brought me. The first says, "I've commanded you to be strong and brave. Don't ever be afraid or discouraged! I am the Lord your God, and I will be there to help you wherever you go."

Relief flows over me. I'm not alone in this. Never alone.

I open the second Relic: "Now go! When you speak, I will be with you and give you the words to say." I gasp at how perfect the words are — for me. For me right now.

I bow my head and give thanks to the Keeper who thinks of everything.

**

I stand across from the door that leads to the Workers. People walk by, but no one gives the door — or me — a second glance. I'm used to being ignored, but them not seeing the door seems odd because it's falling apart and stands out amid the simple doors and white walls all around us. Why isn't anyone curious?

But then I have a thought. They don't notice the broken down door as they don't notice me, the broken down man. Both of us are eyesores and an affront to the routine of their lives. Perhaps the greatest sin of Legalis is blinding its people to anything that sits outside their carefully controlled world. Perhaps the greatest sin of Legalis is killing curiosity.

I am more curious now than I've been in my entire life. I have my new friends to thank for much of it, and the Relics, and Daymon for bringing me those Relics, but I especially thank the Keeper. Seeing him and speaking with him has ignited a hunger and thirst within me to do whatever it takes to reach people. They have to open their eyes and hearts to him! They have to!

But interacting with the Workers is risky.

At the thought I wait for myself to feel afraid. Yet, I'm not. I'm a bit nervous, but knowing that I'll be doing what the Keeper has assigned me to do makes me feel bold. Or at least more bold than I usually am. Which is not bold at all.

But being bold is not being stupid. I wait for a break in the people walking by, then make a beeline for the door, going through it as quickly as possible.

I pause at the top of the spiral stairs heading downward. I'm out of breath. I'm not used to speed. Or stairs.

I slowly make my way down, relieved to feel the cool air from the corridor that leads to the workroom. I take a deep breath, praying the Keeper keeps me safe.

I peek through the window in the door to make sure no one with authority is there. Then I walk inside and close the door behind me.

Zir sees me and shakes his head. "Look who's here."

I walk over to him. "Good morning, Zir."

He keeps cutting out blue fabric. "I didn't expect to see the likes of you again."

"I won't abandon you."

"Hmph. You get arrested like Solana and you won't have much choice."

"I pray that doesn't happen."

Miri joins us. "How is Solana?"

"In jail."

Miri looks worried.

Zir flips away her reaction. "She was arrested. That's what happens."

"Her son works there, so she does have support," I say.

Miri nods, but nervously glances at the door. "We appreciate the visit, Rand, but I'm not sure you should come again."

But I have to come!

I pull out the Relics. "I have two more for you."

Miri takes them and puts them in her pocket. She still looks nervous. "Thank you, but you need to go."

But I can't go. I need to keep coming here to do my work for the Keeper.

"Like the lady said: go," Zir says.

I'm going. But then I have an idea. "Is there a place I can leave new Relics without so much risk?"

Miri scans the room. Her eyes land on an urn filled with spools of thread near the door I enter through. Slip the Relics in there. We'll get them out when it's safe."

"That's perfect. May the Keeper be with you."
She taps her fingers against her chest. "And with you."
I hurry out the way I came.

Chapter Thirty-Nine

Glynis

Friday is my favorite day of the week because it's the one scheduled day I get to see the love of my life. We try to meet more often by leaving notes under a loose stone in the floor near the Sanctuary storeroom, but the timing doesn't always work out. While I was sick I sent Nixi to check to see if my love had left messages under the stone—but she often forgot to go. Thank goodness she has no idea who's sending the notes. If she knew . . .? That's a crisis for another day. But not now. I have enough to contend with.

I enter our secret meeting place through an obscure tunnel. I tentatively open the door to an alley that's a junk dump of sorts. There are unused chairs, a cart that needs a new wheel, some chipped crockery . . . yet despite its distasteful purpose it's a precious place to me, more special than my lavish home. For here, I get to spend time with *him.* Unfortunately, because of my illness, it's been ages since we've seen each other. Before that, we'd never missed a week.

I see people walking on the street at the end of the alley, but no one looks in my direction. The junk is piled high and creates a good hiding place for our secret rendezvous. Over the years we've made this alley ours in simple ways. Our corner consists of two worn chairs next to a table we created from an upended barrel. We leave a skin of water close by. And occasionally I'll pluck a flower out of an arrangement from home. At the beginning we'd bring food to share, but when a pattern formed where the food remained uneaten, we stopped. When all we have is a few minutes, food is inconsequential. Our fuel is each other's company. We only need the sweetness of each other.

I hear his footsteps in the alley and feel myself smiling. He steps around the junk and in seconds we're in each other's arms. We don't even kiss, we just hold each other like two magnets, desperate for the connection. My head fits perfectly against his chest, and he leans his chin against my hair. There is no place I'd rather be.

After basking in our embrace for a few minutes, he pulls an apple from the pocket of his robe. "For you."

I pull back. "What's this for?"

"Happy anniversary."

I clap my hands. "You remembered! And I didn't!"

"No matter. It's been twenty-five years since we first met by the apple tree at the Farm. You wanted one particular apple and couldn't reach it."

The lovely memory rushes back. "But you could."

"I picked two."

"We sat under the tree and ate them."

"Until my boss told me to get back to work."

I remember the panic I felt, knowing he had to leave. "I argued with the farm boss, saying I could do what I wanted because I was the daughter of a Notable. And if I wanted your company . . ."

He laughs. "He suggested—ever so politely—that you go back where you belong, and reminded you that you shouldn't even speak to the likes of me, one of the lowly Masses."

That memory is not so pleasant. "It was the first time I fully experienced and regretted the class separation of Legalis. We were just two young people, eating apples."

"And falling in love."

I hug him again. "Forever and ever. No arranged marriage could ever change that." I look up at his pale eyes. "I am yours, Elum. Always yours."

He kisses me gently, in just the way I like.

"How *are* you?" he asks. "With Varo and Kal arrested . . ."

"I will speak to the Judge about them today."

"Will he be merciful?"

I scoff. "There are no miracles in Legalis."

He runs a finger along the edge of my face. "The Keeper deals in miracles, Glynis. I keep telling you that."

Speaking of . . . "I met a strange man a few days ago. I was in the desert, needing time to think—"

"I've told you not to go out there alone."

"I was fine. But then he was just . . . there. He implied he was sent by the Keeper."

"Then he was."

I jerk back to better see him. "Just like that, you believe him?"

"I know I can seem wary about faith, but considering all that's going on? I believe him."

"Sometimes I think I liked it better when we were totally on the same page, before you chose to believe in *him*."

"But *he* obviously wants you to know him too, dear one. Sending someone to talk to you like that? In the desert? That took effort."

"I guess it did."

"What does he want you to do?" he asks me.

"You assume he wants me to do something?"

"The Keeper is never dormant. Every one of his followers has something to do for him, for the sake of his Kingdom."

"Kingdom. The man mentioned that word." I touch my heart. "He says it's in here. He gave me a piece of paper with that word on it."

Elum's eyes brighten. "A Relic? Do you have it with you?"

"Yes, he called it a Relic. But no, it's back in my room. Though I don't see the significance to a few words on a scrap of paper."

"They are the core of significance," he says with emotion in his voice. "They are bits of wisdom from the Before Times. About him. Next time we meet, bring it to me. I'll share it with the others."

It makes me feel good to know I received something Elum values. "He did tell me to share it."

"See? The Keeper doesn't waste time. He has a plan and needs us to help carry it out."

"If he's so all-powerful, why doesn't he just do it himself?"

"I'm fairly new to believing, but I think he enjoys having a relationship with us, one on one."

"You know him one on one?"

Elum twirls the apple by its stem, then stops. "I'm working on it. It's different to think about connecting with him rather than just have him rule over us as some all-powerful being."

Elum doesn't say, "like the Judge", but I think of it on my own.

"He wants us to turn to him by choice, not because he demands it."

This choice-business is hard to comprehend. "I'm used to dealing with the Judge, who is all about commands."

"Ask the Keeper for help with your meeting. He *will* help you with the right words."

"The man in the desert said the same thing."

"See?"

I sit on my chair and Elum sits on his. "The man made me question my part in creating and supporting the laws of Legalis."

"I've been trying to do that for years."

"He says the **laws might be wrong and destructive.**"

Elum takes my hand. "Glynis, they are. You know they are."

I know they are.

He takes my other hand too. "If you don't get the Judge to change the law about Judging Day, Varo and Kal—and even you and Nixi—are in danger."

The threat of it weighs heavy. "I know."

"And also Helsa's grandmother and Helsa herself," he adds.

"I know that too. Helsa asked me to help."

"Solana's crime was far less serious than Varo's. She was simply caught in the Worker area."

"Giving them Relics."

"She was doing what the Keeper asked *her* to do."

And now I had one too. "How did she know about the Workers?"

"She saw the door while we were winding clocks, was curious, and went in by herself. I told her not to go again, but she's driven. I can't blame her for going. She's very devoted to the Keeper. And now she has to pay for it."

"But how much punishment is right and reasonable? I don't want Helsa hurt. She's become dear to me."

"All the more reason to change the law."

I stand and press my hand against my forehead, feeling my thoughts press against all logic. "It's too much, Elum. I don't know if I'm up to it."

"Are you still weak from the poison?"

It would make a good excuse, but that wasn't it. "I'm feeling fine physically, but mentally and emotionally is another matter."

Elum looks at the blue sky. "Keeper? Provide my dear Glynis with the courage and the words to do your good work. Protect her from all harm."

I stand in awe of him. "He'll do it just like that?"

"It serves his purposes too, you know." He pulls me into his arms again. "I ask and you ask. He listens and answers. I guarantee it."

Somehow, in his arms I believe it.

**

It was hard to leave Elum, but after going home to change into something appropriate for my audience with the Judge, I head out.

Having a meeting is not unusual. As the Head Notable I have weekly meetings with him—or I did, until I was sidelined by Varo.

The poisoning is one of the topics I need to speak to him about. And Varo and Kal in jail. And for a lesser crime, Solana.

Even though I've known the Judge my entire life—he's only two years older than I am—I still get nervous walking through the tunnel that leads from the Notable area to his . . . lair.

That's a vicious word for it, and no one ever calls his compound a lair to his face. But it feels like one: a haunting stone hideout where a monster lives.

For the Judge *is* a monster. Yes, he's just a man from a long line of men who grabbed onto the job at the end of the Before Times. One power-hungry, ambitious family who saw a need and took advantage of our weaknesses. Not that I blame his family. Someone had to restore order to the craziness and chaos.

I suspect their initial intention was honorable. Yet somehow, over the years, their noble desire for order went too far. I can't imagine the Legalis of the present was what they intended.

Then again, my opinion is based on the cracks that are appearing in the legalistic dome that those in power so greedily crafted over Legalis. I'm included in that group.

I never used to think of us as greedy. Yes, of course I've had the occasional thought that we Notables have much and the Masses have little, but I shoved the disparity aside with the excuse that it's always been that way. It's not like I have any revolutionary ideas about how to change things.

Revolutionary? The man in the desert implied a rebellion.

My, I'm having defiant thoughts today, which is not a good frame of mind when I'm going to be with the Judge in a matter of minutes.

I approach the guard at the gate leading to the Judge's compound.

"Good morning, Head Notable," he says with a nod.

"Good morning to you."

He doesn't ask questions for there's no need. When I've come this far it means I'm expected. He opens the gate and I enter an inner courtyard surrounded by a three-story structure, open to the sky far above. All of the Judge's family—his mother, two sisters, a wife, a son, and a daughter—live here, along with the servants needed to sustain such a massive complex.

I enter the main door and climb two sets of stairs to the top level. The Judge's chamber is in the back.

Another guard stands at that door. The two of us don't exchange a word, as I expect to be let through—per usual. But this time he stops me and says, "Excuse me, Head Notable, but the Judge is currently occupied."

I'm taken aback. We had an appointment.

"If you'll wait over there please?" he says.

I step aside and sit on a bench. I try not to feel put-out by it, but sitting here—rejected at the door—is demeaning.

But what choice do I have?

I know this is a good opportunity for me to collect my thoughts one last time, to organize my strategy, but I can't concentrate.

Then I hear commotion and stand. Suddenly, Ivar comes out of the Judge's chambers. My over-eager stand-in.

He sees me, and is startled as well. But he recovers immediately and grins. "Well, well. Glynis. I hope your meeting goes as well as mine did." He makes a condescending bow.

Everything about Ivar is condescending, as if he knows more, is more, and has more than everyone else. I dislike him immensely.

Once Ivar leaves, the guard tells me, "You may go in now, Head Notable."

I don't like that Ivar and the Judge just spoke. What was he doing here anyway? I'm not sick anymore. I'm back.

I find the Judge seated at his massive desk, facing the door. I calm my breathing and put on a respectful — but strong — expression.

Unfortunately we're not alone. His aide sits in one of the guest chairs. He rises when I enter.

"Good morning, Head Notable," the aide says to me.

"And to you." I sit next to him on the visitor's side of the desk. I'm disappointed by his presence. My delicate matters would be more easily discussed if we were alone.

The Judge sets aside the papers he's been reading. "Good morning, Glynis," he says.

"Good morning, Ubel." He's looking older than usual today. He's tall, overly slim — which makes him look taller, and he's always been gaunt in the face. But there are rings under his dark eyes.

"I thought we'd start with an update about the Regalia group and what they're up to," he says.

The Regalia group? What about Varo? But I nod, following his lead.

He looks at his aide. "Wyan, your report, please."

Wyan smiles. I know he thrives on attention.

"I've earned the trust of their leader, Oria." He grins. "She's quite smitten with me."

I didn't know Wyan was involved with her in this way. "You've been spending time with her?"

"I have. I got myself assigned to the food booth where she works."

He seems very proud of himself.

The Judge leans forward, resting his arms on his desk. "I heard you showed Oria the walkway?"

Wyan's face reddens. "Uh . . . it's out of the way and barely used anymore. I wanted her to share personal information, so I thought showing her something special would be tit for tat."

"Your choice was questionable, Wyan," he says. "The place is not known."

His face reddens slightly. "She enjoyed the view. That's the extent of it." He fingers the arm of the chair.

"Don't do it again," the Judge says.

"Yes, Judge. Be assured that my friendship with Oria will give us the information we need about their plans."

"*We* need?" I ask.

"Obviously he is acting at my behest, Glynis. We *need* to know what they're doing that might arouse the Masses. You heard Oria on Judging

Day. She's gutsy. No one has ever questioned our methods. Such attitudes *need* to be curtailed. We don't want a revolution on our hands."

Revolution. There was that word again. "Of course not. Continue."

His right eyebrow rises. He does not need my permission or approval. For anything.

Wyan sits up straighter in his chair. "The good news is that Oria's best friend, Solana, was arrested yesterday. So that's one less of their kind out in public."

Should I speak up about Solana? I wish Wyan wasn't here.

Wyan continues. "The bad thing about Oria is her faith seems unshakeable."

Ubel nods. "Perhaps some additional crises should be inflicted to break them."

I hate the sound of that. Although we are on the same side, the Judge's methods often make me cringe. "What do you have in mind?"

The Judge looks at Wyan. "Do you have anything else to report?"

He seems flustered at his obvious dismissal, and I imagine he's trying to think of something to prolong his moment of relevance. Finally he says, "Not at this time."

Ubel waves his hand at him. "Carry on."

I'm relieved when Wyan leaves. I want to talk about Varo and Solana now but I can't just blurt out my concerns. I've learned the Judge responds best when he is the one initiating the conversation.

Which, thankfully, he does. "I suppose you want to talk about your husband."

"And my maid. And the woman, Solana."

He seems surprised by my mention of her. "The first two I expected but the third? Why should she concern you?"

"She is the grandmother of Helsa, the artist who painted a mural in my home. Helsa is a hard worker, so much so, that she's taking over for Kal. She's a dependable young woman who has earned my respect. And she was the one who saved me from the poison."

"That is commendable."

It seems too scant a word. "Plus, Helsa's grandmother had no bad intentions. She poses no threat." The lie is necessary. Ubel considers all Relics a threat.

"Is she one of the Exiled?"

I have to tell the truth. "She is." But then I fudge by saying, "Even so her crime is negligible."

"Negligible compared to your husband trying to kill you."

There is that. "Just hear me out, Ubel. She admits to being somewhere she shouldn't have been—"

"Talking with the Workers, who are purposely and carefully sequestered from the general population."

"But the Workers are from Regalia. They knew each other. *That* was their only connection. Nothing sinister or dangerous."

"Yet their acquaintance means their bond is stronger than that of strangers."

He's right. "At the bidding of the granddaughter, I ask for Solana's punishment to be commuted. She is new to Legalis and is not fully versed in the laws of the land, and—"

Ubel holds up one long finger, that even without his costume demands attention. "Ignorance of the law is no defense."

"I understand. But perhaps a more balanced punishment would be to give her a Fault. Or two?"

"How many does she currently have?"

"I'm not sure." Hopefully none.

"I shall consider your request." He sits up straighter in his massive chair. "Moving on to Varo . . . he's put me in a difficult situation."

"I understand that. But I ask you to grant an exception in his case, due to his position as a Notable."

"And as your husband."

"That too."

"But you are the victim, Glynis. Surely you want revenge? And it must be noted that you were the one who arranged for his arrest."

All valid points. "The problem with punishing Varo in the same way Legalis punishes others is the means: the Cudgeling Circle."

His eyes show his comprehension. "Either you or Nixi would be punished in his place."

"Obviously, I don't want either outcome." I make a point beyond the personal. "And I don't think it's wise to have the Head Notable beaten in the public square."

"Then let it be your daughter."

"No!"

He cocks his head at my reaction and I force my voice to sound calm. "Of course I don't want that, Ubel. Just as you wouldn't want your daughter punished like that."

"But *I* have broken no laws." He sits forward in his chair. "Have you considered this punishment might have been Varo's fallback plan? If his poisoning attempts were found out—which they were—then he would let himself be arrested and have you killed via the Circle."

I dismiss the idea immediately. "I don't think Varo thought that far ahead. He assumed I would die quietly, in my bed."

"Did he?" The Judge sits back and tents his fingers.

I continue. "One thing I haven't figured out is what Varo hoped to gain through my death. I know he's ambitious, but he won't ascend to my position, Ivar will. Varo will never be voted into such a high station." Thank goodness.

"And then there is the other . . ." Ubel sighs dramatically. "We both know Varo has a hard time controlling his . . . impulses?"

I hate that everyone knows about my husband's infidelities. "His indiscretions have been hard to live with, but I endured them for the sake of Legalis."

"Does he have someone special . . .?"

"No," I say honestly. "Not that I know of." My husband's inability to commit to anything beyond the moment has its advantages.

"So what *is* his motive for poisoning you?"

"You'll have to ask Varo but I think it may be as simple as this: spite. He hates that his wife has a higher rank than he does, therefore, he hates me."

"You deserve the position, Glynis. He never did — and never will."

"I appreciate your support, Judge. I make every effort to do what's best for Legalis."

"Because of that, you can surely see that what's best for Legalis is for Varo to be punished following our laws, as written. It will be best if he is punished via the Circle."

My heart skips a beat. "I don't see that at all."

"Yes, you do. If I show favoritism because he's a Notable then we risk an uprising. You don't want that, do you?"

I'd deal with it. "You're condemning me to death, Ubel."

"Not you," he says. "I can't sacrifice you."

Which means . . . "And *I* won't sacrifice Nixi!"

"The Circle doesn't mean certain death," he says.

"Most of the time, it does. And it definitely means extreme pain. Crushing pain with broken bones and . . ." I shudder.

"If you're asking me for mercy, save your breath, Glynis. Mercy has no place in Legalis. You've had a hand in writing the laws that make it so."

Yes. I am guilty of pursuing laws that focus on judgment, not benevolence.

The Judge stands to his full height. Even without his black costume he's an ominous figure. And despite myself, I feel a wave of fear.

"I'm sorry, Glynis, but the laws of Legalis must be upheld at all cost."

That's it?

He stares at me, waiting for me to leave.

That's it.

I thank him for his time.

I have no idea what to do next. How will I ever tell Nixi?

CHAPTER FORTY

HELSA

I want to talk to Nana first thing but Papa says I need to show up for my new job. Perhaps the Head Notable has good news for us. Papa assured me he will send word if I need to come to the jail.

Nixi answers the door for me—a job that will be mine.

"How are you faring?" she asks me. "How is your grandmother?"

Nixi is so kind. She, whose father is locked up too. "Nana is strong. But of course I worry about her."

"Of course."

We walk into the parlor. "How is your father, mistress?" I ask.

Her hands busy themselves with each other. "I tried to see him yesterday, but they wouldn't let me. But I could hear him yelling, even from the street. He's angry. Bitter. Loud." She snickers. "He's as he always is and always was."

"I wonder if the two of them will get to know each other."

"Not willingly," she says. "I mean no offense, but Father can be quite a snob."

"Understood." It's awkward just standing here. I'd hoped Nixi would immediately tell me her mother had a plan to help Nana. To spur the conversation I ask, "How is your mother feeling?"

"She's surprisingly strong." Nixi looks uncomfortable.

"Did she have a chance to do anything about my nana?"

Nixi hesitates and runs her hand along the edge of a table. Is she stalling? Is it bad news?

Suddenly, Glynis walks in the parlor. "I did have a chance. Good morning, Helsa."

I nod. "Good morning, Head Notable."

She gets right to the point. "I spoke to the Judge and explained the situation," she tells us. "I explained your grandmother's lesser offense."

"And?" Nixi asks.

"He will consider leniency."

It's more iffy than what I want to hear, but it's better than nothing. I dare to ask one more thing. "When will we know, mistress?"

"I have no idea."

She seems weary. I know she's still recovering from the poison, plus dealing with her husband, and now Nana . . .

"Nixi, may I speak to you in private?" she asks.

"Of course." To me she says, "Why don't you see if you can help Bog."

"Yes, mistress."

We part in the hall, with the two of them heading toward Glynis's bedroom, while I go to the kitchen.

Bog is happy to see me. "My new helper! I'm glad you're here, Helsa."

"Thank you. I know next to nothing about cooking, but I'm willing to learn."

"That's all I ask." He's punching some dough, but steps back. "Wash your hands, then you have a try at it."

I pour a few ladles of water into a bowl and wash. "What are we making?"

"Butter buns with cinnamon."

"What's cinnamon?"

His round eyes widen. "Oh my dear. I have *so* much to teach you!"

He shows me how to pinch off some dough, roll it into a ball, and place it on a metal sheet.

"Keep going until the dough's all gone."

While I work he sits and puts his feet up in the way I'd first found him days ago. I don't mind. I like him. Plus, I like learning something new, and I'm hoping it keeps my mind off Nana.

"I heard about your granny," he says. He picks his teeth with a toothpick. "I don't know what she did, but it can't have been as bad as the mister."

"Not near as bad," I say. "The mistress spoke to the Judge about her, trying to get her out."

His eyebrow arches. "That would be a first. Here's hoping it works."

I'm shocked. "No one has ever been freed?"

He shrugs. "None that I've heard of."

My hope is dashed. "No! That's not fair."

He presses his hands down, trying to calm me. "Don't take my word for it. If you asked the Head Notable for help, she'll help."

I take a deep breath to shove my panic away.

"I do feel bad for Kal being there," Bog says. "She's a nice enough girl. Naïve maybe, but . . ."

"She's learning the hard way," I say.

"As do we all," he says. He glances toward the hall. "Did I hear the voice of the mistress?"

I nod. "She's talking with Nixi in her room."

"Hmm," he says, digging at a back tooth. "I suppose they have a lot to talk about with one of 'em going to the Circle and all."

Them? I stop working and look at him. "What are you talking about?"

He looks shocked by my surprise. "That's the way of jail—ignoring that your granny *might* get special help—that's how it works. Surely you've been here long enough to know about Judging Day?"

"I've seen one." I stop forming rolls and let the painful memory claim its moment. "I was one of the Beaters."

He sits up straight, his feet hitting the floor with a clop-clop. "Wow They made you do it even with you being new?"

"Actually, a friend was called up. I volunteered to take his place."

Bog's eyes grow wide. "That was you?"

"It was."

His face grows serious. "Was it awful?"

"Horrible. The entire practice is vicious. Inhumane."

"I won't argue with ya. But it is what it is. It's always been that way."

"That doesn't mean it can't be changed."

He snickers. "Change? You *are* new here. Nothing in Legalis changes: not our weather, not our clothes, not our schedules, and not our laws—unless they spice things up by adding a few more." He shakes his head. "I wish your granny the best—and you the best too since yer her kin—but I wouldn't count on the Judge being lenient."

All hope dies. If Glynis can't even help herself and Nixi, how can I ever hope she can help Nana? "So the mistress or Nixi will have to go to the Circle?"

Bog shrugs. "That's the way of it."

Imagining dignified Glynis or sweet Nixi having to enter the Circle is too much. A wave of anger flows through me. "This isn't right!"

"It is what it—"

"No!" I yell. "It can't happen!" I run out of the kitchen to Glynis's bedroom, where I push open the door without even knocking.

"This can't happen!" I yell. "It can't!"

Only then do I notice that Nixi is crying.

She knows.

Bog appears in the doorway, out of breath. His eyes scan the three of us. "I'm sorry, mistresses." He pokes at my back. "Get outta here, girl. Right now!"

I look down and see that I'm holding a hunk of dough.

Glynis stands. "It's all right, Bog. I'll take care of this." She plucks the dough from my hand, gives it to Bog, then closes the door between us. He looks completely stunned.

As am I.

Yet the full implication of what I've done hits me. "I'm so sorry, Head Notable. I had no right to barge in here, but . . ."

"But you were worried about Nixi. Your friend."

Tears well up in my eyes. My throat is tight. "And you. This isn't right. None of it is right."

Nixi rushes into my arms. I'm surprised by the contact, but I hug her back. Curse the rules. I miss hugs.

We cling to each other. "Mama says the Judge won't let her go to the Circle, so it's me. And you might have to go too."

The reality of her words . . . Glynis must not be hopeful about the Judge being lenient about Nana.

This could really happen. Death could really happen.

To both of us. We're too young to fathom it. We have our entire lives ahead of us.

Lives that might be cut short.

I'm glad — and surprised — Glynis allows our hug to linger.

Finally, Nixi pulls away. Glynis hands me a handkerchief.

"Sit, ladies. We need to talk."

The two of us sit on a bench across from the bed. Glynis stands before us. Her eyes are red from her own tears.

"What happens now, Mama?" Nixi asks.

"First, we don't panic. Some people in jail have been there for months. They will go first."

"For sure?" Nixi asks.

I don't like the way Glynis hesitates. "Not for sure. But that's the norm."

"But Father being there has disrupted the norm," Nixi says.

Glynis nods and bites her lip. I'm not feeling reassured at all.

Nixi takes my hand and squeezes hard. "When will we know a timeline, Mama?"

Her forehead creases. "I don't know."

If *she* doesn't know . . .

Her expression changes as I see her make a decision. "I need to think. If you'll excuse me." She walks out.

Nixi and I are left alone. "This whole thing is horrifying," she says. "I wish Father had never been arrested."

"But then your mother might be dead."

She tosses her hands in the air, then paces between me and the bed. "We should've stopped him another way. Who cares if he's punished — because *he's* not being punished, I am!" Her face is a mask of misery. She stops pacing and faces me. "What if Mama can't fix it?"

"She's the Head Notable. If she can't then —"

"No one can."

I've never felt so helpless and hopeless. My entire body feels heavy with the weight of the violence and pain that seems destined to be Nixi's future—and mine.

Nixi slumps down beside me. "Can you call out to that Keeper you believe in? Maybe he can help."

"Of course I can. We can."

"I can?" she asks.

"Anyone can. He's not just *my* Keeper, he's yours too."

I see a *really?* look on her face. "Tell me what words to say, Helsa. Are there special words?"

"Not at all. You just talk. Say it out loud."

"You go first," Nixi says.

I'm not one to pray for others to hear, but our lives depend on it. I take Nixi's hand and look upward. "Keeper? Please hear our prayers…"

I speak my heart and Nixi speaks hers. I know the Keeper hears us. But how will he answer?

**

Nixi spends the rest of the day in her room. I haven't seen Glynis since she left to think. I am left alone with my thoughts—which run wild and offer no solutions. Bog tries to help by keeping me busy, and I've even dusted the furniture—probably more than once as I quickly forget what I've already dusted.

My prayers are like arrows shot to heaven. Where they land nobody knows. I don't feel any reassurance or peace. I am a mess. Fear is a rope tied around me, tightening until I feel I will collapse in on myself.

Mid-afternoon I can't take it any longer. I ask Bog, "Do you think I could leave? I want to try to talk to Nana, and Nixi and the mistress aren't here to ask."

"Go on with ya. I'll take the heat if they complain—which I doubt they will."

"Thank you, Bog."

I head to the jail. I feel completely vulnerable. Our fate is in the hands of a scary tyrant. Glynis seems afraid of him too. If *she* feels that way . . .

Finally I reach the spot beneath the high windows of Nana's cell. I wait until the street clears, then call out, "Nana?"

A few seconds later I hear, "Helsa! How are you?"

"*I'm* fine." I have to be careful what I say. I don't want to burst any hope she might have. "Hopefully, you'll get out soon."

"I'd appreciate it."

"Are you okay?"

"I am. And I'm not alone here."

Of course she's talking about the Keeper, but I don't dare say his name in public.

"Some other believers are here. We're having good talks."

"I'm glad." It's a relief she has like-minded people there. My thoughts turn to Varo who is in there too. I wonder what he thinks about their Keeper talk.

"Sa-Sa!" Lieb catches up to me. He has whitewash on his cheek. "Are you talking to Nana?"

"I am."

"Hi, Nana," he calls out.

"Hi, Lieb. How was work?"

I can't believe she's asking him about something so mundane.

"It's good. There are always walls to paint. More and more walls. I like it. I get to meet a lot of people."

"Good for you."

The streets are getting busy with people going home. I don't want to get in trouble with a Fault Finder. "We need to go now, Nana. I love you."

"I love you too, child. Both of you."

As we hurry home I wonder if Nana has thought about me or Papa being sent to the Circle. Or is she in denial about it, hopeful that she'll get out?

I've pretty much abandoned that hope.

Lieb chatters on about the people he met today, seemingly oblivious to the life and death crisis we're facing. I envy him.

When we get to Papa's, Elum, Oria, and Rand are already there, getting a meal ready. The atmosphere is grim.

Papa arrives just after we do. We all turn to him, expectantly.

"How is she?" Rand asks.

"In remarkably good spirits."

"That sounds like her." Oria pours water for everyone.

Lieb sits at the table. "Do we have any oranges? I'd really like some oranges."

"I'll try to get us some," Oria says. "There weren't any in the booth today and —"

I slap my hands on the table. "Who cares about stupid oranges? Don't you realize that either me or Papa will go to the Circle?"

They all stare at me.

"We thought you were talking to the Head Notable," Rand says, "that it would be taken care of, that Solana would be all right."

"Glynis tried, but she isn't hopeful." I look at each of their faces. "Papa and I have a slim chance of avoiding that punishment. But Glynis and Nixi won't be so lucky. Nixi is going to the Circle. The Judge all but said so."

Elum drops his knife. "She can't!"

"She can. He's not going to give Varo any leeway just because he's a Notable. So his punishment falls on Nixi."

Papa sinks onto the bench. "In my mother's case . . . if one of us has to go, it should be me. You have your whole life ahead of you."

I appreciate Papa's offer. I know how much he loves me. It's touching he says such a thing—and I don't want to die—but I don't want either of us to go.

We all stare into the air as if answers will appear there. But they don't. There are no answers.

There is only fear. And death.

Oria paces up and back, then stops. "We need to contact the Exiled."

"Now?" I ask. "How can they help?"

"They can pray," Oria says. "Everyone? Let's go."

"That's a great idea," Rand says. "'A cord of three is not easily broken.'"

I'm not so sure. The Judge could break it. Break all of us.

**

We fan out with Devin and Elum going one way, and the rest of us going another. We knock on the doors of the Exiled. A few say they'll pray. A few simply nod. My opinion of them stands: none of them have ever impressed me.

I see Oria wave at someone. "Aury!"

She approaches him and we tag along. He's a nice-looking man, and has a young boy with him. He has four Faults on his shoulder.

They exchange greetings, then Oria looks at the boy. "How are you, Pan?"

"I'm good," he says.

I'm about to head off on my own when Oria introduces us. "Everyone, this is Aury. I worked with his wife, Trina."

I know my face expresses my surprise. "The one who beat you up?"

Oria nods, but smiles at the boy. "And this is Pan. Pan, these are my friends."

He stares at Rand. "I've seen you by the Sanctuary."

"That's me," Rand says.

"You're Marked."

Rand lifts his hair. "I most certainly am."

Aury shushes him. "Stop it, boy. We have no right to condemn others when your own mother was sent to jail."

"How is she?" Oria asks.

"She's dead," Pan says.

Dead? In jail?

"How?" Oria asks.

The father answers. "We don't know for sure, but with her mouth and temper? She probably got in a fight and the guards won."

I'm glad Nana doesn't have a temper.

"I'm so sorry," Oria says.

"Me too," Lieb says.

Aury shrugs. "Yeah. Well." He looks down at his son. "We're doing all right, aren't we, boy?"

Pan peers up at him and I can see the love they have for each other.

"I heard about your friend who was put in jail," Aury says. "I wish there was something we could do."

"There is," Oria says. She seems hesitant but barrels on. "I don't know your beliefs about the Keeper, but we're asking those who believe to pray."

Aury leans close and lowers his voice. "We didn't believe much because Trina hated him, but with her gone, we do now. What do you need us to pray for?"

Oria beams. "That Solana is set free. And ask your friends to pray too."

I interrupt. "It's not just about my nana either. If she's convicted, I go to the Cudgeling Circle. And pray for the Head Notable's daughter, Nixi too. She's going to the Circle."

Aury's eyes widen. "We'll definitely pray." He taps his chest with his fingers, and we do the same as we move along.

"What a victory that was," Oria says.

"Are you sad Trina is dead?" I ask.

"I don't know how I feel. But I'm glad to see Aury and Pan doing so well. Trina used to tell me what a horrible man he is, and she'd tattle about him to the Fault Finders to get him in trouble."

Rand shakes his head. "Some people thrive on causing trouble." Then his eyes light up and he calls out, "Yair!"

A man wearing a dirty white robe walks with his head down. He looks up warily. It's Berit's father. The G branded on his forehead still looks raw.

The two Marked Men meet. "It's good to see you again, Rand," Yair says.

"And you."

Oria nods at him. "How are you faring since . . .?"

"Since I was Marked and set free?"

"Yes."

He shrugs. "I won't complain. My assigned area is near the Farm, so I occasionally get to see something green."

Rand shares what needs to be prayed for.

"I'm so sorry for all of it," Yair says. "I'll pray for a miracle."

"Yes. Please," Rand says. "And if you could ask others to pray, we'd appreciate it."

"I'll do just that. For it is said, 'Ask, and you will receive. Search, and you will find. Knock, and the door will be opened for you.'"

"A Relic?" I ask.

"A good one." He makes the sign of a believer and walks on.

"This is going well," Oria says. "I'm quite hopeful."

I want to be.

CHAPTER FORTY-ONE

GLYNIS

I wander the streets of Legalis.

When I left Nixi and Helsa in my room, they were grieving their shared fates. I know they still hope I can stop the entire process, but I fear their hope is in vain.

Although Nixi enjoys walking among the Masses, it makes me uncomfortable. She loves being around people. I, do not.

I'm glad that I'm wearing a black robe instead of a fancy one, but I still stand out among the sea of white robes. Dirty robes. White cloth can't stay clean with unpaved streets. The bottom inches of everyone's robes are stained. They can never feel good about how they look. Perhaps that was the plan? Though the law making the Masses wear white was made long before my time, it was an ill-advised decision.

One of many?

One of two, at least. Although I've never endorsed the Cudgeling Circle, I've done nothing to stop it. It was always just something that *was*. I fear it says too much about my character that I've only cared about it now that it affects me personally.

People step aside as I pass. They stare, recognizing me from my weekly presence on Sanctuary Day. I wonder what they know about my weeks-long absence. Do they know Varo poisoned me? If they do, are they glad or sympathetic? I have no reason to believe the latter. What have I ever done for them?

It takes conscious effort, but I keep my head up and even offer the occasional small smile and nod. No one smiles back. Many talk to each other behind their hands.

I am not their friend. I am an authority figure who has power over them.

I suffer a small twinge of self-doubt. I want them to like me.

Stop it, Glynis. They don't need to like me. It's best if they don't like me; best if they fear me like they fear the Judge. That's the way order is maintained.

Isn't it?

I find myself looking down as I walk, unnerved by my pathetic thoughts—which are *not* appropriate for someone who is the Head Notable.

Suddenly, the clocks start to chime. I jump at the shocking din.

It's the Count.

Which applies to everyone but me.

Everyone heads to the nearest door and within a minute I am the only one on the street. I turn full circle and shudder at the sudden realization that I am alone. It's eerie and unsettling.

I suddenly wonder about the logic of the Count. Why should everyone stop what they're doing once an hour and scurry away into a random house or shop? What good does it do? What purpose does it serve?

I hear faint clinks and see marbles being placed on the sill outside a door nearby. Four black marbles and one white one.

Four visitors and one inhabitant.

The one has to host four strangers, probably multiple times a day.

Again, why?

Two Counters come into view. They see me and pull up short as if uncertain what to do. They give me a little bow and I nod in return. They walk by the house where I'd seen the marbles put out, but go into the next one.

"Here to count!" they yell as they open the door without knocking.

I hear voices, and as quickly as they entered, they leave and move on to another random unit to check.

It's utterly pointless. Again, why? To my knowledge the hourly numbers are never added together in any checks and balance system. And there's no reason for anyone to lie about how many people are in a building. It's inane, stupid, and pointless. Something really should be done to put a halt to it.

By me?

I continue walking, alone except for the occasional Counters barging into people's lives.

Although I started my walk aimlessly, I find myself near the jail cells where Varo is held. The subconscious is a powerful thing. Perhaps I'm here because I need him; need to see him. Need him to rescue me from having to deal with his crimes?

He's powerless, so my thought makes no sense, but since I'm here I decide to make good use of him. I step into the building. Two guards are sitting in the foyer. One is napping.

"Wake up!" says the second man, slapping the napper.

They both stand.

"Head Notable," one says with a nod. "How can we help you?"

"I wish to speak with my husband."

The guards look at each other. "That's not allowed, mistress."

I cock my head, dumbfounded by his words. "Not allowed?"

"Prisoners may not have visitors."

"That's absurd," I say.

The guard looks uncomfortable. "It's the law, Head Notable."

Implied — but not spoken — are the added words: *Your law.*

"I insist on seeing him," I say boldly. "Alone." When they still look uneasy I add, "I take full responsibility." I look around the wide corridor. "Is there an empty room we could use?"

Another guard points to a room on the left. "In there, mistress."

"Very good. Bring him to me."

The room has a table littered with leftover food and bowls. A guard quickly clears it, and arranges two chairs close.

I am left alone. I brush crumbs to the floor and wonder what I'm doing here. I have no idea what I'm going to say to my husband. We have nothing to talk about — beyond the fact he tried to kill me, and I had him arrested.

I realize how ridiculous it is, and get up to leave.

But too late.

I hear movement in the corridor and Varo appears in the doorway. He's genuinely surprised to see me.

"Glynis! What are you doing here?"

"Come in," I say. "Sit." I wave the guard away, indicating he should close the door.

My husband sits across from me. His skin is pale and his hair, messy. He has a three-day beard. I understand his disheveled appearance, but there's something else different about him. His attitude seems changed. I expected a belligerent bully, screaming at me for having him arrested. What I don't expect is this pensive man before me.

"Thanks for coming," he says.

I don't think Varo has ever thanked me for anything.

"How are you?" I ask. I wait for him to complain about the food, the bed, the lack of privacy.

Instead he says, "I'm kind of a mess."

"I understand that this situation is —"

"I'm really confused."

I'm puzzled by his admission. "About?"

"There's a lot of talk about . . . the other prisoners talk a lot."

"About?"

He shrugs, but I can tell whatever was said concerns him greatly.

"Tell me, Varo."

"They talk about the Keeper."

I'm shocked. "Ignore them."

"I tried. But a few of the things they say intrigue me."

"Like what?"

His hesitation is unlike him. Varo has strong opinions about everything—right or wrong.

"Varo . . ."

"They said when we're discouraged the Keeper will rescue us. He's a protector. And he's always with us." He shrugs. "We're not supposed to be afraid."

I'm impressed by all he retained—even if it is Keeper-propaganda. "Did it make you feel better?

"Well, yeah. I guess. Like I said, I'm confused."

I can imagine. It confuses me too, but I have other things to talk to him about. "But you're not confused about why you're here, are you? You didn't really think you'd get away with it. Poisoning me, Varo? Really?"

He avoids looking at me. "I didn't think much about it."

What an awful thing to say.

I lean on the table. He smells rank from going days without a bath. "Why did you do it? I know we aren't particularly close, but—"

"It was Ivar's idea."

I sit back in full shock mode. "Ivar. My stand in."

"He's the one."

It makes sense in a sick sort of way. "He *is* power hungry. But he'll probably get my position at some point—if he behaves himself. He didn't need to have me killed for it."

"He said he'd kill *me*."

I'm not following. "He'd kill you for killing me?"

He shakes his head. "If I didn't kill you he'd kill me."

This doesn't add up. "Why?"

"Well . . ."

The way he stares at the table and avoids my eyes says there is a lot more to it. "What did he have on you?"

He fidgets in the chair. "I don't want to say."

Again, who is this meek man sitting before me? "Considering the circumstances, Varo, I'm afraid you have no choice but to say."

He wipes a drop of water from the table with his sleeve. "I slept with Ivar's wife." He rushes to add, "It didn't mean anything, Glynis. You know it didn't."

I'm crushed. And horribly disappointed in him. "Just like all the others didn't mean anything—to you, Varo. But to me? Let me summarize here: you slept with Ivar's wife, he wanted to kill you, but wouldn't kill you if you killed me so he could step into the Head Notable position permanently."

He nods once. "You can see I was in a no-win situation. I didn't have a choice."

"Your choice could have been to be faithful to your wife."

He shrugs. "Yeah. Well. You know that's hard."

He says it flippantly, as if infidelity is a mere annoyance to me, like him biting his fingernails or chewing with his mouth open.

"It's been hard for me too, Varo." I glance toward the door and consider walking out, leaving him here to rot. But it's not that simple. "There's a good chance the Judge will convict you."

He seems puzzled. "But I'm a Notable. I'm the husband of the Head Notable."

"Who you tried to kill. The Judge can't risk the example leniency would set," I say. "The laws need to apply to everyone."

"But they don't," he says. "We don't have to participate in the Counts, or only eat food that's allotted to us, or wear stupid white robes, or only work in jobs we're assigned to, or —"

"Why not though?" I ask. "Because we're above all that?"

"Well . . . yeah."

"The Judge doesn't see it that way. Your crime has put him in a unique situation — a difficult one, without precedent. And so, you *will* be convicted. Which means . . .?" I need him to think it through.

He touches his forehead. "I'll be a Marked Man."

I'm not surprised he thinks of himself first. "It also means . . ."

He sits there, blinking. Thinking. Then his eyes widen. "The Circle. It means you or Nixi will go to the Circle!"

"Not me — because of my position, which is sacrosanct. So Nixi will go. Our daughter, Nixi, will be beat to death. Because of your crime."

"No!" He jolts to standing, making his chair fall backward.

The door opens and a guard peers in. "Everything all right in here?"

"It's fine," I say. "I'll let you know if I need you."

He gives Varo a stern look and closes the door.

"Sit down," I tell him.

He does, but looks even more deflated. "What are we going to do, Glynis?"

I feel sorry for him — for my murderer. "I'm not sure there's anything we can do," I say. "We can only hope she lives through it."

"Even if she does, she'll be hurt. Badly."

"I know." I reach out and touch his hand. "I know." I realize there's nothing more to say. "I should go."

He looks at me, imploringly. "When will this happen?"

"The Judge didn't say."

He only nods. "I'm glad you came, Glynis. I appreciate it."

It's my turn to nod.

I open the door and let the guards take my husband back to his cell. I realize our conversation was the longest talk we've had in months. Maybe years. Which makes me sad.

Once outside, I see a pretty redhead talking to the air. She's looking upward as she speaks. I overhear the name "Helsa."

She stops talking when she sees me. I can tell she has no idea who I am, but by her red hair I recognize her. She's Oria. She's the one the Judge is concerned about. The one Wyan has been assigned to befriend. And . . . "You're that woman who spoke on Judging Day," I say.

"I am. And you are?"

"The Head Notable."

Her eyes widen. "Excuse me. I didn't know. I haven't seen . . ."

"I've been absent from Sanctuary Day for a few weeks. You mentioned Helsa? My Helsa? The dear girl who saved my life?"

She smiles. "She's *our* Helsa. Her grandmother is in jail. I was just speaking to her."

I look at the building and only see a few high slits. "Through those?"

"It's all we have."

No, it isn't. "Come with me." I go back into the jail and she follows.

The main guard steps forward. "Yes, Head Notable?"

"This is Oria. She wishes to speak with . . ." I suddenly forget the grandmother's name.

"Solana," Oria says.

"Please arrange it," I tell the guard. "Let them use the same room I used."

"As you wish, mistress."

His quick compliance makes me go further. "From now on allow all prisoners to speak in private to one visitor a day. Understood?"

"But it's not—"

"Understood?" I ask again.

"Yes, mistress."

I suddenly get an idea and turn to Oria. "May I join you?"

"Of course. Mistress."

I return to the room and Oria follows. I pull a third chair up to the table. Oria doesn't sit, and I realize she's waiting for me. So I sit first.

"This is very, very nice of you to arrange, Head Notable," she says.

I feel oddly embarrassed by her compliment. "Yes. Well . . ."

Solana is led inside, and Oria rises to hug her, then they quickly pull apart. "Sorry," she says. "No touching."

I sigh. "Yet another absurd, indefensible law. Sit. Please sit, both of you."

Solana is quite short compared to Oria's height. She's in her sixties, with her gray hair pulled back with a cord. Her skin is wrinkled, yet in all the right places, like the corners of her eyes when she smiles.

Which she does.

"Head Notable," she says. "When they said you wanted to speak with me . . . Helsa has said so many nice things about you. How are you feeling?"

I'm touched. "I am well, thank you—thanks to your granddaughter."

"She often spoke of your illness, and how bad she felt for you. We prayed for your health. Obviously, the Keeper answered."

I'm stunned to hear her speak so openly about him. "I appreciate the sentiment, but I have no wish to seek the intercession of . . . of . . ."

"He likes to intercede. To provide. To guide. It's what he does."

I glance at Oria, who is smiling slightly, as if she expects nothing less from Solana than what she's hearing.

"You spoke with your husband?" Solana asks.

I'm not used to people speaking to me so freely. "I did."

Solana nods. "We've been talking to him. Mostly *past* him actually, as there are other believers being held here as well. We've witnessed quite a change in him."

"How so?"

"At first he was all blustery and yelled at us; real belligerent." She grins. "We kept talking anyway, sharing Relics we knew and —"

"Relics? You have Relics in the cells?"

She taps her head. "They're in here." Then her heart. "And here." Solana looks at Oria. "I learned some new ones you'll like. I taught them to Devin."

"I can't wait to hear them."

"We've even done a little singing." She chuckles. "Now *that* annoyed your husband something awful, but Kal . . ." Her face softens. "Kal has a wonderful voice and is very interested."

"Really."

She nods. "Facing drastic punishment tends to nudge people toward faith. The Keeper's always willing to step up in times of dire need."

Step up?

Oria taps the table. "That's one thing I wanted to tell you, Solana. We've been spreading the word about the Keeper, getting people to pray for all of you." She looks at me. "We're praying for you and your family too, Head Notable."

I'm shocked, and somehow moved. "Thank you."

"It's all good as he is all good," Solana says. "That's what I was saying about your husband. He started out nasty, but he *has* been listening. He's even asked a few questions."

Hence, the calmer version of Varo.

Solana shakes her head a quick bit, then says, "Helsa said you were going to speak to the Judge on our behalf. Is that why you've come here? Is there news?"

I hate to disappoint her. "Not as yet. I did speak to him, pointed out your lesser offense, and recommended that you be given Faults instead of . . . the other."

Her pale eyes are hopeful. "And?"

"He said he'd think about it."

"So the Judge is definitely a man," Solana says. "Someone you can talk to?"

I realize I've damaged his public persona. "He only speaks to an elite few. But he's ultimately in charge. As you've seen on Sanctuary Day."

They seem to discount this as the hasty explanation it is. "When will we know?" Oria asks.

"That, I can't tell you."

Solana's face grows serious. "I will *not* have Devin or Helsa sent to the Circle for my crime." She straightens her back. "*I* will take my own punishment."

Such a thing is unheard of — though others *have* offered. "That's not possible."

"It is if I walk into that Circle myself."

The thought of this tiny woman striding into the Cudgeling Circle is disturbing. Yet I don't doubt her resolve.

"Solana," Oria says. "Hopefully that won't be necessary. Hopefully the Judge will show mercy and you'll be set free with a few studs on your shoulder."

"Mercy?" I say. "The Judge doesn't commend or portend mercy."

Solana shrugs. "If the Keeper wills it, it will happen." She presses her hands flat on the table. "I had a dream about the Circle."

Oria perks up as if Solana's dreams are notable. "What happened? Who did you see there?"

"Unfortunately, that wasn't clear." She inhales deeply. "But everything felt all right . . . all good . . . resolved."

"Did you see my daughter there?" I ask. "Nixi?"

"Not specifically. Again, the details were hazy. It was more of a feeling." Solana changes the subject again. "How is Lieb?" she asks Oria.

"Worried. You know the depth of his heart."

Solana explains. "Lieb is a grandson in all but blood. He's the sweetest, most innocent boy I've ever known."

I remember a scene from the last Judging Day. I wasn't officiating, but Nixi got me there to watch. I remember looking down on the scene from the walkway. All in all, it was a much better way to attend than being in charge. "Was Lieb the one who was assigned to the Circle — the one Helsa replaced?"

"That's Lieb. His name means 'lion' but he's gentle as a lamb."

"Unless one of those he loves is hurting," Oria adds.

"Very true." Solana moves on to other members of her family. "How is Rand?"

I begin to stand, to leave these two to themselves, until she says, "And Elum?"

I sit back down. "Elum?"

Solana cocks her head. "He's the roommate of my son, Devin. Do you know him?"

My heart beats faster, just thinking of him. "I do. He's a good man."

"Yes, he is. How do you know him?"

Now it's *really* time to leave. "If you'll excuse me. Continue your visit. I'll make sure the guards allow the other prisoners to have visitors too."

"That's much appreciated," Oria says.

"I'll keep talking to Varo, mistress," Solana says. "We'll soften him up yet."

"That remains to be seen."

When I leave the jail my mind is a jumble. I head home but don't pay attention to the Masses around me. I'm too absorbed in my own thoughts, for so much has changed.

Have I changed?

I've witnessed a Count. I've had a chastened Varo confess his sins to me. I've found out that Ivar wanted me — wants me? — dead. And I met Oria and Solana, two Regalians with an immoveable faith in the Keeper.

Yet one of the most satisfying events was getting the idea to change the prisoner policy, by allowing visitors.

All accomplished by my order. Just a few words from my mouth and something good came about.

It makes me want to do more. As the Head Notable I have the power.

I start to get all sorts of ideas . . .

But first things first.

I need to talk to the Judge.

**

It concerns me when I see Ivar leaving the Judge's chambers. Again. Since when are they so close?

When he sees me, he smiles smugly with a curt nod. "Glynis."

There's a threatening undertone in the way he says my name. Or maybe I'm reading into things. After all, now I *know* how far he'll go to gain power. "Ivar," I say with a confidence I don't feel.

He pauses. "Are you feeling well enough to take over the Sanctuary Day service tomorrow? If not, I'll—"

"I am fully and totally well," I say. "Thank you for stepping up in my absence."

His left eyebrow arches. "Of course. I've glad to do it."

That's an understatement.

He gestures toward the Judge's door. "He's all yours."

Hopefully.

I knock and wait to hear, "Come in."

Ubel seems surprised to see me. "Glynis. Twice in two days. To what do I owe this honor?"

For a moment, my mind goes blank. Then unbidden words come to me. "I have a proposition for you." I'd meant to ask about his decision regarding Solana, but find my thoughts going in a different direction.

He gestures for me to have a seat. "I'm listening."

"I believe Legalis needs to do away with the Cudgeling Circle. Completely."

He leans forward. "Whyever would we do that?"

"Because it's inhumane, unjust, and does nothing to promote good will among the Masses."

He leans back in his chair. "I didn't know good will was a priority."

I'm fidgeting in my chair and force myself to be still and sit up tall. "It hasn't been, but perhaps it could be. Should be."

"Toward what end?"

"Happiness?" I realize I've said it as a question, so I say it again. "Happiness."

He snickers. "Since when is it our concern whether the Masses are happy?"

"It isn't essential, but what would it hurt? Doesn't it make sense that happy people are more productive people?"

"They produce nothing now. More of nothing is nothing."

I find it hard to put my abstract thoughts into words. "But what if they did produce something? Like the Workers who weave and sew our garments. Their work makes our lives better. And I have to believe it gives them *some* satisfaction."

"But the skilled laborers are all from Regalia. The Masses have no abilities beyond making a few bowls or a table here and there."

"But what if they could be taught?" I think of Helsa. "The young woman who painted a mural in my room? She had no idea she had any artistic talent until Nixi discovered her painting a tree in whitewash — which was her assigned job."

Again, an eyebrow. But the right one compared to Ivar's left.

"We might be amazed at the hidden talents among the Masses." I can't believe I'm talking about talents. I haven't given two thoughts to anyone's talents before. Where is this coming from?

His eyes graze the room while he thinks. "What could they possibly provide that we need? Are you in want of something?"

"Actually, no." I change direction a bit. "But *they* need a lot. They have the bare minimum of housing, food, and even clothes. And why do we force them to wear white robes? White is not conducive to dusty streets."

The Judge waves his hands at me. "Stop right there, Glynis. You're talking drastic changes that interfere with the essence of Legalis. None of these things are your concern. And I don't hear complaints from the Masses."

The logical answer sticks in my throat. It takes effort to let the words out. "They don't complain because they fear repercussions if they speak. They fear jail. They fear the Cudgeling Circle."

I feel relieved to get back to my intended subject. "As I stated, I strongly believe it should be abolished. It serves no intrinsic purpose for our society."

"It punishes wrong-doers."

"Who have no chance to defend themselves."

Ubel clears his throat. "You question *my* judgments?"

I stifle a shiver. Have I gone too far? "I believe the crimes of each offender should be considered individually. We need alternative punishments. Not the all-or-nothing punishment of the Circle."

"I'd ask where this is coming from, Glynis, but I know. You want me to terminate the Circle because your daughter will enter it. And a relative of this Solana woman."

I pause a beat, then say, "Yes." I sit forward, nearly touching his massive desk. "Why not show mercy? That will go a long way to —"

"Mercy?" Ubel scoffs. "For centuries Legalis has curated the ominous figure of an almighty Judge. It has worked seamlessly in keeping the Masses in line. I see no reason to change it now. I see no positive outcome from being lenient. It will only lead to rebellion and chaos." He stands. "There will be nothing more said about the matter, Glynis. And I strongly suggest you set aside any notion of such change in Legalis. Also, I insist you curtail all talk of happiness and purpose. *It serves no purpose. It does* not *serve Legalis.*"

His voice is so forceful that I stand to leave. He usually doesn't use this tone with me.

"By the way," the Judge says. "I have just decided that Varo and Solana will be judged next Wednesday."

"No!"

He waves me away.

"No, Ubel. Please."

"Guard!"

A guard enters the office. I have no choice but to leave.

What have I done?

**

When I go home, I find Nixi reading in the parlor. I hang back and look at her in secret. My darling, beautiful daughter who has done nothing to deserve her dreadful fate.

She reads a few lines, sighs, looks up, then tries reading again. I'm sure it's hard for her to concentrate.

I make my presence known by clearing my throat. "I'm home," I say.

She snaps the book shut "Where have you been, Mama?"

"I saw your father. I spoke with him."

She stands. "You did? Can I see him?"

"Not yet." I motion to her to sit again. "There's more. I met with the Judge. Things did not go well."

Her hopeful expression disintegrates. "And?"

"Your father and Helsa's grandmother will face Judging Day next Wednesday."

She lets out a puff of air as if she'd been holding hope inside as a breath. "Which means I . . ."

I kneel beside her. "I'm so sorry, Nixi. I wish there was something I could do."

"Does Helsa know?"

"She'll know tomorrow, on Sanctuary Day. I'll be back in my position. It will be my job to announce it."

"This isn't fair, Mama. I don't want to die!"

I pull her into my arms. I can do nothing now but stand by and accept that I failed.

Chapter Forty-Two

Oria

I awaken on Sanctuary Day feeling optimistic, though I'm not sure my feeling is warranted.

Solana is still in jail. Devin or Helsa might still go to the Circle.

Yet while visiting her yesterday, witnessing the strength of her faith and knowing she is sharing it with the other prisoners . . . she's an inspiration. I understand why the Keeper put her there.

I was also inspired by Glynis. Seeing her recognize a flaw in the system and arranging for the prisoners to have visitors? Helsa always speaks of her fondly. Now I see why.

I leave my unit, hopeful that Solana will soon return to share it with me. I meet up with the others and walk to the Sanctuary. It's hard to believe this is our fourth Sanctuary Day. In some ways the time has gone by quickly. In other ways it seems like we've been stuck in Legalis forever. Many of my memories of Regalia are fading. It's hard to comprehend that I was a woman of significance there. A Patron. A fashion icon.

I look down at my shapeless dirty robe whose only adornment is a black stud on my shoulder. If only the Favored could see me now.

If only Mother could see me. Or my brother. And of course, Xian.

The Keeper mentioned him during our last meeting. He said he had plans for him. I know in my heart we will see each other again. It's definitely something to look forward to.

We walk up front to the same part of the Sanctuary where we always stand. It's odd how people do that, find the place they've been before and claim it. There must be a deeply seeded need for constancy within each of us. We like what we know.

Unfortunately, I now know Sanctuary Day serves no meaningful purpose other than to make our feet hurt from standing, our minds hurt from the mindless repetition of oppressive directives, and our souls hurt from having Legalis drown out any thoughts of hope, love, or purpose.

I wish the Keeper would walk in, shove the Judge off the balcony, and show everyone who's really got the power. What a battle that would be! I'd come every day of the week if the Keeper ran the service.

I love the memory of him sitting at my kitchen table. I'm so blessed that he visited me here. Without his encouragement I might have broken under this crushing tyranny. Even with his visit it takes effort to stay upbeat and to keep the faith no matter what.

My attention is drawn up front when Glynis steps into the place of the Head Notable. There's a low murmur in the crowd as others realize she's back. It's the first time we've seen her in her rightful position, wearing the black robe with the four-pointed-star medallion around her neck.

The people repeat the Motto and the Ten Directives without emotion. I've memorized them without trying to; ten laws meant to diminish the individual and turn all allegiance to Legalis and the Judge. Or else.

The Head Fault Finder lists the newest offenders. It's getting to be old hat now. I feel no emotion. I'm sad about that.

I glance at the hooded Fault Finders who pace the aisles. I'm used to them now, always vigilant, always looking for offenders. I think their presence is overkill. Who would dare break a law in the Sanctuary? Though I do remember Coli rushing forward during our first time here. That didn't end well.

As I think of Coli's arrest I notice the Fault Finders pause at the end of our row. Helsa is here. And Devin. Are they coming for one of them?

They are! The Fault Finders shove people aside to get to us. In a moment of déjà vu, they grab Helsa as they grabbed Berit.

"Wait!" Helsa yells.

I hear more commotion coming from the front of the Sanctuary, on the sides where the Notables sit. I see a pretty Notable being brought to the platform. It must be Nixi!

My mind repeats one word: no, no, no, no, no, no… I want to scream it and hear the word echo until it dies.

The two friends stand side by side, one in black and one in white. They exchange looks of panic. Then Nixi gazes at her mother, who looks as if she's been knifed in the heart. Helsa looks at us. Devin whispers, "I love you." Lieb cries.

And I want to rush forward and grab both of them. Tell them to run! Hide in a tunnel, or go out to the desert! Be anywhere but here.

Then everyone looks at the loft as if they have no choice but to look. The Judge stands front and center. His mirrored eyes catch the light. He points a long, sharp nail at the two women.

Everyone kneels.

Then Glynis clears her throat, unfolds a scroll, and reads in a shaky voice. "As of this day, Criminals Varo and Solana have been sentenced for their crimes against Legalis. The Judge hereby proclaims that Varo's daughter, Nixi, and Solana's granddaughter, Helsa, will be punished in the Cudgeling Circle on Judging Day—" She falters, then finally reads more. "On Judging Day tomorrow. Monday. So sayeth the Judge."

"No!" Devin yells. "You said you would fix it!"

I shush him as he shushed me when Berit was dragged up front. Helsa is returned to us where she falls in a heap. We want to reach down, hug and comfort her, but we can't. Devin kneels beside her, but doesn't touch her. I can tell Helsa wants to lean into her father's arms, and I almost wish she'd do it. What can the Fault Finders do to her now?

Tomorrow? Nixi and Helsa will die tomorrow? I can't wrap my head around it.

Glynis says blandly, "Go forth in the name of the Judge."

The Judge withdraws and people file out. They don't even look at us, as if by making eye contact our pain will become theirs.

Helsa cries quietly. Lieb cries because his Sa-Sa is crying. I don't want to cry, I want to scream! I want to unburden my soul and vent. I feel the words gather in my throat, ready for me to let them loose.

But somehow they remain there, feelings felt, thoughts thought, but neither expressed.

For now.

I sense that something is coming. Someday I will speak out. But today is not that day.

After the service we head home, but Helsa balks, her face frantic. "I need to see Nana!"

Devin goes with her to speak to Solana.

Who will soon be a Marked Woman.

What a mess.

Chapter Forty-Three

Solana

"Mother." Devin stands at my cell, his eyes downcast. "Will you come with me please?"

"What's wrong?"

He shakes his head, and again avoids my eyes. "Just come. Please."

A guard leads us to the same room where I talked to Oria.

Helsa is there. Her eyes are red.

She's been crying.

Which can only mean one thing.

I pull her into my arms. "You dear child," I say. "I'm so sorry."

She lets go of me. "You know?"

"I knew as soon as I saw you." She sits. "What happened?"

She tells me about the Sanctuary service, where Glynis proclaimed that Nixi and Helsa would go to the Circle.

"Tomorrow, Nana," Helsa says. "We go tomorrow!"

"I'll go," Devin says. "It should be me. I'll volunteer. It has to be me."

"Actually, it doesn't," I say. "Coli says the Judge chooses which relative goes to the Circle."

Helsa wraps her arms around herself. "He chose Nixi rather than Glynis. And he chose me rather than you, Papa." She shudders. "I don't want to die."

I pull her close, wishing I could press her pain into myself so she wouldn't have to feel it.

"How can we stop this?" she asks.

"I wish I knew," Devin says. "If Glynis couldn't stop it happening to her own family, then what hope is there?"

There is only one answer. "The Keeper is our hope."

They look skeptical. "He didn't help before," Helsa says. "Berit died."

"And lots of people before her," Devin says.

They are right. History says it *will* happen. Yet somehow . . . "I don't think you'll die," I say.

"Did you have a dream about it?" Helsa asks.

"Actually, yes."

"Yes?" Helsa's eyes grow large. "And you saw that I didn't die?"

I wish I could give her something definitive. "The image was vague, but left me knowing everything will be all right."

"How?" Helsa asks.

"I don't know exactly."

"Sorry, Nana, but I'd like something more specific."

"I can't give you that," I say. "But I can tell you that in my sixty years I've learned that gut feelings are often sent from the Keeper, like nudges and intuition. He uses whatever works in the moment."

"And at this moment . . .?" Devin asks.

"At this moment, I embrace the dream and the gut feeling that Helsa will not die. I don't know how he'll do it, but I trust him."

"I hope you're right."

Suddenly we hear a loud "No!" It's Varo, shouting from his cell. He must have gotten the news.

"Poor Nixi," Helsa says. Then her face grows hopeful. "If the Keeper saves me, will he save Nixi?"

"I'm praying for that too," I say.

"I need to find Nixi right away," she says as she steps toward the door.

But just then the door opens and a guard says, "Devin. We need your help."

"Go," I say. "In fact, I'll go with you. Maybe Varo needs a Keeper kind of help."

"He believes in the Keeper?" Helsa asks.

"That's between the two of them. But I know he believes in him more now than he did before he came to jail."

I hug Helsa tightly, feeling stronger together than apart. "We've been through a lot, you and I. We'll get through this too."

"Promise?"

"I promise." I'm sincere but feel the smallest stitch in my stomach. What if I'm wrong?

In the hall the guard takes me back to my cell. Varo rants loudly, reverting to the first Varo I met. I hope the progress he's made toward believing hasn't been wiped out by this shocking new reality.

Despite my positive attitude in front of my family, a hint of fear hides in the back of my mind. I know the Keeper is our protector, and I believe in my inner being that Helsa will be all right. But that doesn't mean there won't be pain. Prayers are answered in different ways. Believing doesn't give us a pass on pain.

Yet Helsa is strong. She survived the agony of being assaulted by Bru, the manager of our factory back in Regalia. She survived standing up to the authorities, which led to his arrest and death in the Swirling Desert. Bru died because of her courage. Justice was done.

Where is justice in Legalis? I'm in jail because I dared to speak with friends from home. I can rationalize my actions, but they *were* secret people, hidden away. So yes, that made it wrong. But Helsa doesn't deserve to be beaten for it, and I don't deserve to become a Marked Woman.

Does Varo deserve to be punished? I'd say yes. But Nixi doesn't deserve to be beaten. From what I've heard she's a very nice woman.

Yet does that matter? A broken law is a broken law. It's not up to me to pick and choose which laws to follow—even if they make no sense. But who has the right to *make* the laws? What criteria do they use?

Nothing is logical here. Nothing is based on morals and honor, or what's best for the Masses. Nothing uplifts and encourages. Nothing makes people's lives better.

I sink onto my cot, feeling heavy with the weight of the Legalis delusion that fear, repressive control, and oppression work. Especially since my opinions don't matter—even if they're right.

Right loses to might, and in the case of the Cudgeling Circle, might will kill.

I fall onto my side and draw my knees to my chest.

And sob.

Chapter Forty-Four

Oria

After the service Rand, Lieb, and I stand outside the Sanctuary, looking in the direction of the jail, waiting for news. Dreading news. Needing news.

Rand leans against the building. "I wonder if Solana was told about her fate before it was announced. Or are Devin and Helsa telling her?"

"I don't wish that conversation on anyone," I say. "Either way it will be an dreadful meeting."

Lieb bites his fingernails. "Are they going to be okay?"

Rand and I exchange a glance. We don't want to upset him unnecessarily.

He sees our glances and points at us. "I heard the head lady, I saw Helsa crying. But can we stop it?"

"I don't know," I tell him.

"I don't think so," Rand says.

Lieb draws in a deep breath. "Then the Keeper will have to protect them."

I think of Berit's death. I don't understand the Keeper's ways. Why do good people die? But I manage a smile and say, "That's what we pray for."

Lieb fidgets. He can't stand still. The streets are full of people enjoying their day, free of the Counts. Some people look at us warily, branding us as one of *them*. I feel exposed. We need time to think things through.

Then I remember the walkway.

"Come with me," I say.

"Where?" Rand asks.

"Somewhere we can think and talk in private."

They follow me through the streets to the small alley with the hidden door. Once we're on the walkway Rand gives me the reaction I'd hoped for. He moves to the edge and peers out at the desert. When he speaks his voice is soft. "I'd forgotten it was out there."

It seems an odd statement, yet I understand how it's true. "I wonder how many of the Masses forget about it."

"Especially the Workers," he says. "Their world is so dark."

Lieb stands beside him and smiles. "I like the desert. I go there a lot."

"What are you talking about?" I ask.

He points to the right. "If you follow the walkway around, there are other stairs. The third one leads all the way down into the tunnels — and outside."

I'm shocked. I thought I was the only one who knew about the walkway. And the tunnels? I know Rand has seen some of the Notable area, as has Solana. Helsa has been in the tunnels. And now, add Lieb to that list? I feel left out. "Show me," I say.

He starts to walk, but Rand stops him. "Wait. We were going to talk about Solana and Helsa."

"Maybe we could hide Sa-Sa," Lieb says. "I know lots of places. I've explored all over."

I haven't seen anything that hasn't been shown to me. Have I been slacking? I don't feel like the leader the Keeper charged me to be. I —

"Oria!"

I look behind us and see Wyan. He does not look happy to see us.

"What are you doing here?" he asks. Demands.

"I . . ." I don't have an answer for him. "These are my friends, Rand and Lieb? Gentlemen, this is Wyan, the man who saved me when I got beat up."

"Hi, Wyan," Lieb says innocently.

Wyan discounts his greeting with the flip of his hand. He's fuming. "I showed you this place in confidence, Oria."

Had he made that stipulation? "I'm sorry. One of our friends was just sentenced to the Cudgeling Circle and we wanted a quiet place to talk about it."

"To scheme?"

I'm shocked by his accusation. "We have no schemes. But we do wonder if there's any chance of mercy."

His jaw tightens. "There is no mercy in Legalis."

"Perhaps there should be," Rand says.

Wyan's eyebrows rise. He points at the G on Rand's forehead. "I hardly think a Marked Man has the right to offer opinions."

"Who more than me?" Rand says. "I've suffered under this lack of mercy and reason."

"Are you calling the Judge unreasonable?"

My heart pounds as we wait for Rand's answer.

"Yes," he says.

Lieb takes a step forward. "I think he's unreasonable too. Sa-Sa is my best friend in the whole world and she doesn't deserve to go to the Circle. And Nana shouldn't be in jail either." He nods once. "So there."

I have never heard Lieb say so much about anything. I want to couch his words to calm things down, but I agree with what he said. I'm proud of him for speaking up.

Wyan points back at the stairs. "Leave. Now. Or I will have all of you arrested."

Where's this coming from? "Wyan . . ." I take a step toward him and smile. "I apologize for bringing them here. We just wanted a place to talk, and I wanted to show them the view." Which is partially true.

He waves his hand toward the desert. "There. You've seen it."

"You don't need to be rude," I say.

He gives a quick shake of his head, dismissing me. Then he sighs deeply. "Just get off of here, Oria. Please."

We retreat down the stairs to the street and Wyan stands at the entrance of the alley, as if guarding it against our return.

I'm surprised to see this authoritarian side of him. When we get to the street he storms past us.

We're not sure where to go. Then Lieb says, "I need to go home to see if Helsa and Devin are back." He immediately heads in that direction.

Rand says, "I'm going to check on the Workers. They'll want to know what's happening to Solana."

He also walks off, leaving me alone on the street among strangers.

Some ambassador of the Keeper I am.

Chapter Forty-Five

Glynis

Everyone left the Sanctuary an hour ago. I sit alone in Nixi's seat, where the Fault Finders so ingloriously yanked her up front to hear her fate.

I'm furious.

How dare Ubel make me announce the death of my own daughter and Helsa—tomorrow. Not Wednesday. Not weeks from now. Or never. Tomorrow. He can be extremely cruel sometimes.

Most times.

Poor Nixi.

I suddenly realize too much time has passed. I need to find her. I assume she's gone home without me, but has no one there to comfort her except Bog. I feel guilty for wallowing in my anger when she needs me.

As the Head Notable, I use the tunnels to enter and exit the Sanctuary. But today as I approach the storeroom that will lead me home I check the small stone outside its door. My heart flutters knowing a note from Elum could be beneath it. One is there! I retrieve the tiny note before going into the storeroom.

I move through the stone door and down the stairs, then pause in the corridor to read it: *How can I help? Meet me.*

I want to meet Elum, but I don't know if it's possible. Firstly, I need to get home to see Nixi.

I startle when I hear footsteps coming toward me. The Judge pulls up short, dressed in his full regalia. Seeing him encased in black, with those disconcerting mirrored eyes . . .

"You're coming back?" I ask.

"I forgot something."

I bobble the note and it falls to the floor. He picks it up for me between his pointed nails, opens it, and reads. "Meet? Who are you meeting, Glynis?"

I think fast. "Nixi. She's obviously very upset."

"She sends you a note?"

"She knew I wasn't planning to go home right away." I take the note from him. It's daunting to speak with him when he's standing so tall in front of me, but I forge on. "I want you to know how devastating it was to read that announcement today."

"It's part of your job. If you're not up to it, I know someone who is."

The always hovering Ivar. "You should have let me know about your Solana decision, and about the timing of Judging Day. Tomorrow? Why the rush? And actually . . . why are Varo and Solana pushed ahead of others who have been in jail longer?"

"You're questioning *me?*"

Just the way he says it . . . But I stand strong and say, "Yes, Judge, I am. When I last left you, you'd indicated you were thinking about leniency for Solana. And now —"

"Now, I have proclaimed my judgment."

"But it's wrong!"

His whole body turns slowly to fully face me. I hate seeing my reflection in his mirrored eyes. I wish he'd take his costume off, but I know he never does so outside his lair.

"You're pushing me again, Glynis. Do you really think that's a good idea?"

My heart skips, but then I think *What more can he do to me?* "As the Head Notable you should know that I intend to declare Judging Day inappropriate, cruel, and unfruitful to the legacy of Legalis."

If I could see his eyebrows, I'm sure they have arched. "With an agenda like that, perhaps you shouldn't *be* the Head Notable. That can be arranged, Glynis."

It's hard to breathe.

"At any rate," he says with a flip of his long razor fingers that he could easily slash across my face, "whatever you intend to do will be too late to help your family, won't it?"

I want to grab the black fabric covering his chest and shake him. Pound my fists against him. Hurt him.

He points in the direction of the tunnel leading home. "After you."

I hurry through the tunnel, my nerves on edge, feeling like there's a monster nipping at my heals.

The image suits him.

**

I find Nixi and Helsa in the parlor, hugging each other.

Two doomed girls.

I hesitate to join them. There is nothing I can say to make it better.

Nixi sees me and runs into my arms. "Why didn't you tell me it's happening tomorrow?"

"I didn't know until I opened the proclamation."

"Did you know about Nana?" Helsa asks.

"I did not. I'm so sorry, Helsa." I hold Nixi's hand. "I'm so sorry, dear daughter."

Nixi shakes my hand away. "The whole thing is absurd, Mama! Why should we—two girls, innocent of any crime—have to endure a punishment for someone else's crime?"

"And Nana didn't even commit a crime," Helsa adds.

Nixi begins to pace. "Who came up with Judging Day?"

"People long ago, right after the Before Time."

She shakes her head vehemently. "You can't always blame the past. *You* have power, Mama. Why haven't *you* changed it?

I shake my head, at a loss.

"Why haven't you banned it?" she yells.

I have no answer for her. Or for myself.

Nixi flicks her hand at me. "If you don't mind, Helsa and I want to be alone."

I'm stunned, but I understand. I have no defense and can offer no comfort. So I leave. Not just the parlor, but the house. I must see Elum. Elum will know what to do.

**

I descend into the tunnels and hurry to our alley. And there he is.

He pulls me into his arms and I let the tears flow. "I can't believe this is happening," I say. "Tomorrow."

He lets go of me. "Why the rush? Why them and not the other prisoners?"

I can only shake my head. I slump onto my chair. "What are we going to do, Elum? We can't let our daughter die."

We share a moment of silence. But then I let my words take root. New thoughts flow. Important thoughts.

Elum must see the aha-look in my eyes. "What?"

"She's *our* daughter. You're her father."

"Yes . . ."

I stand. "Varo is not her father, therefore she can't go to the Circle for him. They are not related!" I grab his arms. "Elum, she doesn't have to be punished!"

I see relief wash over his face, but then it turns serious again. "Leaving you as Varo's only relative. *You* will go."

I attempt to push the thought aside. "But the Judge said I wouldn't be punished because I'm the Head Notable."

Elum scoffs and counts off on his fingers. "Number one, by today's surprise, he's shown himself to be untrustworthy—though we already knew that."

"True."

"And number two, if we reveal Nixi's paternity, there will be a scandal. And if there's a scandal, you will surely lose your Head Notable position, meaning . . ."

"I can be sent to the Circle."

His shrug is not indifference but resignation. "We can't win."

"*We* can't. But at least Nixi can." The repercussions swim through my mind. "She'll be saved from the Circle, but her life will be turned upside down by the truth coming out."

"I think *ruined* is a more apt word," he says. "She'll lose her standing, her friends, her home."

"But she'll be alive."

He nods. "She'll be alive."

I pinch the bridge of my nose, trying to sort it all out. "Varo has already disgraced the family. With our revelation, I will merely be disgracing it further." I realize the harshness of my words and extend my hand to Elum. "No offense, my love."

"None taken. The reason we aren't together now is because it was unheard of for a Notable girl to love a lowly man of the Masses."

"My parents . . ."

"Were good parents and kept you from making a horrible mistake."

I slip my arms around his waist. "Being your wife would not have been any sort of mistake."

"Maybe not for us, but for Nixi? I had — I have — nothing to offer her. Or you."

"Except love. You love us."

"Love only goes so far."

There's a bitter truth in his words but I say, "Better to have love and poverty, than no love and riches." I'm not sure I totally believe that, but I hope it sounds true for Elum's sake. I lean my head against his chest, and hear his heart beating wildly.

"May the Keeper save us all," he whispers into my hair.

"How can he possibly do that?" I ask.

"I have no idea, but I'm going to keep asking. You need to ask too, sweet lady."

"I don't pray, Elum. You know that."

"You haven't, but you could. You should. What can it hurt?"

I nod against his chest, but have no intention of bringing the Keeper into this. Elum holds me tighter. How I wish I never had to leave his arms.

**

I leave Elum reluctantly and still without a plan. I wander the tunnels until my legs threaten to give out. I need to sit, yet the tunnels offer no such option. I think about going out to the desert, but I don't want to risk running into the bald man who will push the Keeper on me again. So I end up in the back tunnel leading to the Sanctuary. It's as good a place as any to wallow in my pain. I reach the corridor near the shops and restaurant, relieved to have side-stepped any public encounter. Then I hurry up the spiral stairs to the secret storeroom door.

But once I get there I pause. What if some of the Masses have come back in the Sanctuary? I don't want to risk being seen.

I look to my right and see the narrow spiral stairs leading to the loft.

I suffer a chill because the loft is the Judge's domain. I've never been up there. Has anyone? Yet it's the perfect place to be alone.

I lift my robe and ascend the dark stairs. At the top I trip and stumble my way into the loft, the sound of my clumsiness echoing.

The area is narrower than I imagined it would be. It's barely eight-foot deep, yet it spans the width of the Sanctuary. The railing is solid, but low—which probably adds to the visual of the Judge seeming incredibly tall. He *is* tall but having him loom far above the low railing adds to his ominous presence. I peer over it. I am alone in the Sanctuary.

I look up at the back wall and see the four-pointed star that dominates the view from the floor. I mentally recite: Duty, Deference, Dedication, Dependability. Yet the rote words created long ago have lost their noble intent. I hear four other words in my head: Dissention, Disdain, Depression, Desolation. These words are more honest than the ones our forebears came up with.

I stand against the back wall, off to one side, not wanting to be directly under the star or anywhere near the place where the Judge usually stands. Then I slide down the wall to the floor. Other than my heart beating in my ears, there is no noise but the faint sound of people's voices in the Sanctuary square—the square where Nixi and Helsa will meet their fate.

Tomorrow.

Unless a miracle happens.

I lean my head against the wall, close my eyes, and whisper, "Make me a miracle."

My eyes shoot open. Did I just pray?

That makes no sense. I don't believe in the Keeper. He's for Elum and the others, not for the Head Notable of Legalis.

I shake my head against all thoughts of him and try to tap into my logical self. I need to solve the problem, not waste time appealing to a being that may or may not even exist. And even if he does exist, why would he listen to my pleas for help? I've never done anything for him, in fact my job is to work against him and all who believe in him.

Actually, my job is to save Nixi. And Helsa. The job of a mother, not of a Head Notable.

But how? What are the facts?

I draw in a deep breath and let it out slowly. Varo tried to kill me. His punishment is for a member of his family to go to the Cudgeling Circle. The Judge declared me off-limits because I am the Head Notable. So, as his daughter, Nixi has to go.

Only she isn't his daughter.

Elum is.

Elum, one of the Masses, who stole my heart twenty-five years ago. Elum, who my parents deemed unworthy of my love.

But then I found out I was pregnant.

A marriage with Varo was quickly arranged. I was a pretty young girl from a prominent family, and he was a widower, ten years older than me. He was childless, but wanted a family.

He didn't suspect anything was amiss when my parents insisted on a quick marriage — he probably thought I was simply eager to be his.

I was not eager. At all. Marrying Varo was the hardest thing I ever did, and being with him . . .

I shudder. Even after all these years.

I don't know if he ever suspected Nixi wasn't his. That her "early" birth wasn't early at all. In his favor, he was a good father. She softened him in a way I never could. It was the only thing that made being apart from Elum bearable. At least Nixi was happy. Even if Elum and I were not.

I did everything Legalis asked me to do. I earned my position as Head Notable. I took my duties seriously.

Until now. Until I don't want to be Head Notable anymore. I don't want to be a part of the Notables at all. I don't want to have meetings with the Judge. I just want to be with Elum and Nixi.

I fall onto my side on the cold floor, drawing my knees to my chest. I cradle my head in the crook of my arm and let myself cry. I stifle my sobs, not wanting anyone to accidentally hear, but I have to set them free.

It's like my entire life played out wrong. Elum and I weren't together. Nixi wasn't raised in our loving home. And now she's going to experience the most horrible kind of pain — if not death. Because of something her duped non-father did to her mother.

And there is nothing I can do about it. I can't prevent her suffering. Or Elum's. Or Varo's. Or my own.

I draw my knees tighter and wrap my other arm around my head wanting to block out my appalling reality. Our incomprehensible fate.

Please, please, please, please, please . . .

The word repeats itself as a mantra. *Please someone. Please anyone. Help me!*

I feel a gentle hand on my arm. My eyes fly open and I uncurl to see who's in the loft with me.

But there's no one here.

I touch my arm where I felt the touch. I can still feel it, like a kiss that lingers beyond the moment. I close my eyes, longing to hold onto the memory of the soothing touch.

I suddenly feel heat upon my face.

I open my eyes and see a bright light shining in from the opening in the roof. But it doesn't shine on the spot in the center of the loft where the Judge stands. It shines on me.

Yet instead of panicking and moving out of its reach, I savor it. I raise my face to it, letting its warmth wash over me. And as I do, the light dissolves my agony like a sore body slipping into a hot bath. My doubts and fears dissipate like the glimmering particles dancing around me in the sunbeam.

And I laugh.

I don't clap my hand to my mouth to stifle it—even though I know I should. I let the laughter come, drinking in the liberating joy of this foreign sound.

The joy of the Keeper.

For I know everything that's happening is from him as surely as I know everything will be all right.

But there's more. Unexpectedly, I'm filled with an idea. An image without form. A single word shines in my heart and mind, a word I willingly accept as a promise.

"Miracle," I whisper. "You're going to give us a miracle."

There's never been a more delightful, delicious word!

Suddenly all things are possible. My worries fade into the shadows as the light of hope and promise envelops me.

I raise my arms toward the light, basking in the fullness of the Keeper.

**

I don't go home through the tunnels. I can't, for their darkness and dreariness would not be able to contain the brilliance and lightness in my heart.

Instead, I walk through the streets of Legalis—the exact thing I usually avoid.

I don't look down as I walk. I don't stare straight ahead in an aura of stateliness and self-importance. I look at people. I smile.

At first, they are taken aback. Some even step aside as if my foreign attitude is something to be feared. They have nothing to fear from it—or from me. It's like the old Glynis doesn't exist anymore. I am someone new.

A little girl of three or four stares at me as I pass. I give a little wave and she grins.

Impulsively, I walk toward her, kneeling down to speak to her at her level. "Hello," I say.

She smiles but leans into her mother's leg.

"What's your name?"

The mom spurs her to answer. "Tell the Head Notable."

"Opa."

"That's a very pretty name for a very pretty girl."

The mother beams and says, "May the Keeper be with you, mistress."

I'm thrilled with her words, and nod. "And also with you. "

She touches her fingers to her chest. I've seen that gesture before, and I return it—to her delight.

I notice a small crowd has formed. Before today that would have concerned me, but now . . . I relish it.

I stand and slowly turn to make eye contact with all of them. "Good day to you."

There are murmurs of "Good day, mistress" and "Good day, Head Notable."

I'm not sure what to say to them. But then I see a woman with a bandage around her wrist. "How did you get hurt?" I ask.

"I was clumsy. I fell off a chair."

"I'm so sorry. Is it broken?"

"No, mistress. Just sprained."

"My daughter sprained her ankle once," I say. "She was told to rest, and wrap it for support, but not too tight."

She nods. "Thank you, mistress. I'll do that."

A little boy says, "You're pretty."

"Thank you, young man." The sincerity of his compliment touches me deeply.

A man asks, "Your daughter . . . is she really going to the Circle tomorrow?"

I feel a stab of my old pain, and try to push it away. "So I've been told."

Another man raises his hand. "I just got notice I have to be a Beater."

"I'm sorry to hear that," I say.

Suddenly, he shakes his head. "I'm not going to do it. I won't hurt your daughter."

A few people cheer him on and he drinks it in. "No Circle!" he yells.

The few take up the cry. "No Circle! No Circle!" More chime in until everyone around me is chanting together.

I feel a twinge of panic. What if the Fault Finders start arresting people?

And yet . . .

I raise my fist in the air and join the chant. "No Circle! No Circle!"

I walk on amid their astonished cheers of support.

The chant continues without me.

But *for* me.

For Nixi.

For the good of Legalis.

And suddenly, I realize I have more to share with them. My revelation with the Keeper is not for me alone. I walk back to the group and they stop their chant.

"Good people! Look for a miracle tomorrow," I say.

"What are you going to do?" a woman asks.

I smile. "The miracle belongs to the Keeper. Watch for it."

"What's it going to be?" a man asks.

"We'll find out together. Spread the news."

I walk on, my heart pumping.

But then, I feel a catch in my breathing. I'm suddenly frightened. For now I've upped the ante by throwing my name in with the Keeper. And by sharing his promise I've made it my own.

I'm all in.

There's no turning back now.

Chapter Forty-Six

Rand

What is Glynis doing?

I saw her coming out of the Sanctuary and watched her stop and talk with the Masses. She even knelt down and spoke with a little girl. I wanted to move closer, but as a Marked Man, I knew I might be a distraction, so I watched from a distance.

I've never seen her smile — I've never seen any Notable smile during the rare times they've shown themselves up-top, much less talk to anyone.

And then I heard the people start to chant, "No Circle! No Circle!" What?

I expected Glynis to stop them or call the Fault Finders, but instead she joined in! And then she made a pronouncement about watching for a miracle.

What is going on?

I see by the expressions of her audience that they're as confused as I am. Yet they enjoy what's going on. They enjoy her.

What happened to Glynis in the Sanctuary? For I saw her there.

After being on the walkway with Oria and Lieb, I was too drained to visit the Workers. Instead I found a place to rest inside the Sanctuary. I needed shade and a place to sit apart from the busyness in the square. I needed a place to try to grasp that Helsa and Nixi are going to the Circle. Tomorrow. The gap between going *someday* and *tomorrow* is huge.

That's when I saw movement in the loft. I nearly panicked, thinking the Judge was back. But it wasn't the Judge. It was Glynis, peering over the railing. She disappeared from view, but when I heard her quiet sob my heart broke with hers. She's going to lose a daughter tomorrow. I remember that pain, knowing my mother was going to die.

But then, I heard Glynis laugh — a laugh of pure delight. It echoed in the volume of the building, as out of the ordinary as the sound of screams.

Two expressions of high emotion in a short time — opposite emotions. What was going on?

When Glynis came out of the storeroom and left the Sanctuary, I followed her and witnessed her friendly displays of affection with the Masses, her chant of "No Circle", and the promise of a miracle.

I'm beyond confused.

I spot Elum. I'm about to wave at him, but he's staring at Glynis. He seems fascinated. And pleased. It's not the stare of a citizen seeing the Head Notable, it's the stare of a man seeing something good happen to a friend.

And when she sees him . . .

Whoa.

She excuses herself from the group and walks toward him. He seems surprised, and even a bit nervous, but he waits for her.

She greets him with a smile, and he returns it. There's an undeniable connection between them.

How does Elum know the Head Notable? What hasn't he told us?

They step aside to gain privacy, and she talks intently to him. She points toward the Sanctuary. She makes a gesture to the sky. Her face is animated and hopeful. She's not a woman of authority speaking with a stranger, but a woman sharing something important and meaningful with a dear friend.

Elum's face lights up as she speaks, and for a split second, I see him make a movement as if to give her a hug. Of course, he doesn't, but in that moment, I know that he could. And I know more than that. I know Elum *has* hugged her.

Which changes everything.

With a final nod, she moves on. Elum watches her go. He stands straighter, his jaw raised, his expression confident.

Something important passed between them and I need to know what it was. I call to him. "Elum!"

He looks in my direction, and walks toward me. He's never shown much interest in me, and usually makes me feel like an outsider in our little group.

But now his face is animated. He has something to tell me.

"Rand," he says. "Just the man I need to see."

Before he tells me why, I ask my question. "Do you know the Head Notable?"

"I do. Very well."

"How? Why haven't you said anything? Why didn't you tell us?"

He shakes his head as if that's a subject for another time. "I need you to do something, Rand. Something very important. Life and death important."

"Anything."

"I need you to tell people to pray."

This is not like Elum. "Pary for what exactly?"

He smiles broadly. "A miracle. Tell them to pray for a big miracle tomorrow." He taps his fingers to his chest.

He walks away with purpose in his step.

Although a have a hundred questions, I set out to do as Elum asked. One miracle, coming up.

Chapter Forty-Seven

Helsa

I'm going to die tomorrow.

The best case scenario is this: if I *don't* die from the beating in the Circle, I will still be severely beaten.

Or maybe that *isn't* the best case.

I walk home from spending time with Nixi. I'm not sure being together was good for either of us as we basically whipped each other into a frenzy. I felt bad for Glynis when Nixi sent her away. None of this is her fault.

Or is it?

She's one of *them,* one of the elite who rule over this stupid place. I still don't understand what good comes from their laws *or* their punishments. Both stir up resentment, anger, and . . .

Legalis is due for a revolution.

I shake my head against such a thought. I've done my part in bucking the system. I saved Glynis from poison and Lieb from the Circle. But I haven't seen any signs of others stepping up to do the right thing. Actually, I'm not even sure what the right thing is anymore.

Just before I reach home, I see Papa. I've never admitted it, but he looks much older than he did in Regalia. And why not? After being exiled his wife died. Even though he was reunited with Nana and I, as of tomorrow, Nana will be a Marked Woman and I'm going to die. That would age anyone.

We don't speak until we get inside. Oria, Lieb, and Rand are already there, and Elum stands at the end of the table, his face animated, his eyes bright. I've never seen him look this way before.

"Good, we're all here," he says.

Everyone's face looks hopeful. What's there to be hopeful about?

"What's going on?" I ask.

Elum motions for us to sit. Then he says, "I was telling everyone there's going to be a miracle tomorrow at the Circle."

He certainly has my interest—and my skepticism. "What kind of miracle?"

"I don't know exactly. But Glynis told me it's going to happen and we're supposed to spread the news to pray to the Keeper about it."

Wait. There are so many things. "You spoke to Glynis?"

"I did."

"About a miracle?"

Rand interjects. "By the way, he knows her. All this time, he knows her."

"You know the Head Notable? Why didn't you tell us that?" Papa asks.

Elum shakes his head. "The point is, she's had an experience with the Keeper and it's changed her." He holds his hand up, as if taking an oath. "Truly. I saw her. She *is* changed. He's infused her with some kind of knowledge that there's going to be a miracle tomorrow."

"I don't believe it," I say. "I saw her earlier at her house. I was there with Nixi. She didn't say anything then and she certainly didn't seem optimistic at all."

Elum nods. "I talked to her right after she left you. She wasn't optimistic then either."

"So what happened between all that and now?" Oria asks.

"I know." Rand raises his hand. "She was in the loft. In the Sanctuary."

Papa looks confused. "No one goes up there except the Judge."

"She was there," Rand says. "I was in the Sanctuary and heard her cry. And then laugh."

"Laugh?" I ask.

"A laugh of delight."

"Was someone with her?" Lieb asks.

Elum beams. "The Keeper."

"Really?" Oria asks. "He was there?"

Elum shakes his head. "She didn't *see* him, but she experienced him. She felt his touch on her arm."

"I'd like to feel that," Lieb says. "A lot."

Elum continues. "Then the sun came through the roof and shone right on her. Not somewhere else in the loft, *on her*. She *felt* him. And she was changed." He looks at each one of us, then continues. "Then instead of going home through the tunnels, she walked through the crowd and talked to people. Interacted with them. She's never done that. And above everything, she was . . . happy."

I know Glynis is rarely happy. I'd like to see her happy.

Elum has more. "The people started chanting 'No Circle!' and she joined in. Can you believe that? She chanted with them."

"They all could've been arrested," Papa says. "She could've been arrested."

"I know. But they weren't. She wasn't."

"We're supposed to do what with the miracle?" Oria asks.

"Spread the word that there's going to be a miracle tomorrow, and get people to pray for it—and for the safety of Helsa and Nixi," Elum says. "I need all of us to go out and do it. Like we did before, but this time with even more urgency."

Lieb jumps up from the table. "Let's go!" He turns to me. "Coming, Sa-Sa?"

I'm hopeful because they're hopeful, but I hesitate. "I want to see Nana again before tomorrow. The rest of you go."

"Good idea," Papa says. "Tell her to pray too."

As we fan out Elum stops me to say, "It will be all right, Helsa. I know it."

I want to have faith in all this miracle stuff, but I don't. All the others seem to accept it without question. Elum says Glynis had an encounter with the Keeper and they all believe him? Believe her? She said there's going to be a miracle, so just like that it's going to happen?

Where's the proof?

And to be blunt . . . I'm the one who's going to be beaten. I'm the one who might die. Shouldn't the Keeper come to me? It's like all my faith is second-hand. Somebody else has it first and wants me to try it on to see if it fits.

I'm not sure it does.

I want it to.

I hope Nana can help.

Chapter Forty-Eight

Solana

"Solana! You have a visitor," the guard barks.

Varo calls out. "Again? She gets another visitor? What about me?"

"I can't conjure up a visitor where there ain't any, Notable," the guard says. He unlocks my cell and I follow him into what is now called the visiting room.

Thanks to Glynis.

Helsa waits there. As soon as the guard leaves I pull her into my arms. "My dear, dear child. You're back. It's so good to see you."

We sit. Helsa hesitates, then jumps to the point. "I've been told there's going to be a miracle."

My heart leaps. "I thought there might be one coming."

"Really, Nana?"

I put my hand on my heart. "It's just a feeling." But truthfully it's more than that, it's a knowing. "Who says there's going to be a miracle?"

"Elum. Actually, Glynis told him about it — and yes, they know each other. Well."

How interesting. "Tell me what was said."

"Glynis was upset and went to the loft where she felt the Keeper's presence. A beam of light came through the roof and somehow he told her there's going to be a miracle. It really changed her."

I clap my hands, delighted. "Praise the Keeper! I sensed she had an open heart."

"Then she walked among the Masses and interacted with them. They all started shouting, 'No Circle!' and she joined them."

I'm stunned. "That was bold of her."

"Very. And then she told everyone that a miracle was coming tomorrow."

"That sounds amazing!"

"So you believe it? All of it, Nana?" she asks.

The question catches me off guard and I take a minute to look hard at my granddaughter. "Of course I do. Don't you?"

Helsa's eyes meet mine and I see a longing there, like she wants to feel what I feel, and know what I know.

"I want to believe it," she says.

"Oh sweet child. I understand believing can be hard. But you have to do it. Just open yourself up and do it." I squeeze her forearm. "Here's a key point about faith. To have faith, have faith."

Helsa seems to be repeating the words in her head. "It sounds good, Nana, but it's not that easy."

"It is good, and yes, it is that easy. Faith is all about choosing to believe. It's not something you have to force—in fact, it shouldn't be forced. Can't be forced." I spread my arms wide and take a long, deep breath, then let it out. "You should pull faith in like drawing in air. You can draw deep or draw shallow, but the amount of faith you let out corresponds to what you draw in." I tap a finger on her arm. "Eventually, you will breathe faith in and out without even thinking about it, just like you breathe air in and out."

I see her skepticism. "What do you have to lose by believing, child? Fear, doubt, panic, anger?"

"Well . . ."

I take her hands in mine and close my eyes. "Dear Keeper, replace Helsa's fear with your calm; her doubt with your certainty; her panic with your peace, and her anger with your love. Let her know you are with her as we witness your miracle together."

Helsa's forehead furrows with emotion. "I want to believe all that, Nana. I really do."

"Then do it. Believe!"

She nods, and I sense a glimmer of hope there. There's always been hope between us, and we need it now more than ever.

"Helsa, you and I have been through more than most." I touch her cheek. "We're in a horrendous situation here. I get that. But the Keeper is not unaware."

She bites her lip. She's trying so hard . . .

Then she says, "Elum told everybody to spread the word about the miracle, telling people to pray for it and for Nixi and me too."

"Look at that, Helsa! All these people praying for you and Nixi? Isn't that a marvelous thing?"

"If it works."

I shake my head vehemently. "We will have none of that!" I swipe my hand in the air. "Shoo, doubt! Away with you!" Helsa's smile is a good sign. "We must believe the miracle will happen."

"But Glynis was the one who told us about the miracle. She's not one of us."

"She is now."

Helsa makes a face. "So she says. But should we believe her?"

I can't help but sigh. "I heard stories from the Before Times of prophets who foretold what was going to happen. People could believe them, or not."

"Did what they say happen?"

"Some of it. From a few prophets."

"So who are we supposed to believe?"

That's a tough one. "I figure we need to look at the speaker. If they're an honorable person, then maybe they should be believed."

"Glynis is a Notable. They make ridiculous laws and oppress the Masses. I'm dying because of their stupid laws."

"But look at her personally, is she an honorable person?"

Helsa doesn't hesitate. "Yes, I know she is."

One point in Glynis's favor. "I also think we need to consider if the prediction is good and does good for people. Or if it's self-serving for the speaker."

"If you're asking if Glynis would benefit — of course she would. If there's a miracle her daughter is spared."

"That *is* a miracle. Yet, she's endangered her position as Head Notable by speaking in public about the Keeper. That takes courage. That adds credibility to what she said. She wasn't thinking of herself."

I look at the door leading to the cells. I don't know how much time I have. "Most miracles aren't a group project. They just happen. God doesn't need our participation beyond prayer. If we could do it ourselves it wouldn't be a miracle. A miracle is beyond us. *This* miracle is beyond us."

"What's the miracle going to be?" she asks.

I laugh — not at her, but with her. "That's something we'd all like to know. You and me especially."

Helsa hugs herself. "I don't want to die, Nana. I don't want Nixi to die. And I don't want to feel all that pain either. I'm scared."

I feel her doubt try to infect me and will it away. "Although we don't know the details of the miracle, we can assume it means saving your lives."

"I hope so."

"Yes, Helsa. Hope. Cling to hope. And as Elum asked, pray to the Keeper for the miracle." I have to say one more thing. "And remember everlasting life."

"You mean death?"

I shake my head. "Something better, beyond death."

"That we have no proof about."

I sigh. "Faith is believing without proof. The Keeper spoke of everlasting life, so it must exist."

"So he might use the miracle to prove it? Did you ever think of that, Nana? We all saw something rise out of Berit when she died. I don't want that. I want to live. Here. Now. With you."

I take her hands in mine. "So do I, Helsa. Let's pray for it to be so."

The guard comes in. We stand and hug tightly. It might be the last time we do so.

Doubt can be such a pesky emotion.

**

Back in my cell, Coli asks, "Who was your visitor?"

"My granddaughter."

"I bet she's a mess," Sar says.

"She is understandably scared. But there's good news from Glynis."

"Glynis?" Varo chimes in. "I certainly hope she's getting me out of here."

As expected he thinks of himself and not Nixi. And honestly, I'd like to be able to tell Coli, Sar, and Kal about the miracle without telling Varo, but that's not possible.

"Glynis had an experience with the Keeper and is telling everyone that—"

"The Keeper?" Varo asks. "Glynis doesn't believe in the Keeper."

"She does now. She says a miracle is going to happen tomorrow."

"That's ridiculous. My wife does not believe in miracles either. And neither do I."

I'm tired of him. "*She* believes now. *You* can believe as you wish. Yet maybe the miracle involves you. Or Nixi. Did you ever think about that?"

There is an extra beat of silence as the realization kicks in. "Nixi?"

Maybe he does have a heart. "Glynis is asking us to pray for the girls, and for the miracle."

"Like that will do any good," he says.

"It won't hurt."

"We'll pray," Coli says.

"I'll pray," Kal says.

"Well, I won't," Varo says.

"Suit yourself. But as a favor to the rest of us, can you be quiet so we can do what *your* wife asked us to do?"

It's a miracle he complies.

CHAPTER FORTY-NINE

ORIA

I hobble home. My feet are swollen from all the walking I've done. I've spread the news about praying for a miracle and the girls across Legalis. Actually, the Legalis grapevine worked for the Keeper's good, because many people had already heard about the huge change in the Head Notable.

There were stories about her mysterious experience with a divine being. The way the news multiplied, then multiplied again is its own miracle.

When I reach home my neighbor Frin runs out to meet me.

"Is it true there's going to be a miracle tomorrow?"

I smile. The news got here before I did. "It's true," I say.

"Does that mean Solana will be set free, and her granddaughter…?

Here comes the hard truth I've also had to repeat dozens of times. "I don't know, but I assume something good will happen." I repeat a Relic that someone handed me. "'The Keeper is good and does good.'" I add, "Good. Not bad."

Frin lets out a sigh. "I'm so glad. I don't want anyone to go through what Berit went through."

"Neither do I."

"Can I do anything?" she asks.

"Spread the word and tell people to pray for the girls, and the miracle."

She nods enthusiastically. "I can do that. I will do that, right now."

Frin walks away. I'm happy to let her take over where I left off.

I slowly climb the stairs and fall onto my cot. My feet and legs throb.

I listen to my own breathing. It's too quiet in here. With Solana gone . . . I don't like being alone.

As a Marked Woman, Solana will live alone on the streets. She will be shunned—though as we've helped Rand, we can help her. But strangers will still treat her badly. How will that work?

It doesn't have to work. Not if there's a miracle.

Some faith I have. I feel like a hypocrite for spreading news about the miracle when I suffer doubts it will happen. It would have helped if Glynis offered more details, but even as I think that, I know the Keeper doesn't work that way. He even chided me for wanting more details about Xian, saying, *I will give you wisdom. You must do the rest.*

Do I have wisdom? Does Glynis?

I turn on my side, trying in vain to get my legs to stop hurting. I need to raise them so I lay on the floor and put my feet up on the cot.

Now my back hurts.

I move from dealing with physical, to emotional pain. I have a question for the Keeper: what am I supposed to do during this miracle? Am I going to be a part of it? So much of the faith movement in Legalis seems to be going on without me, as if Solana and now Glynis have usurped the position I was given in Regalia. Even Rand is busy reaching the Workers.

Other than my first outburst at Berit's Judging Day, I am reaching no one. Not even one-on-one. Not even Wyan. After he caught us on the walkway I'll probably never see him again. Though our friendship was often rocky, it was a friendship. Without him, I know no one beyond our small group.

"You're too proud, Oria," I say aloud. "And needy." I'm glad no one can hear, for I am ashamed. Where is the strong Oria?

There *is* no strong Oria. Only the strong Cashlin of the past.

I awkwardly move from the floor to sitting on my cot, moaning all the way.

It's sobering to realize I was more useful to the Keeper as Cashlin than I've been as Oria.

Yet the Keeper gave me that name.

I dig deep into my memory and remember the precious time in the garden when he said that the name Cashlin had suited me for a time, as it meant vain. But one day I would be called Oria — one who is humble in spirit and manner.

I'm not humble at all.

I let out a breath in a huff. Isn't wanting to be *the* one to do something in Legalis the epitome of vanity? Isn't it the opposite of being humble in spirit and manner?

I clasp my hands, bow my head, and call out to the Keeper. "Help me be worthy of the name Oria. Forgive me for caring about what part I'll play in the miracle. Use me how you can use me. Let the miracle play out exactly as you planned."

I pray a long time. I have much to atone for.

Much to aspire to.

CHAPTER FIFTY

GLYNIS

What have I done?

Why did I tell everyone that a miracle is happening today?

When I got home yesterday, I was flying high from my interaction with the Masses and Elum.

And the Keeper. He started all this.

Yet did he? How can I be sure it was him? Although the memory of his touch lingers, it was just a *feeling* that someone touched me. How can I prove a feeling? As for the sun streaming through the roof on me? Perhaps the sun always does that at that particular time of day. Who's to know, since the loft is restricted?

I have no proof it was real. Or special. Or from the Keeper — whom I don't even know. Yet by the time I got home even Nixi had heard about it. She'd run to me, her face hopeful. "Mama? Is there really going to be a miracle tomorrow?"

The gravity of my promise — the Keeper's promise, for I was merely his mouthpiece — hit me hard. I didn't want to dampen her hope, so I said, "That's what I believe." Which was true.

Partly. *Was* true. Today, lying in bed in the predawn hours of Judging Day, I'm less certain. Unfortunately there's no one I can talk to about it.

I toss and turn, but soon get out of bed. I need air. And space. And sky. I get dressed and head down the tunnels, out to the desert.

As soon as I open the door, I balk. I've never been out here at night.

Yet maybe darkness is just what I need.

I tentatively step outside and close the door behind me — making sure it doesn't latch.

Once my eyes adjust I realize it's not dark at all. The stars! Oh my, the stars! And the moon! I turn in a full circle, gazing upward. "Wow," I whisper.

"An apt reaction," comes a voice.

I turn toward it. "Who's there?"

The bald man steps forward. "Glynis. I was hoping it was you."

"What does that mean?"

"I was sent here to wait for someone. I'm glad it's you."

"Do you often come out in the desert at night, alone?"

"I do as I'm told."

I remember our last encounter. This strange man was all about the Keeper. "So the Keeper sent you."

"As he sent you."

"He did *not* send me here, I came out of desperation. I'm still hoping for the miracle tomorrow, but I'm not sure . . ."

"He can use desperation to get us where he needs us to be."

"So I'm supposed to be out here?"

"We both are."

"To do what?"

He gazes at the sky. "Be amazed."

I gaze upward again and involuntarily take a deep, cleansing breath. "That, I am."

He nods. "'He will have as many people as there are stars in the sky.'"

I look at him. "Really?"

"It's his promise."

The implications rush in. "So does the Keeper getting my attention make me one of his 'stars in the sky'?"

"Absolutely."

"But . . . what if everything that happened to me was a farce? A figment of my imagination? Wishful thinking?"

"Do you usually take action based on figments and wishes? Or are you a woman of facts?"

"Facts."

"So . . . did it happen?"

"I . . ." I want to say it. Admit it. Accept it.

"Did you tell people about real events that happened to you?"

"I did."

"How did they react?"

"They were happy. Hopeful."

"Which was the Keeper's intent."

"He wanted me to tell people."

"Is that a question?"

Was it? "Not really."

"Because you know the answer, Glynis. Of course your good news was supposed to be shared. The light of revelation is not to be placed under a basket, but needs to be set free for all the world to see."

"But the idea of a miracle gained a life of its own."

"It is not merely an idea," he says.

"Until it happens, it is. But now the whole of Legalis is talking about it. Expecting it. What if nothing happens?"

"I guarantee you, something will happen. The Keeper keeps his promises."

"But what if I misunderstood what he told me?" I say. "There were no words exchanged. Just a feeling. I feel things all the time that I don't understand. I could have gotten it wrong."

I hear his sigh. "Glynis. Stop processing with your head. Include your heart—which is just as, if not more important, than your mind."

I give my own sigh. "I feel like a hypocrite for doubting something I presented as true."

"You feel human."

"A flawed human who isn't used to being the bearer of good news."

"Isn't it refreshing?" He takes a deep breath. "As refreshing as the cool night air after a hot day."

I draw in my own breath and feel revived. "Do you have any instructions for me?"

He chuckles to himself. "Go with the flow."

Excuse me? "That doesn't sound like Keeper words."

"He, who created all words, enjoys using the ones that suit the moment. 'Go with the flow' suits the moment."

"I was hoping for some profound wisdom and direction."

"This is his show, Glynis. You are but a player. Keep your mind and heart open and go—"

"With the flow."

"Exactly. Let him do the rest. He's quite good at miracles, you know."

"I'll have to trust you on that."

"You'll have to trust him. You'll have to have faith."

It's a lot to take in. "So many people are depending on me."

"So *you* depend on him." He points toward the door. "You need to go home and get some sleep. It's going to be a very eventful day."

I shiver at the implications. "Will Helsa and Nixi be saved?"

"I don't know. But The Keeper's miracles are always good."

"Will you be there?" I ask.

"I wouldn't miss it."

**

Oddly, after I return home, I *do* fall asleep. Perhaps the assurance that something good is going to happen supersedes my previous fears that the day will bring inevitable horror and pain.

I wake up when Nixi knocks at my door, opening it just a crack. "It's breakfast time, Mama. Though I'm not sure I'll be able to eat a bite." She's dressed in her black caftan, ready to go into the world.

The world that will be changed today. Somehow. Some way.

I put on my robe and we go to the dining room where Bog has prepared a feast. He carries in a tray of scones.

"This is too much, Bog," I say.

His eyes graze over the spread. "I didn't know what you'd feel like eating, and I was nervous, so I kept cooking. Eat what you can."

"I appreciate the effort," I say.

He lingers longer than normal.

"Is there something else?" I ask.

"I was wondering . . . since there's going to be a miracle, I was wondering if I could go to the square with everyone else. I've never seen a miracle before."

"I'd like you to be there," Nixi says. "Can he come, Mama?"

"Of course he can come."

He offers me a nod. "What kind of miracle is it gonna be, mistress?"

I can only say, "A good one."

After he leaves, we nibble at breakfast. We don't talk much, as we're both focused on our own thoughts.

But then Nixi says, "Mama, I want to apologize for my attitude yesterday. When I so rudely sent you away? I know none of this is your fault."

"Thank you, dear girl."

"But you leaving turned out to be good, because you had your Keeper-experience after you left me, right?"

"I did." After I talked to her father.

"Tell me more details. Tell me everything."

I tell her about the loft and the touch and the light. And the Keeper's message.

"Did he actually talk to you?"

I shake my head. "I felt it inside. But not just a thought in my mind, but also a knowing in my heart."

"It must have been powerful for you to go into the streets and tell people."

"It was all powerful," I say.

She pulls a croissant apart but doesn't eat it. "So . . . he's real?"

My answer might be the most important answer I've ever given to my daughter. I'm glad the words come out with strength and certainty. "He is. I know it, Nixi. I know the Keeper is real."

"So we can trust him to do the miracle—whatever it is?"

I draw in a deep breath. "We can. We have to."

"Have to?"

I'm not sure how to answer. How do I describe an intangible tangible? "I know so little about him, but I have the feeling that his miracles are intertwined with our faith; inseparable. Or maybe they're just strengthened by it."

"So it won't happen if we don't believe?" she asks.

"I don't know about that, but maybe the best version of the miracle will happen when we do."

"Then I'll believe," she says. "Yesterday a woman stopped me on the street and said, 'The Keeper says, "Fear not."' I guess I've grabbed onto that. The only way I'm not on the floor blubbering is by believing the miracle is possible. Even though I'm still scared, I feel hopeful."

"Fear not . . . I'll grab onto those words too."

Nixi gets up from the table and kneels beside my chair. "No matter what happens today, Mama, I love you deeply and forever."

I look into her lovely eyes that look like her father's. "I love you too, my darling girl."

We hold each other as if our lives depend on it.

Chapter Fifty-One

Helsa

Today I'm going to die. Or not.

Today we're going to see a huge miracle. Or not.

At breakfast, everyone is quieter than usual. I don't blame them for their silence, for I don't know what to say either. Besides, we've said everything there needs to be said — and a few things that don't.

Like Lieb rambling on about the people who have been called to be Beaters. He wonders who they are. I don't care. And I don't blame them for doing what they have to do.

I did it. I beat Berit.

I don't let myself remember how it felt to have my club hit her flesh and bone. The shock of it. The sound. And her screams of pain.

Which may soon be my screams.

I want to talk about the miracle, but they know as much as I do. Which is next to nothing.

Glynis made big promises. Or maybe the Keeper did. To her? Through her? He's never contacted me in any way, so I don't know how it all works.

I wish he would contact me. Rand and Oria have had experiences with him. And Nana has her dreams. Me? I got nothing. I did see the sands part in Regalia, but they parted for Oria, not me. Again, I grabbed onto someone else's coattails.

At this point, I just want it over. I'm tired of being afraid. I'm tired of being hopeful. At this point . . . whatever.

We all jump when there's a knock on the door. Papa opens it and two hooded Fault Finders barge in. "Citizen Helsa, come with us." I stand and Papa and Lieb give me a hug.

"Now," they bark.

I go outside and they walk on either side of me. I'm glad they don't touch me.

My family follows behind and join others walking to the spectacle. I don't look at any of them. I don't want to see their sympathy. Or their glee.

As we reach the square I see Nixi being led forward. The Fault Finders deposit us in the very center. The star attractions.

"Are you okay?" she asks me.

"No."

"Me neither."

The crowd settles around us, leaving room for the Cudgeling Circle to be formed. Then I see Nana and Varo being led toward us. Their hands are tied in front of them. They stand opposite the entrance to the Sanctuary. Nana taps her bound hands to her chest.

Yes, yes, the Keeper.

Where is he?

As on Berit's day, there is little preamble. Everyone looks behind us as Glynis walks out of the Sanctuary to do her duty as the Head Notable. How horrible for her to preside over this day.

She raises her hands to call the Beaters to the Circle.

But she doesn't say anything. She just stands there. And stands there.

The people get restless.

"What's wrong?" I whisper to Nixi.

"I don't know."

Something's up.

Hopefully a miracle is coming.

CHAPTER FIFTY-TWO

GLYNIS

Everyone waits for me to say something — to call the Beaters to the Circle.

But I can't say the words. My mind wars with my heart and tells me, *Speak!* But nothing comes out.

Suddenly, Ivar comes out of the Sanctuary and hisses at me, "Stand aside!"

He raises his arms to say the words, but I speak first.

"I, Glynis, will take the place of my daughter, Nixi, in the Cudgeling Circle!" I don't wait for permission, but walk toward Nixi and Helsa.

Nixi looks panicked. "Mama, don't do this," she says.

"I have to."

The crowd rumbles and mumbles. Ivar peers at the balcony, no doubt waiting for the Judge to come out and make things right again.

But then Devin steps forward. "I Devin, will take my daughter Helsa's place in the Cudgeling Circle."

He joins us, and father and daughter embrace. The law against such touch is meaningless, so I hug Nixi.

"Order!" Ivar yells. "Quiet!"

No one listens to him.

Then Bog steps forward. "I, Bog will take the place of Mistress Nixi in the Circle."

Then a young man steps forward, "I, Lieb, will take the place of Sa-Sa, my very, very best friend."

"All of you! Get back where you belong!" Ivar shouts.

And then I see Elum step forward. Our eyes lock. "I, Elum, will take the place of my daughter, Nixi, in the Circle."

There's a moment of silence.

Then Nixi says, "Mama? What is he talking about?"

I glance at Varo, who gawks. "What do you mean, your daughter? She's my daughter! If anyone goes, it's me." He takes a half-step forward.

Elum stares at him. "Will you go in her place?"

Varo steps back.

"But I *will* go!" Elum says, turning fully around to speak to everyone. "For I *am* Nixi's true father."

"No, you're not!" Varo screams.

"Yes, he is!" I proclaim. I step toward Elum. "Elum, this very honorable man, is the love of my life. He is Nixi's father."

The crowd gets loud, talking amongst themselves.

Ivar huffs and puffs toward me from the Sanctuary Steps. "This can't be! You can't . . . If you admit to such sin . . . you can't be Head Notable."

If you say so.

I lift the gold Medallion of Power over my head and toss it toward him. It lands in the dirt. "I hereby relinquish my position. Take it, Ivar. It's yours."

Ivar leaves the medallion where it lies, but raises his hands. "All who dared to speak, will endure the Circle as their punishment! All will be punished!"

The crowd immediately goes silent.

Nixi holds me tighter. "Mama . . .?"

So nothing was gained by our sacrifice? Where is the miracle I was promised?

Ivar lifts his arms high. "Those who have been chosen to serve in the Cudgeling Circle come forward."

Two men step forward, but hesitate when they realize no one else is moving.

"Come on, people," one of them says. "It's yer duty."

The second man backtracks. And no one else steps up. I turn to scan the entire crowd. No one is coming forward!

Then I hear the chant from yesterday, "No Circle! No Circle!"

The entire crowd takes up the chant, fists pumping the air. Ivar sends Fault Finders to stop them, but their shouts are ignored. One man from the crowd grabs a club and threatens them with it. They back off.

Then six men rush toward Ivar. He cowers. "Leave me alone! Don't you dare touch me!"

It's chaos. It's anarchy. It's wonderful.

A new chant is added, "No Judge! No Judge!"

Oh my. Those are fighting words.

Suddenly the crowd runs toward the middle, runs toward me, Nixi, and the rest who've volunteered. It's exhilarating, but also frightening. What do they intend to do to us? Congratulate us? Or take out their anger against us?

But then I feel a hand on my arm. "This way!" It's Elum. I grab Nixi's hand and we follow him, weaving our way through the throngs of people. Once we get past the crowd and onto an empty street, we run.

I know where we're going. And nothing pleases me more.

We arrive at the alley and quickly hide ourselves behind the debris.

Nixi throws herself into my arms. "Mama, what's going on? What did you do?"

"She started a rebellion," Elum says.

Nixi stares at him, her chest heaving. "Are you really my father?"

"I am." He holds out his hand. "I'm very honored to finally meet you, Nixi."

She looks at his hand as if she's not sure what to do. "If you're my father, why haven't I known about you?"

I never ever expected to tell her the truth, much less in a cluttered alley. "I never told you, because my parents forbid us to marry. I was with child, so they arranged a quick marriage with Varo." I take Elum's hand. "But I have always loved Elum and only Elum."

"And I you," he says with a smile.

Nixi presses her hand against her forehead, clearly overwhelmed.

"We both love you, Nixi," I say.

"Always have," Elum adds.

She shakes her head as if she can't deal with that now. She looks around the alley. "What is this place? Why did you bring us here?"

I link my arm with Elum's. "For twenty-five years this has been our own special spot where we meet as often as we can."

"But how do you arrange—?" She stops her own words and I see her thoughts falling into place. She looks at her father. "The messages under the little stone by the storeroom? Were those from you?"

"From your mother to me, and me to your mother. It's how we arranged our meetings here."

"So I've been helping you see each other?"

"Your help has been invaluable but we always found a way to check on one another," I say.

She begins to pace in the small area between us. We give her a minute to absorb the shock.

"Are you all right?" I finally ask.

She stops and nods, though she doesn't look at either of us. "Actually, I'm not okay. And forgive me if I can't deal with who my father is right now. I almost died. I still might die. Is the Circle going to happen or not?"

"I'd guess not," I say.

"I don't think the Masses will allow it to ever happen again," Elum says.

"But we'll all be punished for the uprising," Nixi says.

"Some will be," I say. "But I truly doubt we will ever see another Cudgeling Circle in Legalis."

"*That* would be a miracle," she says.

"Speaking of the Keeper's miracle," I say. "I'm disappointed it didn't happen."

Elum is surprised. "But it did, my dear lady. The miracle was you, Glynis!" He laughs and holds my shoulders. "You stood up to the system, stepped up to save your daughter—spurring others to offer the same sacrifice. You got the crowd to chant, 'No Circle' and 'No Judge.' You stood up to abominable traditions that have existed for generations. Think about it: you stood up to the Judge!"

I gasp. "The Judge! Did he ever come out to the balcony?"

"I didn't see him," Elum says.

"Will he come after us?" Nixi asks.

The tension in my gut is my answer. "I'm sure he will. And he has eyes everywhere."

"Which means we need to leave," Elum says.

"But aren't we safe here?" Nixi asks.

He shakes his head. "We are not safe here. We need to not just leave *here* but leave Legalis completely."

I'm taken aback. "I can't leave."

"You're not the Head Notable anymore," he says.

I'm not. I quit. I tossed the Medallion of Power to the ground.

"Since *you* quit, then who am I?" Nixi asks. "What about our house? My friends? Will everybody shun me?"

"Shunning is the least of our worries," I say. "The Judge will be furious and want revenge. He'll be desperate to regain control."

"He may want to make an example of you," Elum says. "Of all of us."

Nixi glances at the alley entrance. "That includes Helsa and her friends too?"

"I assume."

"You say we need to leave Legalis," Nixi says. "No one can live in the desert."

"Remember the oasis?" I say. "Jass keeps it supplied. We can go there."

"And then what?" she asks. "With its Swirling Desert there's no access to Regalia. If there was, I'm sure Solana and her family would've gone home."

I'm surprised by her statement. "Are you sure about that? They were exiled. Surely going back—*if* that were possible—would have harsh consequences."

"And living in Legalis doesn't?" Elum says. "What about our harsh consequences? Our laws and restrictions?"

"Now's not the time to renew our discussions about Legalian society, Elum," I say.

"It's exactly the time. Stripped of your position and status, you and Nixi are no better off than one of the Masses, with no perks, advantages, or luxuries. Plus, you'll always be fearful for your life. There's nothing here for any of us."

"Mama . . ." Nixi looks pained.

Varo and I always made sure she wanted for nothing. Now, she has nothing. We have nothing.

"Maybe I should've just taken the beating," she says. "Not everybody dies from it."

"Nonsense!" I say. "All this happened to save you and Helsa."

"So it's my fault?"

Sometimes she seems far younger than her twenty-four years. She's been *too* protected. Too pampered. I take her in my arms. "Enough second guessing. What happened today needed to happen for the good of Legalis. The fact your life was at risk spurred me to take an action I should have taken years ago. Your need made me brave."

"The Keeper had something to do with it," Elum says.

He speaks the truth. "You're right. At the moment I offered myself, I knew it was the Keeper who spurred me to do it. Without his prompting, who knows how today would have turned out."

Nixi sinks to sitting. "You still haven't told me what we're going to do. Where we're going after the oasis."

And suddenly I remember something I read . . . the knowledge comes back to me in a flash, the perfect answer to our problem. "I know of a destination, though getting there is fraught with danger and uncertainties. But there *is* a place beyond Legalis and Regalia."

Their eyes widen. "What are you talking about?"

"Remember when I was sick and couldn't go anywhere, how bored I was?"

Nixi nods.

"I asked you to bring me the box of Notable Writings so I had something to read."

Elum scoffs. "Notable Writings sounds a bit pretentious."

"I suppose it is. But it's also useful. It's a collection of essays by past Head Notables going back hundreds of years. It was quite interesting."

"Why does that matter now?" Nixi asks.

"Because one of the writings mentioned another land besides Regalia and Legalis."

"A third society?" Elum says.

"Yes. They called it Nimbus."

"That's news to me," he says.

"If it exists, why doesn't everybody know about it?" Nixi asks.

"I only saw it mentioned the one time. Apparently someone got lost in the desert and discovered it."

"What did they say about it?" Nixi asks.

"Not much, but . . . oh, I wish I'd kept the essay out . . . they said it was a place totally incompatible with the structure of Legalis. 'Structure.' I do remember it used that word."

Elum's face is hopeful. "That detail could be bad or good. It might mean it's a place where people can be free."

"Or it could be a place where people are hostile. Legalis doesn't have an army or soldiers to defend ourselves, Elum. We've had no need. Maybe this past Head Notable didn't spread the word about Nimbus to protect Legalis from an enemy."

"Or from progress and change," he says.

"But after today everything's changed *here*," Nixi says. "Everything's a mess. I hate to admi it, but we can't stay."

"We are agreed," I say.

"So how do we get to Nimbus?" she asks.

"The essay didn't give directions other than to say it was south."

"We have to try," Elum says. "It's our only hope."

I wish I had a good argument to stay, but I don't. "I can at least get us as far as the oasis for supplies."

"We can't go out the entrance, Mama," Nixi says. "We can't go the way Jass goes. They'll catch us."

"You're right. But I know of a tunnel that leads outside."

"You do?"

"It's where I go when I need to think."

"Who knew your tunnel would be useful to us," Elum says.

"We have to go now?" Nixi asks.

"We can't wait until things have calmed down, because then Ivar and the rest of them will have had time to make a plan. They'll realize they need to find us. We have to go now."

"Can I go home and pack a few things?" Nixi presses her hands against her black robe.

We pause but a second before Elum answers, "No, you can't. That will be the first place they look for you two. I will be less noticeable. I'll go collect a few skins of water and some other essentials, then I'll come back for you."

"Be careful," I say as he leaves us.

Now it's just Nixi and me. The weight of our plan wraps around us like a hot blanket. It's smothering. I want to throw it off and breathe free.

But that can't happen just yet.

"Mama, do we really have to run?" Nixi asks.

I brush a strand of hair behind her ear. "We do."

"I'm afraid," she says.

So am I. But I say, "Remember, the Keeper says 'fear not', so that's what we have to do."

"Is all this really a part of *his* plan for us?" she asks.

"I think so."

"Can I argue with him about it?"

I chuckle. "You can try."

She sighs and takes in our little sanctuary. "How often did you two come here?"

"We tried to meet at least once a week. We just celebrated our twenty-fifth anniversary here."

"Here? In this back corner of a back alley?"

"Our corner in our alley."

Nixi shakes her head, then sighs. "Elum seems like a good man."

"He is good. And generous. And wise. And honorable."

"But Father did a good thing by marrying you, didn't he?"

"He did. And there *is* good in Varo. He assumed you were his. In a way he saved us. And for that, I will always be grateful."

"As you saved me today." She tucks her hands in her long sleeves. "I do appreciate what you and Elum did today. But all the rest that happened . . . did you expect that?"

"I did not. I didn't know what to expect. Even when I first stepped out to call the Beaters in, I didn't know what I would say or do."

"Ivar pushed you into doing something."

I chuckle again. "I guess he did. And the rest just . . . happened."

"I hope the rest just . . . happens."

"I do too."

**

Elum returns with supplies. Now it's up to me to get the three of us to the desert safely.

I lead us through my secret tunnels to the outside world. It's a very convenient secret today. If I'd never been brave as a young woman, never explored the tunnel to the desert, we would have no way to escape.

As I expertly turn left, then right, Nixi begins to ask questions. I shush her. Not now. We must be quiet now.

Our lives depend on it.

Chapter Fifty-Three

Rano

It's chaos.

I stand in the square while the rest of Legalis yells, pumps their fists, and runs amok. Some people stand in shocked silence, yet I see movement in their eyes. I can see them thinking whether they should join the pandemonium or run and hide. It's their chance to set their frustrations free. It's their chance to *be* free. "No Judge! No Judge!"

Speaking of . . . I glance upward at the balcony and spot him. But only for the briefest moment. He appears, then withdraws immediately. Out of fear?

The Judge feels fear? We were taught that it could sweep down over the square and rip people to shreds. I know now that it's a man, but he still could order others to stop all this. That he doesn't, speaks volumes. That he retreats, emboldens me. Suddenly he isn't this ominous *thing* to fear, he's a man with emotions.

And weaknesses.

Follow him.

It's a wild thought, two startling words that become action, almost against my will. I rush into the Sanctuary and remember the stairs to the loft and the balcony that we assumed the Judge used for moving around. And the tunnels beyond that Helsa and Lieb have explored.

Everyone is out in the square so I have the Sanctuary to myself. I slip into the storeroom and push open the secret door, revealing the stairs. I hesitate. Should I be doing this?

I am a small, crippled, defenseless man with no power. The Judge is tall, strong, and fierce. Do I really want to meet up with him in an unfamiliar passageway? Alone?

Go. Now.

I draw a deep breath and whisper, "Yes, Keeper." Then I quietly descend the stairs and see the domain of the Notables. There are a few people walking about. They aren't acting the way I imagine they would act if the Judge had just passed through. And I won't last three steps if I walk that way.

Then I notice a discreet opening off the corridor to the left. It's lined with stone and is dark. Uninviting. Is it a tunnel? If so it seems the perfect avenue for the Judge to use to bypass the Notables and maintain his mystique.

And so I put one crippled foot in front of the other even though all of my instincts scream to go back.

Trust me.

Although these inner nudgings spur me on, I consider ignoring them. Yet, I can't. If the Keeper is guiding me, I have to trust he will *fully* guide me. Protect me. And enable me to . . .

To do what, I have no idea.

I walk in darkness, feeling my way along. This can't be the right way to anything. But then the tunnel widens, and there are periodic lanterns lighting the way.

I come upon a single Notable. "You! What are you doing here?" he asks.

I quickly walk past hoping by my boldness he won't choose to physically confront me.

And he doesn't. He has enough to worry about up-top.

I come to a junction of three tunnels and pause. Which way? The passageways all look the same. There is no clue as to which one—

Then Daymon walks out of the shadows.

"You scared me," I say.

He points to the right. "'Be confident, Rand, and do the work you have been assigned.'"

"Assigned?"

He nods toward the tunnel. "Go. Quickly."

I run in my awkward way, but necessity helps me find a rhythm. And then . . . I see the flutter of black up ahead, at a bend in the tunnel.

It's him!

I balk. No. This can't be happening to me.

Go.

I nearly feel a physical push, so I move along, praying constantly, a desperate plea: *Help me, help me, help me . . .*

The tunnel narrows and twists some more. I'm out of breath. I can't keep this up much—

I turn and pull up short.

It's the Judge! Standing there, looking directly at me!

His bulk seems to consume the tunnel. He has to bend down because he's so tall. He points a knifed finger at me. "What are you doing here, drudge? Get back where you belong!"

My heart drops to my feet. I see my reflection in his mirrored eyes. I look as small and insignificant as I feel.

I hold my crutch in front of me like a sword but I'm shaking. "I come in the name of the Keeper!" I proclaim.

He laughs at me, a deep, guttural laugh of contempt.

In a surge of stupidity I rush forward and thrust my crutch toward his eyes.

It knocks into the corner of the mirrors and I hear them crack.

He recoils and screams. Shards of mirror fall to the ground. He rips off the razor fingers and I realize they are only gloves. Human hands claw at the jagged pieces of mirror left behind. Blood flows from his eyes.

He desperately peels off a black head covering, then the band that holds his mirrored eyes in place.

The Judge is just an ordinary man with matted black hair and cuts on his face.

"What did you do?" he shrieks, holding his hand against his eye.

On impulse I grab his gloves, his hood, and a large piece of his broken eyes, and run away. My crutch is left behind so I lumber and limp, trip and stumble, but I also find an energy and strength borne of panic and fear.

And victory.

I just unmasked the Judge!

This time when I pass some Notables, they hug the walls, as if I'm a rabid animal on the loose.

At the junction, I see Daymon. "This way!" He leads me away from the tunnel that leads back to the Sanctuary.

My lungs burn and my legs ache so much that I know each step could be my last.

"I need to rest!" I gasp.

"Not yet," Daymon says. "A little farther."

Finally he opens a door. We spill out into blinding light.

I squint at the light's intensity. "We're outside?"

He shuts the door. "We are. Sit."

I slump to the ground and lean against a wall. He hands me a skin of water and I drink greedily.

He points to the items around me. "You beat him?"

I fully see my spoils for the first time. "I guess I did." I pick up the face mask. "It's all a disguise."

"Evil often wears disguises."

"Everyone was afraid of him. They thought he was a supernatural monster. He's just a man."

"So what will you do with this new information?"

I look up at him, shielding my eyes from the sun. "People need to know."

"They do."

I stare at the debris of the Judge's disguise and nudge a razor finger with my foot. His 'hands' are empty, without power. Useless. "All of these pieces of him are rubbish, the remains of a façade."

"Listen to me, Rand," Daymon says. "Whatever you learn in the dark, you must share in the light. You need to tell everyone what the Keeper has shown you."

"How do I do that? I'm a Marked Man. I'm invisible."

He smiles at me. "No man is invisible who speaks the truth."

"I'm not so sure about that."

Daymon holds out his hands and pulls me to standing. "The people of Legalis think darkness reigns, but it doesn't. The Keeper's light shines in the dark, and darkness has never—and can never—put it out." He bends down and retrieves the remnants of the Judge's costume. "Go and speak the truth."

I wobble. My legs feel like jelly.

Daymon takes a few steps to the side, then brings me a crutch. "A gift."

It's not just *a* crutch, but my crutch. "How did . . .?"

"He knows what we need and provides. Let me show you the way back to the square."

"I'm not sure I want to go back there. It's madness."

"All the more reason to go." Daymon puts a hand on my shoulder. "You are protected by the armor of the Keeper. Truth *will* be victorious."

My stomach clenches so tightly I'm not sure I can move. But I have to move. The Keeper has given me a mission.

May he help me and keep me safe.

**

The tunnel that Daymon leads me to exits on a side street near the Sanctuary. I've seen this door before but had no idea it led to a tunnel. I wonder how many doors there are. How many tunnels.

One thing I do know is there are too many secrets in Legalis. It's time for the truth to come out.

And then I see another door. One that I'm familiar with.

I postpone my return to the square to do something I've wanted to do for days.

I enter the door that leads to the Workers and boldly step into their workroom. As I step in, they all look at me with surprise and wariness.

"Listen, dear Workers!" I raise my hands to them. "The Judge is no more! Today is the day of freedom for all of Legalis!"

Miri steps toward me. "We heard the ruckus up-top. What's going on?"

"Revolution and rebirth." I hold out the clawed gloves, the coif, and shards of his eyes. "See this? This is the costume of the Judge. I injured him. This is his blood."

Zir sets down the fabric he's been sewing and walks toward me. He takes the glove. It hangs limp, without power. "Well I'll be . . ." He hands it back. "Come on, everyone. This is our chance."

Some balk. I understand. I've lived in fear too. "Please come," I say. "Now is the time. There may never be another."

Mir joins in, urging everyone to follow me outside. When they enter the sunlight, they are blinded and cover their eyes. But then, one by one, they see — truly see the world that has been kept from them for too long.

"Come to the square," I say.

But most of them disperse, as if running for their lives.

Perhaps with good reason. For at the moment *reason* is lacking in Legalis. Even Zir runs away.

Miri is the only one who stays with me. "Are you sure we'll be safe?" she asks.

I hesitate, but tell the truth. "No. But isn't the chance of freedom worth the risk?"

She nods.

"Come with me, Miri. I need to show them what I showed you."

Together we approach the square. The shouting has died down but people linger, talking in small groups. They look excited but cautious. The Fault Finders are present, but seem uncertain what to do.

I'm uncertain what to do. I spot a friend. "Oria!"

She sees me; sees what I'm holding. She hurries to my side. "What is that?"

"*That* is proof the Judge is just a man."

She fingers the glove. "How did you get it?" she asks.

"I fought the Judge and unmasked him. I'll explain more later. First, I need to show the people, but I'm not sure how."

"I'll help you. Come with me." We move to the top of the steps leading to the Sanctuary. Miri follows us, standing on one side of me with Oria on the other. "Wave your crutch to get their attention," she says.

I do that as she calls out, "Good people of Legalis! Listen to important news!"

Miri calls out too, and soon a crowd gathers. My stomach is in knots. My mouth is dry.

"Rand has conquered the Judge!" Oria nods at me. "Hold up the glove."

I do so, and hand the shards to Miri and the hood to Oria, who also hold up the evidence.

When I speak my voice is far louder than I thought it ever could be. "The Judge is not a monster, nor an unearthly creature. He is not an all-knowing demon! I fought him and won! The razors he threatened us with are merely metal tips on gloves."

Oria shakes the face covering and puts her fingers through the eye holes. "And his eerie black face is but cloth."

Miri holds up the mirror remnants. "And his eyes are not made of mystical glass — they are merely glass that shatters."

The people stir and talk amongst themselves. "But he flies!" someone shouts.

"He does not!" I say. "He walks like you and I. And he falls."

Oria points at blood on the hood. "And he bleeds! See the blood of the Judge!"

A man steps forward and tentatively touches the razor gloves. Then he puts it on his own hand, curls his fingers toward the people, and snarls.

They recoil, but immediately step forward again. They are not afraid anymore.

Miri says, "Good people of Legalis. I was held prisoner for years, held underground, working for the Notables! Rand has set us free! As we are now free, *you* are now free!"

Oria tosses the hood on the ground and stomps on it. "Fear not! If the Keeper gives you freedom, you are free!" She lifts her arms to the sky. "The Keeper is our protector, our provider, our Lord! Turn your devotion to him and be free indeed!"

The people look a bit hesitant, but when a few cheer for the Keeper, others join in. It's like they finally have someone to believe in, to follow; someone who offers something more than pain and oppression. The change in mood is infectious and joy dethrones every other emotion.

Suddenly a strong wind blows through the crowd — around the crowd. It doesn't just move robes or hair, it seems to infect the Masses, as if fueling them from within. I feel it too. I take a deep breath, drinking it in. I see Oria and Miri breathing deeply with me. It's a breath of something wonderful; a wind that clears minds, nourishes hearts, and fuels souls.

"What just happened t?" I ask them.

Oria grins. "It's like everything that was dormant is now alive; everything that was confused is now clear."

"I feel full inside," Miri says. "Complete."

"Filled and fulfilled," I add.

Suddenly the clocks chime and people startle. They aren't supposed to chime on Judging Day.

The people move toward the buildings.

"No!" I yell to the Masses. "Stop! There will be no more Counts! No more Circles! No more Judge!"

The crowd hesitates, but they stop walking, breaking their blind obedience to the old laws. "No Counts!" they shout.

The Fault Finders see what's happening and scurry away, making the people cheer.

Some even hug each other and dance around in a happy celebration of the new truth that has blown through their souls.

A few swarm around us, congratulating us, clapping for us. For the first time, I see hope in their eyes.

For the first time, *I* feel hope.

CHAPTER FIFTY-FOUR

SOLANA

I feel so useless, hiding away.

And nervous.

My family cowers in Devin's unit, but we don't say much.

Our eyes are locked on the door. Any moment a Fault Finder will burst in and take Helsa and me away.

We've already discussed whether there's a better place to hide. Perhaps the unit I shared with Oria? Perhaps a stranger's unit? No unit seems safer than here.

Where is Oria? And Rand? When Devin whisked us away during the chaos in the square, I lost sight of them.

"I want to know what's going on out there," Helsa says. "We're completely in the dark here."

"It's not dark here," Lieb says.

She pats his arm.

"I still can't believe Elum is Nixi's father," Devin says.

Helsa nods. "She was just as surprised as everyone else. Including Varo. He argued about it."

"Glynis and Elum certainly can keep a secret," Devin says.

"It's not a secret anymore," Lieb says.

"I saw Elum lead Glynis and Nixi away," Helsa says.

"I did too. At least they're together," I say. "She gave up her high position for Nixi. That's very brave."

"Or foolish," Devin says.

"The Judge is going to be really, really mad," Lieb says. "At everybody."

I chuckle nervously. "Let's hope he can't get us all at once."

When the door opens, we gasp and our hearts jump. But then we see it's Oria and Rand. They're out of breath.

"Good," Oria says. "You're all here."

"What's going on out there?" Helsa asks.

Oria's smile surprises me. "Good things. Plus a *very* good thing." She motions to Rand, who holds up a glove with razor fingers, and a black hood.

"I had a run-in with the Judge," he says, smiling.

"And Rand won!" Oria says.

Rand tells us the details. Oria pulls shards of mirrored glass from her pocket. "These were his eyes."

Lieb picks up a piece and peers at his reflection. "These aren't eyes."

"They're part of his costume," Rand says. "He was just a man disguised as a monster to scare us."

Devin touches the points of the razors. "He certainly did a good job of it."

Oria puts her arm around Rand's shoulders. "And this hero just showed everybody in the square all the evidence. People know the truth now."

"And Oria told them about the Keeper," Rand says.

"How did they react?" Devin says.

"It's like once the seed was planted, a new faith started to grow. It was almost something you could watch as it moved through the Masses."

Rand nods enthusiastically. "Then a strong wind blew around the square and over everyone." He presses both hands against his chest. "It was like a breath of *him*."

"Him?" Helsa asks.

"The Keeper," Rand says. "It's like he swept over everyone. But not just over, through everyone."

Oria beams. "It's like I let out my old air and drew in air that was brand new, totally refreshing and invigorating. Life-giving."

"That's exactly what it was!" Rand says excitedly. "And people felt it. You could see it in their faces. It was the Keeper! They felt him!"

"Wow," Lieb says. "I wish I coulda been there. I want him too."

Oria looks pensive, and then her eyes well with tears. "I think you have him, Lieb. I think everyone who believes in him has him, sealed inside." She holds a fist to her chest. "He's been with us before, he's with us now, and he'll be with us in the future. I know it."

Lieb takes a very deep breath as if drawing the Keeper in. I find myself doing the same. Devin follows our lead. We let out the breath, and laugh with much-needed joy.

"Told you," Oria says. "Do you feel him?"

I nod. I really think I do. "So everything that happened out there... it's his doing?"

"It is," Oria says confidently. "He has set us all free."

Rand's eyes light up. "Speaking of free . . . Solana, I let the Workers out. Miri stood up with Oria and me in the square."

"They're all free?" I ask.

"They scattered everywhere."

The thought of them running around, suddenly on their own, concerns me. I hope they find safety.

Helsa shakes her head. "All this talk of freedom sounds great, but facts are facts. People are free—for the moment. As are Nana and I. But are we really free? Do we need to stay hidden?"

Oria and Rand exchange a look. "I think we definitely need to be wise about it."

"Do we continue to hide here?" I ask. "Or is there someplace safer?"

Oria holds up a finger. "I think there is. I'll show you a place that few people know about. In fact, we should go there now, while things are still chaotic. Why don't we all grab food and water, just in case."

Everyone does just that, and Lieb retrieves his mailbag from its hiding place. "I've got all the Relics to take with us."

I should have thought of that. He's such a good kid.

Within minutes, we're ready to go.

"Follow me. Quickly," Oria says.

We go outside where the streets are hectic. Some people seem happy, but many scurry frantically as if they're afraid. My feelings are a mixture of the two.

The woman who first met us when we arrived runs toward us. "Oria!" she says. "What you said is true! He's real!"

Oria beams. "Yes, he is, Durth. Yes, he is."

Durth hugs her and dances away as if a younger version of herself has been reborn.

Then a man approaches Devin—I recognize him as one of the jail guards. Is he going to arrest me? Devin pulls me behind himself. Rand and Lieb move beside Devin, creating more of a barrier.

"Hey. Where are you and your mother going?" the guard asks.

"Leave us alone," Devin says. "It's over."

The guard puts his hands up. "Don't I know it. A crowd came in and released all the prisoners. That's when I got outta there."

I step out from behind Devin. "Soli and her husband? Kal?"

"Everybody." He looks around. "Gonna be a wild time in Legalis tonight, that's for sure." He gives me a salute. "Best to you, Solana. Glad yer free. Tell the Keeper I was always good to you."

"He knows," I say. "And you can tell him yourself."

He smiles at the thought. "I just might." He strides away.

Oria's face is frantic about the delay. "Please. We need to move faster!"

"Are we going to the walkway?" Lieb asks.

"We are. So hurry."

Lieb looks back at me. "It's a good place. You'll love it, Nana."

She leads us to an alley where she pushes on a wall and a door pops open. Inside are spiral steps. "Last one in, close the door," she tells us.

We follow her, with Devin coming in last. The steps lead up and up, many stories. Then they open into full sunlight on a long walkway trailing off in both directions.

"Look over here, Nana," Lieb says, peering over an outer wall. "There's the desert!"

I am amazed. It's where it all began . . .

Rand points at a slit in a taller, inner wall. "And over here we can see the street."

I have to stand on my tip-toes to see it. "Who uses this walkway?" I ask.

"Wyan says it used to be utilized a lot. But not anymore."

Helsa stares down at the street. "I bet the Judge or his goons use it to spy on us."

"Probably," Oria says.

I look around fearfully. "Are you sure we're safe up here?"

"Safe-er," she says. But she doesn't look confident.

Devin turns his attention to the desert. He seems mesmerized by it. I stand beside him and rub my hand on his back. "What are you thinking?"

"As much as I hate Legalis, I'm thinking it may get worse before it gets better."

"I know. Those in power won't stand down without a fight."

Lieb joins us and leans his arms on the chest-high wall. "We could go out in the desert again. We have food and water. And there's that place with food and blankets out there. It has lots of oranges."

"It's called an oasis," Helsa says, as she joins us. "Nixi and Glynis make sure it's replenished."

"It saved our life," I say.

Oria stands beside me. "Perhaps it can save us again."

And yet . . . "I'm not sure I like any talk about going out in the desert. The Swirling Desert prevents us from going back to Regalia," I say. "So what are we going to do? Wander around?"

"That sounds like certain death to me," Devin says.

Lieb shakes his head. "Then why are there doors going outside at all?"

"I've been outside," Rand says.

"When?" I ask.

"Today. Right after I fought the Judge. A friend led me through the tunnels, to safety. He told me to show the Masses the Judge's gloves and hood."

Lieb cocks his head. "Is he really tall and doesn't have any hair?"

Rand looks shocked. "Yes, to both."

"Wait," Helsa says. "Tall and bald? That's my Tunnel Man."

"I think he lives down there," Lieb says. "His name is Day-something."

"Daymon," Rand says. "You met him too, Lieb?"

"Lots of times. He's really nice."

I'm amazed. "Our Tunnel Man gets around."

"Yes, he does," Rand says. "He's also the man who kept leaving me Relics in the Sanctuary."

"He's letting himself be known to us," Devin says. "Maybe he can help us now."

"I bet he can," Lieb says. "I can get you down—"

"Oria!"

We look toward the angry voice of a young man at the top of the stairway.

"Wyan," she says, stepping toward him. She seems afraid. "We came up here to get off the streets," she says. "It's dangerous down there."

Wyan points at Rand. "You hurt the Judge! You will be severely punished!"

Although I see Rand blink, his voice is calm. "Who's left to punish me? Punish any of us?"

He looks confused. "There are lots of Notables who won't take what you've done lightly. And Glynis can't help you anymore. Ivar is in charge now."

"Maybe," Oria says. "But today showed how much the Masses—the people—of Legalis want change. You can't stop it, Wyan. Nobody can."

"I can try." He sighs as if in pain. "None of this was supposed to happen."

"But maybe it was." Oria's voice is soft and placating. "The Keeper detests injustice and lies. He started his good work today by putting a halt to the Cudgeling Circle."

"But it's chaos down there." Wyan's forehead is wrinkled. "People are acting crazy. I saw a bunch of them pulling carts of food from the farm."

"They're hungry," I say.

He ignores me. "But some of them were even holding each other up and taking down the clocks."

Good for them.

"They'll calm down," Oria says. "They've just been set free. They're celebrating."

I have an important question to ask. "How *is* the Judge?"

"A little blood is not going to stop him." He glares at Rand. "He's going to come after you. After all of you."

"So help us," Oria says.

Wyan studies each of us, and I can tell his thoughts are racing. "The Masses may be in charge at the moment, but the Judge or Ivar, or whoever else, will take back their power. And their punishment will make the Cudgeling Circle look like a slap on the hand."

Oria says calmly, "Please Wyan, help us. We're friends. Friends help each other."

There's a momentary softening to his expression. He wants to help, but will he?

Lieb raises his hand. "I can take us out to the desert."

Wyan shakes his head. "Ivar sent guards to the entrance."

The entrance? I never considered going out that way. For him to assume that's our way out . . . is it possible Wyan doesn't know about the tunnel leading outside?

Lieb says, "Not the entrance. The—"

I stop him from saying too much. "Thank you for the warning, Wyan. We need to talk about things. Can we stay here a short while to do that?"

He looks skeptical.

"Please, Wyan," Oria says. "For old time's sake?"

I can see him battle with his decision. I send out a silent prayer, *Help us, Keeper. Help us leave safely.*

Then Wyan points at Oria. "A few minutes, then you're gone. Agreed?"

"Agreed," Oria says. "Thank you for not turning us in."

He nods once, then leaves us on the walkway.

"He doesn't know about the tunnels or the other way out," I say.

"So it seems," Oria says.

"Which means Daymon is truly a guide sent by the Keeper. He is the one who will lead us out."

"Then let's go," Lieb says, pointing to the right. "The third door leads down, all the way to the tunnels. I can get you close to Daymon from there. He'll find *us*."

There's no time for a discussion. We follow Lieb into the bowels of Legalis.

**

"I had no idea," I whisper as Lieb weaves us right and left through narrow tunnels. "Who uses these?"

"We do," Lieb says.

I can't argue with him.

Lieb hesitates at an intersection, looking from one tunnel to the other. "I'm not sure which way . . ." he says.

Rand peers down each path. "I don't know either."

Helsa keeps looking back the way we came. "Choose one. We can't just stand here. They may be after us."

One tunnel is palely lit while the other is brighter. "The tunnel we need isn't used much, right?" I ask.

"I don't think so," Rand said.

I point to the darker one. "Then I choose that way."

"I wish Daymon would pop out and show us which way to go," Helsa says.

"Me too," Rand says. "But until he shows up, I think Solana's right. Let's go this way."

The tunnel is narrow and we have no choice but to walk single file. Add to that the dim light . . . my heart starts beating too fast and I falter.

"What's wrong, Mother?" Devin asks.

"I don't . . . I don't like tight spaces." I cross my arms. "I can't breathe."

He puts an arm around my waist to give me support. "Take slow breaths. In. Then out."

Even in the faint light, I see the worry on their faces. I don't want to be the one to slow us down. Not when we're this close to safety.

But I can't seem to catch my breath. I feel faint but I refuse to let myself give into it.

We turn toward distant voices. They're coming?

Suddenly Rand speaks, "Oh mighty Keeper! You tell us to fear not because you are with us. Make us strong. Protect us and lead us to safety."

I nod over and over, drinking in the words, praying them as my own. And then . . . a breeze blows past us, coming from the direction we are walking.

I inhale the air deeply and let it—and the Keeper—give me the strength I need.

"That's fresh air," Oria says. "We must be close!"

Close is good. Close is excellent. "I'm all right," I tell them. "Keep going."

My heart and breathing settle, and we continue. Soon the tunnel gets lighter, and when we turn a corner, we see an open door at the end. We all run through it, into the desert.

"We made it!" Helsa says.

"I told you it was here," Rand says.

It takes a few moments for my eyes to adjust to the sunlight. I see the boundary of Legalis, its string of buildings snaking their way in both directions.

But when we hear sounds coming from the tunnel we run to one side, away from the door. There is no place to hide. The three men create a line in front of us. Rand holds his crutch across his body, ready to defend us.

I close my eyes and pray. *Fear not, fear not, fear not . . .*

The sounds of my heartbeat are interrupted by Rand, calling out, "Elum!"

Helsa yells, "Nixi!" and runs toward the girl, embracing her.

And then we see Glynis.

She surveils the group. "I'm glad you made it to safety," she says.

"We're glad to see that you did, too," Oria says.

There's an awkward moment. Then I step forward. "I want to thank you for what you did in the square. It was truly a miracle."

Glynis glances at Elum. "That's what Elum said."

I motion Devin and Lieb forward. "You met Devin at the jail, but this is my grandson, Lieb."

She nods. "I thank the both of you for stepping forward, being willing to take Helsa's place."

Rand is next. He gives Glynis a nod of deference. "Head Notable."

She shakes her head. "Not anymore. And you are?"

"Rand." He takes a step back. "I'm a Marked Man. I shouldn't—"

She raises her hand to stop his words. "You are a Marked Man no more. That means nothing now."

"Do you think so?" Elum asks.

Glynis hesitates. "I guess I don't know for sure. The Count, Marked Men, the Circle . . . they are the past. We started something new today."

"And the Judge." I put my hand on Rand's back. "Rand fought the Judge—and won."

Her eyes widen. "*You* did what?"

"I unmasked him. I made him bleed."

She chuckles—which is an odd reaction.

"He's just a man," Rand says.

"That, he is," Glynis says. "A very prideful, power-hungry, vengeful man."

Nixi looks hopeful. "If the Judge has been routed, then maybe we can stay?"

Glynis shakes her head. "A wounded animal is more dangerous than a healthy one. And far more deadly."

"I think we still need to go to Nimbus," Elum says.

"What's Nimbus?" Oria asks.

He defers to Glynis. "It's a society I read about in historical papers. Although I'm not entirely sure it really exists."

"The only thing the account said was that it's not compatible with Legalis," Nixi adds.

"But we don't know what that really means," Elum says. "Considering how horrible Legalis is, it could be a positive thing."

"Where is this place?" I ask.

"South," she says, pointing.

"How far?" Devin asks.

"I have no idea." Glynis points to the east. "We were going as far as the oasis to rest and get supplies." She offers a little laugh. "I never thought *I* would need the provisions that *I* provided."

We hear a loud commotion sounding over the top of the buildings, coming from the core of Legalis. What's happening?

"Is that happy or scared yelling?" Lieb asks.

"Probably some of both," Elum says. He gazes to the west where the sun is beginning to set. "I think we need to get going. I don't want to be caught in the desert after dark."

**

Oria and I walk behind Glynis and Elum. Not because they told us to, or because they set themselves apart, but because they are our leaders.

I hope they know what they're doing.

Elum takes Glynis's arm as we start walking up the first of many hills between us and the oasis.

"They really love each other," Oria says softly.

For an instant I think of the Elum I first met, the man I wound the clocks with. The man I thought—for a few instants—could be *my* man. It's clear that was never a possibility.

Which leaves me to wonder, will I ever find love again?

Oria displays the uncanny connection we share by asking, "Tell me about your husband."

Thoughts of my husband make me smile. "*He* was kind like that."

"How long has he been gone?"

"A long, long time. I moved in with Devin and Fet when Helsa was ten."

"They saved you from being alone."

"That, they did. But when Devin was exiled and Fet died of grief, it was just Helsa and I." I take a deep breath that is needed for the exertion of my legs *and* my emotions. "It was just the two of us until we followed you here."

"I didn't expect anyone to follow."

"And I didn't expect *to* follow. Or that Helsa and Lieb would come with me."

"Are you glad you did?" she asks. "I mean, Legalis wasn't a welcoming place, and now . . . here we are again, out in the desert, going to a place we know nothing about."

"Sometimes I think about what life would've been like if we'd stayed in Regalia," I say.

"Me too," Oria says as she steps around a prickly bush. "Did we cause real change to happen, or is everything back the way it was before?"

"I think the Devoted were strong enough to keep the change going. At least I hope so."

She only nods.

"But we did some good in Legalis, didn't we?" I ask.

"That is yet to be determined."

Suddenly, Glynis stops walking and turns to face us. "You did a lot of good in Legalis. *We* did good." She motions us forward. "Join us."

We catch up with them, and Elum helps me when I stumble.

"Thank you," I say. "You've always been a gentleman."

He shakes his head, but Glynis nods. "That, he has." She takes his arm as we walk on. "Oria," she says. "You need to realize that you're the one who started the change in Legalis."

"Me?"

"You spoke out at Berit's Circle, when Helsa stepped in for Lieb." She glances back toward the young people who walk with Nixi behind us, with Rand and Devin bringing up the rear. "Helsa has been invaluable. She brought me so much joy and peace through her painting, and protected me from my husband's poison. She's a very brave girl."

"What you did today was bravest of all," I say. "You saved Nixi and Helsa. And with the people rallied against the Circle, you've saved many more lives."

"And because of Rand," Oria says, "they can now be free of the Judge."

"Did you always know he was just a man?" I ask Glynis.

"Of course. I had meetings with him in his office. His name is Ubel."

She says this so matter-of-factly that it throws me off.

"The notion that the Judge has a name and an office . . . How did he come to be the Judge and get into power?" Oria asks.

"He comes from a long line of Judges — some worse than he is."

"I can't imagine," I say.

"Imagine," Glynis says. "Ubel's father had a Judging Day every week."

I shiver at the thought. "What do they get out of it?"

Glynis walks a few steps with her head down before answering. "What did *I* get out of being Head Notable? Power. Status. A chance to feel superior."

I hear regret in her voice.

Elum takes her hand. "We're past that now," he says. "Today is a new beginning."

"It is," Oria says. "Because of what you did, *and* because Rand defeated the Judge."

Glynis shakes her head. "I wouldn't count on his defeat being permanent. Ubel will not go quietly."

We walk a bit in silence, letting this sink in. Then Glynis says, "Oria, I have something to tell you. Something you should know."

"What's that?" Oria says.

"Your friend, Wyan?"

"Yes?"

"He worked for the Judge."

"What?" Oria stops walking, as do the rest of us.

"After you spoke at Berit's Circle he was assigned to infiltrate your group to get information about your plans."

"Our friendship was fake?"

"I don't know about that. Maybe not completely."

She shakes her head and huffs. "No wonder he wouldn't budge about his views."

"I'm sorry," Glynis says. "But the Judge does things like that."

"I'm glad you told me. It helps me move on."

Lieb and Helsa have walked ahead, and Lieb calls out, "There it is!"

"It's the oasis!" Helsa yells.

"Our haven," Glynis says with a sigh.

A haven for now, but what comes next?

I keep the question to myself.

Chapter Fifty-Five

Glynis

I haven't been to the oasis in years, not since Nixi was young.

The trees have grown bigger, providing even more shade. Young Lieb rushes toward the oranges and picks two. "My favorite!"

His joy pleases me. "Is he always so happy?" I ask Solana.

"He didn't used to be. His upbringing was rather negative and grim. His father was cruel, and . . ." She shrugs.

"Devin?"

"No, no. Lieb isn't technically related to us. Over the years we just absorbed him into our family."

"How nice of you."

"We've benefited far more than he has."

My legs ache from walking uphill on sand and rough ground. "I need to sit." I point toward some trees.

Elum brushes fallen leaves off the grass. I awkwardly lower myself to the ground with an *oomph.* He sits beside me.

Lieb comes over with two oranges. "Want some?"

"Thank you, Lieb," I say.

"I'll get water for us," Oria says.

"I'll get bread," Solana says.

As the group scatters on their self-appointed errands, I marvel at them. "They're good people."

"That, they are," Elum says. "Their bond is unbreakable. I feel lucky whenever I get to spend time with them."

I see Rand hobbling along, laughing with Lieb. "What about that one?"

"Rand has faith beyond anyone I've ever known."

"Despite the bad lot with his leg and being Marked?"

"Beyond all that."

"I can't imagine him fighting the Judge."

Elum peels an orange, setting the peels in a neat stack. Once done, he hands it to me, and starts peeling another for himself. "I'm learning that brawn does not count as much as bravery."

"Good to know," I say.

Oria comes back with a refilled water skin.

"Thank you," I say.

Solana comes with bread. Soon everyone sits around us. I like that they don't treat me as the Head Notable—though that's not my title anymore.

Hmm. If not the Head Notable, who and what am I?

We share the food as the sun begins to set. I enjoy listening to them chat amongst themselves, the evidence of the bond Elum spoke about very clear.

Helsa brushes crumbs off her robe. "I have a question about Daymon."

Rand snickers. "I think we all have questions about Daymon."

"Who's Daymon?" I ask.

"He's a magical man who helped us," Lieb says.

Helsa shakes her head. "I don't know about magical, but he's guided most of us."

A guide . . . "Is he tall, bald, and muscular?"

"He is," Helsa says.

I'm thrilled that their guide is mine. "I met him more than once," I say. "In the desert."

"That's him!" Helsa says. "He may not be magical, but he's been there when we need him."

Solana's eyes grow large. "We saw this Daymon in Regalia *and* here. Did he get exiled after we did?"

Rand shakes his head. "He was hiding Relics in the Sanctuary long before you arrived."

"But we saw him right before the exile," Helsa says. "Which means he can come and go between Regalia and here."

Oria's eyes light up. "If he can travel back and forth, does it mean we can too?"

Helsa shrugs.

"Do you want to go back to Regalia?" Nixi asks her.

"It's better than going someplace we don't know anything about," Helsa says.

Nixi tears off a piece of bread. "Mama, could we go there instead of Nimbus?"

They are all ignoring a very important question. "Did any of you ever know or hear of any people in Regalia who weren't *from* Regalia?"

They look at each other. "No," Solana says.

Lieb raises his hand. "I was a messenger-Serv. I knew everybody. There was nobody in Regalia who wasn't from Regalia."

"Except this Daymon," I say.

Lieb shakes his head. "He's magic, so he doesn't count."

"Lieb . . ." Helsa says.

He pops an orange segment in his mouth. "How else did he know where we needed him to be?"

I see Rand's eyes widen. It's clear he has a story to tell. "Rand?" I say. "Do you have something to add?"

He runs his hand along the crutch in his lap. "After I hurt the Judge, I grabbed the evidence, but had to leave my crutch behind. But when Daymon led me to safety outside, he handed me my crutch."

"He replaced your crutch," I say.

"No." Rand shakes his head adamantly. "It was *my* crutch. There's no logical way he could have retrieved it for me."

"See?" Lieb says. "That's magic."

"I'm not going to argue with you, Lieb," Solana says. "I can't prove otherwise, so I can only be thankful." She looks at Nixi. "Back to your question: I don't think we *can* go home."

"Unless Daymon shows us the way," Lieb says.

"They wouldn't welcome *me* back, that's for sure," Oria says.

"Maybe they would," Solana says. "If the Devoted kept spreading the news about the Keeper, maybe the Council has been forced to accept them."

Oria continues. "I wish I knew if what I started continued or collapsed when I left."

"What exactly did you do in Regalia that got you exiled?" I ask.

"I was a Patron who spoke about the Keeper."

I know something about the workings of Regalia. I admire her. "You were brave there, as you were brave here."

"As you were brave," she says. "Mistress."

"I regret I didn't do it sooner."

Helsa tucks her robe over her feet. The air is getting cool. "I think there are a lot of regrets floating around Legalis tonight."

I look in its direction, but can see nothing but hills.

"Are people still rebelling?" Oria asks. "Are they rioting or are they peaceful?"

"There's not much to destroy," Devin says.

I beg to differ. "Unless they get underground and attack the Notable homes."

"And the Notables," Elum says. "It could get bad. I'm glad you and Nixi are safe."

"I am too." And yet . . .

Oria stands and brushes off the back of her robe. "There's a big question that needs to be asked: how do we get to Nimbus?"

Nixi stifles a yawn. "I don't know about any of you, but I have to sleep. I planned on dying today, and now that I'm alive, I'd *like* to stay awake for days, but I'm exhausted."

Sleep sounds amazing. I could sleep. By the lack of argument it's clear the feeling is shared.

Lieb scrambles to his feet and says, "Blankets! I'll get some blankets." A minute later he hands them around.

Solana stops us before we scatter. "Before we sleep I think we owe the Keeper our thanks." She holds out her hands and everyone forms a circle.

Holding hands is a new experience for me. But I like the feeling of skin on skin. The connection of it. I almost feel an energy pass between us.

Solana offers a prayer of thanks. Elum squeezes my hand.

Yes, Elum. I get it. I feel it too.

When the prayer is done, Lieb says, "*This* is the right sort of circle."

I agree completely.

Chapter Fifty-Six

Glynis

I open my eyes to moonlight and see Nixi's face an arm's length away from me.

We're lying on the ground in the desert. At the oasis. We've fled Legalis.

Nixi's here and she's safe. She was saved from the Cudgeling Circle. But now what?

I turn on my other side and see Elum. My heart swells. Never ever did I think I would wake up next to the two most important people in my life.

But now what?

The question is unrelenting. The group that shares the oasis looks to me for answers. I gave them one: Nimbus. Yet it was an iffy suggestion, one borne from the need to offer something to these people who risked everything to change Legalis for the better.

But *is* Legalis better now? Or have our rebellious actions made things worse? Only time will tell.

I close my eyes but sleep doesn't come, and I know it won't come until I think things through. *If* they can be thought through. There are so many unknowns.

I carefully set my blanket aside and stand. I'm happy for the moonlight and carefully step around my sleeping friends. I walk to a stand of trees that offers me a place to think. I sit beneath the tallest tree and lean against its trunk. "But now what?" I whisper to its leaves.

My thoughts return to the chaos in the square, as the Masses chanted for an end to the Circle and the Judge. I remember the ineffectiveness of the Fault Finders to keep order. The violence when the crowd turned its frustrated fury on Ivar and the enforcers.

Elum swept me and Nixi away to safety here. But what happened after we left? The Judge was supposedly conquered. But I know Ubel, and I have to wonder if he was defeated or only wounded and angry. Is Ivar in charge? Has the Notable underground been breached? What of Varo, Kal, and Bog? My thoughts swirl.

"But now what?" I whisper again.

"That's for you to figure out."

I whip toward the voice and spot Daymon, standing in the moonlight. "You do like to show up unexpectedly," I say.

"I go where I'm needed."

"You're implying I need you?"

"You need him."

I start to get to my feet and Daymon holds out his hand to help me up. "Thank you. It always seems to come back to *him* with you people."

"His people."

"Same thing."

"Aren't you one of his people?" he asks.

I smooth my robe and adjust its belt. "If so, only recently."

"Time means little to him. A new follower is as precious to him as an old one."

I chuckle, remembering the others. "I feel very old right now. My life was set. I knew who I was and where I was going."

"Did you?"

I toss my hands in the air. "You do like asking tough questions."

He shrugs. "Life without growth is like being chained to a rock; it's hard and uncomfortable and there's no way forward."

"My life as the Head Notable was comfortable. I lived in a lovely home and felt like I was doing something meaningful."

"Ah." He gazes at the starry sky, then says, "You lived in a lovely home with a husband who tried to kill you."

True. But I hedge. "I'm still here."

"You allowed the Masses to remain prisoners under the oppressive laws of Legalis for years."

This hits me wrong. "So you expected me to undo hundreds of years of tradition and laws by myself?"

"If not you, who?"

I pace in front of the tree. "Didn't I just do that by halting the Cudgeling Circle? By offering to sacrifice myself for Nixi?"

"You did. The first sacrificial act in Legalis. He's proud of you for that."

Despite my uncertainty, this makes me happy. "I didn't do it for him. I did it for Nixi."

"To offer your life for another is the greatest act of love. And what you do for others, you do for him."

"I wasn't thinking about the Keeper at the time."

"Consciously, maybe not. But he was thinking about you."

I run my hand through my hair. "This is getting complicated."

"Not at all," Daymon says. "You surrendered to him in the loft and he created a miracle for you. Through you."

"How do you know all that?"

"Is anything I said untrue?"

So many questions. But I came here to get answers. "Let's say the Keeper is responsible for spurring me into that moment."

"And this one," Daymon says.

He's unrelenting. "What next?"

"That's your choice. The Keeper is keen on free will."

I lift my hands, stopping his words. "We're going to Nimbus. We've made that choice. I was just wondering how we get there. And what we'll find there. And do there. Plus a hundred other unknowns."

"Nimbus *is* a choice. Between Nimbus or . . .?"

The emphasis is odd. "Or?"

He looks back toward Legalis.

His meaning suddenly hits me and I gaze into the darkness. "I can't go back."

He cocks his head. "Why not?"

"It's like Oria said about going back to Regalia. She can't go back because she was a rebel. So am I. I started the chaos. And as you just said, I was the Head Notable who condoned everything that made the lives of the Masses miserable. I will not be welcomed."

"You're not the Head Notable anymore."

His words hit me like a slap. "True. I gave that up."

"Which means . . ."

"I have no power."

He shakes his head. "You have none of *that* power. But now you have more power—power *he* gave you."

That may or may not be true. "I knew how to use the power from my position as the Head Notable. I know very little about how to use any power from the Keeper."

"He'll teach you."

Now, I'm skeptical. "And how will he do that?"

"One step at a time. Change isn't just about overturning laws, Glynis, it's about changing hearts. All he requires is *your* willing heart. Are you willing, Glynis?"

I hesitate. "You're asking me to go back into enemy territory."

"The Masses are not your enemy."

"The Judge is. Ivar is. The other Notables are." I thought of a question that might help me make up my mind. "Is the Judge gone?"

This time it's Daymon who hesitates. "Let's say, he's vulnerable."

"Let's say? As in 'let us' say? As in you and who else?"

There's that smile again. "The Keeper will not give you more than you can handle. You will not go back alone."

"So Elum and Nixi can come with me?"

"They can. But that's not who I was talking about."

"Oh. Him."

"Oh! Him! Say it with enthusiasm, Glynis. Fear not! The protector and provider of the universe will be with you!"

That *is* comforting, but I'm a woman who likes a plan. "So I'm supposed to just walk back into Legalis and take over? Will anyone — on either side — let me do that?"

"That depends on what you offer them."

"Which is?"

He cocks his head, waiting for me to supply my own answer.

"Freedom from the repressive Decrees of Legalis?" I ask.

"And . . . ?"

"Freedom under the abundant promises of the Keeper."

"Which are?"

I sigh. "I'm new. Give me a hint."

"The love, protection, and hope that they just experienced. And so much more yet to come."

"Really?"

He laughs. "Really. It's a promise."

"Of course I'd like to see that the freedom earned is kept. But when we go back—"

"Daymon!"

We turn toward Lieb's voice. He rushes into Daymon's arms. "You're here! Did you come to show us the way to Nimbus?"

Daymon hugs him back. "I did."

He did?

Lieb starts running back to the group. "I'll get everybody up."

Daymon calls after him. "Tell them to gather their things and extra food and water."

Lieb waves his hand, indicating he heard.

"Did you really come to show them the way?" I ask.

"Show all of you the way," he says. "Correct?"

I hear voices. "But how am I going to tell Elum and Nixi about going back? And the others? They depend on me."

He shakes his head. "They depend on him more."

I let this settle. I'm relieved. I don't want to be responsible for the others. To know that *he* is, and they trust him . . .

Elum is the first to arrive. He hands me an orange. "You must be Daymon."

"I am. Glad to meet you Elum."

To me he says, "How long have you been up?"

"Long enough."

"For—?"

Nixi arrives next. "We folded the blankets for the next people," she tells me.

"That's good of you." I say. "But the food and water needs to be replenished."

"That's for someone else to do now, Mama."

Uh . . . maybe not.

I want to tell her more, but she has Helsa and Oria with her. There will be no chance to speak to my family alone.

"So," Oria says. "Daymon, I assume?"

He offers a little bow. "At your service, Oria."

"Wow," she says with a laugh. "You know my name. You are magical."

"I'm glad you're here," Helsa says. "I really don't want to wander around the desert. Been there, done that."

Daymon nods in my direction. He wants me to tell them? Now?

"Go ahead," he says.

"Go ahead what?" Rand asks.

I take a breath that feels like it starts in my toes. "I am not going with you to Nimbus."

"What?" Elum asks.

"What are you talking about, Mama?"

I take their hands, making our private talk public. "Daymon has helped me realize that I need to go back to Legalis and see that the right changes are made so the Masses can lead fruitful, free lives."

"But we just got free ourselves. We can be together now." Elum glances at Daymon accusingly. "Why would you tell her to do that?"

"I didn't tell her. I offered her the choice."

"That, he did," I say, defending him. "And it's the right choice. For me . . ." I squeeze their hands. "And for us, together. As a family."

"You want *me* to go back?" Nixi asks.

I don't want to give her a choice, but I have to. "Yes. We have work to do and people to help."

"If we're allowed to do it," Elum says. "Who's to say the Judge and Ivar will relinquish control to us? To new ideas?"

"We're to say. *We'll* have a say and offer the Masses a say in creating a new and better Legalis."

After only a moment's hesitation Elum says, "I'll go. I'll go wherever you go. I will never leave you."

I lean over and kiss his cheek. "Nixi?"

Helsa rushes forward. "Nixi, don't go! Come with us!"

Nixi's expression is one of anguish. She looks at Helsa then me. And then Elum. "Is it really my choice?"

My heart screams *No!* But I say, "It is."

She studies Daymon, who to his credit, makes no attempt to persuade her.

"It might be terrible back there," my daughter says to me. "I was sentenced. We'll be considered traitors. We may not even have a home anymore."

"You are right on all accounts," I say.

Elum crosses his hands above his heart. "You and your mother are my home. We'll start over. We'll do the good work together."

Nixi's breath is labored. I can almost feel her pulse against my hand. My heart beats faster too. *Please have her say yes*, I pray. *Please.*

With one final look at Helsa, Nixi says the word I long to hear. "Yes," she says. "I'll go back to Legalis with both of you."

The three of us share an awkward embrace.

But then Rand says, "What about me? I'm from Legalis too."

I'm ashamed that I never thought about *his* future. "Of course, Rand. You are welcome to come with us."

Rand looks down and twists the base of his crutch against the ground.

Lieb rushes to his side, taking his free hand. "Don't go back, Rand. You were my first and best friend in Legalis. Stay with me. Come with us."

I have to point out one thing to him. "What if the Judge is alive?"

Rand nods in full comprehension "If he is, he'll want revenge. If he isn't, will others want revenge?"

It's the truth. I can only shrug.

"She's right," Solana says. "You're safer with us."

"We want you with us, Rand," Oria says. "We need a brave man like you."

He scoffs. "Brave and foolish."

"Brave," Devin says, clapping him on the shoulders. "Come with us."

Rand nods. "I accept your invitation." He looks at me. "Give the Judge my best."

Suddenly Daymon says, "I think it's time for everyone to go."

He must *know* it's time. The others look to me for confirmation. "Let's say our goodbyes."

We hug our friends—old and new. Helsa and Nixi cry and cling to each other. Then I hold Helsa tight and thank her once again for saving me. It's hard to think we will never see these people again.

"Can you get back all right?" Devin asks Elum.

"We can." The roommates shake hands. "May the Keeper protect you and keep you safe."

And so we leave the peace of the oasis for the uncertainty of Legalis and Nimbus.

May the Keeper be with us all.

Chapter Fifty-Seven

Solana

We watch Glynis, Elum, and Nixi walk toward Legalis.

"I'm stunned," Devin says. "They're really going back. After all she said in the square? It's a big risk for all of them."

"The Judge and Ivar will be mad," I say.

"Will Glynis get shunned for having a child with Elum?" Helsa asks.

"Varo will still be mad," Lieb says.

"He might get her put in jail," I say. "Tit for tat."

"Tat?" Lieb asks.

"Revenge," I say.

"Oh. That's not good."

"I don't see why Nixi had to go with them," Helsa says. "She shouldn't be punished for what they did."

"Or who they loved," I say.

Oria adjusts the strap of a water skin over her head and shoulder. "Personally, I understand why Glynis wanted to go back. She feels responsible for what she started and wants to see what's going on."

"And help pick up the pieces," Rand says. "But I'm glad I stayed with all of you."

"I'm glad too," I tell him.

"And now it's time to leave this oasis and go forward," Daymon says.

With all the bittersweet goodbyes, I almost forgot we're leaving too.

"How many days of travel do we have in the desert?" Helsa asks, looking toward the rising sun.

"None."

We all cock our heads as if we didn't hear right. "None?" I ask.

"Follow me." Daymon walks behind a stand of trees to some flowering bushes. He brushes leaves and twigs to the side.

"A handle!" Lieb says.

Daymon lifts a trap door. I get a glimpse of a ladder leading downward. "It's nice and cool down there," he says.

"Another tunnel?" I ask. "I don't do well in tight spaces."

"It opens up fairly quickly," he says.

I already feel my heart beating wildly. Devin puts his arm around me. "You can do it, Mother."

"You can, Nana," Helsa says.

"I'll go first," Lieb says. "I'll make sure it's safe."

I immediately realize how blessed I am to have people who care about me. I can't let them down—or slow them down. "I'll be all right." But then I notice Rand looking at the ladder warily. "How about you, Rand?"

He takes a deep breath. "I'll be all right too."

True to his word, Lieb starts to climb down the ladder. Daymon hands him a flint. "There's a lamp at the bottom. Keep the lamp burning."

At least we'll have light.

It's my turn after Helsa and Oria. Devin holds my hand as I take the first step onto the ladder. I look down to watch my footing, but find looking up toward the narrow slice of sky is more comforting.

"That's it, Mother. Keep your eyes on me."

Behind Devin's head I see a cloud floating by. Somehow it calms me as I keep stepping down. Down. Down.

I feel hands on my arms as my feet feel the ground beneath them. "You made it, Nana," Helsa says.

The lamp light is a relief. I step aside as Rand comes next. "Look out below!" he says, as he drops his crutch down the hole. His descent is awkward, but he makes it. Then comes Devin. And then . . .

Daymon peers down at us, his head a dark silhouette in the circular opening.

"You last," Helsa says.

"I'm not coming," he says.

"What? You have to come!" I say. "How will we know which way to go?"

"Listen to these words I share with you now, and remember them."

I have to force myself to put aside the fact he's not coming, and ready my mind to concentrate.

"We're ready," Oria says.

"A life of self is death, but the death of self is life."

"What?" Rand says.

He does not repeat the words, but drops a piece of paper down the hole. It floats toward us and Oria catches it.

"Follow his directions," Daymon says, pointing at the paper." With that, he closes the trap door, shutting out the sunlight.

Lieb scrambles up the ladder. "Don't leave us!"

If I were younger, I'd scramble too. But I say, "Daymon got us this far. He wouldn't have left us if he didn't know we could get the rest of the way."

Oria opens the note and holds it toward the light. "It's a Relic: 'Prepare the way for the Keeper. Make straight paths for him.'"

"I don't understand," Devin says. "How can we prepare anyone for the Keeper when we don't know how to get where we're going?"

"You're missing the point, son," I say. "We have a job to do, to tell people about him." I look at Oria, wanting her to agree.

Which she does. "It's the charge he gave me back in Regalia. The charge he gave Rand and I in Legalis. The Keeper wants us to keep talking about him, and spread the news."

"We did that in Legalis," Rand says. "At least we started the conversation."

"And Glynis will help keep it going," I say.

"So now we spread the news in Nimbus?" Rand asks.

"If we ever get there," Helsa adds.

Lieb jumps down from the ladder. "Straight! The Relic said go straight!"

It didn't say *go* straight exactly, but since there's only one direction *to* go . . . "We're not going to be any good to ourselves or the Keeper just standing here," I say.

Lieb picks up the lamp. "I'll light the way," he says.

The rest of us are left to follow the light.

CHAPTER FIFTY-EIGHT

GLYNIS

The three of us travel into Legalis via the tunnels. Shockingly, we don't see anyone. Meaning they're out in the streets. Or hiding away. Neither option gives us comfort.

We ascend the spiral stairs leading to the secret storeroom door. We go through it but pause before entering the Sanctuary.

"Shh!" Nixi says as she puts her ear to the door. I stop breathing and also listen but don't hear anything. She stands straight. "I hear a few distant voices, but no yelling or screaming."

"That's a good sign," Elum says. He looks at me. "Are you ready?"

"No." I take a deep breath and squeeze his hand. "But let's do this."

He stops me. "Wait." He bows his head. "Keeper, you led us back here. Protect and guide us to do your bidding."

"I should have thought to pray," I say.

"You will. There will be many more chances."

"*Not* encouraging," Nixi says.

We enter the Sanctuary. The space is empty and intact. "I expected to see people defiling the walls or burning things in the center."

"Does this mean the Judge is back in charge?" Nixi asks. "Are people living in fear again?"

The evidence does point in that direction. "The thought of dealing with an angry Ubel makes me want to retreat to the tunnel. Or . . . maybe catch up with the rest of the group."

"There's no going back," Elum says. "If you don't speak up now, our entire society might *never* get help. Perhaps you were made for such a time as this."

Although my stomach objects, his words of encouragement spur me forward. "Let's see if you're right."

We walk to the main door. I am fueled by the possibility that I *am* meant to be here and I *will* help the people. But not wanting to be rash, We peek outside.

The square is full of people wearing color: spots of purple, yellow, blue and . . . every color imaginable, dotting the sea of white.

"There's color everywhere," Nixi whispers.

"And no studs on their shoulders," Elum adds.

I spot Bog, sitting on the top Sanctuary step. What a stroke of luck. "Elum, will you ask Bog to come in here, please?"

Elum goes outside and talks to Bog, who glances back at the door, and quickly comes inside the Sanctuary to join us. He swipes a blue headband off his head, and bows. "Mistress, I'm so glad you're here. And safe."

"I am too. Please tell me what's happened."

His chubby face beams. "Everything has changed, mistress. Everything *is* changing."

"Is the Judge gone?" Elum asks.

Bog grins. "He's in jail. As is Ivar, the head Fault Finder, and a few others who refused to surrender."

"Was there much violence?" Nixi asks. "People had clubs . . ."

"There was some," Bog admits, "but far less than expected for such a total coup. Even most of the Fault Finders removed their masks and joined the Masses in celebration."

It's nearly beyond my comprehension. "And the Notables?"

"They're under house arrest, told to stay in their homes until they can be dealt with."

"Meaning?" I ask.

"We weren't sure what to do with 'em," Bog admits. "Another reason I'm glad you're here."

"Have people looted?" Elum asks.

Bog chuckles. "What's to loot? No one owns anything, but a bunch went to the Farm and brought back carts full of food. Everybody ate 'til they were more than full." He pats his stomach. "I enjoyed seeing *everyone* enjoying good food."

I notice his white robe has been cut shorter, revealing stubby legs. I point at it. "Another change?"

He giggles. "It's much, much cooler, mistress. And you haven't seen anything yet. Turns out there were some sewing people hidden away, and they emptied their workroom of the fabric, and are even starting to teach some of the Masses how to dye and sew it. Some are dying their white robes." He pulls out the headband, which is a strip of blue brocade. "I like blue."

"Blue is your color," I say.

"I notice the studs are gone," Nixi says.

"We threw them all in a pile and set them on fire. They're melted to nothing now."

"As they should be," Elum says.

Bog smiles. "And the children have gathered all the black and white pebbles and are playing games with them."

"That's wonderful," I say.

"Where is my . . . Varo?" Nixi asks with a glance to Elum.

"Back in jail." Bog shakes his head. "He would *not* stop jabbering and complaining. I think people took him there just to shut him up. Plus, him trying to kill your mother."

I look at Nixi. "Do you want to see him?"

"I do not." She smiles at Elum. "I have the only father I need."

The mention of jail . . . "Is the Judge hurt badly?"

"Pretty bad. He says a huge man attacked him."

I smile. That's hardly a description of Rand, but I'll let the Judge have his story.

"The fact he *could* be hurt . . . more than anything *that* has set the people free. And no more laws either. No more Counts or not being able to touch each other, or having jobs that don't suit us."

"Are you still a cook?"

"I'll always be a cook," Bog says. "But since I can't get back to the kitchen in your house right now, I found a spare unit that has a fireplace and I'm collecting pots and bowls and such. I'll cook for whoever wants to eat my food."

"Which should be everybody," Nixi says.

Trying to take it all in, I begin to pace. My footfalls echo in the empty Sanctuary. I stop and look at the volume of this place. A beam of sunlight shines through the hole in the roof. My beam of sunlight. The light that changed everything.

And then I know . . .

"This Sanctuary will be a gathering place for those who believe in the Keeper. It will be a place where we will learn about him and worship him together. Our motto of Duty, Deference, Dedication, Dependability is good. But the recipient of those actions needs to change."

"Needs to be directed toward the Keeper?" Elum says.

"Exactly."

Bog nods. "That sounds like a very good plan."

My heart races in a most delightful way. "To do that, I need to talk to the Notables."

"What are you going to say to them?" Nixi asks.

I haven't a clue. "The words will come to me when I need them. But basically, I'm going to tell them that I am back and that things have changed in Legalis. If they want to be a part of the change, good. If not?"

"If not?" Bog asks.

"It'll come to me." I walk toward the door. "But first, I want to talk to the Masses." Despite Bog's hopeful report, as I walk outside I feel a stitch of fear.

But then, people see me. They point at me . . . and they cheer.

"Yay! It's Glynis! Glynis is here!"

They rush toward me, their faces exuberant, their cries full of joy and celebration.

Elum steps in front of me, keeping them at a distance.

"You're our hero!" a woman with a red shawl shouts.

Her red shawl delights me.

"All hail, Glynis the Great!"

I touch Elum's arm and he steps aside. Even as the cheers fill my heart with joy, I press my hands downward, quieting their encouraging shouts.

"Good people of Legalis—"

Some cheers erupt, but I quiet them.

"I am here to help guide you toward a new Legalis, a free Legalis!"

More cheers erupt and I let them quiet of their own accord.

"A time of pain, torture, and oppression has turned into a time of rebirth, relief, and revival. What was will be no more!"

Lively shouts fill the square.

I look across the crowd, where people no longer look the same. It makes me happy and hopeful. "Some of the changes will come quickly—like your discovery of color." I gesture toward their bright clothes and many spin around to show me. "But other changes will take time. Undoing hundreds of years of history must be addressed with wisdom, prudence, and . . ." I hesitate only a moment, "And with an ear and a heart tuned to the guidance of the Keeper—my Keeper. Our Keeper."

Across the crowd, fingers touch chests, and the gesture catches on in a wave. I touch fingers to my own chest. "All glory to the Keeper!"

The crowd cheers wildly.

My thoughts move to my next task of speaking with the Notables. And then there's the question of what to do with the Judge, Ivar, Varo, and the others who are in jail. I don't relish any of it, but I know I am the one who can do it.

I am destined to do it.

I raise my hands to the Masses—the good citizens of Legalis. "Now I leave you to your celebration while I go and do my part in effecting permanent, positive change. May the Keeper be with us all!"

I turn to my family and Bog and smile, "Come now, all of you. We have work to do."

Chapter Fifty-Nine

Oria

We stopped talking two hours ago. The tunnel has narrowed and we have to walk single file. It seems endless. And monotonous. The only variation is the dance of light from the lamp Lieb carries as he leads the way.

I worry about Solana. I've never had a negative reaction to tight spaces, yet as the tunnel leads us downward, deeper beneath the desert…

Actually, if I let myself think about that, or that we're in a tube and the only way out is ahead of us at some destination unknown . . . even I could panic.

What stops me is thinking about Daymon. He—and the Keeper—rescued us from Legalis. They wouldn't lead us into this tunnel if it would hurt us.

Would they?

I shake my head adamantly at the thought.

Solana must have seen my gesture because she asks, "Are you all right, Oria?" She walks behind me with Devin bringing up the rear.

"I'm fine. Just thinking too much."

"It's all we can do down here."

I glance back at her. "How are you faring?"

"I just keep repeating 'fear not' in time with my footsteps."

"That's actually a good idea. I'll start doing that."

After a few hundred 'fear not' steps, the tunnel mercifully starts veering upward again—though the climb makes walking more strenuous. I hear everyone puffing at the exertion. I hope going *up* is a sign we're near the end.

A short time later Lieb yells, "Hey!"

He carries the light forward, leaving us in the dark. "What is it?" Rand calls out.

The light comes toward us again, bobbing wildly. "It's a ladder going up! Come on!"

By the time we get there, he's left the lamp with Helsa and has climbed up into darkness. He's either brave or foolish. We'll know soon enough.

Moments later, sunlight streams down the shaft.

Solana and I hug each other. "We're safe!" she says.

"Maybe," Devin says. "But even if we're in Nimbus, that doesn't mean we're safe."

I don't appreciate him bringing us down, even though he might be right.

One by one we climb the ladder. As soon as my head is clear I squint at the sunlight, then gasp and eagerly scramble the rest of the way out. All my senses explode. "It's so beautiful!"

Lieb helps Solana with the last step. Her face beams. "Quite a change from dry and dull Legalis."

"A happy change," Helsa says.

The ladder shaft has brought us to the edge of a meadow. There are stands of lush trees and wildflowers growing everywhere. I pick one and hold it to my nose, basking in its luscious scent. "This is just what we need."

"Don't speak too soon," Devin says. "The scenery is pretty but what about the people? The writings said Nimbus was incompatible."

I remember what Glynis said. "Incompatible to the structure of Legalis."

"Incompatible because it's beautiful," Helsa says as she slips a daisy behind her ear. "Legalis was anti-beauty."

"You look pretty, Sa-Sa," Lieb says.

She curtsies. "Thank you, kind sir."

Rand closes the hinged, wooden lid to the shaft. It's clear it was covered with leaves and twigs to hide it. He covers it again. "Let's remember where this is, just in case."

Helsa shakes her head. "I am *not* going back to Legalis."

"I am not going back in that tunnel," Solana says. "Not unless I'm forced to."

"Let's hope that doesn't happen," I say. I spin in a three-sixty, drawing in deep breaths of the fragrant air. But then I stop halfway around and point. "Look over there!"

Behind us, a short distance away, is water. We walk through tall grasses to its edge, squat down, and put our hands into its sparkling coolness. I can't remember the last time I felt cool in any way.

Lieb cups his hands and splashes water over his face, then washes the dust off his arms. "Sa-Sa, try it. It's wonderful!"

She copies his action and soon all of us are refreshed by the water.

"Can I jump in?" Lieb asks.

"You may not," Solana says. "We don't know what's under the water or how deep it is. You stay right here on its bank."

I stare out over the water. "I can't see land at all."

Rand drags his crutch through the water's edge, making a crunching sound against tiny pebbles. "What's water like this called?

I've never seen such a thing in Legalis."

"We have nothing like it in Regalia either," Devin says.

Solana looks to the right, then the left. "Nice as it is . . . where to?" she asks. "We have no idea which way to go."

Lieb closes his eyes, spins, then points toward the left. He opens his eyes. "We go that way."

It's as good a way as any.

We stroll along the water's edge, through wildflowers and grasses bending in the breeze. I drink in the fresh, cool air. Although most of our time in Legalis was spent outdoors, the air always smelled tight. Dusty. Never like this. This smells of moist earth and leaves reminds me of my garden back in Regalia. How I loved to sit in that garden, the garden where the Keeper visited me.

He said he loves gardens. Maybe he's here somewhere.

We come upon a grove of massive trees creating a canopy. And then I see it. "Look! It's a path leading away from the water."

"Logically, it should lead us to people," Rand says.

"I hope they're friendly," Solana says.

We take the path — which is well-worn. A good sign.

Lieb spots a tree heavy with apples. He plucks one off. "Yum!"

"Don't eat it!" Devin says.

But too late. Lieb's already taken a big bite of the apple. "Hmm," he says with delight. "It's a good one. Come on, everybody. Take one."

We *are* hungry, and the apples *are* refreshing. I hope we don't get in trouble for it.

We walk on, then Helsa suddenly pulls up short and raises her hand to stop the rest of us. "Shh!"

We hear voices. Dozens of voices. Is that singing? I hear a flute, a fiddle, and a drum.

This is definitely not Legalis.

"I love music!" Lieb says. "Let's find it."

Before we can urge caution, he and Helsa run ahead. We have no choice but to hurry after them. I hope Lieb's innocent exuberance won't be the death of us.

We catch up with them at the edge of a clearing. Dozens of people are gathered in the distance. Some dance while musicians play. Everyone sings and claps.

"It's pure joy," Solana says with awe in her voice.

Which is something else that was lacking in Legalis.

I can't help but notice the clothes. They are colorful and flowy, made of brightly patterned fabric. Skirts, pants, blouses, scarves, dresses . . . not a blah robe in sight. The fabrics aren't stiff at all, but float and undulate as if designed for movement.

"I knew I missed fashion, but what they wear is beyond fashion," I say. "It's pure freedom of fashion. Almost freedom *from* fashion."

"Everyone wears something different," Solana says.

"Come on!" Lieb grabs Helsa's hand and runs toward the dancing, bursting through the crowd. He joins in with full abandon. Helsa doesn't dance, but stands nearby, motioning for him to stop. Their dirty white robes stand out amid the colorful, fluid fabrics.

"Oh dear," Solana says. "Lieb shouldn't have . . ."

Suddenly the people stop dancing. The music stops. Everyone backs away from Helsa and Lieb, and stares.

Then someone points toward us. "There's more of them!"

"Helsa! Lieb!" Solana and Devin motion for them to return to us. They hurry back and stand with us.

The crowd is silent. We're silent. I'm not sure what to do. Although we mean no harm, we *are* strangers. "Smile," I whisper to the others. Then I take a few steps toward them, but stop when a tall woman walks through the crowd. She doesn't just walk, she drifts with genuine grace. Even at a distance I can tell she is stunningly beautiful, with black wavy hair cascading down to her waist.

She comes toward us. Her green, diaphanous dress ripples in the breeze. She wears a headdress of silver starbursts adorned with flowers. By the way she carries herself and holds her head regally straight, I know she's important.

I hope she's also friendly.

The people step aside to let her pass. It takes all my willpower not to step back with the others. But I stand tall and try to look confident, yet harmless.

When she reaches me, I nod. I wait for her to speak first.

"I am Mother Nimbus," she says.

An interesting title. "I am Oria, and these are my friends." I don't give names. Yet.

She eyes our pitiful and dirty robes. "Where did you come from?"

"We have just arrived from Legalis."

"Where?"

Her question makes me wonder how much I should say. I can't toss away hundreds of years of ignorance on a whim. "Regalia?"

She shakes her head. "I demand to know how you got here." Her jaw is tight. Her eyes are wary. Even a bit afraid?

Again, I hesitate. To tell her about the tunnel might destroy our only escape route. So I ignore her question and offer some honest flattery. "Nimbus is very, very beautiful."

"As intended."

An unexpected response.

I don't know what to say next. She's clearly in charge. The next step is hers to make.

Lieb takes care of the silence. "Can Sa-Sa and I go dance?" He points at the crowd. "We like the music."

Mother Nimbus blinks, as if his frivolous question has broken through more serious thoughts. "I think not—right now." She raises her hand and a woman rushes forward. "Take our guests to get baths, food, and . . ." She scrutinizes our clothes skeptically. "And something more suitable to wear."

"We'd be very appreciative," Solana says.

"Mother," Mother Nimbus adds.

Solana makes the adjustment. "We'd be very appreciative, Mother."

The woman motions for us to follow her. But as we walk, Mother Nimbus singles me out. "You. Oria."

My stomach flips, but I step toward her. "Yes. Mother?"

"As soon as you are refreshed, I demand a full accounting of how and why you have invaded Nimbus."

What? "We haven't invaded—"

Her dark eyebrows rise.

"Yes, Mother."

I hurry to join the others, thankful for a bath, food, and clean clothes, but nervous about what comes after.

How can I ever explain to the mother of Nimbus about our *invasion*?

The End

**

Finally, brothers and sisters, rejoice!
Strive for full restoration, encourage one another,
be of one mind, live in peace.
And the God of love and peace will be with you.
2 Corinthians 13: 11

**

Continue the story in *A Seed of Change*
(Excerpt following)

Chapter One

Oria

As we walk to who-knows-where, I marvel at Nimbus. The best words to describe it are *lush* and *green*—two words that have no meaning in Legalis.

The woman who walks ahead of us looks to be in her late-fifties. She is as short as Nana, and her light brown hair shows streaks of gray. I didn't have much of a chance to see her face, but I did notice a deep crease between her eyes. What I also notice is her waddling gait, as if a knee or hip hurts. Perhaps both.

Lieb points to the right. "Look at those houses over there! They have flowers growing up the sides of them. Aren't they pretty, Sa-Sa?"

Helsa answers in her patient tone. "Yes, they're pretty, Lieb. Very pretty."

"Will we get to live in one of those?" he asks Solana.

"I don't know," she says.

"Take it down a notch, boy," Devin says. "We just got here. We don't even know if this Nimbus is a safe place."

The woman glances over her shoulder. "It's as safe as you make it."

We all exchange a look. What does that mean?

I walk faster to catch up with her. "I guarantee that we are not invaders. We're not—"

"Don't talk to me about it." She lowers her voice. "I'm not the one you have to convince."

As I did to Durth when we first came to Legalis, I ask her name. "I'm Oria. And you are?"

"Zinna."

"Are you Mother's . . . assistant?"

She flashes me a look. "I am her House Hand."

Her tone indicates it's a high honor.

We turn a corner and have to stop and gape at a building on the top of a massive hill.

"Oh my," Solana says.

"That's the prettiest place I ever saw," Lieb says.

Zinna stops with us. "Of course it is. The Nest is a castle worthy of the mother of all Nimbus."

I've never heard the term *castle*, but if that means an enormous stone building with high walls, and many, many turrets, what stands in the distance is indeed a castle.

"Do we get to stay there?" Helsa asks.

"That's up to Mother Nimbus." Zinna points ahead. "Quit yer dallying. I ain't got all day."

We start walking again, but gather around Zinna. "Did Mother Nimbus have the castle built for her?" Devin asks.

"Nah. It's been here forever. Since the Before Times as far as I know."

"Does she have a husband?" I ask.

Zinna flashes me a look. "Eye, yer nosey. Do you?"

"I do not."

"Neither does she."

"But as *Mother* Nimbus she must have children," Rand says.

Zinna snickers. "She has a few of those. A few hundred."

What?

Zinna points ahead, then studies Rand with his crutch. Stretching before us are hundreds of stairs leading up to the castle.

"Yikes," he says.

"Is there any other way up there?" I ask.

"Nope," Zinna says, with no compassion in her voice. "You can stay here if you want, but the food, water, and clothes are up there."

Rand nods. "I may be slow, but I'll get there."

"Wise man."

Devin offers Rand his arm, and we begin the trek upward.

No one talks, as full attention has to be given to the steps.

Zinna stops periodically, out of breath. Solana struggles too. I'm glad for a chance to rest. We all lean against the thick stone railing that edges the stairs. I look back the way we've come but don't see Mother Nimbus behind us.

Lieb peers over the railing. "We're so high!"

"No wonder it's called the Nest," I manage to say.

"Mother needs to see the entirety of her domain."

I wonder how big Nimbus is, but realize I'll soon see for myself.

After three stops to rest, we reach the top where enormous wood doors greet us. Two guards stand outside. They wear leather breastplates and tall boots. They hold spears.

When they see us they stand at attention and hold the spears in front of their bodies. Are they afraid of us?

Us?

Zinna slaps one of them on the arm. "Open the doors, ya idgits!"

They do as they're told, and the heavy doors are pulled outward. We follow Zinna into a grand room that's two stories tall, with log rafters overhead.

"Wow," Lieb exclaims.

That sums it up nicely.

There are two round chandeliers with at least a dozen candles each and a stone fireplace at the far end, with intricate carvings from the mantel up to the ceiling. The room is further lit by multiple tall windows created from individual small diamond panes. An intricate red and blue rug sits atop large slabs of stone flooring. The room is populated by numerous chairs and carved wood benches.

"May I?" Rand asks, pointing to a bench.

"That's what they're there for," Zinna says.

He sits with his bum leg extended.

A clock over the mantel starts to chime, and all of us — as one — gasp and tense up.

Zinna looks at us warily. "What? Ya never heard a clock chime before?"

I start the laughter, and the rest join in.

"Now you laugh at the clock?"

"Excuse me," I say, getting myself under control. "It's just that clocks chiming have not been a pleasant experience for us."

Zinna studies the clock. "I can't imagine why not."

I'm sure there's a lot she can't imagine . . . (continued)

Dear Reader:

When I write, I don't plan. I don't outline. I grab a few characters, set them in a location, kind of know what the end of the book might be, and start writing. That may work for my regular contemporary and historical books, but not as well for my fantasy books. Creating an entirely new society on the fly is like designing a wedding gown with no pattern and no picture, just a hunk of fabric, some lace and beads. It's possible, but difficult.

So it was when I began to write *A Count of Courage*. Setting my characters in Legalis was hard on them—and me. As I learned about this horrible society, so did they. Or maybe they learned and *then* I learned? It's entirely possible. I swear I often don't know what I'm writing until after I write it. Then I read it over and think, "Huh. That's a good idea. Where did that come from?"

The other issue with creating a new—very odd—society is that I don't know what details I need until I need them. Like the Decrees of Legalis, or what food they eat, what they wear, what's the hierarchy? What do the Fault Finders say when they hand out a Fault? How does the Count work? There are hundreds of questions that I have to answer as I weave the story together.

And the characters change constantly. At first I thought Elum would be a spy for the Judge. I thought Elum and Solana might have a romance. Or maybe Wyan and Oria? No-go on both of those. Rand was going to be a minor character—certainly not the hero. As for Glynis? I never planned on her even *being*, yet she turned out to be my favorite character in the whole book—and essential to the story. I am SO proud of her and what she did. I feel like a proud mama.

Want to see an image of the Judge? At first I had his eyes glow, until I realized there's no technology in Legalis, so I had his eyes be mirrored.

So many changes. As Daymon told Glynis: "Go with the flow." I should have that cross-stitched for my office.

A note about the "miracle." That was unplanned too. When Glynis was up in the loft having an encounter with the Keeper, he told her there would be a miracle. As soon as I wrote that I thought, "Really? What miracle?" So the next day I started to brainstorm what the miracle would be, but I stopped myself. God had nudged me to mention a miracle in the first place, so I decided not to think about it, but just write Glynis's next chapter and let the miracle reveal itself without me. Or with me. Or . . . I don't know how all this happens, but it does. I wrote the chapter and what do you know, there was the miracle. Moments like this are why I write. And why I write for Him.

I used a lot of Scripture in this book. There are 15 or 16 Relics, which are of course Scripture — though often paraphrased — but there are at least that many other verses that people share — without quoting — in their conversations. I'd be writing along and a verse would come to me, and then it would come out of a character's mouth. Whatever the number, there are dozens of Biblical truths in the story that show how alive and active the Bible can be. All to prove that God's Word *is* interwoven in our lives — whether we realize it or not.

When my dear editor (my amazing daughter, Laurel) read this book she mentioned that my agenda was very clear. That threw me a little (was it a good or a bad thing?) but then I embraced it. You bet my agenda is clear! I am a devoted Christian, a child of God who worships Him and basks in His unconditional love. All of my books — but especially the Last Call series — shine a bright light on faith and God, and showcase how much He wants to know us. The story also hints that time is short. As Elum says to Glynis in Chapter 58: "There's no going back. If you don't speak up now, our entire society might *never* get help. Perhaps you were made for such a time as this." Perhaps I was made to write this series for such a time as this.

Of course that can be argued, but don't even try because I'm not going to argue back. I know that *we* have been set in place for "such a time as this." Don't waste your chance. Don't be shy. Don't be scared. Fear not! Speak up and let the world know that your loyalties and devotion lie with Jesus. You have been created by the Almighty God with a unique purpose. Find it and step into your purpose with gusto!

May the love and protection of the Keeper be with you always.

Nancy Moser

About the Author

NANCY MOSER is the best-selling author of 47 novels, novellas, and children's books that focus on discovering your unique purpose. Her titles include the Christy Award winner *Time Lottery* and Christy finalist *Washington's Lady* and *A Slice of Sky*. She's written 21 historical books including *Mozart's Sister, Love of the Summerfields, Masquerade, Where Time Will Take Me,* and *Just Jane. An Unlikely Suitor* was named to Booklist's "Top 100 Romance Novels of the Decade." *The Pattern Artist* was a finalist in the Romantic Times Reviewers Choice award. Some of her contemporary novels are *If Not for This, An Undiscovered Life, The Invitation, A Steadfast Surrender, The Good Nearby, Crossroads, The Seat Beside Me,* and the Sister Circle series. *Eyes of Our Heart* was a finalist in the Faith, Hope, and Love Readers' Choice Award. Nancy has been married fifty years—to the same man. She and her husband have three grown children, eight grandchildren, and live in the Midwest. She's been blessed with a varied life. She's earned a degree in architecture, run a business with her husband, traveled extensively in Europe, and has performed in various theaters, symphonies, and choirs. She knits voraciously, kills all her houseplants, and can wire an electrical fixture without getting shocked. She is a fan of anything antique—humans included.

Website: www.nancymoser.com
Facebook: www.facebook.com/nancymoser.author
Bookbub: www.bookbub.com/authors/nancy-moser?list=author_ books
Goodreads: www.goodreads.com/author/show/117288.Nancy_Moser
Pinterest: www.pinterest.com/nancymoser1/boards/
Instagram: www.instagram.com/nmoser33/
Substack: www.substack.com/@nancymoserwrites
X: www.x.com/MoserNancy
Blogs: Author blog: www.authornancymoser.blogspot.com
History blog: www.footnotesfromhistory.blogspot.com

www.ingramcontent.com/pod-product-compliance
Lightning Source LLC
Chambersburg PA
CBHW071226300726
48975CB00002B/312